D0048809

The Old Man and Mr. Smith

WORKS BY PETER USTINOV

House of Regrets
Blow Your Own Trumpet
Beyond
The Banbury Nose
The Tragedy of Good Intentions
The Indifferent Shepherd
The Man in the Raincoat
Plays About People
The Love of Four Colonels
The Moment of Truth
No Sign of the Dove
Romanoff and Juliet
Add a Dash of Pity
Ustinov's Diplomats
The Loser
Photo Finish
The Life in My Hands
The Frontiers of the Sea
Half Way Up the Tree
The Unknown Soldier and His Wife
Krumnagel
Dear Me
Overheard
My Russia
Ustinov in Russia
The Disinformer

PETER USTINOV

The Old Man and Mr. Smith

A FABLE

Arcade Publishing • *New York*

LITTLE, BROWN AND COMPANY

Copyright © 1990 by Dunedin N.V.

All rights reserved. No part of this book may be reproduced in
any form or by any electronic or mechanical means, including
information storage and retrieval systems, without permission
in writing from the publisher, except by a reviewer who may
quote brief passages in a review.

First U.S. Edition 1991

Library of Congress Cataloging-in-Publication Data
Ustinov, Peter.
    The old man and Mr. Smith / Peter Ustinov.—1st U.S. ed.
    p. cm.
    ISBN 1-55970-134-X
    I. Title. II. Title: Old Man and Mister Smith.
PR6041.S7304 1991
823'.914—dc20   90-27617

10 9 8 7 6 5 4 3 2 1

RRD VA

Published in the United States by Arcade Publishing, Inc., New
York, a Little, Brown company, by arrangement with Michael O'Mara Books
Limited, London

Printed in the United States of America

FOR MY CHILDREN
Tamara, Pavla, Igor, Andrea
IN ORDER OF APPEARANCE

There is a remote chance that none of this ever occurred; what is much more likely, however, is the fact that, if it did occur, it will never occur again.

The Old Man and Mr. Smith

1

'God? Presumably with two "d"s,' said the concierge, without looking up.

'With one "d",' said the Old Man, apologetically.

'That's unusual,' remarked the concierge.

'Unusual? It's unique.' And the Old Man laughed mildly at his own observation.

'Given name?'

'I haven't one.'

'Initials will do.'

'It stands to reason – since I haven't a first name, I haven't initials either.'

The concierge looked at the Old Man penetratingly, and for the first time. The Old Man fidgeted, eager to put an end to the awkwardness.

'Are you going to say that that's unusual too?' he suggested, and then went on, reassuringly, 'There's a perfectly normal reason for it, which should satisfy you. I had no parents, you see.'

'Everyone has parents,' stated the concierge, dangerously.

'I haven't,' retorted the Old Man, hotly.

There was a moment while the two protagonists weighed each other up. The concierge resumed the verbal contact in a tone of enforced relaxation.

'And this for how long?'

'I can't say. I am subject to whims.'

'Whims,' echoed the concierge. 'And what will be your method of payment when you leave?'

'I have no idea,' said the Old Man, betraying signs of weariness. 'I would have thought that in a hotel of this class—'

'Of course,' the concierge replied defensively. 'Although even a hotel of the highest category must ask itself questions when a potential client declares himself to be a Mr God with one "d", and isn't even the possessor of initials, let alone luggage.'

'I told you, my luggage is on its way.'

'With your friend?'

'Yes. We both realize it is practically impossible to get a hotel room without luggage.'

'Oh, you've tried before?'

'Oh, yes.'

'And so? If I may ask?'

'And so, he has bought some luggage.'

'Just luggage? With nothing inside?'

'How inquisitive you are!'

'I beg your pardon. But I'd still like to know your method of payment. I am *not* particularly inquisitive, you understand, but my employers . . .'

'I have been asked for much more than mere method of payment . . . health, peace, victory, salvation . . . substantial things, you understand, often involving nations, or at least peoples. I must say, I usually turn such requests down as too imprecise, too vague. I wonder then why I am so irritated by your quite rational request? It must be old age creeping up on me . . . Here, is this of any use to you?'

And he dredged a fistful of coins out of the cavernous depths of his pockets, spilling them in great profusion over the glass top of the concierge's desk. Some fell to the floor, and rolled away, but not far, for few of them were perfectly round.

'Chasseur!' called the concierge, and a small boy in uniform crawled about on the floor, collecting the coins. The concierge examined those that remained on his desk. 'I hope you are not thinking of paying with these.'

What's wrong with them?' asked the Old Man.

'They look Greek to me, and ancient at that.'

'How time flies,' sighed the Old Man. And added, 'I'll have another go.'

The concierge tapped his pencil on the glass top of his desk in a rhythmic tattoo while the Old Man patrolled his pockets for something more viable. He seemed at one point to be making a physical effort, as though his activity were both more obscure and more complicated than he allowed to let on. Then he produced green notes as if they were parts of a disintegrating lettuce.

'This any good?' he enquired, rendered breathless by his activity.

The concierge examined the notes, which opened up like flowers as though they had a life of their own.

'On the face of it . . .'

'How long can we stay on that?'

'We? . . . Oh, yes, your friend . . . On the face of it, about a month, but it naturally depends on room service, the valet, mini-bar, all that . . .'

'A month. I don't think we will possibly stay as long as a month. We have far too much to see.'

'You are sightseeing here in Washington?' asked the concierge, trying to be agreeable in order to disperse any possible traces of friction.

'We see new sights wherever we go. Everything is new to us.'

The concierge was at a loss how to deal with this exultant innocence, which seemed oddly self-sufficient, and unwilling to communicate. He doggedly continued to take the initiative. As a concierge of note in the profession, he had to be able to recognize a nuance when he observed it, and to ignore it when it suited his professional purpose.

'There are excellent tours arranged by the Yankee Heritage people,' he said, producing a handful of brochures. 'They enable you to visit the National Gallery, the Smithsonian—'

'The White House,' suggested the Old Man, consulting a piece of paper.

'That is more difficult,' smiled the concierge. 'They don't allow groups any more, owing to security.'

'I wouldn't want to go with a group in any case,' said the Old Man. 'When I go I will want to go alone, or perhaps with my friend.'

'For that you have to have an invitation.'

The Old Man took on a surprising air of authority. 'I have never had an invitation in my existence, and it's not now I intend to begin.'

'*Never* had an invitation?'

'No. I've had prayers, intercessions, even sacrifices, burnt offerings, in the old days, but never an invitation.'

At that moment, another old man attracted attention to himself by attempting to negotiate the revolving doors leading to the street while carrying two revolting plastic suitcases. His hair was black and dank, and hung around his face like the physical expression of despair itself. His face was in marked contrast to the porcelain chubbiness of the Old Man, a lined and terrible object, pitted, prised, and pummelled into a mask of melancholy, the black eyes, which seemed to have reticently observed all that is horrible, afloat on tremulous tears, which every now and then shook free to lose themselves in the crevices in the damaged parchment of his cheeks.

'*Mon Dieu*,' said the concierge, watching the struggle. 'He looks older than God.'

'No, we're roughly the same age,' observed the Old Man.

'Bertolini, Anwar,' ordered the concierge.

The two employees of the hotel were too fascinated to move without being called to order. They now rushed forward, and helped the newcomer, whose bags seemed of suspicious lightness.

The newcomer walked unsteadily towards the desk.

'At last!' said the Old Man, pointedly.

'What do you mean, at last?' snarled the newcomer.

'I have been engaged in small talk while waiting for you. You know how tiring I find it. Where did you get the bags?'

'I stole them. You don't expect *me* to buy them, do you? In any case I had no money!'

'And your name is . . .?' the concierge asked, pretending not to hear the rest.

Before the newcomer had time to reply, the Old Man said, 'Smith.'

The concierge didn't raise his eyes from his register. 'In hotels Mr Smith is invariably accompanied by Mrs Smith,' he said.

The Old Man seemed as mystified as the newcomer was antagonistic.

'There is no Mrs Smith in this case,' stuttered the Old Man. 'Marriage always took too long, was too binding, too much of an obligation.'

'It was your fault! Everything was always your fault!' yelled Mr Smith, his tears flying into the air like moisture from a horse's nostril. 'I could have settled down into a sweet and sunny domesticity if it weren't for you!'

'That's enough!' thundered the Old Man with such astonishing vehemence and sheer volume that the few people passing through the foyer panicked and ran for cover.

'Rooms 517 and 518,' shouted the concierge at the top of his lungs, which seemed awfully puny after the majestic sound which had preceded it. Never mind; in the hotel business, one had to do what one could. It was essential to see only half of what happened, on condition one saw through more than half of what didn't.

'And take your money, please.'

'Keep it for me.'

'I'd rather you kept it yourself,' said the concierge with enormous courage.

The Old Man took a handful, leaving another handful on the desk.

'That's for you. For your pains.'

'This is for me?' asked the concierge steadily.

'Yes,' replied the Old Man. 'Just out of interest, how much is it?'

The concierge glanced at it. 'It looks like – between four and five thousand dollars.'

'Ah. Are you happy? I have no idea about the value of money.'

'I can believe that, sir. In answer to your other question, sir, I am neither happy nor unhappy. I am in the hotel business. If you should change your mind—'

It was too late. The ornate gates of the lift were already closing on the two old gentlemen, Bertolini, Anwar, and the two hideous bags.

*   *   *

Once in their rooms, they managed with much difficulty to open the communicating doors. The Old Man had absent-mindedly given some Greek coins as a tip to Bertolini and to Anwar, who didn't quite know how grateful to be, if at all. Now that the two old gentlemen were alone, they began a conversation in Mr Smith's room. Mr Smith opened his bag as it stood on the collapsible stand.

'What are you looking for?' asked the Old Man.

'Nothing. I've merely opened my bag. Isn't that normal?'

'It isn't normal if you've got nothing inside it. Shut it at once. Lock it, and keep it locked until we leave.'

'You're the same old bully you always were,' grumbled Mr Smith, doing what he was told.

'There is a reason for everything I do,' pontificated the Old Man.

'That's what makes it so irritating.'

'The one chance we have of succeeding in our mission is to seem as normal as possible.'

'Fat lot of chance we stand, with our great manes of hair, and curious dress.'

'We may have to change that, too, before we can say we have done what we set out to do. I am aware that people no longer dress like us. Some of them still wear their hair long, as nature demands, but they either train it or cut it so that it imitates the appearance of animals, or they grease it to stand in sticky stalagmites on the head, like oily black coxcombs.'

'Black? Yellow, blue, red, green in their crudest forms. I hope you don't expect us—'

'No, no, no . . .' The Old Man was irritated by this continual opposition to anything he said, this nagging contention. 'I merely don't wish us to become the butt of the inquisitiveness of chambermaids, who notice phenomena like empty suitcases and tell their fellow employees, and the news spreads like wildfire.'

'You made it clear they were empty to the man at the desk by asking me where I had acquired them—'

'I know, and you, with exemplary tact, stated that you had stolen them.'

'Correct. Is that man any more reliable than the other domestics?'

'Yes!'

There was a pause while the echoes of the Old Man's voice died away.

'Why?' asked Mr Smith, in a voice like a rattlesnake.

'Because I tipped him five thousand dollars, that's why. I bought his silence!' The Old Man over-enunciated his reply to give it added weight.

'All you have to do is to leave a few thousand dollars for the maids,' murmured Mr Smith.

'You think I am one to throw my money around? Certainly not when it is far less trouble to lock your bag.'

'It's not your money in any case.'

There was a pause while Mr Smith turned the key in the padlocks.

'When you're finished, we'll go down and dine.'

'We don't need to eat.'

'Nobody need know that.'

'Everything for show.'

'Yes, remember we are on Earth. Everything for show.'

As they moved to the door, Mr Smith suddenly recovered his energy. With a cry like an outraged crow, he stopped dead.

'Why did you say my name is Mr Smith?'

The Old Man shut his eyes for a second. He had been expecting this reproach; in fact, he was surprised it had not occurred earlier.

'Listen,' he said, 'I have had enough difficulty identifying myself. I wasn't going to go through all that again.'

'What did you call yourself?'

'I foolishly identified myself correctly.'

'Ah. Honesty was your privilege.'

'Well, has dishonesty not been yours throughout history?'

'Thanks to you, yes.'

'Oh, I hope we're not going to have that all over again. I must point out that the restaurant closes in a short while.'

'How do you know?'

'I am guessing. And as usual, I guess correctly.'

Mr Smith sat down in a deep sulk.

The Old Man appealed, 'Do you seriously think that it will help us in our investigations if it gets around that not only do we not need clean linen, but that we don't even need sustenance? I leave it to your sense of fair play.'

Mr Smith rose, with a sinister cackle. 'That was a frightfully silly thing to say. So silly, in fact, that it appealed to my acute sense of the ridiculous. All right, I'll go down, but I can't guarantee not to bring up the subject again, so deep is my wound, so searing is the pain.'

There was something about Mr Smith's last words, uttered slowly and with total simplicity, that sent a shiver down where the Old Man's spine should have been.

* * *

'And with that, may I suggest a Christian Brothers Cabernet or a Mondavi Sauvignon, both fine wines, or, if you are looking for something older, but not necessarily better, there is the Forts-de-la-Tour, 1972, from Bordeaux, France, or, at two thousand and eighty dollars a bottle, La Tâche, 1959, from Burgundy, France, or any amount of fine table wines in between,' declared the sommelier without taking a breath.

'To us, all wines are young,' smiled the Old Man.

'The joke is well taken,' said the sommelier

'It's not a joke,' spat Mr Smith.

'*Touché*,' said the sommelier, for something to say.

'Bring us a bottle of the first wine you lay your hands on.'

'Red or white?'

The Old Man glanced at Mr Smith.

'Is there no compromise?'

'Rosé.'

'Good idea,' said the Old Man.

Mr Smith nodded curtly, and the sommelier went off.

'People are staring at us,' muttered Mr Smith. 'We were wrong to come.'

'On the contrary,' replied the Old Man, 'people are wrong to stare.' And the Old Man stared at the other diners, one at a time, and one by one, they went back to their food.

The dinner was not a success. Neither had eaten for so long that every taste had to be acquired, and the delay between dishes seemed interminable. There was little else to do but talk, and whenever these two talked, they attracted attention. Even if the other diners had been inhibited both by the penetrating glance of the Old Man, and by a lugubrious atmosphere which had descended on the dining room, even affecting the usually insensitive pianist, who struck several discordant chords in his rendering of 'Granada', and eventually left the room mopping his brow, they now stole furtive glimpses of the two old men, who, like two small tents, one black, one white, were pitched under the disgusted mask of a triton, in a niche, spewing water from its mouth into a marble fountain.

'Out with it,' muttered the Old Man discreetly. 'Unlike what you usually say, your final reproach as we were leaving our rooms was so heartfelt that I was touched. I don't want you to suffer, whatever you may think.'

Mr Smith laughed in a manner more unpleasant than ironical. Then he grew serious, seeming to have some difficulty in forming his words.

'It was your motive which I always found particularly transparent, and hurtful,' he managed to say eventually.

'Is this something you have said to me before, or is it something quite new?'

'Oh, how can I remember?' Mr Smith cried. 'We haven't seen each other for centuries! I may have touched on it, but I believe it to be a very old reproach, which I have never mentioned before.'

The Old Man tried to help. 'I remember your sickening cry as you plunged overboard. That was a cry that was to haunt me for many years,' he conceded.

'Years . . .' echoed Mr Smith. 'Yes . . . yes . . . that was bad enough. I had my back to you, was looking over the side of a cumulus cloud, and then, suddenly, without warning, this callous shove, and the sickening fall. In mortal terms, it was murder.'

'You are still here.'

'In human terms, I said.'

'I apologize,' said the Old Man, clearly expecting that to be the end of the matter.

'Apologize?' cackled Mr Smith in amazement.

'When have I had an earlier opportunity?' asked the Old Man.

'Never mind about that,' Mr Smith went on. 'It's not the fact of my expulsion. That I have had to live with and I would probably have left on my own sooner or later. It was the motive! You had to rectify a terrible oversight in the Creation, which was otherwise handled with competence.'

'An oversight?' asked the Old Man, betraying what almost amounted to nervousness.

'Yes. With everyone white, how could they recognize you for what you are?'

'What are you saying?' The Old Man licked his lips.

'White needs black in order to be recognized for what it is,' said Mr Smith with terrible precision and lack of his usual fuss. 'When all is white, there is no white. You had to push me in order to be recognized yourself. The motive was . . . vanity.'

'No!' the Old Man protested. Then, as an afterthought, he added, 'Oh, I hope not!'

'You have a debt of gratitude towards me which no amount of contrition can ever hope to repay. Until my expulsion, nobody, not even the angels, understood you or felt the warmth of your radiance.

With me to supply the background of darkness, the contrast, you became visible for what you were, and still are.'

'It is to find out if I still am, if we still are, that we are here on Earth.'

'Without my sacrifice – without *me*, you are invisible!' Mr Smith spat.

'I am willing to believe that that is partly true,' said the Old Man, having recovered his composure, 'but don't pretend that you did not enjoy your experience, at least at the beginning. You yourself graciously, and accurately, said a moment ago that, had you not been pushed, you would probably have left of your own accord sooner or later. That means the seeds were there. I pushed the right angel.'

'I don't dispute that. The colleagues you created for me were entirely without character, with the possible exception of Gabriel, who was always volunteering for difficult missions, ready to carry complicated messages over long distances. And do you know why? He was bored. As bored as I was.'

'He never showed it.'

'You wouldn't know boredom if you saw it.'

'I would now. I would now. But I admit that then, when the world still smelled of newly aired linen—'

'And those ghastly seraphim and cherubim, with their unbroken voices, shrieking their choral evensong in unbearable unison, not a sweet dissonance, not a cajoling harmony or a subtle shift of emphasis among the million or more of them, dreadful little garden ornaments, fashioned out of marzipan, too pristine, too dainty to need a single diaper or chamber pot among them . . .'

By this time the Old Man was rocking with a laughter as generous as it was silent. He extended his hand. Surprised, Mr Smith took it.

'Those seraphim and cherubim were not a success,' he chuckled. 'You are right. You often are. And above all you are a born entertainer. Your descriptions of things are a joy, even though at times the mixture of your metaphors threatens to obscure some of the darker of your pearls. I am so pleased I took the initiative at last – the initiative which led to this reunion.'

'I bear no malice. I just see things clearly.'

'Too clearly . . .'

'It is the centuries of deception, of festering resentment.'

'I understand.'

The Old Man looked Mr Smith deep in the eyes, and enclosed Mr Smith's freezing hands in his warm ones.

'If it is true that without you I am unrecognizable, it is equally true that without me you don't exist. There is no need for either of us without the other. Together we constitute a gamut, a palette, a universe. We dare never be friends or even allies; we cannot avoid being at least nodding acquaintances. Let us make the best of a difficult situation by retaining our civility towards one another as we find out if we are still necessities, and not just luxuries, or even superfluities. In success or failure, we are, for better or worse, inseparable.'

'I find nothing to quarrel with in what you say, except . . .' Mr Smith seemed brimful of sudden mischief.

'Be careful,' the Old Man appealed. 'I have succeeded in re-establishing a kind of equilibrium between us. I have made concessions. Don't spoil it all, I beg of you.'

'There is nothing to spoil,' Mr Smith croaked. 'I'm no fool. I understand the geometry of our positions, what is possible, what isn't. I am not here to score points which, after all this time, are not worth scoring. I merely think—'

'Yes?' interrupted the Old Man, hoping to provoke Mr Smith into thinking again.

'I think it's ironic that, in order to create a new function for me, you had to play a dirty trick on me, worthy of me, but not of you.'

The Old Man grew immensely sad. 'That's true,' he said in a voice which suddenly showed his age. 'In order to create the Devil, I had to do something diabolical. Push you in the back when you were least expecting it.'

'That's all I wish to say.'

The Old Man smiled sadly. 'Do you wish any more soup? Trifle? Venison? Trout? Grouse? Mint tea?'

Mr Smith brushed all this off. 'It was inevitable,' he said. 'Thanks for the invitation.'

The two of them had not noticed, in the ebb and flow of their conversation, that the lights had become dimmer and dimmer, the usual subtle hint that the kitchen is irrevocably closing, and that the last diners are infringing on agreements between the hotel and the unions. All the other diners had sidled out, although some of them had

11

experienced some difficulty in getting their bills. At the height of the argument, most of which was clearly audible, the waiters had become nervous of re-entering the restaurant, while the remaining diners were rooted to the spot.

'Let's just go,' said the Old Man. 'We can pay tomorrow.'

'Give me some money while you're about it, otherwise I'll have to steal some.'

'Of course, of course,' said the Old Man happily.

Nobody had noticed that the pianist was once again at his instrument, probably in the hope of at least a show of gratitude. He broke into song as the old men were picking their way among the tables towards the exit. 'Pennies from Heaven . . .'

2

It was the next morning. They had no need of sleep so the night had seemed long, especially since they were shy of conversation now that a degree of harmony had been established between them. The Old Man had just created some pocket money for Mr Smith, which the latter was placing carefully in his pocket. There was a discreet knock at the door.

'Come in,' called the Old Man.

'The door is locked,' said a voice.

'Just a moment.'

When he and Mr Smith had finished their transaction, the Old Man went to the door, unlocked it, and opened it. Outside stood the concierge and four policemen, who immediately pressed forward with quite unnecessary urgency.

'What is this?'

'I must apologize,' said the concierge. 'I must thank you once again for your excessive generosity, but must also regrettably inform you that the banknotes are forgeries.'

'That is not true,' declared the Old Man. 'I made them myself.'

'Are you willing to sign a statement to that effect?' asked the leading policeman, whose name was Kaszpricki.

'What is all this about?'

'You can't make money all by yourself,' said Patrolman O'Haggerty.

'I don't need any help,' retorted the Old Man haughtily. 'Look!'

He dug into his pocket, and after a moment of concentration, hundreds of shining coins cascaded onto the carpet as from a fruit machine.

Two of the policemen half kneeled before being called to order by Kaszpricki. The concierge did kneel.

'OK, what are they?' asked Kaszpricki.

'Pesos, I guess. Philip II of Spain.'

'Is numismatics your business? Is that it?' enquired Kaszpricki. 'But that don't allow you to monkey with green backs. That's a federal offence, and I got to take you in.'

'Handcuffs?' asked Patrolman Coltellucci.

'Yeah, we might as well do this in style,' Kaszpricki answered.

Mr Smith panicked. 'Shall we disappear? Use our tricks?'

'Hold it right there,' snapped Patrolman Schmatterman, drawing his gun, and standing with it in both hands, as though urinating over a great distance.

'My dear Smith, we must subject ourselves to these little inconveniences if we are to find out how these people live, and above all, how they treat each other. Is that not why we came?'

The handcuffs were snapped into place, and the cortège left the room. The concierge brought up the rear, reiterating his regrets at the incident, both on his behalf, and on that of the hotel.

Once at the police station, they were stripped of their outer garments, and grilled by Chief Eckhardt, who stared at them unblinking from under an iron-grey crew cut and a forehead lined like music manuscript paper. He wore rimless glasses which enlarged his eyes to the size of small oysters.

'OK, your name is Smith, I got that. Given name?'

'John,' said the Old Man.

'Can Smith not speak for himself?'

'Not on . . . personal matters . . . He had a bad fall, you understand.'

'How long ago?'

'Before your time.'

Chief Eckhardt gazed at them for a while.

'Is just he crazy – or are you both nuttier than fruit cakes?'

'There is never an excuse for rudeness,' admonished the Old Man.

'OK, so we'll try you. Name?'

'God – frey.'

'For a moment I figured we was going to be subjected to blasphemy. What did you find in their baggage?'

'Nothin',' replied one of the two policemen who had just entered the room.

'And nothing in the pockets neither,' added the other, 'except forty-six thousand, eight hundred and thirty dollars, all in notes, in the right-side inner pocket.'

'Forty-six thousand?' yelled Chief Eckhardt. 'In whose pocket, in which pocket?'

'Dark fellow's.'

'Smith! OK, so who made the money, you or Smith?'

'I made the money,' said the Old Man, with an opulent weariness, 'and I gave it to Smith.'

'What for?'

'To spend. Petty cash.'

'Forty-six thousand bucks, petty cash? What do you consider real money, for crying out loud?' cried Eckhardt.

'I haven't given the matter much thought,' said the Old Man. 'As I explained to the gentleman at the hotel, I have no idea of the value of money.'

'You know it well enough to forge it.'

'I don't forge it. I have pockets like cornucopia, virtually bottom-less, pockets of plenty, if you will. I only have to think money and my pockets gradually fill with it. The only difficulty is, after a fairly lengthy history, I find it difficult at times to remember where and when I am. For instance, I have no notion why I spilled so many Spanish dubloons, or whatever they were, on the hotel floor this morning. Inspired by the furniture in our room, I must have fleetingly spared a thought for poor Philip II, who had such a tortuous way of expressing what he imagined was his love for me, half sunken in moth-eaten ermine, the smell of camphor mingling with the incense in the icy corridors of the Escorial.'

Mr Smith laughed joylessly. 'My moths won the day against the camphor by sheer force of numbers.'

'That's enough,' snapped Chief Eckhardt. 'We're straying way off the point, and I don't intend letting that happen. The two of you's is going before the magistrate in the morning, charged with forgery and attempt to defraud. Which way do you intend pleadin', and do you require a lawyer?'

'How would I pay the lawyer?' asked the Old Man. 'I could only create money for the purpose.'

'You can have a lawyer allotted, as a public service.'

'No thank you, I hate to waste people's time. But tell me one thing, so that Mr Smith and I have at least a little chance on our side as we defend ourselves. How can you tell that my money is forged?'

Chief Eckhardt smiled with grim satisfaction. He was happier when the matter at hand was down to earth and crystal clear, supported by irrefutable facts, and therefore accurately illustrative of the technical superiority of the US of A.

'We got a lot of ways, all of them the result of state-of-the-art technological know-how . . . and they're changin' all the time . . . gettin' more refined. I'm not going to let on what these methods are, 'cos in a sense we're in the same business, you trying to get away with it, me successful in stopping you. But let me say this. This great country of ours is a great place for private initiative, but I got to tell you, forgery's not one of them. I'll see to that. Me and other law enforcers.'

The Old Man took on his most disarming air. 'Tell me one thing as a courtesy before you relegate us to the impersonal powers of the law. How does my money compare to the real stuff?'

Chief Eckhardt was a fair-minded man. Fair-minded and ruthless, reflecting a world in which even justice was subject to a deadline, and in which even a snap decision was better than the embarrassment of doubt, which smacks of incompetence. He took up a note and looked at it with studied negligence.

'On a scale of zero to a hundred, I'd give you thirty. Careless watermark, a bit of imprecision in the brushwork, and the signature is legible – it shouldn't be. As a forgery it leaves a whole lot to be desired.'

The Old Man and Mr Smith looked at one another in some alarm. Things were not going to be as easy as they had hoped.

Chief Eckhardt placed them in the same cell, out of compassion. It happened to be cell No. 6, for quite another reason.

*　　*　　*

'How much longer are we going to stay here?' asked Mr Smith.

'Not much,' replied the Old Man.

'It is very unpleasant here.'

'It is.'

'I can feel hostility all around me. For some reason, I don't inspire confidence. And then you don't want me to talk. That makes it even worse. I had a bad fall, indeed. A joke in frightful taste.'

'Nobody knows it's a joke.'

'You do, and I do. Isn't that enough? Down to fundamentals.'

The Old Man smiled as he lay on the iron bed, a little on his side, his hands folded benevolently on his stomach.

'How things have changed,' he mused. 'Within twenty-four hours of our reunion here on Earth, we are already in prison. Who could have guessed it would happen so quickly? And who could have foreseen the reason for our undoing?'

'You could have, but you didn't.'

'No, I didn't. I have never been very quick in noticing, let alone foreseeing change. I remember during the time of our adolescence, before we were confirmed in our divinity, when mortals still thought we were installed on the peak of Mount Olympus. They saw us as a mere reflection of their own lives, a kind of endless domestic comedy as seen from below stairs, with a mass of endings, happy and unhappy, the result of superstition, fantasy and innuendo. Nymphs turning into trees and heifers and mournful little rivulets. All manner of nonsense, with me alternately a bull or a fly or a lost wind from the flatulent bowels of the Earth. Those were the days, in a way. Every deity had his handful of shrines, his or her ration of prayers. We were all too busy to be consistently jealous of one another – we were only jealous, in fact, when jealousy moved the plot forward. Life was an adventure, or perhaps what I have heard referred to as a soap opera. Religion was an extension of life itself on a higher but not necessarily better plane. Guilt had not yet been thought of as a poison in the sacramental wine. Mankind was not yet tortured by imponderables and the inventions of middlemen.'

Mr Smith suddenly laughed merrily. 'Remember the panic when the first Hellenic mountaineer reached the top of Mount Olympus and found nothing there?'

The Old Man refrained from joining in the laughter. 'Yes, but the panic was only ours, not theirs. The man was too frightened to describe the pinnacle as empty when he returned, for fear of being torn limb from limb by believers. He did the second most foolish thing for fear of doing the first foolish thing. He confessed this state of affairs to a priest. The priest, who was probably a political appointee, told the man that the news must go no further. The man swore not to tell anyone. The priest said, "How can I believe you, once you have told me?" The man found no answer, and died under mysterious circumstances the very same night. But, as they say, the cat was out of the bag. People had seen an adventurous mountaineer going up – others had seen him come down, dour and silent. Gradually, as the quality of sandals improved, people began to climb to the top in order to picnic, and the place acquired in litter what it lost in divine mystery.'

'And gradually the seat of the gods rose into zones of mist and rainbows, both physically and in the imagination. Symbolism reared its muddled head, and we were off into the era of the smothering of primal truths in the opaque sauce of mumbo-jumbo. The simple melody was subjected to a glut of orchestrators,' said Mr Smith.

The Old Man was moved. 'How can you speak with such emotion about things which no longer concern you?' he asked.

'Must I lose my interest in your Heaven just because you kicked me out? Remember, criminals haunt the scene of their crimes, children revisit their schools when grown up. I have certain interests as a one-time angel – and then, Hell has changed much less than Heaven over the ages. It is not a place which encourages change, whereas you have had to adapt to every new moral perception, every whiff of theological fashion.'

'I don't think so. I don't agree.'

'In my day, you insisted on the irksome idea of perfection as our guiding principle. In the nature of this, perfection is the antithesis of personality: we were all identical, and perfect. No wonder I was subject to twinges of revolt, Gabriel too, and probably even the others. It was life in a hall of mirrors – wherever you looked, you saw yourself. Yes, I admit it: when you pushed me out, I felt an immense sentiment of relief even as I fell to an uncertain eternity. I am myself, and alone, I thought, as the air around me became warmer and more agitated. I have escaped! It was only later that I grasped at the idea of bitter resentment, which I nurtured as one nurtures a plant, in case we ever met again. But now that the reunion is a reality, I find it more interesting to tell the truth. Evil often bores me, for evident reasons. Virtue also is dull, but there is nothing in all of your Creation as sterile, as lifeless, as overwhelmingly negative as perfection. Dare to contradict me!'

'No,' said the Old Man reasonably, but with a trace of sadness. 'I agree with far too much of what you say for comfort. Perfection is one of those concepts that looks so foolproof in theory, until practice turns it into a contagious yawn. We soon gave it up.'

'Have you ever given it up – entirely?'

'Oh, I think so. It perhaps still exists as an ambition in some particularly subservient minds, those who are so saintly they think that boredom is merely an extended pause before an eternal truth is uttered, and who spend their lives waiting, with sickly little smiles of imminent omniscience on their lips. But to most of us – even to the angels, who are so emancipated I hardly ever see them these days – it is recognized that insistence on total good and total evil are archaic concepts. I don't like to speak of myself, simply because I can see you with greater clarity than I can lavish on myself, and without seeking to flatter you, or indeed to insult you, I must tell you from our brief re-acquaintance that you are far too intelligent to be entirely evil.'

A pulse of irony seemed to spread over Mr Smith's craggy features, like mottled sunlight over water. 'I was once an angel,' he said, and in the depths of his black eyes there was a flicker of tenderness. Then his features hardened again. Warmth was expelled. 'The cases are legion of great figures in villainy throughout history who had received their education from priests. Stalin, for instance.'

'Who?' asked the Old Man.

'Never mind. It was merely an example of a seminarist who became dictator of a land dedicated to atheism.'

'Ah, Russia.'

'Not Russia. The Soviet Union.'

The Old Man frowned as he tried to work this out, while Mr Smith reflected that to know everything is not necessarily to be very alert in selecting items from the vast inventory at one's disposal.

'In any case,' Mr Smith went on, when he estimated that the Old Man had had enough time to bring a little order to the celestial computer lodged in his mind, 'we will have plenty of opportunities for further ethical meanderings in all the prisons in which we are destined to find one another while here on Earth. My growing concern is how to escape from this one.'

'Use your powers, but for my sake, don't wander too far away. I will feel lost if I lose you now.'

'I only want to see if my powers still work.'

'Of course they work. Have faith. You know how to do that. And then, they must have worked for us to meet with pin-point accuracy on a sidewalk in Washington after millennia of absence.'

'They work all right, but for how long? I have this worrying sentiment of their being rationed in some way.'

'I know what you mean. There suddenly seems a limit to one's possibilities, although this may well be an illusion brought about by longevity. I don't think it's true.'

'I shall feel emasculated if one day I am completely without tricks.'

The Old Man expressed a momentary irritation. 'I wish you wouldn't refer to them as tricks. They are miracles.'

Mr Smith grinned one of his ghastly grins. 'Yours may be miracles,' he said. 'Mine are tricks.'

There was a silence.

Chief Eckhardt, established in a soundproof room in the basement together with members of his staff, looked up. His face expressed all the puzzlement of an average policeman confronted by the obscure. Cell No. 6 was, of course, bugged, and they had been listening to the conversation of the two old men, their brows knitted like those of schoolchildren in an exam, their jaws rippling with determination in its purest and most meaningless form.

'What do you make of it, Chief?' Kaszpricki ventured.

'Not much,' Eckhardt replied, 'and I wouldn't trust the guy claimed he knew what the hell they was talkin' about. Lookit, O'Haggerty, go up to the cell and see what gives. I don't like this silence, and all this talk of tricks and gettin' out.'

O'Haggerty left the listening room and went up to cell No. 6. He noticed at once that the Old Man was alone.

'Hey, where's your friend?' he asked dramatically.

The Old Man appeared surprised to find himself alone. 'Oh, he must have stepped out for a moment.'

'The door was triple locked!'

'I have no other contribution to make.'

This Eckhardt and the other eavesdroppers understood.

'Kaszpricki, go up and see – no, on second thoughts, I'll go up myself. Schmatterman, keep that tape going. I want all of this on the record. The rest of you, come on with me.'

When Eckhardt reached cell No. 6, he found Patrolman O'Haggerty inside, with both old men. 'What's been going on round here?' he asked gruffly.

'When I got up here, this old guy was alone in the cell,' panted O'Haggerty.

'That's what I understood,' said Eckhardt, who then looked at Mr Smith. 'Where was you?'

'I never left the cell. I was in here all the time.'

'That's a lie!' cried O'Haggerty. 'He got back just seconds before you got here, Chief!'

'What do you mean, got back, O'Haggerty? He entered the cell by the door?'

'No. No. I guess he materialized.'

'Materialized?' Eckhardt said slowly, as though he had yet another nutcase on his hands. 'And what are you doing *inside* the cell?'

'I got in to see if I could get out,' O'Haggerty said.

'And can you?'

'No, I can't. So I don't see how Smith did it.'

'Maybe Smith didn't do it. Maybe Smith was in here all the time?'

'Exactly,' said Smith.

'We don't need no help from you. Do me a favour, just button it,' replied Eckhardt.

'I can't countenance all these lies,' said the Old Man.

Mr Smith tut-tut-tutted.

'I mean it,' the Old Man went on. 'As I told your delegate, Mr Smith stepped out for a moment.'

'He couldn't have,' said Eckhardt sternly. 'These locks are the latest state-of-the-art pickproof types from the Safe as Houses people. There's no way you can get out without dynamite.'

The Old Man smiled. He felt the time had come. 'You want me to show you?'

'OK, show me,' Eckhardt drawled slowly, allowing his right hand to find the revolver in his open holster.

'Very well, but before I go, let me thank you for your charming hospitality.'

An engaging smile still on his lips, he vanished into thin air. A split second later, Eckhardt shot twice into the space where the Old Man had been.

The shock of this was instantly superseded by a cry from Mr Smith

21

as eerie as that of an aviary of winter birds, a desolate, discordant shriek.

'Shoot, will you! Think you can better *our* tricks with tricks of your own. Do your worst! I'm off! Try to stop me!' And Mr Smith laughed in their faces, cruelly, disdainfully.

Eckhardt shot a third time. Mr Smith's laughter turned to something between physical pain and surprise, but he disappeared before any of them could draw any conclusions.

Eckhardt was instantly apologetic. 'I tried to get him in the foot.'

'Let me outa here,' implored O'Haggerty.

On the pavement, Mr Smith materialized beside the Old Man, both bubbling with relief and pleasure at their double success. As they walked away, Mr Smith loitered by a trashcan, to the momentary displeasure of the Old Man. Fumbling among the refuse, he withdrew a soiled newspaper and placed it in his pocket. Then they walked away.

Inside the police station, Eckhardt's mind had cleared even if his ears were still ringing with the impact of the shots.

'OK, Schmatterman. You can stop the tapes,' he called up to the ceiling. 'Pack them, mark them, and file them. And meantimes, guard them with your life.'

'What you going to do, Chief?' asked Kaszpricki, every bit the right-hand man, boosting his boss's confidence by forcing him into powerful decisions.

'This thing is too big for us,' muttered Eckhardt, but so that all could hear. 'I'm going to do the only responsible thing. I am going to call in the highest possible authority.'

'The Archdiocese,' suggested O'Haggerty, who was Catholic. Eckhardt glanced at him with disdain.

'The President?' Coltellucci was a Republican.

'The Federal Bureau of Investigation,' Eckhardt said, with painful slowness. 'The FBI . . . Ever heard of it?'

He neither expected nor received an answer.

3

It was when Mr Smith had removed his third stinking newspaper from trash awaiting removal on the sidewalk that the Old Man remonstrated for the first time.

'Is it necessary to steal old broadsheets from garbage?' he asked, as they walked along one of Washington's many tree-lined avenues.

'It is hardly stealing it if it is taken from materials by definition rejected by their owners, otherwise they would not be in shining black bags by the roadside. You want me to pinch them from newsvendors? That *would* be stealing,' Mr Smith replied, as his eyes scanned the greasy pages, to which bits of apple peel were still gamely sticking.

'What are you reading?'

'Is there a better way to understand the mentality of those who have so far made our existence on Earth unpleasant than by reading as a duty what they read for pleasure?'

'And what have you discovered?' enquired the Old Man, with a trace of scepticism in his voice.

'I have skimmed through three or four editorials while we have been walking, and I think I begin to understand that these people are very well informed and even extremely efficient about everything which concerns them, and almost totally ignorant about that which does not. Counterfeit money, for instance, concerns them, since it exploits their prosperity in a way which flouts their acute sense of legality. It is for that reason they have developed highly sophisticated ways of discovering that money, even if it is of divine origin, is not manufactured in an authorized mint.'

'Legality? Do you mean that they are law abiding?'

'No. I mean they have a horror of using counterfeit money in corrupt operations. It seems to them that, for corruption to count, the dishonest transactions must be conducted with legal tender.'

The Old Man frowned. 'I can see your mind has been sharply focused while mine has been meandering hither and thither. Why do you say they are uninterested in that which does not concern them?'

'There are one or two editorials about changes in the Austrian Government, deadlocks in the Israeli Cabinet, and the Pope's visit to Papua, and so on, which appear to be written by people both very well informed, very conceited, and very ignorant in their use of the information at their disposal. It says that they are syndicated. I have no idea what that means. The word is a new one.'

'I'll say this,' said the Old Man, a little depressed, 'you have weathered the passing centuries better than I have. I had no idea that Austria had a government, that Israel has a cabinet, or that – where did you say the Pope is?'

'Papua. Fiji tomorrow. Okinawa and Guam the day after. Rome on Tuesday.'

'Don't laugh at me – where is Papua?'

'New Guinea, north of Australia.'

'And what, for my sake, does Israel need with a cabinet?'

'Everyone else has a Cabinet. They need one also.'

'Are they not content with being chosen?'

'They wish to be on the safe side. They choose themselves as well. And for that, of course, they need a Cabinet.'

'I have a lot to learn.' A cloud passed slowly over the Old Man's pensive face. He cheered up suddenly. 'And have you any practical solutions to our predicament as a result of reading soiled newspapers?'

'Yes,' said Mr Smith. 'We must change our physical appearance.'

'Why?'

'We are far too easy to identify. Remember, we may enjoy ambling down leafy streets among neo-Georgian houses, it may seem a civilized pastime in fine weather, but we are criminals on the run.'

The Old Man's eyebrows raised. 'Criminals?'

'Certainly. We were apprehended as counterfeiters, and we escaped from justice.'

'Go on.'

'And now, I have a plan, based on my perusal of the financial pages.'

'Oh, is that what you were doing? I have never known you as incommunicative as you were during this walk, even in the old days.'

'There is no time to lose, that's why. My plan is this. I will disguise myself as an oriental—'

'Whatever for?'

'It is quite clear that the one burning anxiety of the Americans is the immense upsurge of oriental competition. Once I have become transmogrified, you will concentrate hard and produce a large quantity of their banknotes, known as yen.'

'That is still forgery.'

'What other way is there, apart from stealing? We can't very well earn it. Or do you think I have a future as a baby-sitter?' The giggles of Mr Smith rang out like a carillon of cracked bells.

'Tell me your plan,' said the Old Man, wincing.

'They know every detail of their own money,' replied Mr Smith, slowly recovering from his outburst, 'but they know little or nothing about Japanese banknotes, with a calligraphy which is to them indecipherable. The fact that I look Japanese will be a guarantee to any American bank clerk that the notes are genuine.'

'What do you intend to do with these notes if I succeed in creating them?'

Mr Smith was a little pained that the Old Man had not yet understood. 'I shall change them at the bank.'

'For what?'

'For *genuine* dollars.'

The Old Man stopped walking. 'Brilliant,' he said, quietly. 'Absolutely dishonest, but brilliant.'

At that moment, a car with a blue light on the roof squealed round the corner ahead of them, grazed and buffeted several stationary cars, and slewed sideways to block this quiet residential street. Instinctively, the Old Man and Mr Smith turned round to go the other way. A policeman on a motorcycle was riding up the sidewalk, followed by a second one. In the roadway, another police car drove up with as much fuss and hysteria as the first one. Men jumped out, but they were all in civilian clothes. Some of the older ones wore hats. They all brandished guns, and they shepherded the Old Man and Mr Smith to one of the cars. Here they were forced to place their hands on the roof while the newcomers frisked their ample robes.

'What did I tell you?' said Mr Smith. 'We must change our appearance, either now or later.'

'What was that?' snapped the senior of the frisking officers.

'Later,' replied the Old Man.

They were bundled into the cars and driven to a huge building in the outskirts of the city.

'What is this – police headquarters?' asked the Old Man.

'A hospital,' answered the leading FBI officer, Captain Gonella.

'A hospital,' echoed the Old Man.

'On account you are a very sick old guy,' crooned Gonella. 'In fact, the two's of you is. We're going to try to show you didn't know what you was doing when you made all that money. That you did it while the balance of your mind was disturbed, see. We're going to give you every chance. Only you got to help us. I want you to answer every question the doctor may ask. I ain't telling you what to say, see . . . just don't step outa line, don't start talking unless you're talked to . . . easy on the words. Just take it easy. Act as crazy as you like, they're expecting it, only just don't confuse the doctors with a lot of words . . . hell, I don't have to tell you what to do . . . and – oh, one final word. Quit disappearing, will you? The FBI don't appreciate it. I don't know how it's done. I don't want to know. All I'm saying, don't do it. That's all.'

They were paraded before a terrifying woman dressed as some sort of superior nurse or matron, who sat at a reception desk. In fact, at first glance, Mr Smith and the receptionist scared each other, with good reason. The woman wore a plastic card proclaiming her name to be Hazel McGiddy. She stared inquisitorially at the newcomers with her bulbous blue eyes, so light as to be almost egg-white. Her eyelids seemed to keep the eyes in their sockets by sheer determination, and the mouth, like a scarlet wound in the centre of a shrivelled, inanimate face, was the only feature which had any movement in it, since it twitched almost imperceptibly as though she was continually trying to remove a remnant of yesterday's lunch from a cavity in her teeth.

'All right,' she barked. Such women, and sergeants of both sexes, always start any disagreeable military litany with these two words. 'Which one of you two is Smith?'

'Him,' said the Old Man.

'One at a time!'

'Me,' said Smith.

'That's more like it, young man.'

'It's not my real name, nor am I young.'

'You're down as Smith on the police report, and you got no right to change it. If you didn't want to be called Smith, you should have thought of that before you got yourself on the computer. Now, you're Smith for life. Religion?'

Smith began a long, silent peel of laughter, during which his lanky figure shuddered with a suppressed and evidently painful rhythm.

'I'm waiting, Smith.'

'Catholic!' he screeched, as though posing for El Greco.

'I won't allow you to say such things!' thundered the Old Man.

'One at a time!'

'No, no. It's too much. Why do you have to know our religion in any case?'

Miss McGiddy closed her eyes for a moment, as though registering the fact that she was so used to dealing with idiots that it wasn't lightweights like these who were going to get her down.

'We do it,' she replied, as though dictating for schoolchildren, 'so as if one of you seniors should see fit to pass away while in our hospital, we will know in which church to bury him or where to send the ashes in the event of incineration.'

'We haven't died for centuries. Why on earth should we develop the habit now?' asked the Old Man.

Miss McGiddy glanced at Captain Gonella, who shrugged it off with a look full of meaning. Miss McGiddy nodded briefly.

'OK,' she said to the Old Man, 'we'll give your friend a rest, and turn to you. You are Mr Godfrey.'

'No,' replied the Old Man, coldly.

'That's what it says here.'

'It is bad enough that we are forced by circumstances over which we have no control to manufacture money – but this continual fibbing is beginning to annoy me. My name is God, pure and simple. God, with a capital "G", if you feel inclined to be polite.'

Miss McGiddy raised a quizzical orange eyebrow. 'You expect me to be surprised?' she enquired. 'We have three inmates undergoing treatment right here who believe they're God. We have to keep them apart for their own safety.'

'I do not believe I am God,' said the Old Man. 'I am God.'

'That's what the others said. We call them God One, Two and Three. D'you want to be God Four?'

'I am every God, from minus infinity to plus infinity. There are no others!'

'Keep him away from the others. I'll call Dr Kleingeld,' Miss McGiddy informed Captain Gonella.

The Old Man looked at the Captain, who smiled.

'There are seven hundred and twelve men and four women in the United States who believe they're God. FBI figures. That includes Guam and Puerto Rico, of course. You got plenty of competition.'

'How many claim to be Satan?' asked Mr Smith suddenly.

'That's a new one on me,' replied Gonella. 'None that I know of.'

'It's wonderful to feel exclusive,' Mr Smith said softly, with a little camp preen, to the Old Man's evident annoyance.

'Is that who you are? Satan?' laughed Gonella. 'Great, great. Satan Smith. I'd like to have been at your baptism. What was it, total immersion, in fire? OK, Miss McGiddy, just mark down the essentials we know about, I'll countersign the entry form. We gotta get a move on—'

'The essentials?'

'God and Satan. It's a bumper day for us. We oughta feel proud.'

'I've already marked Mr Godfrey and Mr Smith, and that's the way it's going to stay.'

'OK, OK, it's all phoney anyways, whichever way you look at it.'

'How's about the statutory deposit?'

'We'll handle that, unless you're prepared to take counterfeit?'

'Are you kidding?'

With this frosty badinage, the two captives were led to their physical examinations prior to their interview with Dr Mort Kleingeld, the renowned psychiatrist, author of *The If, the It, and the I*, as well as the more popular and accessible, *All You Need to Know about Insanity*.

They tried to take the Old Man's pulse, but couldn't find it. They made X-rays, and nothing appeared on the plates. In the words of Dr Benaziz, the co-ordinator of the examining team, 'We found no heart, no ribs, no vertebrae, no veins, no arteries, and, I am glad to report, no signs of disease.'

Among the remarks on the report was the observation that the Old Man's skin had at moments the consistency of 'ceramics', at other moments 'a rubbery feel quite unlike that of human flesh'. He appeared to be capable of changing his texture at will.

Mr Smith caused even greater perplexity, owing to the astonishing heat he emanated when stripped, including little puffs of smoke which burst almost imperceptibly from his blackened pores, filling the ward with a vague and unpleasant smell of sulphur, and this although he was normally ice cold to the touch.

They tried to take his temperature, but the thermometer exploded in his mouth. He cheerfully munched the glass, and swallowed the mercury as though it were a thimbleful of a rare vintage. They tried to place a replacement thermometer in his armpit, but once again it blew up. The last resort was a rectal thermometer, and he joyfully turned his body over in bed, since he was by inclination an exhibitionist. The doctor came back to the others with the alarming news, 'No rectum.'

'Come on,' cried Gonella, 'he's got to be hiding it someplace.'

'Have you any ideas where?' asked the exasperated Dr Benaziz.

'There's people had operations, shit out their hips, am I right?'

'That's even more evident than an outlet in the place nature intended.'

'Christ!' cried Gonella, now losing his temper. 'Let's get them to the shrink. That's what we brought them here for. We know they's alive, and they don't look like they's at death's door. If they do, they've been at death's door so long it don't make no difference. We need the evidence of the shrink.'

'You won't get that in a hurry,' remarked Dr Benaziz. 'Kleingeld takes his time.'

'Everyone's time,' commented another doctor.

'Everyone's money,' added a third.

'Everyone's time *is* everyone's money,' stated Dr Benaziz.

*   *   *

Dr Kleingeld was a man of small stature with a disproportionately large head, who spoke in whispers. He evidently thought it expedient to dominate his clients by undercutting their volume, by making them strain to hear, by inducing in them the feeling that if they so much as breathed too hard, they might miss something. He studied his notes from the depths of an all-embracing easy chair with a smile of self-assurance and superior knowledge on his thin lips. The chair was only just slightly more erect than the couch on which the Old Man was stretched.

'How do you like my couch?' Dr Kleingeld whispered.

'I don't know the difference.'

'The difference?'

'Between your couch and other couches.'

'I see. Because you're God?' Dr Kleingeld was amused by the idea.

'Perhaps. Probably.'

'I had a man in here a little time ago who said he was God. He said he liked my couch enormously.'

'That proves, if proof were needed, that he isn't God.'

'What proof have you that you *are* God?'

'I don't need proof. That's the whole point.'

There was a pause while Dr Kleingeld made a few notes.

'Do you remember the Creation?'

The Old Man hesitated. 'What I remember would mean nothing to you.'

'That's an interesting observation. They usually repeat long passages out of Genesis, as though they had remembered the events. All they have remembered is the text.'

'Whom are you referring to?'

'Patients who say they're God.'

Kleingeld wrote a few more notes.

'May I ask why you came back to Earth?'

The Old Man reflected. 'I don't really know in so many words. A sudden . . . surprising loneliness. A desire to see for myself the peculiar variations on the theme I thought so splendid long ago. And then . . . it's too difficult to put into words . . . for the time being. May I ask you a question?'

'Of course, but I haven't as many answers as you have.'

'Do you . . .? You seem to believe I am . . . who I say I am.'

Dr Kleingeld laughed silently. 'I wouldn't go as far as that,' he said softly. 'You know, I don't find it very easy to believe in anything.'

'That is the mark of your intelligence.'

'How nice of you to say so. I am not afraid to change my mind. In fact, I encourage myself to do so, regularly. To worry my sense of the truth as a dog worries a bone. Nothing is constant. Everything changes all the time. Humans age. So do ideas. So does faith. All things are eroded by life and that is why I find it not too difficult to talk to you as though you are God without really knowing or caring much whether you are or not.'

'How curious!' said the Old Man, very much alive. 'I never realized how embarrassing it would be to be believed. It is so unexpected. When you said just now that you don't really care much whether I am God or not, it came as a relief after a moment of panic. You see, down on Earth, it's so much easier to pretend to be God than to actually be Him.'

'It's easier to be considered mad than to be blamed for all that seems to have gone wrong with the world—'

'Or praised as omnipotence personified. There is no more terrible pressure than to be the object of prayers.'

Dr Kleingeld wrote again.

'May I ask the identity of your travelling companion?'

'Ah!' cried the Old Man. 'I knew you would ask sooner or later.' There was a brief pause. 'You asked me why I came down to Earth after so long a time . . . Well, please don't tell him, but I have had for ever so long a recurrent twinge of conscience about him . . . You see, I pushed him out.'

'Out?'

'Perhaps I am asking you to accept too much all at once – but – Heaven.'

'It exists?'

'Oh yes, but it isn't quite as enviable as it has always been painted. And the solitude is at times quite oppressive.'

'Solitude? You surprise me. I didn't think you would be prone to such human vulnerabilities.'

'I am alleged to have created man in my own image. I have to keep in touch, do I not? I must have the mechanism for doubt, even the capacity for joy and anguish. If I created man, I must know *what* I created.'

'Does that mean that there are limits even to God's imagination?'

'I never thought of it like that, but of course, there must be.'

'Why?'

'Because . . . because I can only create that which I can imagine, and there must be things I can't imagine.'

31

'In the universe?'

'The universe is my laboratory. I'd go mad in the wide sweep of Heaven without having the universe to play with. It keeps me fresh and youthful – up to a point – but even the universe is largely there for discovery, and human interpretation, since it is made up of matter known to man. It is in the universe that the limits of my imagination become evident – but of course, immortality requires a frame just as mortality does. Mortality has the very necessary frame of death to give life its meaning. Limits to the imagination are equally necessary for immortality, for without them it would quickly become chaos, out of the sheer fatigue of eternity.'

'That is most enlightening,' muttered Dr Kleingeld, 'but you have, of course, in the thrill of elucidation, avoided telling me who your companion is. Is it Satan?'

'I thought I'd said as much.'

'You did, in a way – but remember, I don't necessarily believe *all* you say. Did he once work in the circus?'

The Old Man looked mildly perplexed. 'I have no idea. He may have done. I had lost touch with him since he . . . he left . . . up to yesterday. A circus? Why a circus?'

'I don't know. He seems to be able to make things vanish, even parts of his body, and his relationship with fire appears to be friendly. There are those who swallow fire and do tricks. They usually work in the circus.'

'Tricks! He even calls them tricks. He is rather more extrovert than I am, and he likes surprising, and showing off his powers. I prefer to live like a man while on Earth, if such a possibility exists.' He pondered. 'I wished to see him again, after all this time. I sent a rather furtive message. He responded like a shot. We met the day before yesterday for the first time since prehistory, on the sidewalk before the Smithsonian Institute here in Washington, at twenty-three hundred hours, by mutual arrangement. We went straight to a hotel, where we were denied access because we had no luggage. We spent one night between the Smithsonian and the National Gallery.'

'Which are both shut at night.'

'Walls are no problem, nor are heights. What we saw encouraged me enormously about certain of man's achievements, and bored Mr Smith almost to distraction.'

'The next night you found accommodation, and had to create money in order to pay the hotel. Is that what I am to understand?'

'Precisely.'

Dr Kleingeld looked at the Old Man with a look both mischievous and challenging.

'The FBI brought you here for a psychiatric assessment of your sense of responsibility, or sanity if you will. We will come to the second part of the test momentarily. But first, may I ask you to make some money?'

'I'm told it's illegal.'

'I don't intend to use it. It's just so that I can testify, in confidence of course, about your ability, or lack of it.'

'How much do you need?'

There was a glint in Dr Kleingeld's eye. 'If you were a normal client,' he said, 'my fee would be in the region of two thousand dollars per session. And judging by what you have told me so far, you would need between ten and twenty sessions before I could assess whether you needed more. As you can see, such things are terribly difficult to judge. Say thirty thousand dollars, which is a conservative estimate.'

The Old Man concentrated hard, and suddenly money flew from his pocket like liberated pigeons. The notes fluttered all over the room, but they were not green in colour. Dr Kleingeld caught one in the air.

'These are not dollars,' he cried, out of character. 'This is Austrian currency! Did you know I was born in Austria?'

'No.'

'It's entirely worthless. It was minted during the German occupation of Austria just before the war.'

'Ah,' said the Old Man, with some satisfaction. 'Probably I'm not a normal client. It's a pity, because you are really very perspicacious in other ways.'

*   *   *

It may have been animated by a spirit of revenge, or may have been merely the reckless inquisitiveness of men dedicated to research, but whichever it was, Dr Kleingeld had Luther Basing let out of his confinement and brought into his study. Luther Basing, an extremely stout young man with his hair cut close to his head and the dangerously sleepy expression of a sumo wrestler, was locally known as God Three, reputedly the most dangerous of the three.

'Ah. I thought you two should meet. God Three, meet God Four.'

Luther Basing trembled slightly as he looked at the Old Man, and he even seemed to be on the verge of tears. Dr Kleingeld briefly gestured to the two male nurses who had entered with God Three. They advanced quickly and silently, standing behind Dr Kleingeld.

Meanwhile the Old Man and Luther Basing faced one another, locked in an ocular embrace. There was no telling yet which one would win the test of strength.

'Amazing,' murmured Dr Kleingeld to the male nurses. 'Normally God Three would have torn into a newcomer, and destroyed him. That's why I asked for you to come with him and stay in my study during—'

He had not finished speaking before Luther Basing slowly lowered his enormous frame to the floor, and knelt before the Old Man.

The Old Man advanced slowly and extended his hand. Luther Basing refused it, looking down at the floor, turning his thoughts inwards as perceptibly as though he were folding a tablecloth.

'Come, let me help you up. With your great weight, I cannot allow you to kneel.'

Meekly, Luther Basing extended a hand which looked like a bunch of stunted bananas.

'The other one too. I need both.'

Obediently, Luther extended the other hand. The Old Man took both hands in his, and with a rapid twist of the wrist lifted the huge hulk high off the floor, and held him there.

Luther Basing screamed in a high-pitched, feminine voice, and kicked the short columns of his legs in a panic. The earth was his element, for reasons which were obvious, and he could not bear being removed from it.

The Old Man let him down tactfully, and opened his arms to console the whimpering giant, who laid his head on the Old Man's shoulder and made little noises for a while, like a child seeking to recover from a tantrum.

'With Gods One and Two, he goes wild,' said Dr Kleingeld, 'and with you he is meekness itself. Why?'

'In his heart of hearts, despite his arrogant claim to be God, he knows he isn't. With the other two pretenders he knows that, although he is not God, they are not God either. The secularity of the situation brings out the belligerent in them. In my case, he recognized some quality other than arrogance, or even the desire to convince. I don't claim to be God. I don't need to.' And the Old Man glanced at the immobile mammoth leaning on him. 'He's fallen asleep.'

'He hasn't slept for weeks,' said the first male nurse.

'Can you take him back without waking him?' asked Dr Kleingeld.

'We can try.'

The nurses tried to take charge of Luther Basing. He woke with a roar, and sent both nurses flying. Dr Kleingeld rose in terror.

The Old Man reached out, touched Luther, and asked with great directness, 'How did you recognize me?'

Luther's eyes disappeared in the folds of his face as he strained to remember. 'A celestial choir . . . I used to sing in one . . . till my voice broke . . . a million years ago . . . more.'

'You can't have been a cherub. Their voices never break. Unfortunately. Their voices are as shrill as they always were, but they are more often off the note than before, out of sheer routine.'

'I don't know where it was . . . but I knew you straightaway, see . . . when I came in here.'

'Don't allow it to worry you. The imagination is an uncanny substitute for experience. Nothing that has ever lived has truly died, it has merely changed. Nature is a grand dilapidated library of all that has ever been. You cannot find your way about it, and yet it is all there, somewhere. Often humans can catch a glimpse of this or that as it passes by on the wavelength of their minds. A moment of comprehension, a spark of light is all that is necessary to briefly illuminate previously unsuspected places in unknown worlds or long-past times. Everything is available to everyone, sometimes only inches out of sight.'

The big man grinned. 'I know now where I know you from,' he said.

'Where?'

He tapped his grotesque head with a chubby finger. 'The mind.'

The Old Man nodded gravely, and said to Dr Kleingeld, 'He'll give you no further trouble. And incidentally, he's not mad. He is merely visionary. It is the rarest, the most precious form of sanity.'

Luther Basing turned to the two male nurses. 'OK, fellers, let's go. Time for dinner.' And he picked them up, one under each arm, and carried them squirming out of the room.

'I suppose you're very proud of yourself,' said Dr Kleingeld, resentfully.

'I never think in those terms. I have nobody to compare myself with.'

'What can I say in my report?'

'Tell the truth.'

'You want them to think I'm crazy?'

4

The Old Man had been given a tranquillizer, and was pretending to sleep in order to avoid conversation with the pretty black nurse who had administered the pill. He just had no stomach for small talk. There was too much to think about.

When she had left the ward, he noticed between half-open lids that an oriental gentleman in hospital clothes was picking his way among the beds in the half light of the late afternoon.

The Old Man opened his eyes. 'What are you doing here, Smith?' he asked sternly.

'Sh! Sh!' the oriental gentleman implored. 'I am trying out my disguise. I am Toshiro Hawamatsu. So far, so good. I'm leaving soon, whether you accompany me or not.'

'Where are you going?'

'New York. Washington is for you. Big moral issues, pressure groups, corruption in high places, all of that. New York's for me. They even call it the Big Apple. Remember the small apple, in that garden whose name always escapes me, the one in which I had to learn to slither? It's all physical. Drugs, prostitution, accompanied by high moral postures. It's my scene, as they say.'

'What are you going to do about money?'

Millions of yen began to materialize between the sheets and blanket of the Old Man's bed.

'Thanks, or rather, *Domo aregato gozaimas*,' said the grateful Mr Smith, as he swept the money into his meagre pockets. 'I had already stolen some. Nothing easier in hospital. There's a room downstairs where the patients' valuables are kept. All I need now are some clothes, and a pair of glasses. Oh!—'

He had spotted a pair of reading-glasses on the bedside table next to that of the Old Man's, belonging to an invalid who was at present asleep. Mr Smith removed them deftly from an open paperback, the pages of which began to close slowly.

'Why did you do that?' chided the Old Man. 'You don't even need glasses. Neither of us do. That poor fellow does.'

'If you're going to be convincing as a Japanese, you've got to have glasses, whether you need them or not.'

'What do I do if he wakes up and asks me if I know where his glasses are?'

'If he wakes up, you go to sleep. Simple as that.'

'And what about my legal dollars?'

'Come with me. I'm going down to the X-ray room to collect some clothes. There's bound to be money in the pockets. Enough to see us through. Then I'm catching what is known as a Greyhound bus at seven thirty. It gets us to New York around midnight or just after.'

'You go ahead. I'll follow.'

'But if you miss the bus?'

'I'll find you in some den of iniquity.'

'There are many in New York, I'm glad to say. I've heard of a gay bath-house and sauna called Oscar's Wilde Life on 42nd Street.'

'I dread to think what a gay bath-house is – aquatic orgies of some kind?'

'No. Rather, homosexual low-jinx.'

'Really? Are there such things?'

'I always forget how naïve you are.'

'Why would a Japanese businessman go there?'

'By the time I reach the place, I'll no longer be Japanese. I will have changed my yen into dollars at a bureau de change, and can revert to being myself, or rather, a version of myself acceptable to the Americans. I am going to the baths not so much in order to begin a form of inspection of the Earth's depravities as to find some imaginative togs left by the naked bathers in the locker room.'

'Gracious, you simply can't acquire a wardrobe by stealing, I won't allow it. Not while you're with me.'

'I won't steal indiscriminately. I'll leave the clothes there that I steal here. Exchange is no robbery.'

'*Fair* exchange is no robbery. What's wrong with the clothes you hope to steal here?'

'I can't imagine myself eager to keep any of the clothes I steal here.

Have you seen some of the people who come here to have X-rays done?' He lifted his eyes to illustrate the incurable dullness of such people, and therefore of the clothes. Two FBI men entered the ward, as inconsiderate of those asleep as if they had been parked cars.

Mr Smith disappeared with alacrity.

'Smith's got out again,' said one of them.

'Who was that standing by your bed just now?' asked the other.

'Nobody.' The Old Man blushed as circumstances compelled him to fib again.

'I coulda sworn I caught oriental features, Korean or Vietnamese . . .'

'I saw no one. Look, gentlemen, Mr Smith is a gregarious character. He may be anywhere in this vast hospital, making friends and gossiping. Have you tried the coffee shop?'

'OK, Al, let's get going. We gotta find him. He's gotta be some place.'

'Maternity?' quipped the second FBI man.

'That'll be the day,' laughed the other.

As soon as they had gone, Mr Smith materialized. 'I'm off now,' he said.

The Old Man started. 'You gave me a shock. I thought you'd gone.'

Offended, Mr Smith disappeared again.

The sick man in the next bed had been woken up by the FBI men, and had sought consolation in his bedside thriller.

'Have you seen my glasses?' he asked.

The Old Man was about to answer in the negative when he reflected that the telling of white lies was in danger of becoming a habit, a dangerous habit which could chip at the very base of his morality.

'Yes,' he replied robustly. 'They were stolen by Mr Smith.'

'Smith,' echoed the sick man. 'That's too bad. I can't see a thing without them.'

'Those were FBI men in here just now,' said the Old Man by way of encouragement. 'They're looking for Smith.'

The sick man brightened. 'Because he stole my glasses?'

'Yes,' the Old Man surrendered. The truth was a confounded nuisance at times, and prolonged uninteresting conversations indefinitely.

*   *   *

The conference in Dr Kleingeld's study was a difficult one. The doctor now sat at his desk, on a swivel chair, which he used incessantly to engage in, or disengage from, conversation. At the moment, he had his back to the others. Gonella walked hither and thither nervously, whereas the other FBI men sat perched on the arms of chairs, or else leaned against other furniture. Chief Eckhardt of the 16th Precinct was also present, as was Deputy Director of the FBI, Gontrand B. Harrison, whom Gonella had urgently asked to be present. Both were seated in armchairs.

'Where do we go from here?' he asked.

'Let's retrace our steps, shall we?' suggested Gonella.

'That's constructive thinking,' declared Harrison.

Gonella read from notes: 'Chief Eckhardt, you were called in, as I understand it, when the cashier of the Waxman Cherokee Hotel, Doble K. Ruck, took a series of banknotes given to the chief concierge of the hotel, René Leclou, by Godfrey, to the Pilgrim Consolidated Bank for verification. After only about a minute to a minute and a half, the manager of the "K" Street branch of the bank, Lester Kniff, pronounced the banknotes to be forgeries . . .'

Dr Kleingeld spun round in his chair to face the assembly. He spoke in his non-consultancy voice, loud, clear and discordant.

'We've been through all this before, and several times, gentlemen. This is not a trial as yet, but merely a psychic phenomenon. No amount of reiteration of insignificant details is going to help. And I deny that it's constructive thinking, Mr Harrison. It's just a muddle-headed bureaucratic time-waste, a favourite time-waste in high places.'

'I resent that,' said Mr Harrison.

'The fact is that I am neither willing to confirm or deny that those two men are not who they say they are.'

'Are you out of your mind?' snarled Harrison.

'I questioned that too. I asked God Four what he expected me to do. He replied, "Tell the truth." "D'you want them to think I'm crazy?" I remember saying. I knew full well the natural reaction to my stance, and yet I see no alternative to it.'

'Doctor,' appealed Gonella, 'we're four men who hold down great jobs. Can we afford to go on record as saying that a couple of old guys who've developed a repertoire of parlour tricks are conceivably God and the Devil? Come on – we'd be laughed out of court. And – well, there's enough people out there just waiting to take our jobs – but that's a subject I'm not even going into.'

'Let us, for a moment, look at it another way,' said Dr Kleingeld, recovering his composure, and with it, most of his somewhat suspect authority. 'Let us divorce this incident from religion. Religion, supposedly the great consolation, the great uplifter, actually makes people nervous.'

'I resent that,' said Mr Harrison.

'It is nevertheless true, in my experience. Let us treat what has happened as science fiction. Judging by the television, the invasion of this planet by a wobbling jelly, or wise little sexless busybodies with huge heads and the bodies of starved children, is quite rational, and the forces of law combat the invaders, eventually involving the armed forces of the nations, or else the saccharine goodwill of mankind, helped by all the violins Hollywood can muster. Millions follow such stories, and are deeply affected by them. They are entirely credible as the next step for the testing of our military capacity to its utmost, or else as hymns to universal peace, love spread on man's soul like honey on yesterday's toast. Remember, way back in the days of radio, how Orson Welles panicked the American public by graphically broadcasting, blow by blow, the invasion of the world by Martians? Nobody has ever panicked the public by suggesting God and Satan have paid us a visit.'

'That's what you're asking us to do,' said Gonella.

'I'm saying it can't be done. What's wrong with us that it can't be done? Every presidential candidate has to pretend to be deeply involved with prayer, even if he only goes through the motions for the sake of appearances. Prayers at home, on solemn occasions – it's part of the American tradition – and yet the idea of the physical apparition of the object of our prayers is deemed impossible, even blasphemous. Easier to believe in a menacing jelly or a dinosaur survived from the time of the Creation.'

'Do you pray, sir?' Harrison asked.

'No,' replied Dr Kleingeld.

'I thought not. I happen to. That is perhaps why I so bitterly resent all you say. Let me add that this is not a university lecture, but a very precise and very real emergency. Tomorrow morning, Godfrey and

41

Smith are coming up before a judge on a charge of forgery and grand larceny. In view of their age, we hoped you could suggest some kind of extenuating circumstances of a mental nature which would militate in their favour before a judge who only has limited time at his disposal and no opportunity to find out even that which I have managed to find out about the case. But obviously, such help from you is too much to ask.'

'You want me to cheat, as we all cheat all the time, with little things, in little ways. You want me to say that the two old men are not quite responsible for their actions, that they require probation, to protect society, like delinquents in their second adolescence, that they need help, which sounds so generous, but is the first of the very few steps leading to permanent incarceration. I just want to say that the words used by God Four in calming God Three displayed enormous authority, absolute intellectual integrity, and an enviable economy of means, which all of us could emulate with advantage.'

'That is your last word?'

'Oh no, I have no knowledge of what my last word will be. I can only say that while you were speaking, I prayed for the first time in my life . . . as an experiment.'

'Come, gentlemen,' said Mr Harrison, rising. 'I won't dwell on my disappointment. Chief Eckhardt, you'll just have to go ahead with the prosecution, treating this as a normal case. As for the abnormal aspects of the case, we would be best advised to forget them, and never bring them up again.

'Yes, sir. OK,' and Eckhardt added, as a quiet afterthought, 'What if they disappear *during* the hearing?'

'The FBI will do all in its power to prevent such an event.'

'Easy to say, sir. You haven't seen the way it happens.'

'We've got quite an armoury of tricks up our sleeves too, Chief.'

'Yes, sir. That's wonderful to know.'

'Yes, sir.'

Gonella summed up. 'So let me get this straight, just so we all understand. We charge these old guys as common criminals, and we try to avoid all reference about how the money was produced, i.e., from a pocket. No mention of the Spanish or Greek coins. Just the plain facts, as it relates to the phoney notes, and nothing else.'

'Right,' said Harrison with a cursory glance at Dr Kleingeld, who was sitting with a smile on his lips, his eyes shut, his fingers forming a tent before his face. 'We can discuss the technicalities back at the office, or else at the 16th Precinct. This is internal business. OK, let's go.'

The door opened before they had a chance to reach it. It was the two FBI men.

'They've gone,' said the first one, breathless.

'Gone? Both of them?' cried Gonella.

'Yeah. The old guy, goes by the name of Godfrey, he was in bed, see, at four forty-three, and he said like he thought the other guy, Smith, might be in the coffee shop, seeing as he was outa his bed at that time. We couldn't find Smith, so we returned to talk to Godfrey, but he'd gone, see. Mr Courland, in the next bed, says he was there one moment, gone the next.'

'That's it, that's it,' wailed Eckhardt, who recognized the symptoms.

'Also said Smith stole his glasses.'

'One thing at a time,' Harrison snapped. He was all for clarity.

'Smith, or Godfrey, or some other person, stole the clothes off this guy, Mr Xyliadis, while he was down in the X-ray unit.'

A dark, bald, stout man appeared, dressed in striped undergarments, with a borrowed dressing gown over them, and clearly very angry indeed.

'It's a goddam disgrace,' he shouted. 'I come here for my half-yearly check-up regular as clockwork – have done every six months for the last ten years – except last year when I was in Salonika – I leave my outer garments in the changing room same as always—'

'Take down the particulars, someone,' cried Harrison.

'OK, I'll handle it,' snapped Chief Eckhardt.

'The rest of you – listen here – I'm going to take this matter as high as it will go – to the President himself if need be.'

'The President?' asked Gonella, incredulous. 'Isn't it just a little premature?'

'No, sir,' hissed Harrison, between dentures set in determination. 'You realize this may be a patrol from another planet, or something the goddam Soviets are trying out before they use it? This is too big for us to hold, and it may just be that time is of the essence. Let's go, fellers.'

They were averted in their departure by a merry peal of laughter from an unusually serene Dr Kleingeld.

'A patrol from another planet? What did I tell you? That is easier for us to countenance and lay on the President's desk than a divine visitation.'

'Is that all you have to say?' asked Harrison, resentful of even seconds wasted.

'No. I have just had a most uplifting experience for someone who has spent over sixty years without a prayer. The first time I try it, it is answered.'

'What did you pray for?' asked Gonella, already sneering in advance.

'I prayed for the two old boys to disappear. Lucky judge in the morning. He'll never know what he has missed! And lucky us!'

'Come on. We've wasted enough time,' ordered Harrison, and the officers streamed back to their squealing tyres, their screaming brakes, and their wailing sirens, the signature tune and incidental music for the Valkyries of public order.

Only Chief Eckhardt remained behind, taking down the tedious deposition of Mr Xyliadis, who had already produced four different versions of what he had had in his pockets.

*   *   *

Once out in the open, Mr Smith moved with an energy and determination which were impossible when in the company of the portly Old Man, whose natural rhythm was moderate, not to say ponderous.

He hailed a taxi, and found out from the driver that he could reach New York quicker by shuttle than by Greyhound bus, and also that there was a bureau de change at the airport. This solution was also better for the driver, as he himself pointed out, since the fare to the airport was higher than that to the bus terminal.

'So everyone's happy,' he chortled as they drove off into the evening.

Mr Xyliadis' clothes hung from Mr Smith's slender frame in folds. There had not been much choice. The only other person being X-rayed at that time of the afternoon had been a little girl of eight. Now Mr Smith looked as peculiar as an unpregnant woman wearing the clothes of her pregnancy. In fact, a large lady stopped him on his way to the ticket counter, asking him if he was undergoing the Westwood Wideworld Diet, and if so, in which week he was. Mr Smith replied that such a diet, 'Unknown in Japan.' The elephantine lady reacted as though it wasn't particularly gracious for an oriental visitor to deny that he was undergoing a Californian diet when it was perfectly obvious that he was.

The yen were changed without any difficulty, and the ticket on the shuttle purchased. Mr Smith flew without luggage, but left La Guardia airport in New York with a smart new grip which he stole without a second thought from a conveyor belt bearing luggage arriving from Cleveland. He then took a taxi to Oscar's Wilde Life. The driver was a garrulous gentleman from Haiti, who asked Mr Smith if there were many gays in Japan.

'Kindly keep eyes on road,' was all that Smith would say. The reason for his unwillingness to talk was that he was, like a salamander in spring, shedding one disguise for another, and it required concentration.

The Haitian's driving became more and more erratic as he noticed changes in his client's features in his driving mirror. In fact, he seemed absolutely petrified as the client emerged in 42nd Street, no longer oriental but now vaguely Anglo-Saxon, with flowing red locks and a mass of freckles on a face as disturbing as ever, the mask of centuries of unshared vices.

'I haven't overdone it, have I? With the freckles I mean?' he asked the driver as he prepared to pay. On an impulse, the driver accelerated away without waiting to be paid.

Mr Smith was delighted, realizing he had saved quite a sum in genuine dollars. He reflected that it was the first of his tricks which he had, in some way, commercialized.

He walked over the street, which was still very much alive, despite, or rather because of the late hour. Electric signs stuttered out their unsubtle promise of titillation, if not of vice. Vice was left to the shadowy figures on the sidewalk, who all appeared to be waiting for something to happen, or, like spiders waiting for unsuspecting flies to become entangled in their invisible webs, remaining as still as possible.

Near the entrance to Oscar's Wilde Life, there stood a girl of noble proportions, her legs visible up to the hips, in wide-meshed stockings, torn in places. Her shoes had stiletto heels, which, when she moved a little, gave the impression that she was standing on stilts. She wore a mini-skirt which looked as though it had shrunk in the wash, and her breasts were like swimming dogs, eager to keep their nostrils above the waterline. Her face was young, but worn out. Their eyes met for a moment, and there was a flicker of some kind of recognition.

'Coming with me, hun? . . . Show you a good time . . .'

'Later perhaps . . .' said Mr Smith, and brushed by her and her cloud of floral perfume.

'There may be no later . . .'

He ignored her and went into the brightly lit entrance to Oscar's Wilde Life. Behind a curtain it became dark again. An effeminate brute dressed as Popeye the Sailorman stopped Mr Smith. He was joined by an elderly man with white hair brushed forward over his eyes, also dressed in a manner redolent of yacht clubs.

'I'll have to see in that bag, sweetheart,' said the brute. 'Security. We've had two bomb alerts already from Fascist heterosexual organizations.'

Mr Smith opened up the bag. The contents were a make-up case, a silk camisole, silk panties, a bra, and a pair of salmon pink pyjamas.

'Come on in,' said the older of the two men. 'I'm Oscar. Welcome to the club. Come, I'll show you round. What's your name?'

'Smith.'

'We're all on a given name basis here.'

'Smith is my given name.'

'Right. Come this way, Smith dear.'

Mr Smith followed Oscar through a mass of exotic plants, which suddenly gave way to what appeared to be a clearing in the jungle. There, miraculously, was a swimming pool made of marble, with neo-Roman motifs, and some heavy-handed visual eroticism worthy of Pompeii. The water pouring into the pool flowed out of a gilt male organ, as shoddy in its brilliance as a piece of costume jewellery. The two appendages, also in a blinding gold finish, produced waves and treacherous currents at will. The water, of an evil green, was full of naked men, shrieking, and manifesting their gift for over-statement. By the side of the pool stood two nude blacks, their ears studded with rhinestones. One had ropes of Majorcan pearls round his neck.

'These are my native porters,' giggled Oscar. 'Fellows, welcome Smith.'

'*Jambo, jambo, bwana,*' cried the two men in a complicated rhythmic patter, ending with a highly synchronized dance and hand-slap.

The men in the swimming pool roared their approval.

'Boys and girls,' called Oscar, with a suggestive roll of his eyes. Applause. 'This is Smith.' Hoots of derision. Oscar clapped his hands in reprimand. Cajolingly he went on, when silence had been re-established, 'Smith is *all right.* Oscar's seen inside his *suitcase.*' All in an alluring cantabile. 'Now go and get rid of those *dreadful* clothes in our baroque *un*-dressing rooms, and show yourself in your *true* glory!'

An outbreak of enthusiasm. While Oscar led Smith away, one swimmer called out, 'I'm just crazy for freckles,' to be playfully bitten by his lover, who hadn't a freckle to his face.

'I'll leave you *alone* here. But not for *long. Dig* that *hair!*'

Mr Smith looked round in this red plush and bone-white changing room, with its statues of Roman youths in inane poses. He pulled aside the curtains to the alcoves where the clothes were hung, and his eyes fell on a pair of jeans, hand painted with peacocks and birds of paradise. He felt the stirrings of a deep enthusiasm which he had not experienced for years. He tried them on. They fitted. Nothing else left there by the bathers went terribly well with the trousers, but he slipped into a loose, tarnished T-shirt of a tender violet hue with the words 'Call Me Madame' printed on the front. He looked at himself in a mirror. He was amused by what he saw.

Seizing his suitcase after he had hung Mr Xyliadis' formal suiting on the hangers from which he had stolen his new clothes, he rushed past Oscar, pushing him aside, as well as the muscular Popeye at the entrance, and gained the street. The prostitute was still where he had first seen her. Seizing her hand, Mr Smith hissed, 'Quick! Where do we go?'

She ran with him on her stiletto heels, sounding like a colt.

'A hundred bucks, I don't take no less!' she panted.

'All right, all right!'

She pulled him into a dark doorway. A man sat there, busy not looking up.

'It's me, Dolores,' she said.

'116,' said the man, giving her a key attached to a label.

She took the key, and climbed a narrow staircase to the first floor. When she had found the door, she opened it, turned on the light, and ushered Mr Smith in to share the spartan misery of this alcove dedicated to vice for a few precious moments.

She closed the door after Mr Smith, and locked it. She then invited him to sit on the bed, which he did. Then she turned a switch near the door, and the blinding white light was replaced by an ugly red. She lit a cigarette, and offered one to Mr Smith, which he refused.

'Dolores,' he said.

'Yes?'

'That's a pretty name.'

She wasn't here to waste time. 'What are you into?' she enquired.

'Into? I don't understand the question.'

'You're not here for straight sex, are you? That's not the way you look.'

'I don't know.'

She puffed on her cigarette in irritation. 'OK, so I'll give you the tariff,' she said. 'The prices may seem steep to you, but I'm very experienced in every variant from straight to kinky. Basic is a hundred bucks, like I said. Then straight is twenty bucks every ten minutes after.'

'Straight?' asked Mr Smith, his face gnarled.

'Sure. Straight intercourse, without none of the trappings. Then if you want to be spanked like a schoolboy, that's fifty bucks every ten minutes over and above the basic hundred bucks basic. If that's the way you want to go, I go upstairs to the wardrobe, see, and dress up like a schoolmarm, or else if you want to be a slave, that's seventy-five every fifteen minutes, and I dress up as a mistress or as a goddess, whichever takes your fancy. If you want to whip me, that's going to cost upward of a hundred bucks every fifteen minutes, and I don't take no hard strokes. I got French maid outfits, and schoolgirls, studded leather handcuffs, collars, wooden ankle restraints, and nipple clamps, or vibrators and dildos. What's it to be?'

'Where is the passion?' cried Mr Smith in a voice like a chord on an organ.

'The what?' asked the frightened Dolores.

'The passion,' spat Mr Smith. 'There can be no vice without

passion, a precipitate voyage to the very extremes of human possibility, a delirium as close to death as can be, a kaleidoscope of the senses, something which defies description. Passion. It has no price.'

'Then get outa here,' cried Dolores, emboldened by her terror. 'I got nothing to give without a price.'

'Here's a thousand dollars,' said Mr Smith, suddenly reasonable. 'Do what you think I deserve.'

'A thousand dollars!' Dolores was staggered. 'You want to tie me up?'

'I don't want to make any effort. I am extremely tired.'

'How do you want me to dress up?'

'I paid for a body, not for clothes.'

'Get your clothes off then.'

'That's asking for effort again.'

Dolores was lost momentarily. 'Care for Greek?'

'Greek?'

'Body, body?'

'I don't know what you are talking about.'

'Brother, where you been all these centuries?'

'Well may you ask . . .'

Dolores found some rock music on the aged little bedside radio, and began swaying to the music, which was a kind of return to sanity for her. Moving her hips in what she took to be a sensual way, she responded to the monotonous beat of the music, and to the incomprehensible lyrics, which consisted of a single phrase in no particular language, repeated over and over again.

Mr Smith watched her through half-closed eyes. While she began a routine which was to her the gateway to sex in all its rhythmic insistence, it seemed to Mr Smith that he had wandered in on a journey to the very depths of boredom.

Bouncing away, she undid the fasteners on her mini-skirt, and it slid obediently to the ground. She tried to dislodge it from her feet by stepping out of it while maintaining the rhythm, but it caught on one of her heels, and she nearly fell over. A split second of amusement threatened to break Mr Smith's surrender to tedium, but Dolores recovered, and Mr Smith was once again enveloped in his torpor. Dolores undid her brassière to music, and liberated her breasts, which tumbled to their natural position, wobbling to the beat as though they had a life of their own.

Mr Smith noticed the traces of sharp lines where the garment had bitten into the flesh. After the net stockings had been rolled down, the panties followed, causing the body to pass through a diversity of graceless poses, and once again, as Dolores became visible for the first time in all her arrogant nudity, Mr Smith's last impression before being overtaken by oblivion was of the marks of elastic, cutting like the traces of a centipede's progress around the waist and diagonally across the buttocks.

When Mr Smith awakened, the radio had been reduced to an unpleasant crackle. He looked around, and realized that a naked woman had achieved what centuries of existence had been unable to: she had put him to sleep. He felt into his pocket. His money had gone. In a fury, he rushed to the door, and downstairs. The unseeing man was no longer there. The light over the desk was out.

Mr Smith emerged into the street. It was beginning to be light, and the street was relatively empty. He ran back along the pavement to the entrance of Oscar's Wilde Life. There was no trace of Dolores. Instead, the Old Man stood where Dolores had been, his white hair and beard cascading over his robes as before. Beside him were two small suitcases.

'How did you know?' stammered Mr Smith.

'You gave me the address, remember?' replied the Old Man. 'I've booked us into a transients' hotel round the corner. It's called the Mulberry Tower. Not the best perhaps, but we are not on Earth to experience the best.'

'You can say that again,' mused Mr Smith resentfully, and he added, 'Did you ask for me in Oscar's Wilde Life?'

'No. I thought it wiser not to.'

'You really are amazing.'

'Not really. I just feel I know you, that's all.'

'What are you doing with two suitcases?'

'One is for you. I thought you might have lost yours by now.'

Mr Smith burst into tears suddenly, and quite embarrassingly.

'What is the matter now?' sighed the Old Man.

'It's not all I've lost,' sobbed Mr Smith. 'All my money's gone! Stolen! Stolen!'

The Old Man sighed deeply. He dug into his pockets, and produced a few hundred yen.

'Oh no, not again!' pleaded Mr Smith tearfully. 'I can't bear being Japanese. I'm so bad at it.'

The Old Man began to lose patience. He concentrated briefly and ferociously. Then he produced a fistful of notes. 'These any better?'

Mr Smith took them. 'Swiss francs. You are a sport. How can you ever forgive me?' The tears were back.

'I don't know, but I'll find a way. All I refuse to do any more is to carry your luggage. Kindly pick it up and follow me.'

5

The Mulberry Tower was not the kind of hotel that insisted on unrelated people of any sex having separate rooms. Mr Smith and the Old Man consequently shared a pretty abominable little box in which the feeble lighting was amplified by the bright and neurotic neons from outside, to say nothing of the shadow of the metal fire escape which was cast on the damp walls in a variety of geometrical patterns. The fact that an unhealthy-looking dawn was breaking only added to the disharmony.

'Please try to compose yourself,' said the Old Man to Mr Smith, who had taken to blubbing again, at times like a punished child, at times with a towering anger and disgust.

'Remember, we who do not need sleep have to put up with the nights so that men and women may recuperate from the ardours of the day. It is a tribulation for us, this nightly passage from light to darkness, and then back to light again. But we must accept it. It was part of the original blueprint, and there's nothing we can do without affecting the ecological balance. We must be patient.'

'Oh God,' grumbled Mr Smith, 'you talk like one of your own bishops, platitude upon platitude, generality upon generality. You think the night is respected by all those pederasts, splashing the dark hours away in Oscar's Wilde Life? They tuck each other up during the day, take the phones off the hooks, and snatch what rest they can, with eyeshades and earplugs in place, and electronic devices imitating the noise of a waterfall. There are no rules governing human behaviour as there were in the Middle Ages, when candles were the only alternative to daylight, and curtains the only alternative to night. People can sin round the clock now, whenever and wherever their stress allows them to. I've seen them plugging electrical devices into wall-sockets to make them function. They do the same with parts of their body, plug them into one another for moments of snatched ecstasy, and the burping, farting satisfaction afterwards, with a few words, a bottle of fizzy elixir, and a mentholated cigarette weak in tar.'

'There are those who treat the act of procreation with the piety it deserves,' admonished the Old Man.

'There are those, there are those, there are *always those*,' cried Mr Smith. 'But there are others, the outnumbering multitude. Why, you still speak as though examining the blueprint, the grand design. Reality is what the blueprint has become. They know how it works. They no longer have to read the instructions on the lid of the box. They've thrown the box away! That's why we came back, isn't it? On a fact-finding tour? Didn't you wish to remind yourself of how mankind has adapted itself to survival on this planet? Wasn't that the idea? A renewal of acquaintance? For better or for worse?'

The Old Man smiled. 'Of course. Your question is merely rhetorical. You don't really expect me to answer.' The Old Man knitted his brows. 'Bear with me for a moment. Try to be frugal with repartee and with undue facility. They come too easily to you, but there are times when one must forego the temptation to be entertained, since amusement too easily deflects us from the course of an investigation.' The Old Man left a pause. Then he went on, slowly and deliberately.

'You see, to exist as a pervasive atmosphere, a formless spirit, lending a landscape its sudden stabs of sunlight or sheets of mournful rain, stage-managing natural disasters with as fine a touch of macabre magic as the centuries have taught me, is all very well, but I found that I had to return to the limitations of a human shape if I wished to help my memory in its task of reconstructing life as we had once imagined it. I needed a feel of those mortal restrictions, inability to fly without an aeroplane, to cover distance without an automobile, to change altitude rapidly without a lift, to speak to the ends of the Earth without a telephone. These are all things man has invented to give himself the illusion of being a god. And they are brilliant inventions, considering the fact that I left no clues how they should be done. The last time I saw man, he was still trying to fly by launching himself from high places and flapping his arms about. No amount of broken bodies would dissuade him from his efforts. For centuries he slaved away trying to find a less capricious substitute for a horse, and gradually he bent metals and mineral oils to his will, until today he is able to emulate us in many of our powers, by sheer stubbornness and that private and personal elysium called the intelligence; the ability to join even abstractions together to form a pattern, held in place by the cunning logic of existence. I admire what the infant I first saw reaching for blurred objects in his line of vision has achieved. He can talk in seconds from one end of the Earth to the other. If what he says has not much improved from the time he could only be heard as far as his voice would carry – well, let's not be too readily disappointed. Wisdom is far slower to mature than scientific knowledge.'

'You always see the positive side,' grumbled Mr Smith. 'I suppose it's normal. Virtue is somehow tied to optimism. The vocational beatitude of priests is its trademark, and it drives me down a pole. But in all this, can there be no thought for how vice has become degraded? Mechanical and cold? I shall never forget that bulbous whore with her vulgar catalogue of pleasures, catering for the preselected delights of dull man. What is the point of carnality if it is not the result of a kind of burning folly, something uncontrollable and yet, in the act, controlled? If whip you must, whip like the divine Marquis de Sade, right up to the gates of death. If you must suffer, suffer like a martyr. If screw you must, screw like Casanova –'

'He only wrote about it –'

'So I chose a bad example. You know what I mean. There is no price for passion except the gift of oneself. Only tarnished illusions can be for sale, and they are so far from the truth they are as counterfeit as your money, and yet the commerce of the body is legal tender.'

'As long as it is paid for in legal dollars,' added the Old Man with a twinkle, and then he went on, in a different tone, 'You know, we have found out so little thus far, there is really not much point in exchanging impressions. Admittedly you know more than I do, since you keep reading your soiled newspapers so assiduously. But there must be a quicker way by now to place a finger on the public pulse.'

'There is,' said Mr Smith, pointing to a small cube.

'That? What is it?'

'Television. I saw a child fiddling with one at the airport. The father was intent on watching some kind of ball game. The child kept turning the knob to glimpse other channels. I don't know who won. I had to run for my shuttle.'

'How does it work?'

Mr Smith, despite his pleas for passion, was good with technical things, far better than the Old Man, whose plane was loftier and less down to earth. In a trice the set was switched on, and revealed a group of middle-aged men with long hair and curious headgear shooting indiscriminately in a supermarket with all manner of firearms. One woman shopper had her head literally blown off by machine-gun fire. A man loaded with supplies was punctured, red holes appearing in his back, charred ones in the supplies. The whole exercise went into slow motion in a hideous choreography of death, blood splashed like milk in a wild exaggeration of factual possibility, while on the soundtrack, besides the obligatory screams of panic, there was an infuriating little tune played by a reduced jazz combo, with a piano as calculatedly out of tune as the events it illustrated.

Once the carnage was over, and staff and shoppers lay strewn in every alleyway like broken toys, the intruders began to load up the supermarket carts with supplies, and then found, to their evident annoyance, and amid bouts of filthy language and wild hoots and indistinguishable dialogue, that it was tough work lifting the full carts over the dead bodies.

The Old Man and Mr Smith watched the horror with stony faces until the end, or rather, till just before the end, since by the end Mr Smith was asleep again.

The film was apparently called *Return from Strawberry Bunker*, and was advertised in the guide which the hotel had placed on the TV set as a serious drama about the disenfranchised men back from the nightmare of Vietnam faced with both a hostile homecoming and supermarkets swollen with goodies. It said, gratuitously, 'This is a film which no thinking and feeling American can afford to miss.'

The Old Man nudged Mr Smith, who woke with a start.

'What happened in the end?' he asked, but then modified his eagerness. 'No, don't tell me, I don't give a shit.'

'Your language is influenced by what you heard.'

'That could be, and I apologize. There is nothing I would less like to be influenced by than that film.'

'Is that what it was, a film?'

'Yes, and it succeeded in putting me to sleep – twice in twelve hours! It's a disgrace.'

'I failed to understand the film, although I succeeded in staying awake. So, be reassured, you have missed nothing. It says in the little book that the film's rating is PG. And then, in an explanatory note, it further states that PG stands for Parental Guidance. Can you envisage a parent worthy of the name actually advising his child to witness such a mindless carnage?'

'To keep the little bastards out of mischief, some parents will choose almost any solution.'

'Even watching this?'

'Listen,' said Mr Smith, 'in some less developed parts of this world the sight of their parents copulating goes under the name of children's entertainment, and there is far more reason to label such activity as PG, since, in a very real sense, it is educational.'

The Old Man was saddened by this revelation, and fiddled disconsolately with the knobs. The Mayor of Albany appeared briefly to explain why trashcans were sometimes collected by non-union labour, and a hall full of women exchanged confidential information about the sexual shortcomings of alcoholic husbands. On yet another of the innumerable channels, three rabbis argued about what constituted Jewishness. They were, of course, not in agreement, and were, moreover, impervious to compromise in any form. There was a man selling used cars with the help of an Old English Sheepdog, who had been trained to leap onto the roof of the cars and bark. There was a woman explaining the latest natural disaster, a flood in Utah, to the Portuguese community. And, at last, another film, in which five policemen, recognizable as such, though walking with the hesitant gait of robots, or with artificial limbs all round, limped down a street, taking up all the sidewalk. Their eyes were glazed, their features stiff; only their trigger-fingers seemed to have the sensibility required by a full life.

Before them, a handful of evident gangsters stumbled over each other trying to get away. There was the inevitable black man in a knitted tam-o'-shanter and dark glasses, who expressed his fear in high coloratura shrieks. The leader of the mob, a white sweatband round his hair, mean eighteenth-century glasses and a cigarette in a holder, seemed less inclined to flight than the others, only retreating grudgingly. He was wrong, for the shooting began on a signal from a zombie in an armoured command car.

The policemen began shooting in a wild cacophony, their eyes even more glazed than before. It seemed as though they were lousy shots since only one gangster was mortally wounded, leaping high in the air, diving over a parapet, and landing in a cement mixer in a building-site crater, some forty feet lower than the level of the street.

'Re-load,' instructed the zombie in the command car, his face expressing a kind of vacant satisfaction. The uniformed puppets did as they were told, as though by numbers.

It was time for the gangsters to fire back. Some bits of uniform were charred, but the police were evidently bulletproof.

'Fire,' said the zombie, and once again the police let loose a blinding, ear-splitting barrage, once again only managing to kill one more gangster, who was blown through the glass of a shop window, ending up dead in the arms of a manikin in evening dress.

Since there were upwards of a dozen gangsters, and the police could apparently only manage to kill one per five magazines, this butchery took quite a time, and only terminated when the chief, who was, of course, chased over rooftops as the end of the film approached, in order to have further to fall, laughed insanely at the irony of fate. The noise attracted the attention of one of the mechanical police, who lifted his eyes upwards, unlike the others who were still awaiting instructions. A twitch indicated a subtle return to a degree of humanity. His gaze switched from the glazed to an expression which suggested that he was recapturing the horrors of past events. With a terrific effort of concentration he aimed his pistol, and with a great cry of, 'That's for my dead buddies!', shot the chief at a range of three hundred yards.

The chief swayed, and then launched himself into space, falling at the foot of a pump in a gas station. The expression on his face was beatific considering the extent of his fall, and to match this miracle with one even more impressive, the cigarette in the holder was still alight, clenched between locked jaws.

The last embers fell into a pool of petrol, and the screen blew up in a fitting coda for such a story, a blaze huge enough to devour all questions and all answers, all details and all broad story lines, all credibility, everything.

'What was all that about?' asked Mr Smith.

The Old Man looked it up in the brochure. 'It was called *Phantom Precinct*, and it was the story of dead policemen resuscitated by a dead sergeant who had found a way of bringing them all, including himself, back to a sort of half-life. They existed as automatons, bent on nothing but vengeance. The sergeant, being a sergeant, had a superior half-life to the men, able to take limited initiatives. In the end, Patrolman O'Mara rises to the rank of semi-posthumous sergeant by shaking himself free from the constraints of blind obedience. He wrenches himself back to a fuller consciousness by shouting, "That's for my dead buddies!" as he topples the arch-villain from the roof with a single shot, a feat which speaks volumes about the rigorous training at the Police Academy. It once again ends with the claim that no American family can afford to miss this inspiring story of courage and refusal to accept death as a final answer. And I don't have to tell you the rating.'

'PG?'

'PG.'

*   *   *

They watched movies unrelievedly from five thirty in the morning until half past three in the afternoon. Every hour or so an irritating maid tapped her keys on the door with a sing-song call of 'Just checking,' but apart from that there was no interruption to the spate of lunatic senators and the chiefs of secret government laboratories eager to seize power for themselves in the name of patriotism, democracy and the rest, only to be thwarted in the nick of time by the initiative, vision, or special powers of an individual.

'The desire for immortality is everywhere evident, and it is most disturbing,' said the Old Man, as he lay on the bed exhausted by ten hours of crossfire with virtually nothing to engage the mind. 'Suppose they really find a way not to die? It will be too expensive at first for most people, and so only the idiots with inherited wealth or the criminals with new wealth will survive to give the immortal world its standards. The poor fools. Don't they realize that it is mortality which gives the world its yardstick of quality? If Beethoven had been immortal, there would have been hundreds of symphonies, infinitely repetitive, and eventually indistinguishable from each other even in degrees of mediocrity. In such a world senility would be as contagious as the common cold, and births of children would be rarer and rarer, each one being eventually heralded by a national holiday, while civilization, all that man has painstakingly built for himself, which went by the name of progress, would be frittered away in the growing darkness of incapacity, toothless grins, rivulets of saliva from the corners of the mouth, mucus moving like ice-cold lava from the encumbered nostrils being the last signs of life of my most happy daydream.'

The Old Man's eyes were moist with tears.

Mr Smith spoke compassionately, but still with a pinch of self-deprecating irony. 'You need no eloquence, my dear,' he said. 'As an argument against immortality, need you look further than you and I?'

The Old Man grabbed Mr Smith's extended hand and gripped it tightly, closing his eyes and assuming an air of majestic gravity.

After a moment, Mr Smith wanted his hand back, but could not think how to engineer this. 'I don't see why any of the murderous stuff we have observed is commercial,' he said, trying to change the subject. The Old Man failed to reply, so Mr Smith went on, 'Do people pay good money to be scared out of their wits, deafened to a point of utter stultification, dazzled, bullied, and bastinadoed into submission? Is what we have seen entertainment?'

The Old Man opened his eyes without releasing Mr Smith's hand. 'It's like the old arguments of the Jesuits. Admittedly, Cesare Borgia and the Sacred Inquisition were reprehensible moments in a sublime history, but what a religion to be able to survive such moments, and emerge the stronger for them! America sees itself as a society so infinitely desirable and indomitably powerful that it is capable of encouraging every challenge to what it imagines to be its moral supremacy, and still come out on top. All the films we have seen express the same absurd optimism, in which the dice are loaded in favour of the righteous, while giving the impression until the denouement of being loaded in favour of the corrupt. In any case, there's one thing you can count on, that the dice are loaded. And the moral posture is inflexible, even if vice seems to be rampant and dishonesty rewarded. But it's always a photo finish. Always. That, I suppose, is where entertainment must come in. Although right must win through (that is statutory), the risk must be made to seem enormous, even opposed to the law of averages, unfair. The ultimate glory is all the greater.'

'Strange to hear you refer to optimism as absurd. It is what I have sometimes called yours. Stranger still to hear you refer to the inheritors of old wealth as idiots and the creators of new wealth as criminals. Those are overstatements worthy of me. Uncharacteristically, you took the words right out of my mouth.'

'We cannot avoid influencing one another,' said the Old Man emotionally, tightening his grip on Mr Smith's hand.

Mr Smith continued, 'I think, you see, that in this country the pervasive corruption alleged by the films we have seen is a necessary and indeed flattering adjunct to its immense wealth. Without such wealth, such opportunity for wealth, there would be no reason for corruption, no reason for poverty, no reason for practically everyone to carry guns. Did you notice in the films, as danger approached, several times a hand would slide open a drawer to make sure the gun was still in place? In practically all the films we saw this happened at least once. And yet we saw none of the poverty we could notice out of the corner of an eye as we rode through the city – the derelicts asleep, or drunk, or drugged, or dead, on the sidewalk, the tenements with broken glass in many windows, the streets as playgrounds. I suspect there is a reason for this.' And his eyes narrowed as he searched for the right words.

'I have read and heard much about the American Dream. Nobody defines it. Nobody dares. It sits, an ectoplasmic presence as hard to crystallize as your obscure invention, the Holy Ghost, on the altar of American consciousness. It is, by definition, unattainable, and yet no effort must be spared to attempt the impossible. At its most tangible, it is an extension of the hopes and prayers of the Founding Fathers, adapted by endless amendments to the constantly changing conditions of the modern world. At its most irritating it is a glow, silhouetting gothic shapes, and vibrating with voices singing in unison. But, you see, I think it already exists, this dream, or compendium of dreams, in a form both nefarious and deeply destructive.'

'Oh, where?' asked the Old Man, slightly nervous.

'Here,' replied Mr Smith, tapping the television affectionately, as though it were the head of a child.

'The television? The television is a means, not an end. Like the telephone, or the aeroplane. You can't blame the wretched instruments for the uses to which men have put them!'

'The end is served by such means. My whole point. The American Dream is an ongoing fantasy, as they would say, an endless parade of notions too advanced for others to have, but with solutions too simple for others to countenance. The dreams are contained in half-hour, hour, sometimes two-hour segments. Their message is that bullets settle arguments, that faith is not so much simple as simple-minded, and that whereas men are free, they are expected to submit themselves to the dictatorship of righteousness as spelled out in the Bible. It is not only entertainment which has to obey these pious strictures, but politics is also a branch of what is known as show business. And, without wishing to shock you, so is religion.'

'You do shock me. Of course you do. But what a relief and an inspiration it is to have a serious conversation with you. I will go as far as to say, one can learn a great deal by disagreeing with you,' said the Old Man, cozily.

Mr Smith turned on the television.

'Oh no, I don't want to see any more television, not just yet,' the Old Man cried.

'You don't believe me. There are upwards of forty channels. There must be something religious going on somewhere.' He switched from one channel to another with growing impatience. Suddenly the screen filled with a face of a man who seemed to be in the last throes of agony, tears mingling with perspiration, vibrating on his cheeks and forehead like tapioca.

'This looks like religion,' muttered Mr Smith.

'It could be delirium tremens,' suggested the Old Man coyly. Just then, the man found a voice, a poor cracked organ pushed beyond its normal capacity by sheer will-power.

'I have been tempted to sin!' cried the man, choking a sob.

'That's better,' said Mr Smith.

The pause the preacher left was enormous, impertinent. There was a shot of the congregation. Oval heads with rimless glasses, women with lined faces, holding their hands close to their faces, ready for emergencies, young people, open as books, but with traces of scepticism here and there.

'I have been tempted to sin!' said the preacher, in a normal voice, as though recapitulating a dictation for schoolchildren.

A man in the audience shouted, 'Yeah.'

'Glory be,' echoed another.

The pause went on while the preacher seemed to try and meet every eye in the house.

And finally he whispered, 'I have been tempted to sin!'

'Get on with it,' cried Mr Smith.

The preacher shouted once again, pointing a trembling finger at the space before him.

'I have had the Devil in my parlour!'

'Liar!' yelled Mr Smith, wrenching his hand free from the Old Man's grasp.

'He appeared to me just as Mrs Henchman was preparing for bed, after a hard day helping in my ministry . . . Charlene Henchman is a wonderful human being . . .'

Shouts of 'Yeah,' 'Amen,' 'Alleluia,' and 'They don't come no better.'

'I said to her, go to your room, honey, I got old Satan here for company, and I've got to find my own way of showing him the door.' He paused dramatically. 'Mrs Henchman went up to her room, and never so much as asked a question,' he said softly. Then, with rising emotion, 'I turned to Satan . . . I turned to the critter, looked him straight in the eye, and cried out, and I quote: "Take Linda Carpucci right out of my life, Satan" . . . I got a wife already . . . I don't need no Linda Carpucci to fill my idle moments with thoughts of sin and the desires of the flesh. Mrs Henchman has given me six wonderful kids, from Joey Henchman junior right down to La Verne, our youngest. You gotta be crazy if you think I'm going to sacrifice all of Almighty God's bounty, showered around my unworthy head, just because that old son of a gun Satan lays Linda Carpucci in my path, one night, when my precious Charlene was working late at the ministry, sealing envelopes so that our great message could be carried to the hundred and upwards foreign countries in which we operate.' His voice rose again, and he sobbed, 'I paraphrased the words of our Lord to Satan, and I called out, "Get thee behind me, Satan, and take Linda Carpucci with you!" '

There was a great show of applause and approval from the hall, while Mr Smith was stung into a transport of anger.

'Liar! Filthy, scurrilous liar! I never saw you before in my life! And who the hell is Linda Carpucci?'

On the screen the Reverend Henchman was nodding gratefully to his public, like a game-show host, mouthing mute thank yous and thank you very muches.

'I've got to go there! Now! This is provocation of the most intolerable kind! I'm off!'

'We have no money.'

'To hell with money.'

'We can't pay the hotel.'

'To hell with the hotel.'

On screen, the great hall faded, and a voice took over: 'We will return to the Reverend John Henchman live from the Stained Glass Church of Many Colours, University of the Soul, Henchman City, Arkansas, after this word from our sponsor, Whistler's Mother Cake Mix.'

'That's the address,' snapped Mr Smith. 'Are you going to bestir yourself, or shall I go alone?'

'Think again. This is probably only one of many such outbursts . . .'

'This one has struck me straight between the eyes. I have been slandered, libelled. I'm impulsive. I can't take it. I won't! It's too unfair!'

He held out his hand, and the Old Man took it.

Just before they vanished into thin air, the Old Man had time to ask, with a trace of malice, 'What does it feel like to be part of the American Dream? A negative part, but oh, how important. Eh, old critter?'

'Just checking,' called the maid, and when she heard neither human voices nor the television, she went in. 'Baggage still here,' she murmured. 'Funny, didn't see them go out.'

And she switched the bedside radio on. Light music, without which no bed could be made.

'Funny,' she said aloud, 'they never slept in the beds. Guess it takes all sorts . . .'

And she turned on the TV as well as the radio in order to have her fill of entertainment. Then she sat on one of the beds and lit a cigarette.

6

In a rush of warm wind, which dislodged one or two hats, the Old Man and Mr Smith landed in the aisle of the Stained Glass Church of Many Colours, a surprising building made up entirely of translucent bible scenes held together by a modern tent-like structure, the fierce southern sun bringing out the blues and reds and yellow ochres in all their primal intensity.

A group of men in green tuxedos and women in old-fashioned rose-coloured party dresses constituted a choir which sang the occasional hymn or religious jingle in a syncopated harmony, clicking their fingers and flexing their knees to the rhythm.

The freely perspiring preacher, the Reverend Henchman, was on the stage, exactly where he had been before the commercial break, but he seemed almost pathetically small after the magnification of the television screen. Only on the television monitors, which were everywhere suspended, could every bead of sweat be seen.

'I will pause in my sermon, to allow our fine choir to sing the hymn I wrote with my own hands, inspired by . . . you know who . . .' (A huge roar of confirmation. This was evidently a conditioned reflex, a signal for Alleluias and Ri-i-ights and You'd Better Believe Its, accompanied on Henchman's face by a wink of confirmation, which dislodged some perspiration from his brow like a flight of frightened insects.) '. . . on the occasion . . . on the occasion of our second son's birth . . . of Lionel Henchman's coming, right here, on campus . . . the music . . . the music was composed by Charlene Henchman . . .' (Another roar, while a big, flat-chested lady with a keyboard of large teeth and a bouffant hairstyle, like petrified candy floss, muttered, 'Praise the Lord,' on the monitor, her streamlined glasses, with their motif of stylized butterflies, reflecting the many-coloured spotlights.) '. . . she dictated the tune right from her bed of labour . . . by humming it into the ear of our wonderful orchestrator and resident organist, Digby Stattles – take a bow, Digby . . .' (And an organ appeared from nowhere, rising into view with a man in a white bolero, smothered with sequins, who sat at the keyboard and played a saccharine voluntary while turning round as far as possible on his seat to acknowledge the anticipated applause. The notes trembled like jelly, while the imitation organ tubes, which were fashioned of some material like perspex, and contained strip lighting bent into religious symbols, such as crosses, stars, and stylized hands, two fingers raised in benediction, as well as crowns of thorns and halos, changed colour endlessly in a computerized orgy of pastel shades.)

'The hymn will be rendered by our Church of Many Colours Male and Female Choir . . . yes, folks, give them a hand . . .' Henchman ranted when the organ had fully risen. 'This is not a ministry which insists on silence . . . With what . . . with what is silence most often associated? . . . The tomb . . . Right! . . . This is a ministry of enthusiasm. Of life! Yes – of humour!' (And he laughed breathlessly.) 'This is a ministry of humour! God has a sense of humour! Heck, he must have! . . . Judge by some of the creatures he decorated his green Earth with . . . hippopotamus . . . Ever see one of those?' (Yeah!) 'Now, whoever thought up a hippopotamus, he just got to have a sense o' humour, know what I mean? . . . Know what I mean? . . .' At this point, Henchman glanced at Charlene, who had lost her smile in a big way. 'However, I digress,' he said, gravely. 'OK, folks . . . Charlene's hymn!' (The smile was back.) ' "Come Join Your Tiny Hands in Prayer", and I want you all to join in to the chorus, which goes "Hands in Prayer, Hands in Prayer, Hands in Prayer" repeated just three times. Got it? Take it away, Digby.'

As the hymn began, some members of the congregation, imbued with the spirit of sharing, pushed up to make way for Mr Smith and the Old Man. Mr Smith sat with alacrity, right onto a newspaper which his neighbour had left there. The Old Man settled on the aisle with some difficulty, since the space left him by Mr Smith was hardly adequate for his large frame. Mr Smith lifted himself slightly, and removed the newspaper from under him. The headline caught his immediate attention. 'Evangelist Henchman slapped with $6 million paternity suit by ex-stripper.'

It appeared that Linda Carpucci had sung in the choir a year ago, having allegedly caught the Reverend Henchman's attention in a nightclub in Baton Rouge, where her principal activity had been to rotate tassels from her nipples. This task she accomplished with such application and such diligence that the Reverend, with uncanny perception, recognized great new material for the musical section of his ministry. She was subsequently initiated, according to the newspaper, finding both Jesus and the Reverend Henchman at one and the same time. One curious fact, remarked the journalist, not without malice: nine months to a day after being born again, Miss Carpucci passed on her knowledge of these wonders to a curly-haired little daughter named Josie. Weight six and a half pounds, eyes blue, distinguishing marks a tendency towards excessive perspiration and a predilection for screaming. From these facts it was almost automatic that a great lawyer, Sharkey Pulse, always poking round the trashcans of society for what he called angles, should quote $6 million as a decent fee for a paternity suit.

'Don't even ask about what's just or unjust,' he said on the phone from his Portland, Oregon office. 'Just ask if the son of a gun can afford it. And if it happens to come out of the pockets of the born again, that's just too bad. Thanks to me they'll become wise again.'

Mr Smith nudged the Old Man, who was unwilling to take the newspaper. He was rather taken by the simple-minded jingle and joined in in a stentorian diapason every time 'Hands in Prayer' was called for. As far as church music was concerned, Bach rather frightened the Old Man by his ferocious logic and extraordinary inventiveness, which demanded, in all serenity, a devotional enslavement. Handel seemed to the Old Man more flamboyant, more theatrical, suggesting that a glut of grace notes inevitably culminated in a state of grace. This kind of nursery-rhyme tune, as pristine as blancmange, offended nothing but the occasional intelligence, and gave time to the Reverend to wipe his brow with a couple of bath towels.

When the young adults had finished their paeon to infantile piety on an acidulated final chord, the Reverend, now dried off and pomaded, came forward out of his corner for the next round of the Good Fight, while his seconds retired into the wings with their combs, brushes, and towels.

'I'm through with Satan,' said Henchman jovially.

There were stirrings of enthusiasm in the church.

'You know where Satan can go as far as I'm concerned? He can go there where he chose to set up house. There's nothing bad about the word I'm about to use. It's merely descriptive of a state of mind. Satan can go to hell.'

Great excitement, while Smith tried to struggle to his feet. The Old Man restrained him with superhuman strength.

'Don't be a fool!' hissed the Old Man. 'There are bound to be better opportunities than this if you must lose your composure.'

Mr Smith waved the newspaper before the Old Man's face, and the Old Man understood that his perusal of it was the price of Mr Smith's good behaviour.

Just then the tension lapsed. The Reverend Henchman relaxed, the audience began to gabble.

'OK, folks. Relax. We're in a commercial break!' shouted the floor manager.

'What has happened?' asked the Old Man, trying to read the article.

Mr Smith chuckled. 'This American Dream has been temporarily interrupted by this message from its sponsor.'

'You mean, they interrupt church services for commercial messages?'

'Yes, every few minutes the money lenders are allowed back into the temple in order to sell their wares.'

'It is not a practice I can possibly approve of. I say, this is an astonishing article. The Reverend Henchman seems to be unusually vulnerable to feminine pulchritude.'

'Well, you saw his wife. It's almost understandable.'

'I don't like to be unkind. But I must say, she did look rather like one of nature's aunts.'

'What do you mean by that?'

'I shouldn't have said that. I shouldn't have said most of the things I have said since I met you again.'

There was warmth between them.

'Stand by!' shouted the studio manager. 'Transmission resumes in thirty seconds. Let's have a devotional atmosphere now, folks. This is the last segment before the faith healings. All of you with sickness who registered before the show with either me or one of the assistants, be prepared to line up in the place indicated. Ten seconds. Let's have a great show, folks, and don't hold back with your applause. Joey! Take it away!'

Henchman returned to the matter-of-fact style, the valleys of his emotional landscape. 'Folks . . . some of you may think I have treated the Devil in a somewhat cavalier fashion . . .'

'Well, I do for one!' shouted Mr Smith, in his most grating voice.

Henchman looked surprised for a moment.

'I'm sincerely sorry to hear that, sir.' And he broadened his approach for the audience to bear witness. 'There's a gentleman here thinks I have treated the Devil in a cavalier fashion.'

There was a groundswell of 'No way,' 'To hell with Satan,' 'Get thee behind me,' and so on.

The Reverend held out a hand indulgently, for silence. 'There's a reason I don't want to spend more time with that old critter, Satan. You see, he may be right here in the church, although I gotta say, I saw him clearly the other night, and there's no one answering to that description here today. But – ' (and his voice rose and trembled) 'there's one presence here you don't have to identify . . . you just feel it in your sinner's heart . . . My friend, God is here tonight . . .'

'Did you hear that?' whispered the Old Man.

'He's talking about God. He doesn't mean you,' cackled Mr Smith cattily.

'God is here tonight. This is his house. These are his stained-glass walls . . . his home movies all around us . . . we his sinning children . . . He lives right here, with us . . . right in our hearts and minds . . . and let me tell you this, folks . . . If he were to decide to materialize here today . . . to turn up in any guise . . . he, in his infinite wisdom, chooseth . . . I'd recognize him instantly, and I'd say . . . on your behalf . . . O Lord God, we greet thee in all simplicity, in awe of thine majesty, wrapped in the swaddling clothes of thy love . . . cosseted in the warmth of thy affection . . . and on behalf of the congregation of this consecrated Church of Many Colours on the Campus of the University of the Soul, in Henchman City, Arkansas, with its radio or TV outlets in upward of a hundred countries . . . we just say to thee the loveliest words in our language . . . Lord, welcome home . . .'

There was a tumultuous ovation, and the Reverend was in tears again, moved by his own sentiments and the beauty of his words.

The Old Man rose, and began climbing onto the stage. A security man stopped him.

'You can't go up there, old timer. Healing's in the next segment.'

'I have been recognized,' said the Old Man.

'What seems to be the trouble, Jerry?' Henchman asked. He could not believe that an old man in flowing robes could constitute a menace, or a disruption of the programme. On the contrary, Henchman had a gut feeling that an old man with such childish openness on his face might even help the illusion of pervading sanctity.

'You have recognized me,' called the Old Man, with immense force, 'and I am deeply touched.'

Back at home, in West Virginia, Gontrand B. Harrison, the Deputy Director of the FBI, who was a fan of the Reverend Henchman, knocked over his highball when the Old Man appeared on the screen.

'There's the son of a bitch!' he cried to the startled Mrs Harrison.

'Who?'

'Switch on the video, will you honey? Clean tape. I'll phone Gonella. Remember the Identikit photo I showed you?'

'God?'

'Right. That's him. Arkansas. Hello, Mrs Gonella? Is Carmine at home? This is urgent.'

Back in the church, Henchman, obeying his intuitions as a TV star, called on the Old Man to come up onto the stage.

'Don't be afraid,' he called out charmingly, believing that an old man like that might legitimately be timid.

'Why should I be afraid after the welcome you have given me?' called the Old Man in a voice which filled the church with sound, and even provided its own echo.

'Give him a mike,' said the Reverend.

'He don't need no mike,' replied the sound man, intimidated.

'I gave you a welcome? Who are you, Old Man?'

'I have only been back on Earth for a few days. You are the first man to discover my identity in a public place and I congratulate you. I am God.'

The Reverend looked desperate. He had miscalculated. If the Old Man had said he was Ellsworth W. Tidmarsh out of Boulder City, aged 95, he would have brought the house down, but God was the last kind of competition he needed. And you couldn't very well ask God if he was a regular watcher of the Joey Henchman Hour.

'Old Man, do you realize you are guilty of blasphemy?'

'Oh, don't spoil it all now,' said the Old Man, pained. 'You were doing so well . . .'

'Shall I tell you how I *know* that you are *not* God?'

'You cannot know that,' cried the Old Man. 'You said yourself, in *whatever* guise I chose to appear.'

'I did indeed. You are right. I said that indeed. Those very words. I'd welcome God in *whatever* guise he chose to appear. After all, unlike Satan, I've never seen God. He could turn up here in any form, and while I'd recognize his sacred spirit, I couldn't recognize him physically.'

'He could even turn up looking like me,' said the Old Man.

'He could indeed. Looking like you. That's a possibility. Although I'd expect him to have a little better taste perhaps . . .'

The crowd laughed its approval, while Henchman, who did not wish to give the impression of making fun of a harmless old lunatic, added, 'Sartorially, you understand.' And then his voice rose and developed a snarling aggression.

'But there's one thing you're doing which God would never do. This is a multi-million-dollar enterprise serving God and his message in upward of a hundred countries. Knowing the cost of air time today, for God knows everything – he is *om*-niscient – God would never, ever, waste this precious air time by taking it unto himself and away from its rightful owner, its purchaser, the Reverend Joey Henchman who is, round the clock, and at his own expense, spreading the holy word. God would be better informed than that, better briefed. Am I right?'

There was a great yell of approval, with the usual shouts of 'A-men,' 'Sit down,' 'Go back where you came from.' Even the Old Man, with all his abilities in the field of acoustics, could not make himself heard against the rising tide of righteous indignation. He just stood there helplessly, while a couple of security men tried to pull him from the stage. The well-trained cameras avoided him, training on either Joey Henchman's nodded satisfaction at having made a religious point so succinctly and so well, or the ugly mood of the congregation, which seemed almost to lose control of itself.

It needed a dramatic act to recapture the initiative. In a flash, Mr Smith was on his feet and streaking up onto the stage. The security men were too encumbered with the Old Man to react as quickly as they were supposed to. Mr Smith shouted and gesticulated wildly, but he could penetrate the barrage of noise no more easily than the Old Man. He burst momentarily into flames.

There was a shriek of horror from the auditorium, and then a stunned silence while people asked themselves if they had really seen what they thought they had, or whether it was a low trick of the collective imagination.

'Joey Henchman, you are a cheat and a liar, and I can prove it.'

The Reverend was covered in perspiration once again, but it was not due to his exertions.

'Go right ahead. Prove it,' he said recklessly, licking his lips.

'Remember me?' cried Mr Smith. 'Full face?' He turned sideways. 'Profile?'

'Can't say as I do,' said Henchman, steadily.

'And yet you claimed that you knew me very well. You were lying. You associated me with Miss Linda Carpucci. I've never had the pleasure of meeting the young lady. Another lie. You said you remembered my physical presence, and that I was not in the church although I was sitting in the first row, just in your line of vision. A third lie.'

'OK, OK, don't tell me, let me guess. You're Satan,' said Henchman, absolutely unimpressed, even mocking.

Before Mr Smith had time to confirm this educated guess, Henchman reverted to the congregation, his great ally.

'Isn't that great?' he asked rhetorically. 'The *Devil* comes to *God's* assistance. Is that *some* scenario? The two of them on the same side, trying to make a monkey out of Joey Henchman and a multi-million-dollar enterprise, dedicated to the Word of Almighty God?'

The laughter swelled, and changed to acclamation.

'That's it, folks. It's time for a message from our sponsor once again, and I guess I've shown you how we deal with false prophets and those who would twist holy writ for their own murky and sombre purposes.' There was great applause, and Joey Henchman and his electronic amplifying system had won the day.

Mr Smith and the Old Man, threatened from all sides, held hands. Desperately Mr Smith waved his other hand, and the building burst into flames.

'Don't be a fool,' cried the Old Man, putting out the blaze. There was another collective scream, followed by silence.

'I won't be told that I'm not bona fide!' Mr Smith yelled, and a fire broke out behind the congregation.

'I forbid you!' shouted the Old Man, putting it out again.

'Leave me alone,' wailed Mr Smith, setting fire to himself again.

The Old Man blew and the flames died.

'I am my own master,' yelled Mr Smith. 'Let me destroy what deserves to be destroyed. Mammon's temple!'

'I refuse to allow you to do my work to my face,' snapped the Old Man. 'Behind my back, you may do what you like. Even pray, should you be overcome by nostalgia.'

'Hold it right there!'

Another voice entered the argument. A man in a panama hat stood at the entrance, holding a card in one hand and a gun in the other.

'Smith and Godfrey!' he called out.

The Old Man and Smith blinked, but failed to respond.

'Gardner Green, FBI, Little Rock, Arkansas. You're under arrest for forgery. Throw any weapon you might have on the floor in front of you.'

Mr Smith trembled. 'What do we do now?'

'Hold my hand and clear your mind.'

'Of what?'

'Of anything.'

'No talking!' said the FBI officer, advancing up the aisle. 'And don't try to disappear.'

'Where are we going?' cried Mr Smith.

'A mountain top in Arizona, free of men.'

And they disappeared. There was a gasp of amazement, but the commercial had just begun, and those watching TV were spared the actual disappearances. The FBI man swung round to face the congregation. An aide ran forward with a microphone.

'OK, I don't want any panic. What you have just experienced is perfectly normal, and well known to all students of extra-sensory perception and other psychic phenomena. These guys, of uncertain origin, first escaped from custody in Washington DC, just a few days ago. They are classified as unconvicted petty criminals and have no record of physical violence. Now, enjoy. And leave the rest to the FBI, one of the elements which make this country great.'

There was clapping, and the FBI man exited from the scene, replacing his gun in its holster.

The healings went as well as ever, incontinence, asthma, blindness, piles and AIDS being among the scourges handled with Old Testament directness by the Reverend Henchman, the last case, that of AIDS, being dealt with in the remaining thirty seconds of the programme. The victim claimed to feel much better after being knocked on the head with a few insulting words directed at Satan.

It was only after the programme was off the air, and while the Reverend Henchman was having his make-up removed, that the full impact of what had happened began to sink in. Gardner Green, the FBI officer from Little Rock, sat on a stool and sipped a dry martini with a twist of lemon, the way he liked it, fixed by Joey Henchman himself. The Reverend was in need of allies. People to talk to. He had been extremely courageous and professional in moments of great difficulty, but now things were perhaps a little out of hand. The telephone never stopped ringing. Many of the callers praised the Reverend Henchman, but there were those who said, what if it really was God, really was the Devil? How could they be sure they were not who they purported to be? Others actually felt positive vibrations when the Old Man was on the air, negative vibrations when Mr Smith burst into flames. The newspapers would probably have their own comments. The major TV companies had already planned to buy the right to air the tapes in their evening news broadcasts.

Gardner Green was quite relieved that the story had, to quote him, gone public. 'It's a toughie,' he mused, as he swilled his drink around and watched the olive bounce about in the glass. 'See, these old guys have a knack of disappearing, and turning up again elsewhere in a matter of seconds . . . and by elsewhere, I mean one or two thousand miles away. According to the manager of a hotel in Manhattan, the maid heard their TV at four thirty, when she did her rounds. At five o'clock . . . seventeen hundred hours . . . she passed again . . . it was her last chance to do the room before she went home, and she found it unoccupied . . . two suitcases, unopened . . . both of them empty . . . the beds not slept in from the night before. Now, the interesting part of all this is that when she passed at four thirty . . . that is sixteen thirty hours . . . she distinctly heard your voice. They were listening to your show.'

'Well . . . that's right . . . it would've been fourteen thirty hours mountain time. We're on the air right then. I must just have gone on.'

'Right. Now it must have been something about your show which made them take off some time between four thirty and five o'clock mountain time. Can you imagine what would have excited them sufficiently to cause them to cover the distance from New York to Henchman City in a coupla seconds?'

Joey Henchman laughed as a soothing balm was applied to his face by the pretty make-up artist. 'Well, first of all I got to put it on record that nothing on God's Earth would make me travel that fast.'

'On account of you couldn't if you tried.'

'Right, right. No, in answer to your question, I don't know what could've sparked their decision. I started off my midweek sermonette . . . I preach it once a week . . . rest of the time, I'm on evenings . . . Joey Henchman's Hour of Many Colours . . .'

'I know that,' said Green.

'Do you watch it?' asked the Reverend, beaming.

'Not if there's anything else on.'

Henchman was momentarily stung by this unexpected note of hostility, but pretended Green had said yes.

'No, I started the sermonette by passing over briefly my experience when Satan visited with me, and made a passing reference to all those rumours about . . . you know . . . Linda Carpucci . . . It don't do nothing for you to be seen to be running away . . . not by that . . . that rabble . . .'

'Which rabble?'

'The goddammed press . . . 'Happy Hour at Henchman City' . . . 'Fun and Frolic in the Topless Pit' . . . 'Joey does his homework behind teacher's back' . . . you've seen the headlines.'

'No.'

Joey Henchman was incredulous. 'You must'a done.'

'No.'

'Why not?'

'Guess I just wasn't interested. That satisfy you?'

Henchman returned gallantly to the attack. 'That Carpucci is one ba-a-d girl, I'm telling you. Only one thing matters to her. Money. Money in any form. And she'll give anything for it, body, soul, you name it.'

'Sounds like your ideal companion. Must have been a lot of unspoken bonds between you. You were too busy to speak.'

Joey Henchman pushed the girl to one side, and sat up in the make-up chair, angry. 'Whose side are you on, anyway?'

'Me? I work for the FBI. I guess I'm on the side of justice. When I'm lucky. But I tell you this, my boss, Gontrand B. Harrison, old Gonner Harrison, he's a fan of yours . . . never misses the Joey Henchman show unless he's on duty, of course . . . He caught your confrontation with the old guy . . . you know, Godfrey . . . and he had the presence of mind to call the Little Rock office . . . and I was actually in my car, not far from here . . . and I could come right over when I did, getting additional input on my car phone on the way, see.'

'Well, I got to hand it to the FBI. They sure work fast. How did you know which hotel to find him in?'

'They phoned us. We've had an Identikit likeness of the fat old guy out for best part of a week, circulated to all hotels, and the hotel recognized them after they'd disappeared.'

'Great. But tell me . . .' Henchman became confidential, and gave the impression of being deserving of trust. 'Tell me . . . they're just small-time counterfeiters, is that right?'

'I don't know about small-time, but sure, the warrant's out for forgery—'

'Why no Identikit picture of the skinny guy?'

'He keeps changing identity, from an old artist type to a Japanese industrialist and now a Village gay. Tougher to pin down.'

'But . . . who do you think they are?'

'Me? I don't count. I'm just a link in a chain of command. My only duty was to come here and try to arrest them on the information at my disposal, and prevent a panic. Now, during the end of the programme, the faith-healing part, I was able to call ahead to our people in Phoenix, and they will go to every mountain top in Arizona by jeep, by helicopter, and on foot, trying to succeed where I failed.'

'But it's very important I know . . . for obvious reasons . . . Who does the FBI think they are?'

Green took a sip of his martini, savoured it, and swallowed with a sigh of satisfaction. 'There are two theories at this time,' he said. 'Others will surely develop later as the first two are discredited. The first, developed by the Head of the Joint Chiefs of Staff, General Anzeiger. He believes in extra-terrestrials more than he does in the Soviet Union. He figures they are a patrol from outer space testing our defences. This theory seems a little romantic to a down-to-earth guy like the President's security advisor, Pat Gonzales, who is, of course, a civilian. He believes in the Soviet Union a little more than he does in tiny marzipan men from the planet Moron. He thinks the Soviets and not the extra-terrestrials are trying out something new, which already goes by the code word ISLE, Isle, and which sounds like yet another futile treaty organization, Individual Supersonic Location Exchange. Personally, I think they're the kind of juvenile theories which constantly emanate from highly placed officials who won't risk being considered old hat.'

'What do you think it is? You've said nothing yet, except that it's not up to you to have theories.'

'Right.'

'Christ, how humble can you get? There's nowhere in the Good Book it says you've got to turn the other cheek before the first one's been struck. We're a democracy, feller. Even a wino in the Bowery rates a theory.'

Green smiled. 'OK, so you insist,' he said. 'Well, my theory is that the old guys might be just precisely who they say they are, God and Satan.'

'You're just aiming to make me nervous, that's all!' Henchman cried. 'Get out of here!'

'As you wish. But as my boss pointed out, whatever the truth, this event has sure taken the heat off your fling with Miss Carpucci.'

Henchman overlooked his anger, considered this for a moment. 'You think so?'

'Oh sure. Who's going to worry about a paternity suit when the FBI's on the trail of two old guys calling themselves God and the Devil, and they can travel faster than the fastest jet on Earth *and* escape arrest by vanishing into thin air?'

'Hey, you may be right at that. Wait till I tell Charlene . . .'

'You bet.'

The smile suddenly left Joey Henchman's relieved face. 'Do you pray, Mr Green?'

'No, sir.'

'Are you a Christian?'

'No, sir.'

'Are you ready to be born again?'

'No, sir.'

A sob appeared in Joey Henchman's voice as he closed his eyes. 'I'll pray for you.'

'I could think of better ways to waste your time.'

Joey's eyes opened again, surprised, unused to this attitude of detachment. 'You are an agnostic,' he accused.

'I am.'

'And yet you are willing to believe that a couple of mountebanks really are who they say they are, to wit, God Almighty and Satan?'

'Yes, sir. Has it occurred to you that I may well regret not believing?'

'You *could* believe, if you wished to.'

Henchman advanced, and tried to take Green's hands in his. Green avoided this manoeuvre by retreating while holding out his empty martini glass, which Joey took by reflex.

'No, sir. I could never believe, nor do I wish to under prevailing conditions. My job has shown me that some of the worst gangsters in this country are those who commercialize their belief.'

'Commercialize their belief?' echoed Henchman, incredulous.

'Yes . . . in upward of a hundred countries . . . isn't that the formula? Well, even if I cannot be born again, thanks for the martini . . . it was . . . divine?'

7

The Old Man sat on a rock in the rich, late-afternoon sun, basking in the incredible beauty of the red-gold hills and the mauve distance. The air was pure and tepid as the heat of the day had drained slowly away. Mr Smith lay flat on the ground behind him, exhausted by the speed of the journey. He watched the agitated progress of ants with fascination. It was their rush hour, and they tumbled over each other in their desperation to reach their destinations. Evidently, with all their intelligence, they had not yet reached a pitch of cohesion which compelled one line of ants to stick to one side of the pathway, the opposite stream to the other.

'This makes sense,' said the Old Man expansively.

'What does?'

'It reminds me of so many things, sitting in a high place, out of the reach of influence. The time of our adolescence, remember? Olympus?'

'Olympus was cold, shrouded in clouds, miserably uncomfortable. It wasn't a bit like this.'

'Well, I remember it like this – not in my celestial memory perhaps, but in the mortal one I assumed in order to assess the human condition. Moses, too. Moses and the Tablets. A high place.'

'I wasn't there.'

'My attention was attracted. That's why I remember.'

There was a silence while each pursued his own thoughts.

'Where will we pass the night?' asked Mr Smith.

'Here.'

'It's infested with insects.'

'Levitate,' said the Old Man, as though it was the most normal thing in the world.

'Levitation takes energy. I'm absolutely exhausted by all these rapid trips in succession.'

'I'll lend you my robe to rest on. Nothing will touch you. You may even find it in yourself to sleep a bit.'

'No,' grumbled Mr Smith, 'only two things seem to put me to sleep, sex and television. Come to think of it, that's what I miss up here. Television. Can't we go and rest somewhere there's television?'

'No,' snapped the Old Man, in a surprisingly bad temper.

'Why not?' grumbled Mr Smith peevishly, sounding like a child. He had found the wavelength of the Old Man's thoughts, and he was jamming them with the selfish perversity of a malevolent infant. 'Why not?' he repeated, and after a while, louder and more drawn out, 'Why no-o-ot?', and suddenly the kettle came to the boil. 'Why not?' screamed Mr Smith, kicking unreasonably with his legs and beating the ground with his fists.

The Old Man shut his eyes as though to keep his patience within bounds. 'You really are the limit,' he said. 'After all we have undertaken together, after all the moments in which we have exhibited kindness and consideration towards one another, you have found a way to disrupt my cosmic ruminations. What are you up to back there?'

And the Old Man noticed a quick defensive movement as Mr Smith turned, like a schoolboy covering up his schoolwork from the eyes of a prying neighbour.

'Take your arm away!' commanded the Old Man.

Grudgingly, Mr Smith did as he was told, to reveal a ring of small fires surrounding a scorpion, which held its tail high above its body, as though ready to throw a javelin. The corpses of other scorpions lay around like devoured shrimps.

'Ugh . . . ugh . . . that's dirty, like picking your nose,' said the Old Man. 'I'm surprised at you. Poor little scorpions.'

'Poor little scorpions indeed!' cried Mr Smith. 'You talk as though it's murder. It's not, I hasten to point out! It's suicide.'

'Suicide? Trust you to make use of a technicality in your defence.'

'I miss my television.'

'I thought you hated it.'

'I hated many things when I first tried them, Camembert, oysters, mentholated cigarettes, marijuana. I easily become addicted to things which I find repellent on first contact. You see before you a TV addict in urgent need of a fix.'

'What is there about it you find fascinating?'

'I don't know. I haven't analyzed it. Perhaps because thousands of people are killed without anyone getting hurt. These little scorpions I killed to while away the time, they're all really dead. They won't come back to menace the barefoot or the imprudent sunbather. And d'you know why they're dead? Because they weren't on television.'

The Old Man smiled grimly. 'Since when do you care whether death is real or feigned?'

'Since I began travelling with you, O Lord.'

'Hypocrite.'

'Oh yes! What flattery!' and he giggled insanely for a moment. Then he became serious. 'I would be failing in my mandate if I suddenly began to distinguish between real death and false death, between real suffering and false suffering, between the truth and theatricals.'

'I am very relieved to hear you admit it.'

'There's no risk of that,' said Mr Smith darkly. 'But I hope you realize that I should have come to the Reverend Henchman's rescue and not to yours. He is my man.'

'If you had come to his rescue and stated your reasons with the kind of moderation it requires to be convincing in American politics, you would have destroyed his ministry with a single body blow. You would have blown his cover for good, with or without Miss Carpucci. But you are far too highly strung for such a complicated strategy. You lose your head, forget your original intention, panic and set fire to things.'

There was a long moment of silence.

'Why don't you answer?' asked the Old Man.

'Is it really in my interest to destroy his ministry? He is my man, as I said, not yours. See those poor invalids who were beginning to form a line when we made our getaway – their dashed hopes, the illusions of improvement, their psychosomatic sentiment of sudden well-being. They are all in my province. Only their inherent optimism about their condition derives from you. The irrefutable reality is mine. And that is perhaps why I find television suddenly to my taste. There is nothing intimate or discreet about it. It is as vulgar a market place as they come, with everything for sale, every bad example offered for emulation, with no time wasted on reflection. Everything is action, go, go, go!'

He snapped his fingers and invented a quick routine redolent of exuberance and abandon.

'We watched part of a programme about the mating rituals of penguins, done, I thought, in excellent taste, but you insisted on switching to another channel, remember? Not all television is the kind you like. In fact, I would go so far as to say that if we stayed together for any length of time, we would have to have separate sets.'

There was another pause, as it grew visibly darker. A deep-orange sun lost its intensity behind voluptuous clouds, which caught various reflections in their folds, as though they were abstract paraphrases of the human body. At least, that is how Mr Smith saw them, with a kind of sad enjoyment. The Old Man saw them as the unravelling of great truths, too obscure to bear translation into the coarse vehicle of language.

'I think,' said the Old Man bluntly, 'that so far our adventure, however necessary to our well-being, has not been entirely successful.'

'I agree.'

'I had envisaged it as far simpler. I had no idea that sophisticated society had so evolved itself as to be practically impenetrable to a couple of old eccentrics on safari in its midst.'

'May I utter a word of criticism?'

'Since when have I ever tried to muzzle you?'

'Never mind. We won't go into that. Don't you think we were wrong to attempt this experiment at the sophisticated end of the scale? After all, we have so far made only one big mistake, and that was within the first full day on Earth. You let fly with fistfuls of dollars, which turned out to be counterfeit. That was the only mistake we needed to make. After that, our life has become progressively more precarious, with uncouth men brandishing revolvers telling us to hold whatever it is right there and trying to put us on our honour not to disappear before they even had an opportunity to punish us. I never want to feel those ice-cold handcuffs again, nor sit behind bars, nor submit to a medical examination.'

The Old Man smiled. 'I admit there have been moments both embarrassing and disagreeable, but we have learned more than we think. And if we had effected our landing in the African bush or in the jungles of India, we would have told ourselves that not much had changed, and we would probably have been wrong even then. But I somehow don't think the authenticity of money would be so important in a place bereft of it and, true or false, it would be welcomed with equal delight and gratitude.'

'Then why did we start with America?'

'It is certainly the most difficult of our hurdles, and I think that before we return to our usual existence, maybe even long before we return, we will be forced to leave the United States.'

'Do other countries have television of the same intensity?'

'What a curious question. You really are bitten by it.'

'Well, I had my moment of glory on it yesterday, against enormous odds. I flatter myself I would be recognized almost everywhere today, if we hadn't now come to a place entirely devoid of an audience.'

'That is probably why we will have to leave the United States, because of your hankering after publicity. But remember, they are so embedded in their scepticism that you will never be recognized as Satan, only as the guy who thinks he's Satan!'

'Well, at least I have changed my appearance to avoid detection. You make no effort. Have you seen anybody remotely like you in our travels? And would we have gone to Africa or India looking the way you do? How would you have explained away the fact that you are white to the point of tastelessness? Not only is your skin white, your hair and beard are white, your robe is white, and you even wear what look like tennis shoes on your feet. Why? Are you so scared of the slightest blemish? You don't merely wear your perfection on your sleeve, you are dunked in it. Hell, do I remember Heaven when I look at you!'

'That's enough!' cried the Old Man, with something approaching stridency, and became instantly black.

Mr Smith began to splutter and choke as he was invaded by irrepressible laughter.

The Old Man blinked in irritation. He was not very adept at being black, since he had never seriously practised and had none of Mr Smith's flare in the art of disguise. He was not very good at being white either, it must be said, because anyone else his colour might have been thought to be not only at death's door, but to have passed the portico. Now the Old Man was so utterly and exaggeratedly black that he lacked authenticity, looking more like a blacked-up night-club performer of the late twenties than the genuine article.

'What is the matter now?' he enquired testily as Mr Smith seemed at last able to control his laughter.

Mr Smith looked at him with grateful eyes, from which a procession of tears had rolled into the furrows of his cheeks, among the half-hidden moles and blackheads, disappearing in tiny puffs of steam to the tune of brief hisses.

'We are not ourselves, are we, when we are forced into the restrictions of human shape? We are not intended to be tangible,' he said, suddenly sober and reasonable.

'How can we embark on a voyage of discovery without making the essential temporary sacrifice of assuming the shape and, if possible the spirit, of our creations?'

Mr Smith began shaking with laughter again, much feebler and more painful than before.

'Oh, please don't embark on a serious conversation looking like that. I mean, your other appearance is just as preposterous, but at least I've got used to it.'

In a trice the Old Man reverted to his old ivory look, but he was far from pleased. 'You really are the limit,' he said, and began to stride off.

'Where are you going?'

The Old Man did not deign to reply.

'I'm sorry! I apologize!'

The Old Man stopped. Mr Smith staggered in his hurry up the gradient.

'Where are we going?' he asked. 'I thought we were going to spend the night here. You even told me to levitate.'

'I took pity on you. It's not in my character to be able to enjoy the ecstasy of high places when I feel that you are miserable.'

'The ecstasy of high places? Now you're taking me even higher, above the snow line. Look, there it is. You can just see it ahead of us. Snow!'

'There's also a cottage up there. You can see a vague glow from the windows spilling onto the snow.'

'Where?' asked Mr Smith, incredulous, his face twisted with effort to see the invisible.

'Trust me. They may even have television.'

'Oh, forget it,' said Mr Smith. 'I can live without television. What have I done for millions of years? I just thought it would be nice, that's all.'

They trudged on in silence, the atmosphere heavy with unsaid things which had accumulated over the centuries.

Suddenly the Old Man stopped. 'Where did you get those scorpions from?'

'I found them,' Mr Smith replied, seeming to wallow in guilt.

'Nonsense. It's far too cold for scorpions up here, apart from a couple of hours around noon, and in the height of summer. If I put my mind to it, I can remember the specification for scorpions quite clearly.'

'Well, if you must know, I brought them with me in a cardboard box, in case I ran out of amusements.'

'Amusements?' the Old Man cried.

'You prefer forged currency in your pockets. That's a matter of taste, isn't it? I happen to like watching scorpions die, and pulling legs off frogs, and drowning insects in saucers – blood sports, you understand.'

The Old Man refrained from answering. He just strode on with thunder in his eyes. Mr Smith assumed an affectation of petulance, as though his democratic rights were being gratuitously infringed.

They reached the door of the house in silence. The Old Man rang the bell. There was an immediate bark from a very aged dog, its voice filled with uncertainty and a sense of recollected duty.

'If we were dogs, that's how we'd sound,' said Mr Smith.

'I'm not going to laugh,' replied the Old Man, stifling his smile with difficulty.

The door was opened by a man in some kind of uniform. His wife stood behind him. As soon as they saw the Old Man, both fell to their knees.

'But I haven't yet explained who I am,' said the Old Man.

'They've got television!' exclaimed Mr Smith, delighted.

In the background, two small children were having their supper and, puzzled at seeing their parents on their knees, started banging their plates with their spoons.

'Quiet, children,' said their mother, in her church voice.

'Welcome, Lord, to our humble abode,' the father intoned.

'Please rise,' the Old Man pleaded.

'It is not seemly that we should rise,' said the father, searching for fitting devotional words.

'Oh, for heaven's sake,' exclaimed the Old Man,' we are not in the Bible. And certainly not in the seventeenth century. May I ask your name?'

'Thomas K. Peace, sir.'

'That's a beautiful name, even if you insist on remaining on your knees. Why do you do it?'

'We caught you on the Joey Henchman show, Lord.'

'It was not terribly successful, I'm afraid. It was naïve of me, but he seemed to sense my presence in the hall. And I was taken in by his words. I thought he was sincere.'

'I could've told you about Joey Henchman, Lord. He's one of the things that's wrong with this great country of ours.'

'It's OK to get up, Tom. The Lord's going to get mad at you if you stay down there,' said the wife nervously, seeking confirmation from the Old Man.

'Go mad?' asked the Old Man in some alarm.

'Get mad. Angry,' explained the wife.

'Ah. I'm afraid I'm not acquainted with the latest linguistic fads. No, certainly I will never be angry. There are religious fanatics and there have been pilgrims who spent most of their lives on their knees. There are those who only understand religion as a form of physical torture, and unfortunately the tendency is particularly prevalent among those who dedicate their whole lives to it. I regret it.'

Immediately on hearing this, Tom Peace sprang to his feet.

'I didn't mean to hurry you,' said the Old Man.

'I served in the Marine Corps, Lord.'

'Oh, hence the abrupt movements?'

'We did everything by numbers, so that everything'd become second nature in an emergency, Lord.'

'The Marine Corps. Is that a military organization?'

'Sure is, Lord.'

'We're just having supper, Lord, with our children, Tom junior and Alice Jayne. We haven't much to offer, but we'd certainly appreciate it if you . . . you and your friend . . . broke bread with us,' said the wife.

'With pleasure. You realize, of course, we don't eat. No, it's not a question of principle. It's just that food is not one of our needs. But we will sit with you, in all simplicity.'

The Old Man and Mr Smith sat shyly on small wooden chairs.

'We want to do the right thing, you understand, Lord,' said Tom. 'Do you expect us to wash your feet?'

'Goodness, no.'

'I wouldn't mind, if it's all part of the service,' remarked Mr Smith.

'No!' said the Old Man sharply.

The dog that had barked before now began to whimper and claw at a door.

'You don't object to animals, do you, Lord?' asked Tom.

The Old Man laughed. 'How can I object to animals?'

'Nobody has yet consulted me,' remarked Mr Smith, with a drop of acid in his voice.

'My question was a general one,' Tom said tactfully.

'My friend and I are not usually at the receiving end of general questions.'

The Old Man interrupted. 'Before meeting the dog, it occurs to me that we have already met everyone except your wife.'

'I'm sorry, Lord. This is Mrs Peace.'

'I gathered as much.'

'Nancy,' said Mrs Peace, feeding the children.

'And my friend's name is – Mr Smith.'

'I'll handle Satan, honey.'

'Satan?' Mr Smith sat up as though stung.

'No offence, sir.' Tom hesitated on his way to liberate the dog.

'Is that the dog's name?' asked the Old Man, brimful of amusement.

'Yes, Lord.'

'Why?' demanded Mr Smith, in a voice which made both children begin to cry.

'I guess on account of he's black.'

Mr Smith, after a moment of imminent rage, relapsed into a baroque sulk.

'Has the dog a lovely character?' asked the Old Man, ever eager to be conciliatory.

'He looks just terrifying, but he's got a heart of gold.'

'Well, then, I think he's aptly named.'

'I guess one of the reasons he scares people is that he's blind.'

'Blind?' asked Mr Smith, as though sensing another insult in the offing.

'Well, he's seventeen years old, sir.'

'Seventeen years!' Mr Smith screeched. 'A mere puppy!'

The Old Man was visibly grateful that Mr Smith had pulled himself together.

Tom opened the door and Satan bounded out, knocking over a coffee table. His yellow eyes seemed to see all too well, although they were totally unfocused. He stood very still, as though trying to assess a new situation by means of hidden sensibilities. Suddenly his tail began to wag and, head lowered, he made his way cautiously towards the Old Man.

'Well, Satan, this is a surprise,' said the latter gently, extending his hand and stroking the noble head with its sightless eyes. Suddenly a passing odour distracted the dog's attention and, turning his head towards Mr Smith, there began a growl so deep it was scarcely audible.

Mr Smith rose precipitately. 'I knew it,' he cried. 'I hate dogs, and they hate me. Nobody consulted me. I knew this would happen! I knew it!'

Both Tom and the Old Man attempted to divert Satan's attention and to reassure him, but it was to no avail. The whiff of sulphur in the air, the stink of original corruption, the draught through ancient keyholes could be hidden from men, but certainly not from dogs. The whites of the yellow eyes began to show as the head was tilted to one side, cocked like a rifle, and the growl passed from bass to the tenor register.

'Easy, boy, come on,' Tom crooned urgently, as the children watched wide-eyed, munching automatically on their rusks.

A dangerous foam began to form around Satan's mouth.

'He wants to kill me,' hissed Mr Smith.

'He can't kill you. No one can!' the Old Man tried to reassure.

'I won't let it happen. If nobody will protect me—'

The dog seemed ready to neglect the darkness in which it vegetated, and plunge into a savage daylight.

Mr Smith's eyes dilated horribly, and just as Satan was about to spring, despite Tom who tried to hold him by his studded collar, Mr Smith transformed himself into a large, slavering, grizzly bear with little porcine eyes and paws with yellowed claws.

'Stop that at once!' cried the Old Man. 'That dog is entirely harmless!'

The smaller of the children was visibly jolted by the sheer size of the bear, and began screaming. The larger one just pointed, as though the others might have failed to notice.

Satan suddenly cowered, sensing a new situation which could not be assessed in a hurry.

'Put the dog back where he came from if you don't mind, Mr Peace. We'll never persuade Mr Smith to revert if you don't,' said the Old Man.

'Thy will be done,' Tom intoned, and then, 'Come on, feller, basket.'

As soon as the door had shut on Tom and the now whimpering dog, Mr Smith reverted to his usual shape.

'It's all very well for you to scold me and tell me the dog is harmless,' he spat out as soon as the transmogrification had taken place. 'He let you pet him. He was going to attack me as though I'd stolen his identity instead of the other way round.'

'Calm down, and wipe up that mess. You've slobbered all over the table.'

'There's paper napkins right there,' said the ever helpful Nancy.

The screaming child was now studying Mr Smith, a slight frown on a face bathed in recent tears. The other child enjoyed the quick changes, and seemed to ask for more by waving a spoon around in the air and eventually dropping it onto the floor.

While Mr Smith was wiping bear saliva off the table, Tom reappeared, smiling grimly. 'We'll have no more trouble from him. Poor Satan's in a state of shock.'

Mr Smith wished to forestall any remarks which the Old Man might have to make. 'I must apologize for any precipitate change of appearance I underwent. It was not my intention to cause you or your children any distress. I was merely acting in legitimate self-defence,' he said, a trace litigiously.

'I've got to say, I've never seen Satan like that before. You live and learn, Lord. It's maybe old age.'

'Might I prevail on you to refer to him as just "the dog" in future conversation?' asked Mr Smith, sweetly.

'Sure, sure. Nancy, honey, I guess there's been a little too much

excitement round here tonight for the junior members of our family—'
Tom said.

'Got you,' replied Nancy, and clapped her hands. 'Bedtime!'

The children looked at Mr Smith for one last time.

'Bedtime!' he cried, clapping his hands in his best nursery manner.
Both children began to cry again.

'They're overtired,' said Nancy tactfully, releasing them from their
high chairs.

'I'll carry them, sugar. If you'll excuse me for a moment, Lord.'

'Of course.'

As soon as the Old Man and Mr Smith were left alone, they looked
at one another with displeasure.

'A bear, indeed,' muttered the Old Man.

'I had to think quickly, once you had decided not to come to my
rescue—'

'Your rescue?'

'You could have put him to sleep with your petting, or plunged him
into a euphoria of canine well-being. I've watched you of old—'

'I've told you once if I've told you a thousand times, I wish to be
sparing with my powers while on Earth—'

'Yes, but not at my expense, I hope. Must I remind you I am here at
your invitation. I am, in fact, technically speaking, your guest here on
Earth. You are responsible for my safety!'

'The dog couldn't have savaged you if it had tried, not even with the
sight of both eyes!'

'I felt safer as a bear, and that's all there is to it. I could've become a
crocodile, but they can't sit at table, and in any case, I would have risked
biting a poor blind dog. I can hear your reproaches now. I could have
become any number of things. A giraffe wouldn't fit into this room, and in
any case, it is entirely harmless. An elephant would have gone through
the floor, and there'd have been much more dribble on the table. No, no,
I believe that environmentally and functionally I did the right thing,
although if the dog should recover its aggressive instincts and reappear, I
would probably go to the other extreme and then no one would be safe.'

'What would you become?'

'A wasp?'

Tom came back. 'It's going to be a problem getting the little critters
off to sleep,' he said.

The Old Man beckoned. 'Tell me, Tom. Or rather, tell us. Why were you so relatively unsurprised to see us?'

'Well, like I told you, we watch the Joey Henchman show—'

'Yes, but why did you watch it, once you told us that he is one of the things which is wrong with this great country of yours?'

'I guess we had a hunch that if ever there was going to be a second coming – and we were both quite sure, Nancy and I, that there'd have to be one sooner or later, the way things is going – why, then, it would most likely happen on a show like Joey Henchman's. There are quite a few of them – the Reverend Obadiah Hicks, Brian Fulbertsen's Whispering Hour – but Joey Henchman has got to be the worst of the bunch.'

'But to recognize us so quickly—'

'I'll be honest, Lord. We didn't recognize – Mr Smith, is it? – at once. Only just before the show went off the air. I guess it's on account of we always thought of you, Lord, or members of your family, in terms of a second coming. The – Mr Smith we figure is here all the time.' He laughed quietly. 'Maybe it's just human nature to think of evil as ongoing and good as something's got to be waited for. Anywhichway, the moment you appeared on the screen, Lord, both Nancy and I fell to our knees. I remember her calling out Alleluia!'

'That's most extraordinary,' said the Old Man soberly. 'And you've never had a moment of doubt as to our – that is, my – authenticity?'

'None, Lord.'

'What if I had turned myself into a bear instead of my colleague?'

'I'd have thought, there's got to be a reason the Lord's worked that miracle – one day, with luck, and faith, that reason will be revealed.'

'That's all?'

'That's all, Lord. Simple as that.'

The Old Man basked for a moment in his amazement. 'But your devotion seems so natural, so free of complexes.'

'I'm a kind of straightforward guy, Lord. I was a soldier, sure, serving my country. They sent me out to Vietnam, see, to fight Communism. Know what that is, sir?'

'I'm not entirely ignorant.' The Old Man smiled.

'I just don't want to take you into territories where there's got to be too much explaining to do to make it meaningful.'

'I know about Communism, without, mark you, knowing much

about the daily changes over there. Is Mr Stalin still active?'

'He died back in 1953, much to my regret,' said Mr Smith scornfully.

'Now you mention it, I seem to remember having made a mental note of it,' said the Old Man doggedly. 'Please go on.'

'Well, Vietnam was a kind of crazy war unlike anything we'd been trained for. I guess if we'd been defending our country we'd have lost our heads at times, and done some crazy and plain disgusting things to the people invading us – so I can understand it with hindsight. But at the time – we weren't told we was invaders, see. They left it to us to find out later, for ourselves. Told us we was the proud carriers of the American Way of Life, the American Dream. Once again, they left it to us to find out it was a nightmare, the way we was ordered to interpret it. Maimed kids, defoliated forests, drink and drugs.

'Well, it was us was maimed, Lord. Some went plain round the bend without showing it, the worst kind of mental disturbance. Others took refuge in hatred. That's no better. There were those fell by the wayside. The whole dumb business put too great a strain on us, you understand. If any soldiers in the whole wide world could've stood up to it, we could've, but – we couldn't either, see, that's the point. They were wrong to expect it of us. And they were wrong not to give us a better homecoming when those of us who stuck it out came home.'

'But you called your country great,' remembered the Old Man.

'It is too, Lord, thanks to you. Only thing, it maybe grew too fast. When there was just thirteen states, like at the outset, we kinda knew what it was all about. We was like a new-born babe, free of sin as yet. We knew our duty, clear as crystal. It was to survive. We was what you'd call today a third-world nation. Then we started to grow, see – all that space. Just like a growing kid, we found out how to walk, by trial and error. We put things in our mouths we didn't ought to. We was hardened by overcoming sickness. Childhood came. Schooldays. The inheritance of great wealth at too young an age. Oil, wheat, all the treasures of your great Earth, Lord. Colossal fortunes was made, while poverty was fuelled by immigration. We grew and grew, began to flex our muscles, took joy in our physical strength, but our ideals remained the same as they had been when we was born, a fledgling nation with a possible dream. I mean, when the slate is clean, all dreams is possible, am I right? Well, I don't want to bore you with all this, Lord.'

'Go on, go on.'

'Well, what we are now is adolescent, see. We like riding our skateboards backwards down hills, our surfboards upwards over waves, trying out new sensations, exposing ourselves and other people to danger, doing all the irresponsible things a teenager enjoys – but our dream has remained where it always was, in the cradle. The dream of openness, of freedom, of good will to all. We, all of us, even the worst murderers, the idlest drop-out or hobo, carry fragments of that dream with us. That's tradition. But what we wake to every morning is reality. The need to earn, to be a success, to scramble, to run, to avoid death, to live by appearances, to treat ulcers, to watch TV, and at the end of the day, just before sleep, to realize there hasn't been much time for the dream – or for love. And, as a last conscious thought, tomorrow will be different.'

'Astonishing,' murmured the Old Man. 'I sometimes hope I have nothing left to learn, but I am always disappointed. When did you think of all this?'

'There was plenty of time to work it all out. In Vietnam, during the lulls in the fighting. After a time, you understand, I figured I wasn't there for combat duty, as I'd been told. I was there to learn, which I'd never been told.'

'And you are still a soldier?'

'No.' A great grin of well-being spread across Tom's face.

'You still wear a uniform?'

'Yeah – well, I guess I went back to the cradle and pieced together that broken dream like a jigsaw. This uniform is not a military one. I'm a ranger now, up here in the El Cimitero National Park. My job is to protect nature. I can't do it for all the world. I don't have the personality or the conviction. Only a madman could have it, and I ain't mad. So – since I can't do it for all the world, I'll do it for a few square miles. At least they are my responsibility. I'll protect my acre of Heaven with my life, Lord.'

'Amazing.'

'Yes, I must say, amazing,' added Mr Smith. 'It's enough to deflect me from the crooked and wide. All that thought! All that wayward meditation condensed into a few drops of clairvoyance! It's enough to disillusion one!'

Just then, a noise, like a great beating of wings, began to grow with a menacing intensity.

'That's funny,' Tom said. 'A helicopter. We don't allow anyone here, and certainly not at night.'

An intense beam of light shone onto the house from the outside, moving hither and thither over its surface.

The Old Man said, 'I have an awful feeling that may well be the FBO.'

'FBI,' corrected Mr Smith.

'Whatever it may be, if you believe you are constrained to surrender us, we will quite understand.'

'Speak for yourself! I have no wish to spend the night in clink because *you* forged some money,' cried Mr Smith.

'Go up into the spare room,' Tom ordered. 'It's second on the left at the top of the stairs. And don't turn on the lights.'

'There are no more dogs up there?' Mr Smith asked.

'No. Keep your voices down. Just don't move around too much. Find seats, and keep clear of the windows.'

The two visitors began to do as they were told under those sharp, precise orders, while Tom, lit by the beam, which was now steady, prepared to face the visitors. The beating of the huge wings began to die down, accompanied by a metallic whirr.

8

Seated in the dark, and speaking in muffled tones, the Old Man and Mr Smith were conscious of the sounds of voices below. Evidently the walls were very thin.

'I'm tired of running. After all, if there are more people like Tom, our visit may yet be turning into something beneficial,' said the Old Man.

'Take it from me, he is unique. Oh, there may be those who are potentially like him, if only they trusted their native intelligence rather than what they are told, or even ordered to do. No, believe me, the denizens of Oscar's Wilde Life greatly outnumber the Toms of this world, although in their way they are equally nonconformist. Most men and women, the vast majority, imitate each other, ape each other's opinions, hairstyles, sartorial cut, and language patterns. To such people, originality is an obstacle to social intercourse.'

'Depressing, if true,' reflected the Old Man. 'I do know, something within me wishes to give up the struggle, to go to gaol, to follow human logic to the end of the road. Without that, I don't think we will have fulfilled the mandate we set ourselves to the full.'

'Sounds like that dreary old death wish rearing its yawning head again.'

'Maybe it is . . . maybe it is.'

The acid burned through Mr Smith's vocal chords again. 'Resign yourself to one thing, my poor old self-righteous buddy,' he said. 'You have done nothing worthy of the death sentence. You have merely forged some fourteen thousand, eight hundred and sixty-four dollars . . .'

'How do you know the exact figure? Even I don't know that.'

'The FBI do. In that awful hospital in Washington, I read it. I'm very good at reading upside-down. I'm a veritable upside-down speed reader. So, the sum is comfortably under fifteen thousand bucks. It is your first offence . . . that they know of. They haven't yet cottoned on to the five million yen and all the other perks of our survival kit, and with luck they never will. In view of your great age, you will probably be put on probation, having to report once a week to a dimwit for whom no better employment could be found. Such a prospect is hardly worthy of the supreme sacrifice, and in any case, as you so disobligingly pointed out to me when I was about to be bitten by a rabid dog, we can come to no harm. So forget it.'

'You are always ready with buckets of cold water to dampen any transitory enthusiasm I might entertain. It's too bad.'

Down in the parlour, Tom was confronted by Guy Klevenaar, Doc Dockerty, and Luis Cabestano, all of the FBI.

Klevenaar was examining the table by walking around and looking at it from all angles.

'I'll grant you no food has been taken,' he said, 'but the chairs are displaced in a manner suggesting that they were recently occupied.'

'What are you trying to prove, fellers?' asked Tom, his light eyes blazing. 'That I'm harbouring criminals, or worse, that I'm in cahoots with them?'

Doc Dockerty leant forward earnestly. 'I just wonder if you fully understand just what dangerous men these are. I don't think I'm betraying any secrets when I say that it has crossed several top minds in this administration that they may well be working for the other side. First of all, they entered the United States illegally, possibly off of a submarine. Then they were caught red-handed in Washington attempting to pass off close to a million forged dollars as legal tender. They disappeared out of police custody. They disappeared out of a psychiatric hospital. We caught up with them again on the Joey Henchman show – you may have read about it – where they attempted arson. They got away again. They're now rumoured to be in this neighbourhood, and *they are dangerous*.'

'You don't say. Tell me, how do they keep getting away? I thought you people were adept at holding on to prisoners.'

The three FBI men looked at each other with glances eloquent of their perplexity.

Luis Cabestano, in a lilting Hispanic accent, said, 'That's classified material. We no' got the righ' to eben so much as tink about it.'

'Right,' Klevenaar confirmed.

'Still,' Doc Dockerty drawled, 'ain't no one can stop a guy from speculating, and from what I hear on the grapevine from Washington, DC, they got some new technique of just disappearing into thin air. Now, if they can do that, it can mean only one thing: they've gotten something we haven't. And who would be able to have something we haven't? An individual? You crazy? An organization? You want your head examined! Another nation? Now you're talking! It needs the full resources of an en-tire nation. Know-how like that don't just come overnight. Now you're beginning to see daylight? Ri-ight! Now you can guess why some informed brass figures they're in the service of the . . . other side?'

'The other side?'

'You don't have to be super-intelligent to know they means the Russkis . . . only we ain't allowed to say so much in case there's a mole around, on account we're getting on so good with them these days, scrapping our obsolete weapons and all that. Shit, I don't have to tell you.'

'Where do these stairs lead?' asked Klevenaar, his foot on the bottom step.

'Where do stairs usually lead?' Tom asked back. 'Upstairs. Only I tell you what, fellers. This door leads out. And that's where I'd like you to explore. We don't encourage helicopters up here. They disturb the wildlife, specially nights, and they pollute. And I hereby order you out of the National Park area, 'cos you're breaking some of the ground rules set for this place.'

'How 'bout in 'n'emergency?' cried Doc. 'You break a leg, your wife's appendix busts?'

'That's different. This is not an emergency.'

'No emergency?' yelled Doc. 'With two dangerous enemies of the United States at large . . . more'n likely in the service of the goddam . . . other side? OK, guys, search the place.'

'There's my wife in her bedroom and the kids asleep!' cried Tom in a ferocious whisper.

'I'm sure Uncle Sam will be ready to apologize to all of them,' Doc replied in a deferential whisper, as ferocious.

Just then, Guy Klevenaar, halfway up the stairs, cried out and shook his hand in pain.

'What is it?' called Doc, ready to draw his gun.

'I've been stung by some goddam thing.'

'Let's have a look at it.' Doc bounded forward.

'Right here, on the back of the wrist!'

'Sure that's not a blowpipe?' said Doc in a low voice. 'Remember we had that lecture on blowpipes and their uses.' And he added, 'Shit!' as he reeled backwards, clutching his neck.

'What's up?' asked Luis Cabestano lethargically.

'I've been stung too!'

'Both o' you's. Dat's a coincidence. Let's have a see.'

Doc allowed his neck to be looked at.

'Dat's a wass.'

'A what?'

'A wass.'

'A wasp?'

'Yeah. Oh-oh.'

'What is it? You too?'

'Yeah. I don't overeac' like you fellows do's. I bit mos' every day in de garden.'

'Where?'

'Here on the ank,' said Cabestano, raising his trouser leg.

'All three of us,' snarled Guy, 'at over ten thousand feet, above the snow line, at night, stung by a wasp.'

'That don't make no sense.'

They looked at each other with a growing sense of the absurdity of the situation.

Doc frowned, and said softly and portentously, 'You think this could be something else they've got . . . which we haven't?'

Tom felt something tickle on the back of his hand. He glanced down, without raising his hand. On it were perched two hornets, one of them dark, the other snow white.

'Jesus, an albino hornet?' he said to himself, and suddenly realized what had occurred. A miracle.

Without moving his hand, he opened the front door with the other one. Then he leaned out into the open air. The hornets took off in formation, seeming to Tom to waggle their wings in salute.

'What you doing there?' snapped Doc, ever suspicious.

'It's stifling in here, don't you think?'

Guy replied, 'I was just going to remark how cold it is.'

'Right,' was Cabestano's comment.

Tom closed the door.

'Feel free to go upstairs, fellers. Anything I can do to help the FBI in their line of duty—'

'What's up there anyhow, apart from upstairs that is?' asked Guy, halfway up the stairs once again.

'Them hornets must have made a nest up under the eaves, like they did last year. Had to smoke the critters out.'

'Hornets? That's worse than wasps!'

'Yeah. Four sting from hornet is enough to ki' a guy. Tree sting if he frail.'

'Hey, know something, that pain isn't getting no better,' said Doc, cupping his hand over his neck.

Guy came slowly down the stairs again. 'Guess we're ready to take your word for it, that you're not sheltering no one.'

'You got my word,' said Tom, every inch the clean-cut, trustworthy American, 'that I never sheltered a human being in here since last winter's blizzard.'

At that moment, the old dog, having woken from a fitful sleep, punctuated by visions of salivating monsters, sensed alien presences, and began to bark.

'You got a dog?'

'Yes . . . I don't like to let him out.'

'What kind is he?'

'A mixture between a Dobermann and a Rottweiler.'

'What do you call him?' Doc asked.

'Satan.'

'Well . . . I guess I'm satisfied if you guys are. I want to get some treatment for this sting,' Doc said.

'OK by me,' retorted Guy. 'I won't get no sleep if this pain gets any worse.'

'Hey, you guys, I was ready to call it a day before ever we got stung,' Cabestano assented.

'Thanks for your help,' said Doc on the way out, and, as an afterthought, he came back. 'Listen, if those suspects do turn up after we gone, just call us at Phoenix 792143 or 44. Here's my card. And don't mention we been here looking for them. We don't want them to know that we're onto them see? If you have to lie, remember, you're lying for your country. Just tell them, no, there just wasn't three human beings in here looking for you. Call us, keep 'em talking. We'll do the rest.'

'OK, Doc.'

Soon after an initial hesitancy due to the cold, the limp rotors tensed up, and the helicopter moved out of sight, and eventually out of earshot.

Tom opened the door once again, and called, 'You can come back now . . .'

He waited a time, then realized they had gone for ever, leaving behind much thought for a man of simple faith.

9

They had flown a night and a day when the darker hornet landed on a railway embankment somewhere in the Middle West. The white hornet circled above it solicitously, until it observed that its companion was changing slowly and very uncertainly into Mr Smith. Then it, too, settled down, and changed rapidly and gracefully into the Old Man.

Mr Smith shook his dishevelled head as though the tangled hair would thereby disentangle. He puffed and moaned and blew out and inhaled deeply.

'Had enough?' asked the Old Man indulgently.

'I couldn't have borne it a moment longer,' proclaimed Mr Smith. 'Mark you, I think stinging those three idiots took a great deal out of me, more than I would have thought.'

'That was rather vindictive.'

'It was well deserved. If there had been time, I'd have stung the dog into the bargain. It's just nightmarish, being confined into a space as minute as the body of a hornet – also to be within a frame of such limited life expectancy! I felt I was getting older and grumpier with every yard I flew. Nothing in my nostrils but the dusty smell of pollen. No interest in life but that bleak industry. No object but flower-hopping. I tell you, I had trouble reminding myself who I really was during the flight!'

'You are too impressionable, dear fellow. I had no difficulty in reminding myself of my identity.'

'Of course not. Whoever heard of a white hornet? Even as an insect, you had to make your identity clear. It was a positive embarrassment flying alongside you. Luckily we encountered nobody who could possibly recognize us on the way.'

'Where do we go from here?'

'Somewhere where we don't have to run away all the time. Somewhere where we have a clean sheet.'

'I shall ignore the allusion.'

Mr Smith reacted with energy. 'It's true. Thanks to my enquiries here and there, editorials in soiled newspapers, and remarks overheard, I know that in this country every misdemeanour, however innocuous, every tiny infraction of the law, every anomaly which marks privately held opinions as being unconventional is registered on a computer endowed with a memory – and every time someone is in trouble, the sordid details are trotted out anew as though they date from yesterday. That underscores equal opportunity for all . . . *all* start at a disadvantage.'

'A computer?' the Old Man asked tentatively.

'A man-made imitation of the human mind.'

'They have succeeded?' The Old Man was full of sudden trepidation.

'There are two main differences. It has and can have no imagination, for the simple reason that, if it should ever acquire an imagination for emulation of human beings, it will begin to be as inefficient as they already are, and therefore of limited use to them. The second difference is that, whereas men tend to forget with time, a computer never does. In the cases I have been describing, it is like a washing machine which, instead of cleaning, produces the same dirty laundry decade after decade, the passage of time only serving to make the filth look worse than it was originally.'

'Why do I know so little of this? It really is discouraging,' sighed the Old Man.

'Rely on me for the details. Your natural grazing ground is the sweep of history, the tapestry of time, gigantic vistas, high places . . . to say nothing of choral singing in a major key. To me it is the gossip, the backbiting, the rumour, and the bitchiness which make human communication bearable. You can't possibly put two and two together. It's too easy. But ask you the square root of nine million, four hundred and six thousand, two hundred and sixty-eight and three-quarters, and you answer absent-mindedly, while seeming to think of something else.'

The Old Man beamed. 'That's an awfully attractive way of saying we are complementary.'

Mr Smith sighed. 'You knew what you were doing when you kicked me out. You are the poet of infinity. I'm merely the journalist of the day to day, hour to hour, minute to minute.'

'They are complementary, too. If I had come alone on this expedition, I would have learned absolutely nothing. While gazing at the horizon, I would have tripped on every pebble.'

'Enough of flattery!' scowled Mr Smith. 'It's unnatural.'

'What are we going to do? I don't think we can stay here much longer. After all, if the FBO follows us up a mountain in a flying machine, they are capable of everything except catching us.'

Mr Smith let the error pass. He was fed up with always seeming to be right.

'We have explored the valleys,' said the Old Man. 'We can't leave without visiting the pinnacle.'

'The pinnacle?'

'The President, who lives in the White Cottage, in Washington. Am I right?'

'Almost. It is a house. But before we go, let us decide in advance about our meeting place afterwards. I'm sure we will not be able to leave the White House with dignity. There are too many security men around it.'

'Good thinking. I suggest the airport. At least we should be able to leave the *country* with dignity.'

'I doubt it. It will mean purchasing tickets, first class for preference. More yen to change. More Japanese disguises.' Mr Smith groaned. 'Where would we go to in any case?'

'The United Kingdom,' said the Old Man, quite decided. 'They used to own far more of the world than was their right, and they thought it was owed to them. I am fascinated by people who can delude themselves to such an extent, and yet come out of it with a quiet self-righteousness, and a conviction that if they hadn't done what they did, someone else would have done it, meaning, as usual in their case, the French.'

'You seem surprisingly well acquainted with them.'

'They themselves claimed my attention throughout the ages, as did many other people, on the eve of war. They had the affectionate habit of holding huge Masses to induce me to bless the arms of one side or another before the outbreak of hostilities, as though I would ever do such a thing. And because they had gone through the mumbo-jumbo, they believed that had done the trick. It never had, as you can imagine. But I gave them full marks for effort. Only the Germans overstepped the limit of decency a few years back by claiming that I was on their side. *Gott mit uns*, if I remember rightly. I refused to listen to this nonsense, but regretfully it didn't make much difference. They behaved as though I had endorsed their bellicosity. In the end, they lost, of course. That was their come-uppance.'

'You never took sides?'

'Never. I had better things to do. I left it to you. The only ones I really hated were the religious wars – the Crusades, and so on. Passions ran so high. I have never tolerated being a bone of contention, torn at by the dogs of war. But recently there have been no more Masses. Funerals, yes, but nobody wants blessings any more. Wars have become surreptitious, swift and secret. No one in their right mind associates them with morality. They are blasphemies against all Creation.'

'What do you expect me to say? That I agree with you? Well, as a matter of fact I do. In many ways. Too much time has passed since the Creation for me to take any pleasure in conflict. Evil, after all, is to be enjoyed. How can one enjoy wars in which the entire planet is turned into a kind of lunatic discothèque? No, evil is dispersed, diluted, worst of all, wasted in big receptions. Evil is for intimate dinner parties. Evil is to be savoured, not consumed.'

They both meditated for a while in silence, resting their bodies on the steep grass bank, already saturated in dew.

'I've never heard myself talking like that,' said the Old Man in growing bewilderment.

'Well, you've never had anyone to talk to. You summoned me out of my depths as a listener.'

'Perhaps. But it was not only that. I needed a contradictor.'

'A sounding-board?'

'No, no. A contradictor. Someone who would rekindle the dying embers of opinion by opposing them, by sharpening my blunted sensibilities, by ending, at least for a few moments, the terrible hibernation I have endured.'

'White calls for black again as a woman calls for a mirror.'

'Well, it's true. My vision of things may have changed temporarily because, having adopted the limitations of a human form, I am influenced in my thinking by those very limitations. I see everything as a man might, without so much as a trace of that post-Olympian detachment which has enabled me to float among the firmaments, untroubled by any sentiment other than a searing boredom, and an occasional sense of deprivation, of being without taste or nerves or even the capacity for exhaustion or for pain. In that sense, my mission here is on the way to being accomplished. I am slowly rediscovering what it is like to be a man. I have a fleeting sense of physical fragility and of intellectual confusion.' The Old Man suddenly laughed softly. 'You won't believe this, but I wouldn't much care for being a mortal. I don't think I could put up with the tension, the sheer stress of having to judge every move in the light of its dangers and the possibilities of failure. And yet, with all that, I am somewhat envious of my creations.'

'What do you mean?' asked Mr Smith.

'When they are tired, they can sleep.'

'Is that all?'

'When they are very tired, they can die.'

The two immortals were so wrapped in their thoughts that they quite failed to hear the freight train as it lumbered clanking through the crystal night and passed close to their heads with a mournful wail. A curious flurry blurred their vision for a moment, and an unkempt and bibulous fellow rolled down the embankment, preceded by an aura of stale alcohol and stinking clothes.

'Hi, fellers,' he called out as he came to rest by their side. He was unhurt, and had evidently developed a technique for rolling off the slow-moving trains without injury.

'Where have you come from?' asked the Old Man.

'From off that train,' cried the newcomer.

'What was your destination?'

'St Louis, Missouri. That's until I saw you two guys lying on the embankment. I said to myself, those two guys must've rolled off the three forty-two from Lincoln, Nebraska to Terre Haute, Indiana, gets here around five. Chances are they've got something to eat. I ain't had dinner, you understand.'

'We don't eat,' said the Old Man sternly.

'What's that? Don't eat? You guys alive?' And the hobo laughed richly and excessively.

'We are not hungry.'

'We are never hungry,' added Mr Smith gratuitously, on the same high moral tone.

'Well . . .' contemplated the hobo, 'there's only one explanation. You must be on drugs, like me.'

'Drugs?' asked Mr Smith.

'Sure. What makes a guy go on drugs, you'll ask me. Well, I tell you. I love this world with a passion, you understand? Only I like it naked, like a virgin. I like what the Good Lord gave us—'

'That's very good of you,' the Old Man interrupted.

'But I hate all we done with it. I know it's hard to credit, but I was born rich. Only son. Had every goddam thing I wanted when I was young. Packard Roadster, polo ponies. I went to military school, Princeton University. Married the daughter of E. Cincinnatus Browbaker, who owned most of the West at that time, including the Rocky Mountain and Pacific Railroads, the Pinnacle Studios in Hollywood, the *Reno Daily Prophet*, the Death Valley District Bank, you name it. It was the biggest marriage in Denver this century. Seven thousand bottles of champagne was consumed, four-hundred-thousand dollars' worth of fireworks were released. How could any marriage survive it?'

There was a silence, broken only by the discreet whistle of the wind in the telegraph wires and the soft moan as it combed the grass.

'No questions so far?' asked the hobo, now with a certain whimsicality.

'No,' said the Old Man. 'It sounds like your average biblical morality.'

'Funny you should say that. My Dad, he made his fortune in toilet flushes. Lamington's Silentflush. He was a regular churchgoer. Somewhere deep inside of him, he held tight to holy writ and wouldn't let it go, however rich he got. That parable about the camel and the eye of the needle always had him worried. So when he finally became wealthy enough not to know or really care how much he owned, he had a huge needle cast in Wilkes-Barre, Pennsylvania. I remember the day it arrived, on fifteen trucks, and they were soldered together on the lawn, right under the balcony of Dad's bedroom suite. Then he bought a couple of camels in Egypt, and every morning one or the other of them would be walked through the eye of the needle, and Dad would look up at the sky and say, "I hope you're watching, Lord. I guess you know why I'm going to these lengths?" And he would chuckle devoutly, and say, as to a business partner, "Let's just keep the secret between us, shall we?" I have no idea where he is now.'

'Is he dead?' asked the Old Man.

'Well, he sure ain't alive, I tell you that,' laughed the hobo. 'Otherwise I wouldn't have inherited . . .' He sighed deeply. 'He didn't trust me, so he made it tough for me to lay my hands on more than a billion dollars before the age of fifty.'

'How terribly inconvenient,' said Mr Smith. 'How did you manage?'

'I tell you how I managed. Once I was sure that my three boys were doing well at school, and my wife was having an exciting affair with my psychiatrist, I just vanished into the landscape, and here I am. Luckily I was crazy about railroads when I was a kid. The only part of civilization I really identified with. Used to have a small schoolbook filled with locomotive numbers and timetables and itineraries, and I've really kept my information up to date. So I travel up and down, the length and width of this great country of ours, avoiding cities, leaping onto moving trains, and rolling down embankments by a special technique I taught myself.'

'This great country of ours?' enquired the Old Man. 'You're the second man we've come across who called it that, only the other one was in very different circumstances to you.'

'Better? Worse?' laughed the hobo, giving his rotting teeth an airing. 'Well, that's because it's a kind of catchphrase, this great country of ours, often used by military personnel under indictment for criminal offences, or by presidents forced to make unpopular moves – but seemingly, it is great. Look over there. The dawn's coming up, just a few streaks of purple and a dash of orange in the sky, like the orchestra of the day tuning up. There's just such a sense of power in the skyline, such a murmur of hidden wealth under the soil. It's so goddam *confident*. I just never tire of feasting my eyes on it, and my ears, and what's left of my friggin' mind.'

'If you are so exultant, by nature, I don't see what you need with drugs,' remarked Mr Smith.

The hobo laughed again quietly. 'How can you tell my exultancy, if there is such a word, isn't due to drugs?'

'Drugs are merely an expensive way of making the worst of a bad job.'

'That's all you know. How old are you?' asked the hobo, beginning to show an ugly side to his nature.

'A little older than you,' said Mr Smith quietly.

'Yeah, I bet you're not.'

'I bet I am.'

'You are *not*,' shouted the hobo, spoiling for trouble.

'Oh, come on,' said the Old Man, 'how can you eulogize about the wonders of nature at one moment, several passages of which I particularly appreciated, and indulge in an utterly fruitless argument the next?'

'On account of I'm sixty-eight fuckin' years old! That's why!' cried the hobo.

'You're a mere child by our standards. Only children use what they imagine to be strong language.'

'How old are you, then?' asked the hobo, suddenly suspicious.

'So old you wouldn't believe it.'

'Yes, and we're about the same age,' added Mr Smith, on a highly moral tone which the information hardly justified.

'How come you haven't objected to the way I smell?' the hobo enquired darkly.

'Why should we?' It was Mr Smith who bothered to continue the conversation, while the Old Man seemed to switch off.

'Everywhere I go, when I get real close to people, the way I'm close to you guys, I'm told I stink. I sometimes get into fights. I always win. The other guys may be stronger and younger, but I got that knock-out odour, like a skunk. I always gets my way.' He looked at them slightly. 'You guys haven't raised no objections. How come?'

'Neither of us has a sense of smell. But we have imaginations. And now you mention it, I can imagine how you doubtless smell. You should be ashamed of yourself.'

'That does it. You want a fight?'

'We are resting. Can't you see that?'

'I killed six men in my time. Six men and one woman.'

'Lucky you, to be able to keep count.'

'Are you telling me you killed more than that?'

'I don't kill. I cause to be killed. Often by negligence. But then,

I can't be everywhere at once.'

The hobo broke off the conversation, and prepared to take a fix by setting up the portable paraphernalia he carried in his voluminous coat. There was no conversation for a while, Mr Smith looking away as though offended. It was the Old Man who re-established a contact.

'What are you doing?'

'I am preparing to bend my mind,' replied the hobo with suppressed savagery. 'Your minds are already bent, and I feel kind of left out of it.'

'Bent?'

'Yeah. You're a couple of lousy old liars. You're on drugs just like I am, otherwise you wouldn't talk the way you do. I'm going to take a fix so we can carry on a normal conversation. And let me tell you something – there's a kind of camaraderie among what I like to call the fellowship of the iron road, a kind of what I might call spirit of belonging and sharing you two old bastards just don't know the first thing about. We all share all we got – food, drink, marijuana, the hard stuff. All for one and one for all. No one's in no one's debt. Money, that filthy cancer of society, just don't exist. We're like open books. And that's one thing you got to learn, if you're going to ride the freight cars. Otherwise there'll come a day when we all get to know you, and there's nothing easier than to push a man off of a train where there's no embankment to roll down – a bridge'd be favourite, or a tunnel – or maybe when another train is passing.'

'What have you against us?' asked the Old Man.

'You're lying. You got secrets and you don't let on. You won't look me in the eye. You're shifty. You're secret drug takers. You're probably a couple of old faggots and I interrupted your tryst, or what the hell you call it. You're trying to keep me out of your lives!'

'Stop blaspheming!' cried Mr Smith, stridently, his voice cutting into the hobo's eardrums like a bistoury.

'Blaspheming?' raged the hobo, who was just in the process of taking his fix. 'What do you take yourselves for – God Almighty?'

'We can't both be God Almighty, and it's certainly not me.'

'Oh boy, you're way past the point of no return,' said the hobo, lying back while waiting for the drug to take its effect.

The Old Man decided to be a calming influence. 'You have such a rich and even febrile imagination by nature – obviously far too gifted to be a millionaire – I don't see why you need additional stimulation.'

The hobo's eyes were shut, and a fine perspiration was just visible on his brow. 'Christ, are you ignorant . . . so easily satisfied . . . confined to the prisons of your own bodies . . . resigned to the bars on the windows, and the darkness beyond, nipping fantasy in the bud . . . Jesus, a man needs help to struggle out of the frame life imposes on him . . . twenty-four hours round the clock, six foot tall, weighing a hundred and eighty-six pounds, blood pressure 198 over 80, social security number 5 dash 28641BH, and so on, and so forth . . . everything charted with pin-point accuracy . . . pin-point, like a butterfly in a showcase . . . no life, no soul, just your true colours . . . O my brothers, what magic in the mass of arteries and corpuscles and cells and pores that make up the human metabolism . . . but of what use if the brain is ossified like a fossil in the desert? But . . .'

He began a discreet, yet still controlled trembling.

'. . . add a little powder, innocent white, or a shot in the vein, and a landlocked man can fly over the landscape, encompass the world, like Puck, in half an hour, career among the galaxies, and rest for moments in the stratosphere at motionless speeds above that of light.' He began to declaim, trying to lift himself off the ground. 'It's a mind-shattering, loin-wrenching amalgam of skiing, snorkelling and sex!'

The Old Man rose effortlessly. 'I can't bear it,' he said sternly, and very much to the point. 'Here I am, making every effort to confine myself and, inevitably, my thinking, within the restrictions of mortality, and here is this more than miserable mortal, rendered incoherent by wine and stimulants, who is straining at the leash in the direction of being a god. That should be enough to cure me of ever attempting this kind of subterfuge again. I'm off. Disgusted.'

The hobo began writhing on the ground as though being brought to an orgasm by an invisible partner.

'Don't leave me alone with him,' warned Mr Smith. 'It's enough to put you off vice for good.'

'I even fancy I can smell him now,' said the Old Man, depressed, his eyes shifting from side to side, his nostrils flared and his lip curled in revulsion. 'What time is it?'

'Why ask me?'

'You know everything.'

Mr Smith looked at the sky. 'I'd say between five and six.'

'What's the time in Washington?'

'If the tramp's information about our whereabouts is correct, I'd say it's between seven and eight.'

'Hold hands,' said the Old Man.

'We'd better say goodbye,' said Mr Smith.

They both looked at the hobo, who seemed to be in the grip of terminal malaria.

'We don't want to disturb you, but we must be off now,' said the Old Man.

'Goodbye, and good luck,' added Mr Smith.

And they vanished.

The hobo was not surprised.

'Hey . . . what kind . . . of drug . . . are you into?' he screamed. 'I'll be up there . . . with you . . . just give me time . . .' and he gripped the word with his mind as though it were a loose trapeze above the sawdust, and clung to it for dear life, shouting in a voice losing itself into hoarseness, into whimpering, into silence, 'Time . . . time . . . time.'

Finally, he was no more than an entity, only certifiable as being alive by virtue of small, convulsive motions and a white foam forcing its way out of his pursed lips and down his chin.

Slowly another train chugged its way along the tracks, moaning its solitude to the deaf landscape.

As it passed, a shrouded figure rolled down the embankment. Evidently this was an accredited meeting place for covens of vagrants.

The newcomer, a small wizened man with a beard and whiskers, understood at once what was needed. He uncorked an old military water bottle and, cradling the hobo's head in his left arm, he forced the water bottle into the quietly bubbling mouth.

10

The Old Man and Mr Smith materialized, still holding hands, in an anteroom of what turned out to be the White House. Through a half-open door a man could be heard humming, and partly singing, in a private and somewhat unmusical manner, 'It Ain't Necessarily So' from *Porgy and Bess* by Gershwin.

'Where are we?' asked Mr Smith in a raucous whisper.

'Ssh. The White Mansion,' the Old Man whispered back, and went on, 'No time to lose. If all goes wrong, our rendezvous is at the airport.'

'Where in the airport? The airport's a big place.'

'So big we can't see each other?'

'Gracious, yes. Remember Mr Henchman's cathedral? Well, it's about fifteen or twenty of those, all separate.'

'Oh dear. That is big indeed. What's it called, at any rate?'

'Dulles International Airport.'

'You mean one man owns it? That's America for you.'

Mr Smith closed his eyes for a moment to give himself patience. 'He was Secretary of State. It is one of the few tributes to his memory.'

'Thank you. What would I do without you? You and your extraordinary general knowledge.'

Mr Smith shrugged modestly. 'It's part of my job. How could I lead people into temptation if I only knew what I was leading them to, and without knowing what I am leading them from?'

'Yes, but that's only temptation . . .'

'Everything's temptation when you come down to it. Ambition itself is a temptation. Drugs in order to rule the world for a paltry quarter of an hour, the quiet life above the snow line, a few illicit moments with Miss Carpucci behind the altar, all that worthless Austrian money, falling like autumn leaves. . .'

'I'll take your word for it. This is no time for a philosophical treatise, especially not one conducted in whispers. There'll be plenty of time for that in the flying machine. Listen! The fellow has stopped humming. Briefly. Can we fly by a British machine?'

'Why?'

'There would probably be less vigilance from those American people with initials.'

'The FBI?'

'Exactly. I daren't say it anymore, for fear of getting it wrong.'

'The Federal Bureau of Investigation.'

'Oh, is that what it is? That's far easier to remember than initials. And then, I imagine the British section would be rather smaller, and therefore it will be easier for us to identify one another in a crowd.'

'Good thinking. The British Airways counter, then, at Dulles airport.'

'Look out!'

A man, athletic for his age, a vocational smile on his somewhat sharp but not unfriendly features, entered the room in his underwear. His clothes were laid out for him. He was carrying his rimless glasses in his hand, and now placed them on his nose. He seemed pleased by the selection of his shirt, and took it off its hanger. Then he turned around in order to put it on. Immediately, he had the shock of his life.

'How did you get in?' he stammered.

'Never mind the details,' the Old Man advised.

'How did you get in?' This time he found more voice.

'We have that capacity . . .'

'It's not possible to get in. Hell, when I'm outside, even I can't get in without a whole bunch of checks and verifications. You can't get in here!' he insisted, almost tearfully.

'Don't you want to know who we are?'

'Hell, no. I want to know how you got in here!' And he suddenly stopped dead. 'I know you,' he said. 'You're those two nut – those two men apprehended by the FBI on several occasions. I've got the full report on my desk. I haven't had time to do more than glance at it, I'm afraid. I'd picked it out as lighter reading at Camp David the coming weekend.'

'Lighter reading?' asked the Old Man with misgiving.

'You should see some of the stuff I have to read,' said the President, almost to himself. 'There are days I ask myself if all that effort . . .'

He drifted off into a momentary daydream, and put his shirt on absent-mindedly. Then he smiled engagingly. 'Well, you're obviously not here to kill me. You'd have done that as soon as I came out of the bathroom.'

'Don't bank on it,' said Mr Smith, looking really terribly sinister.

The President stopped buttoning his shirt. 'Are you serious?' he asked, colourlessly.

'No. But never judge an execution by the speed with which it is carried out. There are sadists who like dragging these moments to infinity.'

'Of course we're not here to cause you harm, or even worry,' said the Old Man, annoyed with Mr Smith and his taste for the oblique. 'It's no use my telling you who we are, you'll never believe us.'

'You're alleged to believe that you are God, and your friend here is believed to be the . . . well, that in itself is preposterous, because God would have no time for the Devil. They most certainly wouldn't be caught travelling together.'

'That's all you know,' chided the Old Man. 'It's clear you have more faith in political values than in human ones. It may well be that we are not supposed to be seen together – it may even seem like collusion, or graft – but, you see, unlike you we are not running for office, we are not in competition, we don't have to justify an existence, or beg for support – we just are. And once we are, and have been, and always will be, we might as well get on together. After all, we are the only beings we know.'

The President looked sharply from one to the other. 'Why are you telling me all this? You know, I only have to press a button with my foot and the boys from security get here in under twenty seconds.'

Mr Smith whistled in mocking admiration. 'Where's the button?'

'I've got one in the bedroom, two in the Oval Office, but in here . . . there's got to be one, but I just never contemplated an attempt in the bathroom area.'

'Think no more of it,' said the Old Man. 'We don't even need a button. If we feel we're not wanted, we just vanish.'

'So I read. There are those like Senator Sam Stuttenberger from Ohio, and representative Newt Cacciacozze of Arkansas, who swear blind you two are sent by the Soviets – that you are, in fact, scientists trying out new espionage techniques on us. You are the reason, the Senator said in a closed-door meeting of the Senate Armed Forces Committee, that the Soviets can afford to make unilateral gestures as far as short-range missiles are concerned. Now, you're going to deny that if it's true, that's obvious – but we're on pretty good terms with the Soviets these days, and will certainly find out sooner or later, whatever you choose to tell us.'

'Why is it,' asked the Old Man in a voice not lacking in amusement, 'that we have had lucid conversations with a park ranger, a psychiatrist, and with a social outcast, one who at least made up for in unfettered cynicism what he lacked in clarity – but for sheer idiocy you evidently have to climb to the peak of power? Certainly we have much more to do than spies have, but we also have much better things to do than spying. We would be wasting our time by emulating that most despicable of activities.'

The President smiled grimly. 'You choose to categorize the suspicions of Senator Stuttenberger and Congressman Cacciacozze as idiotic? I may think so at times, but I can unfortunately never express myself with such baldness.'

'Do you think we're spies?' asked Mr Smith.

'On the face of it, I have my doubts. I can't imagine what spies would be searching for in a bathroom, and dressed in a manner calculated to attract attention to themselves in a crowd.'

'We are not dressed in a manner calculated to produce any particular effect,' said the Old Man. 'We are just a little out of touch, that's all. It's not surprising, after all this time.'

'A T-shirt, with a cute message on it? That's out of touch?'

'I didn't arrive with that,' said Mr Smith. 'I stole it at a gay sauna in 42nd Street.

'You *stole* it,' reiterated the President at dictation speed, 'at a gay sauna?'

'Yes. Ever since coming back to Earth, I have been acutely aware of our quaintness. I hate being stared at. After all, most of my work is subversive, unlike the Old Man's here.'

'You admit it!' cried the President.

'As the Devil! Oh, you do make me furious, you people with your one-track minds! The Devil is not by definition Russian, you know, whatever you have been taught!' snarled Mr Smith, hissing like a pitful of pythons.

Alarmed by this menacing three-dimensional sound effect, the President held out both hands in a gesture of pacification, his standard back-to-square-one body language.

'OK, OK, let me ask you this. What do you fellas want with me?'

'We have spent some time here now,' the Old Man said.

'In this great country of ours?'

'Precisely. We have been behind bars; in a huge hospital, like a city dedicated to infirmity; in hotels both luxurious and shabby; we have travelled by various means; we have been both fascinated and lulled to indifference by the sheer violence on television; we have been outraged and reduced to helpless mirth by the pastoral message of a religious charlatan who pretended to know both of us personally; we have been touched and impressed by the extraordinary power of a simple man's faith; and finally sickened and repelled by the ability of drugs to make a man coherent to himself for a few precious moments and incoherent to those who observe him. These are just a few stray stones from a vast mosaic we will never have time to examine in all its undoubted majesty and bewildering contradictions. I will merely ask you this, sir . . . how does it look to you from your unique point of vantage?'

The President looked reasonable, as he always did when addressing an impossible issue.

'The way I see my country from the viewpoint of my desk?'

'Your great country,' the Old Man corrected tactfully.

A ghost of a smile of recognition passed over the President's face. 'The first thing anyone's got to realize is that no one knows everything about the country. Too much is going on. In four time zones simultaneously. People sleep and wake at different hours. And then no one stays put. There's no time for tradition to get a grip in many of our cities. Right now, the industrial age, polluted, smoky, detrimental to health, is giving way to the informational age, sterile, automated, robotized. The industrial north is being abandoned, leaving great factories like broken and nerveless teeth over the skyline, while old and young alike flood into the sunlight as the hours of leisure increase. What happens next is anyone's guess, but I don't think this restless movement of people will ever really slow down.'

'How very interesting, and succinct.'

The President smiled. 'I'm quoting from my own State of the Union speech, which I delivered yesterday. Then drugs. That's number one on our priorities list. Don't ask me why this is, but the desire for these harmful artificial stimulants is growing all the time. And it's a shame. This great country has so much to offer those willing to accept the challenge. Our immediate task, however, in the light of developments in the urban ghettos, is to prevent by all the means in my power this shame from turning into disaster. When we have accomplished this task, it will be no time to stop our endeavours. On the contrary, we will counter-attack the drug pushers and foreign profiteers, and drive this shame from our land.'

He seemed to be addressing a much larger audience than just two venerable men.

'We asked you a simple enough question,' remarked Mr Smith, 'and you reply with rhetoric. May I ask you a supplementary question, in all intimacy?'

The President cast an anxious eye at the clock on the wall, and said, 'Shoot.'

'I beg your pardon?'

'I'm listening.'

'Oh. Were those words yours?'

The President laughed. 'Hell, no. Nobody in his right mind writes their own words, not if they're in my position. There's no time. They were the words of Arnold Starovic, my second speechwriter. Unfortunately my number one choice, Odin Tarbush, came down with tonsilitis. Arnie's a fine writer, no question, but he's a little too intellectual for the image I'm trying to project.'

'Image?'

The President glanced at the clock again, and seemed satisfied. He smiled. 'We've all got to work on our images these days. Public relations is everything. Politics. Religion. You name it. Now, if you don't mind my giving you a piece of advice, that's the area in which you guys have got to get your act together. You've gotten hold of the wrong image. The American people don't expect God to be . . . to be portly. He can be old, OK. In the light of his experience and longevity, that's understood. But he's got to have a fine face, and well-cut robes, designer robes, know what I mean? Thin hands, tapered fingers, and, if possible, a little diffused light behind the head. What we all remember from our illustrated bibles.'

'Like this you mean?' The Old Man concentrated, and slowly changed into a creature of forbidding beauty, like a figure from a fin-de-siècle stained-glass window, two fingers raised in blessing, his doll-like face quite devoid of expression apart from routine solemnity. His robes became cerulean blue, with gold, violet, and a poisonous green in the trimmings. Behind his head, a hidden light just caught the white curls and made them luminous.

The President's voice faltered as he asked, 'Who *are* you?'

The Old Man reverted to his portly look. 'It's no use. I can't do it for long. It just isn't *me*.'

The President blushed and passed a slightly febrile hand over his brow. 'I didn't see what you just did. It's a trick, isn't it? An illusion.' He laughed mirthlessly. 'How do you fellas do it, or is it a secret? Sure, if I could do tricks like that, I'd keep it a secret.'

'And how about me?' asked Mr Smith. 'Won't you tell me where I go wrong with my image?'

'Well, there you have me guessing,' laughed the President mildly, his inner tensions showing. 'The Devil, in our folk imagery, is supposed to be everywhere, without any clear image, a permanent evil spirit with his many homes on the darker side of our hearts. It's only God the Father who has been immortalized in our imagination.'

'By some of the greatest and the worst painters in history,' sighed the Old Man.

'Right,' laughed the President.

'That's what it takes to achieve universality.'

'We were talking about *me*,' Mr Smith commented pointedly, and without warning transformed himself into a standard Mephisto from a third-rate opera house, black wrinkled tights, black slippers with upturned toecaps, a black hood with a widow's peak, pencil-thin mustachios and goatee. He adopted the stance of an operatic bass of the Victorian era. This apparition served to lessen the tension, since the President was liberated of all his inhibitions as he laughed with the good nature which had been his before he had thought it necessary to think of his image.

Mr Smith milked the moment, smiling himself, while the Old Man chuckled gently in appreciation of his colleague's sense of the absurd.

Slowly Mr Smith melted back into his usual shape.

'You find that funny?' he asked soberly.

'Funny? Listen, it's hysterical,' said the President, drying his eyes on a tissue which he drew from a silver receptacle with an eagle on it. He grew serious immediately, in an unobtrusive sort of way. His advisors had told him that, whereas an occasional joke was a good thing, frivolity was not.

'I tell you, fellas,' he said, expressing a kind of tortured clairvoyance which 64 per cent of the electorate had found attractive (only 19.5 per cent of those asked hadn't known), 'I have no idea how you do it. It's a trick, of course. It has to be a trick. Now there are good tricks and bad tricks – yours are good. They're a hell of a good series of tricks. But there are two bits of advice I'd like to give, and you'll maybe have occasion to remember this some day. The first is this. Leave all allusion to God out of your act. It's a question of taste, see. God is not amusing. And then, many of my fellow Americans have very different concepts of Him, with a capital H. Some of our original inhabitants still bang drums in forest clearings and dance round a totem pole. That's their privilege. Some citizens are Muslim, or Jewish, or Buddhist – you name it – and some of them are pretty damn sensitive about the rightness of their own traditions and the wrongness of everyone else's. All this adds up to only one tough rule. God is a non-starter in show business. He is taboo. TABOO. Now, the second piece of advice I'd like to give you is this. Give your act focus. It's as simple as that. Focus. FOCUS. OK? By which I mean every act's got to have a beginning, a middle and an end. Exposition, Realization, Conclusion. Bear that in mind, and with your talent, you won't go far wrong. Even if you think you may have left it a little late to make a start, don't you believe it. It's never too late for quality. Get yourselves a good agent, and later, when it's justified, a good manager. You won't regret it. And think up a good name for your act, a good regular name. I'll certainly make a point of catching your act when you've worked on it, when you've cleaned it up and honed the rough edges. Know what I mean?'

The Old Man glanced at Mr Smith, who returned his look. Both of them smiled warmly.

'What is written on your dollar bills?'

'One dollar.'

'No, no. A noble sentiment.'

'Oh. In God We Trust.'

118

'What a pleasant thought,' reflected the Old Man. 'If only—'

The door burst open.

'There's no reply – what the hell?' said the newcomer.

'We are being very calm and well behaved,' murmured the President, both hands extended in his emollient gesture.

'Hey, wait a moment – aren't these the two who—?'

'Precisely right,' said the President, smiling. 'Now I can't very well introduce you, since you haven't yet had time to select suitable professional names, but this is the Press Secretary for the White House, Glover Teesdale.'

Teesdale, who sensed that the President was busy defusing a potentially dangerous situation, nodded briefly at the two old men, and then made his way as swiftly as possible without seeming to panic to the full-length mirror on a mahogany stand, where he fiddled discreetly with the brass fittings.

'Glover,' asked the President, keeping his nerves under visible control, 'what in the hell are you doing?'

'Goddam red button,' said Teesdale under his breath. 'I thought I had all these locations memorized.'

'Where is it?'

'Back of this mirror someplace.'

'Is there anything we can do to help?' asked the Old Man solicitously.

'No . . . no,' replied the President hastily, trying not to appear too hasty.

'Got it!'

'Don't push it!' muttered the President. 'We don't want them all in here with their guns!'

'Too late. I just did.'

'Jee-sus.'

'I believe we have twenty seconds' grace,' said Mr Smith.

'Sit down, please,' suggested the President. 'I'll sit down myself. Glover?'

They all sat down.

'They won't mistake us for sitting ducks, I hope.' Mr Smith was irrepressible under such circumstances.

There were muffled vibrations from outside, as though the US Cavalry were galloping on a pile carpet.

The drill had been rehearsed on many occasions, when the President had been away, this or another President.

There were six of them altogether, and they all adopted the same slightly obscene posture, as though straddling imaginary motorcycles. They held guns in front of them, like accusing fingers.

'All right, you two. Get up, face to the wall, hands above your heads, lean forward!' shouted the evident leader.

'Put those guns away,' said the President wearily.

'We got a procedure laid down!'

'Did you hear me, Crumwell?'

'Let me handle this my way, sir, with all due respect.'

'Who am I, Crumwell?'

'My President, sir, and I'm responsible to the entire nation for your safety, sir.'

'I am also your Commander-in-Chief, Crumwell, and I order you fellas to put away your guns.'

Crumwell seemed on the verge of mutiny. Then he subsided melodramatically, making his feelings on the matter painfully evident.

'OK, guys. I guess you heard,' he snarled.

'Oh, Glover, I wish you hadn't pushed that goddam button,' the President scolded, and then turned his attention to the intruders.

'Don't misunderstand me, boys. I appreciate the fact that you got here so quickly. But these are just a couple of old buffoons who have the makings of a great vaudeville act if they can only manage to find a hook to hang it on.'

'I recognize them, sir. I didn't when I first came in. Buffoons or not, they're still on the FBI's most wanted list.'

'They are?' asked the President, genuinely surprised.

'They've been doing their vanishing act all over the country. Every time our agents catch up with them, they vanish. That constitutes a felony in my book.'

'Felony?'

'Resisting arrest, simple as that, sir.'

'Why should they have to resist arrest? I apologize, I haven't yet gotten to reading the report.'

'Forgery.'

'Forgery?'

'Attempted arson. And some smaller items. Non-payment of hotel bills, petty thefts, minor misdemeanours.'

The President turned to Glover.

'Just how mistaken can a guy be? I'd have bet a million bucks that these are just a couple of harmless old idiots. I was actually playing for time, keeping them quiet till someone got here. I figured the best thing to do was to humour them. And now you tell me—'

'We didn't actually forge anything at all,' said the Old Man. 'I just dug into my pockets, and the stuff fluttered out.'

'Show them,' urged Mr Smith. 'Watch this, it's the best trick of all.'

'No,' chided the Old Man, 'they obviously regard it with disapproval. I don't want to antagonize them further.'

'If you really are innocent,' said the President, 'why don't you trust a court of law to acquit you? This country is ruled by the law, and no man, not even the President, is above that law. Give yourselves up, man. You can't spend the rest of your lives on the run, just vanishing. That's no achievement. There's nothing positive about vanishing. It's twisting the law. It's placing yourselves above it.'

'Perhaps he's right,' suggested the Old Man unhappily.

'Don't you believe it,' retorted Mr Smith, aggressively. 'He's talking like the television. It's enough to make me vomit!'

'The television? Explain yourself!'

'I remember enough from that orgy of viewing we had in that hotel to recognize a common denominator in all that enticing rubbish we sat through. There were all the elements calculated to give me pleasure – rape, violence, perversion, cruelty, insensitivity, wickedness, torture, blood-letting, cynicism. And then, to spoil it all in the waning moments, the invariable, ghastly, saccharine gesture in your direction, some cloying nonsense about the law, or even more pretentious and gratuitous, justice, as though mere mortals have more than a hazy knowledge of its nature.'

'Don't be too flagrant in your accusations. After all, we're not here to prove our superiority,' pleaded the Old Man.

'We're not here to sit around meekly while they give us absurd advice either,' stormed Mr Smith, who was clearly very angry. 'Buffoons indeed! To hell with the other cheek! I can stand just so much play-acting and nursery games, but when the music stops, something just snaps in me!'

'It was not my intention to hurt your feelings,' cried the President, his hands outstretched in supplication.

'Well, you did! I have my pride!' shouted Mr Smith.

The President briefly caught Crumwell's eye. At any subsequent investigation, Crumwell could testify that he interpreted the President's wink as an appeal for help. In view of the circumstances it would be believed.

'Operation Jessie James,' he suddenly cried.

The six guns reappeared as though by magic, and the slightly obscene poses were adopted in a trice.

'Don't threaten me with those toys!' yelled Mr Smith.

'Hold it right there,' Crumwell cautioned.

'And what if I don't hold it right there?' roared Mr Smith, as angry as he had been at any time since his fall from grace.

'You're going to get a bullet in you. This is the final warning. Go back to your seat and sit down with your hands on your head.'

Slowly Mr Smith advanced on Crumwell, who retreated slowly.

'This is your last chance!'

'Oh, don't show off!' cried the Old Man, rising. For a moment it seemed as though the Old Man's analysis of Mr Smith's attitude had struck home. Mr Smith hesitated momentarily.

'Show off?' he asked, as though wishing elucidation.

'I know you can do clever things. We both can. There's no great glory in proving it to others. I'm thinking of the wallpaper. You can survive a bullet. The wall cannot.'

'At such a moment, he thinks of the wallpaper!' muttered Mr Smith savagely, showing that his anger had in no wise diminished. 'In the name of the wallpaper, which cannot speak for itself, may I thank you for your solicitude.'

He then returned his attention to Crumwell, advancing on him slowly as though eager to wrest the gun from his grasp.

'This can be negotiated!' said the President. 'I have a gut feeling it can.'

Crumwell fired once. Twice.

Mr Smith looked at him, surprised. He put his hand to his chest, and seemed to see blood on it. Then, without changing his expression, he swayed for a moment, crumpled, and fell. The Old Man made a gesture of irritation, and sat down.

'Why did you do that?' asked the President.

'You can't negotiate with a nut.'

'Glover, this has got to be kept out of the press,' said the President, who knew his priorities. 'Not a word of this must leak out. Can I count on you fellas?'

There was a ragged chorus of agreement.

'Maybe I'd better explain why this little incident warrants an innocent cover-up. Reports of a shooting within the White House will inevitably show our security arrangements in a poor light. It will reflect on the FBI, and may even give pleasure to the CIA.'

There was a little contained laughter. The boys really appreciated the President's objectivity.

'OK. Operation Jessie James is over, fellas.' They all replaced their firearms in their holsters.

'I hope you understand the need for this little strategy, and are willing to give your undertaking not to let on what happened here today.' The President addressed the Old Man.

The Old Man turned slowly to face his interlocutor. 'Who would I tell? And who would believe me? I tell you who I am. You do not believe me. Who would believe I'd ever even been in the White House? Do I look like someone you would invite?'

'No, that's right,' replied the President, reasonably, and then adopted a more vulnerable look, the look he usually reserved for widows. 'I'm awful sorry about your friend there. I can't say the security boys were entirely to blame.'

The Old Man looked down at his prostrate companion. 'Oh, don't worry about him. He's always doing silly things like that.'

'Well, just how often can you do such silly things?'

'An infinity of times. Believe me,' said the Old Man, with the weight of the ages suddenly on him. 'He didn't like it when you referred to us as buffoons. As for me, I couldn't care less what names you call us – but you gave me offence too, at quite another moment . . .'

'I gave you offence?' asked the President. 'I ask you to believe it was quite unintentional.'

'God is not amusing, you said.'

'Well? Is he?'

'You can look at the Creation, and dare to say that God is not amusing? Even Mr Henchman didn't make that mistake. Fish with two eyes on the same side of the head? Bushbabies, wallabies, apes?

The sight of a hippopotamus in love, or lobsters in the mating season, like two broken deckchairs trying to find erogenous zones, or through their eyes, human beings? Not amusing?'

'I meant that God is not amusing to us.'

'You have never said anything as hurtful, or as deeply untrue. Why did I create the unique dimension of laughter, unique to man alone, if I didn't wish my jokes to be appreciated? Laughter is a therapy, a balm, a deflater of all that is solemn and pompous. It is my most refined invention, my most sublime and sophisticated discovery, second only to love.'

Slowly Mr Smith sat up, but so imperceptibly that the men did not immediately notice. When they reached for their guns again, Mr Smith spoke calmly.

'It didn't work the first time. Why do you think it will work the second?'

'You mean you're not even hurt?' blasted Crumwell.

'Surprised? With what vanity you all immediately assumed that I was dead!'

'I didn't,' said the Old Man.

'I wasn't talking about you.'

'Where did you learn to die like that?'

'Television. Where else? And you let me lie there, presumably bleeding to death, while you made plans to draw a veil over this little incident, in the interest of public relations. How attractive you all sounded from my vantage point! But there is one aspect you have overlooked, and which I urge you to deal with before the personnel arrive to clean the rooms.'

'What is that?' the President asked, dismayed.

'Precisely what my friend had envisaged. The bullet holes in the wall. You know how quickly rumours spread in a free society.'

The men rushed over to the wall. They could not find any damage. Mr Smith leaped to his feet, and deposited two bullets in an ashtray with a tinkling noise.

'As usual, I think of everything. You have my word that, as far as I am concerned, this matter will go no further.'

'Thank you very much,' said the chastened President, and added, 'Crumwell, don't leave those bullets in the ashtray!'

'And now, we must be off,' said the Old Man.

'Hey, not so fast,' said Crumwell, as he was pocketing the bullets, 'you guys got charges to answer.'

'You are going to press them, even now that we have proved to you that you can *never* press them?' asked Mr Smith.

'That's right.'

'Don't appeal to me, sir,' shrugged the President. 'The law is greater than all of us, as I tried to tell you.'

'Right,' added Crumwell, 'and you're lucky we only have you up on minor charges as yet. Best come away quietly now than for the charges to accumulate as they're bound to.'

'Oh, come on,' said the Old Man, 'let's face them and get it over with.'

The President beamed with confidence in the American system. 'That's what I like to hear,' he said. 'There's no great stigma attached to it. At this moment in time we have so many scandals going, this will pass entirely unnoticed. Why, we have a justice of the Supreme Court up on charges of sentimental attachment to a male prostitute, a senator on a charge of laundering mafia drug money, a cabinet member accepting bribes from a spark-plug manufacturer and a top-ranking general cheating on his wife with a Nicaraguan air hostess, to name only a few. What you've done is just chickenfeed in this company, and the worst thing is, they all write books about their misfortunes while in prison, implicating a whole new bunch of people we all thought of as innocent until then. Promise me you won't write books.'

'Shall we go?' asked the Old Man.

'No,' came the adamant rejoinder from Mr Smith.

'What difference does it make if we disappear now or later?'

'It's a waste of time. Valuable time.' His eyes swept over his audience.

'If you disappear again, that will be another offence,' snapped Crumwell.

'Why are you so determined to be unpleasant?' asked Mr Smith. 'What offences we have allegedly committed are the result of our inexperience. We have never actually hurt anybody.'

'That is what we are trying to assess at this time.'

'What do you mean?'

'Dr Kleingeld mean anything to you?'

'No.'

'Yes,' said the Old Man. 'He was the psychiatrist who interviewed me in that hospital.'

'Right. He was an accredited FBI psychiatrist. I don't know what occurred during that interview, but his life has changed dramatically since then. He's lost his practice, and the FBI accreditation. He founded a movement called Psychiatrists for God and Satan. As far as we can ascertain at this moment in time, he is the only member of this movement, and he spends most of the day outside the White House, carrying a message on a banner.'

'What is the message?'

'God and the Devil are on the level.'

'What does that mean?'

Crumwell hesitated, then grinned in a humourless sort of way. 'He's the only member of his movement. I guess you have your answer right there.' His tone hardened. 'OK, let's go.'

'Come on, do let's get it over with,' said the Old Man, with a sigh of resignation.

Mr Smith's attitude had changed entirely. He was suddenly affable, yet extraordinarily sure of himself. He smiled, almost engagingly.

'You never think things out to a conclusion which is halfways logical, do you? So keen are you on your confounded pride in your own integrity that you never see the consequences of your actions until it is too late,' he said.

The President was giving way to irritation. This entire episode had told on his nerves far too early in the day, and he was eager to put an end to it.

He smiled mechanically. 'Why don't you just follow your companion, and await due process of law?'

'I tell you why not,' said Mr Smith softly. 'You wish to keep what happened here today a secret. I have already helped you materially by not dying, and by fielding the bullets with my body. Now let me give you the rest of the scenario. We are taken out of here, each of us handcuffed to an agent of the FBI. We go down corridors, with elevators, through doors. Can you guarantee we won't meet anybody? Cleaning women, aides, members of the press corps perhaps? And how will it look? Two old manacled men, one in a nightshift, the other in a saucy T-shirt, being led by grim-faced officers from the presidential suite? Aren't you inviting the very situation you are so eager to avoid? And all out of respect for your sacred law?'

The President frowned. Decisions, decisions.

'He's right, of course.'

'What do we do?'

The President brushed aside Crumwell's question. He spoke to Mr Smith.

'What's your solution?'

'We are accorded the doubtful privilege of being allowed to disappear here . . . with your approval . . . no, better, with your encouragement.'

The movement of the President's jaws betrayed his anguish.

'OK,' he said.

'And the fact that we disappeared with your blessing means that this incident will not be among the charges you intend to press when and if we become available to you.'

'OK.'

'Have I your word?' said Mr Smith, extending his hand.

'You have my word,' replied the President, taking Mr Smith's hand. Then he shrieked.

'What's the matter?' asked Mr Smith, amused.

'Your hand. It's either very cold or very hot. I can't decide. Now get out of here!'

'But, sir—' pleaded Crumwell.

The President turned on him savagely. 'Hell, Crumwell, this is a nation of deals. We invented the plea bargain. There's a time and place for everything. For hand-on-heart high-mindedness. For down-to-earth pragmatism. That mixture has brought both integrity and opportunism to any business ethic. I want these guys arrested, OK? But more urgently, I want them out of here! It's a question of priorities!'

There were sounds of activity in the corridor.

'You are amazing,' conceded the Old Man, as he looked at Mr Smith with admiration. 'I'm thwarted at every turn. After you.'

'No, after you,' said Mr Smith. 'I want to be sure you disappear.'

'Allow me to thank you—' the Old Man began, addressing the President.

'Get out. Vamoose. Scram!' the President hissed.

127

Offended by the tone the President had adopted, the Old Man disappeared.

'Now you!' the President urged, as the noise in the corridor increased.

Mr Smith smiled. 'I'm awfully intrigued to know who's going to burst into the room,' he said calmly.

'No, no, no!' The President doubled up, clenching his fists and stamping his feet.

At the very moment two officers entered the room, Mr Smith vanished into thin air.

'What's going on in here, Mr President?' asked one officer.

'Nothing. Nothing at all, Colonel Godrich.'

'We're sure sorry to barge in here before you're fully dressed, sir,' said the other officer, 'although others seem to have preceded us. We heard that the red alarm had been sounded. Shortly after we heard two shots from this general direction, and we thought we'd best investigate.'

Glover Teesdale spoke. 'It was the President's idea to try out the security systems without prior warning to the responsible authorities.'

'Right,' added the President, who had recovered his Olympian detachment. 'Any security exercise which is announced for a specific hour, like lifeboat drill aboard ship, is not an adequate test of our defences, General Borrows.'

'Good thinking, sir. Although, by lifting the status of make-believe onto the plane of reality, somebody's liable to get hurt. Where'd those bullets go?'

'Out the window, at the Commander-in-Chief's request,' said Crumwell, spinning the magazine of his revolver in order to show the two empty barrels.

'Any damage to property?'

'No, sir.'

The General looked round the room, and then withdrew, saying, 'OK, let's get back to regular business, Lee. Next time, perhaps whoever's on duty in our office might be informed, as a courtesy.'

'General Borrows, total security brooks no half-measures,' retorted the President in quotable words.

Borrows and Godrich left in silence, chastened.

'The incident is closed, Mr Crumwell, in every possible way, and I want to thank you guys for your collaboration.'

'We're going to get those sonsabitches before we're through,' announced the frustrated Crumwell, almost tearfully.

The President made urgent gestures for him to keep his voice down. 'I don't doubt that for a moment,' said the President, very softly.

The FBI men filed out in silence.

'Back to square one,' murmured the President to Glover Teesdale, and then, springing back to life with his customary resilience, added, 'Oh, Glover, before I put my pants on, show me where that goddam red button is.'

11

Mr Smith materialized in the British Airways section of Dulles airport, but in such a way that the man behind him, a brash and choleric English businessman, was convinced that his place in the queue had been usurped.

''Op it,' said the Englishman aggressively. 'You wasn't 'ere a moment ago, and there's no use pretendin' you was!'

'What are you accusing me of?' asked Mr Smith, his face creased like a plumstone.

'Taking my place in't queue. Are you First Class?'

'I haven't a ticket yet.'

'Then you've no business in the queue. Where's your baggage?'

'I haven't acquired any yet.'

The Englishman laughed heartily, and attempted to include other travellers in the absurdity of the situation.

'No bag, no ticket, and he barges into the queue. Wonderful, isn't it? I bet you're one of those religious cranks they warned us of. They're all over the shop today.'

'Religious crank? Me?' Mr Smith laughed a high and brittle laugh, which vibrated unpleasantly in the Englishman's eardrums.

'Go on, 'op it, like I said, or I'll fetch an official. If you need a ticket, you can effect a purchase downstairs. Now. That's all the 'elp you're going to get from me,' said the Englishman, flinching with every peal of Mr Smith's laughter.

Mr Smith made to leave, then returned. 'About the religious cranks – you haven't seen an old man with flowing locks and beard, white of course, with pinkish cheeks and a portly build, wearing robes?'

'I've seen about fifteen of them when I flew in from Columbus, O'io a while ago. They're mostly congregated at the American terminuses, 'cos that's where the money is, you understand.'

'Money? Religious cranks?'

'Well, that's what they're in religion for, aren't they? Stands to reason. Religion's a big industry out 'ere, isn't it? It's the one area in which the Japs haven't been able to compete, 'ave they? Now 'op it.'

The Englishman moved forward towards the desk, pushing his luggage before him with his foot. As a parting shot, he indicated a notice on the wall with a vague gesture.

'You'll find all about the religious cranks on the wall. They've posted notices saying it's legal, and you can't do nothing about it. Bloody disgrace, I call it. Nothing more or less than a licence to annoy. That's carrying freedom just a bit too far. In jug, that's where they belong – or in the Army – at least there they get a free 'aircut.'

Mr Smith walked reflectively over to the notice on the wall and read it. It seemed to apologize for the possible presence of members of religious groups in the airport, dispensing pamphlets or accosting passengers with a view to their conversion. Under the constitution, with its insistence on freedom of religious thought, there was nothing the authorities could do about it, except hope it would not turn out to be a nuisance.

This Mr Smith took to be rather good news. The Old Man and he, with his wild mane of oily hair, could wander with impunity round the airport without attracting undue attention, accepted as militant members of obscure religious fraternities. But where was the Old Man? There was no sign of him. Mr Smith hoped that absent-mindedness had not got the better of him again. That would be too bad. In fact, a cause for panic. Was not the Old Man the fount of all yen? Without his magic, the task would be far more difficult. For all his concentration, Mr Smith had never been able to conjure up more than a few bent or damaged coins, which even phoneboxes rejected.

Mr Smith searched everywhere for the Old Man, but without success. Slowly his growing anguish turned to irritation, and finally to anger. If there was anything he hated, it was inefficiency. The idea of being stranded all alone in Dulles airport with nowhere to go but to Hell filled him with rancour. Then he remembered how he had found the Old Man standing on the sordid sidewalk of 42nd Street with a couple of suitcases in his hands, waiting patiently for his escapade to run its course, and he reflected. Had the Old Man put this memory into his mind, as a plea for understanding? Was the Old Man already there, but still invisible? Was there a reason for this delay?

Mr Smith became more positive in his attitude. They could not waste time if they wished to leave the country before the FBI could catch up with them again. Passports could not be bought. Ergo, they had to be stolen. It would be best to steal them in another terminal. The hue and cry would be local to start with, and only spread later. Tickets, on the other hand, would have to be stolen in the British terminal since they were going to London. Baggage could be stolen anywhere. It would lack credibility for them to travel without baggage, on an airline that is.

He left the British Airways building and walked down till he reached a sign indicating Saudi Arabian Airlines.

The hall was fairly empty, suggesting that departures were not imminent. There was a dark female employee of the airline struggling with a faulty computer, and shouting angrily in Arabic. On various chairs, as well as on the floor, an entire tribe seemed to be draped in various attitudes of slumber, while a couple of small children shrieked and played an invented game with a chipped blue thermos flask. It looked as though no aircraft was expected to leave for a day or two yet. The overhead information panel was devoid of information. Only the chill blast of the air-conditioner suggested that this was New York and not some outpost on the confines of the Yemen, only visited by metal birds every other week.

Mr Smith glanced here and there for any passports left carelessly unguarded, but everything seemed safely packed into ungainly bundles. It was at this moment that the airline official finally lost her temper with her unseen interlocutor and stormed out of the room into the offices behind, muttering darkly. Mr Smith went to the unattended desk and spotted a large collection of passports, attached by a rubber band, and with a short message in Arabic scribbled onto a bit of paper, joined to the passports by a paperclip. He could hardly believe his good fortune. He looked around, his eyes ablaze with the joy of risk. The woman had resumed her diatribe far away, and could be heard exchanging insults with one or two others in the distance.

He moved like lightning, sliding a couple of passports out of the collection. One he replaced, since it revealed the photograph of a veiled woman, who was, of course, totally unrecognizable. It was merely the veil which suggested it was unsuitable. He chose two of men, and rearranged the others as he had found them. Only just in time. The click of the official's heels could be heard returning.

Mr Smith walked away without seeming to hurry.

'Are you on SV 028 to Riyadh?' he heard the woman ask in Arabic.

'I was looking for a brochure,' answered Mr Smith, also in Arabic.

'A brochure? What of?'

'I haven't decided yet, but thank you in advance.'

'Don't mention it. Are you a pilgrim?'

'No. I'm a religious crank.'

'Oh, I only mention it because there is a twelve-hour delay.'

'That is very useful information.'

'They have already received it,' she said, indicating the sleeping figures.

'*Markhaba.*'

'*Akhlin wa Sakhlin.*'

And Mr Smith made his way back to the British Airways section. Here there were fewer people, but more activity. The girls at the desk were as exasperated as their Arabic counterpart, as something was evidently wrong with the computers here too.

Mr Smith walked right to the desk, ignoring the waiting passengers.

'What seems to be the matter?' he drawled in Levantine Brooklynese.

'Are you from maintenance?' asked a girl.

'Sure. Ali Bushiri. Maintenance.'

'Have you got identification?' asked another, more cautious girl.

'Shit, no. How long you been here, girls?'

'What's that got to do with it?'

'Everyone know Ali Bushiri. He don't need no identification. That just shows you how often these crummy machines go on the blink. What's gone wrong this time?'

His languid self-assurance was enough to convince the girls of his authenticity. It was just like the powers that be to employ a hideous creature of indeterminate age, with a mane of greasy hair and a dirty T-shirt with a frivolous message on it, to mend complicated hardware. He had probably graduated from the Massachusetts Institute of Technology.

'OK, just what is malfunctioning?' he asked.

'I'm not getting any printouts,' explained the girl whose computer he was investigating. 'I've got to do it all by hand.'

Mr Smith took the back cover of the machine off.

'It's not just a malfunction here – all the messages are garbled. Look at this, London comes out as LDNOON.'

'A bit of seasonal dyslexia,' said Mr Smith. 'Let me deal with one problem at a time. When do you girls go off duty?'

'In about ten minutes, thank God.'

'Then another shift comes on?'

'Right. We've been here from five this morning. Let the other girls deal with this mess.'

There was a chorus of approval.

'How many flights do you have to London today?'

'One at thirteen hundred hours, that's BA188, and one at twenty forty-five, BA216. They're both practically sold out, which means it's backbreaking work when the computers are out.'

'Both nearly sold out?' Mr Smith frowned. 'Even in First?'

'Especially in First. It's a sign of the times, I always say to my husband. He always used to vote Labour before we came to live over here. Now he doesn't vote any more, and tells me he appreciates democracy for the first time.'

'The Concorde leaves in just under an hour, but it's frightfully expensive.'

'Is that full?'

'There are usually a few seats left. Why?'

'Just curiosity. Does the Concorde have special boarding passes?'

'Yes, these over here. Satisfied?'

Mr Smith grinned, and pretended to be dealing with some frightfully delicate anomaly within the box.

'That's got it, I believe. Let me try this for size.'

He slipped a Concorde boarding pass into a slot.

'And the Concorde number is?'

'BA188,' said the girl obligingly.

Mr Smith typed a few ciphers, and the machine began stuttering obligingly. Out came a boarding pass, seat number 24, non-smoking, in the name of Ali Bushiri.

'Eureka!' cried the girl. 'It's working again!'

'No, I think I can do better than that,' and he briefly consulted the other Saudi Arabian passport, destined for the Old Man.

'What are you looking up?' asked the girl, inquisitive.

'The instruction book,' replied Mr Smith, spelling out other instructions on the keyboard.

Out came a boarding pass, seat number 25, non-smoking, in the name of Amir El Hejjazi.

'That looks OK. As for the jumbled words, I'll have to go and deal with the central computer up in computer control. See you, girls.'

The girls, who were all preparing to leave, echoed, 'See you, Ali.'

Mr Smith was well satisfied with his success so far, but now that so much had been achieved, he was once again annoyed by the Old Man's absence. The Concorde was to leave in under an hour. They had passports and boarding passes, but as yet no luggage, no passport photographs, and above all, no other passenger. He looked into every building on the concourse, but saw no sign of his partner.

Then, in a hall devoted to several minor airlines, he suddenly noticed a photomat, its curtain drawn, with some impatient people gathered around it. An uncanny instinct drew Mr Smith towards the little edifice.

'How much longer are you going to stay in there?' cried a woman.

The reactions of the people had the kind of sombre urgency of those waiting for the liberation of a much needed toilet. Mr Smith's eyes were drawn to the metal tray into which photographs were spewed out every now and then. A new set of four followed the twenty or so already in the tray. They were all of the Old Man, expressing every variety of emotion with the heavy-handedness of illustrations to a Victorian book on the technique of acting. Avarice, Greed, Vainglory, Dourness, were all catered for by distinct grimaces, to say nothing of Terror, Astonishment, Innocence, and Pride.

'What are you up to in there?' Mr Smith's voice crackled with misgiving.

The curtain was pulled instantly. The Old Man looked at Mr Smith with genuine pleasure.

'Ah, there you are, at last!'

'At last?'

'I've been here for hours. But I'm afraid I became fascinated by this new device.'

The small crowd began to push forward, but Mr Smith forced himself into the cubicle with a confidential aside, something to the

135

effect of dangerous homicidal lunatic, and a mutter about being his keeper eager to recapture him after a truant.

'He hasn't threatened any of you, has he?'

Those waiting were flattered by the confidence, and denied any threat, although two or three of them began to allude to misgivings they had felt all along. Mr Smith said in an undertone that he would deal with the situation, and disappeared into the cubicle, which was never really intended for two.

'What did you tell them?' the Old Man asked cozily.

Mr Smith sat on the Old Man's lap.

'I told them you were a homicidal maniac.'

'What?' The Old Man seemed deeply shocked. 'And they believed you?' he went on.

'Evidently, otherwise they wouldn't have allowed me in. Now listen carefully. We haven't a moment to lose. You've taken about twenty photographs of yourself. Now it's my turn. We need them for our passports, you understand.'

'Our what?'

'Never mind. You'll just have to trust me, that's all, since you're determined to leave without magic.'

'How can I trust someone who spreads rumours that I am dangerous?'

'Give me a coin.'

'I've used up all my small change.'

'How selfish can a person be?'

'I am not a person.'

'A person pretending to be a person!' Mr Smith was beginning to lose his patience. 'Were the coins you used genuine or counterfeit?'

'Counterfeit,' said the Old Man, almost inaudibly.

'Then you can jolly well create me one.'

The Old Man dug into his pocket and produced a coin, too new to look authentic.

'You're learning,' said Mr Smith. 'Now, don't move! You have very inhospitable knees. Don't wriggle for a moment, or I'll be out of focus, and you'll have to keep me in coins till we get it right. One, two, three!'

Mr Smith smiled what he imagined to be engagingly; there was a blinding flash of a red bulb, and the whole apparatus seemed to gulp.

'Right.' Mr Smith rose, exaggerating his discomfort. 'Now struggle with me as we leave.'

'I have no intention of struggling with you,' said the Old Man.

Mr Smith was outraged. 'After all I've done for you,' he snarled, 'you can't even indulge in a little make-believe in order to bear out my story.'

'No, I can't,' said the Old Man, with what sounded like a sob. 'It's not make-believe so much as lies. Ever since I assumed the mantle of mortality, it's been an accumulation of petty untruths. I can't bear it. It's beneath my dignity.'

Mr Smith was painfully explicit. 'My dear, that's what it means to be a man. And you had to wait until confined to a photomat, immortalizing your grimaces, to find out!'

'You really think to be a man entails telling lies?' asked the Old Man.

'You knew temptation, didn't you? For the first time in your transcendental career.'

'I've never seen a photo of myself before, you understand. On a cosmic plane, there is no need for these little confirmations of one's existence. Look.'

And from his ample robes the Old Man withdrew yet another sheet of photographs. On each of the four he expressed a different emotion.

'You've been outside the cubicle to collect them?' asked Mr Smith, surprised.

'There was nobody waiting then. I've at least a dozen more. I've been here almost all the time since we left the White – the President.'

'And although you are wanted in the United States for forgery, you calmly went ahead and created a few miserable quarters?'

'I created whatever would fit into the slot.'

'Disgraceful.'

The rumpus outside increased in volume.

'Right march!' Mr Smith twisted the Old Man's arm, and prepared to leave.

'You're hurting,' cried the Old Man.

'Don't lie!'

'All right, then, you would be hurting if I could feel it.'

Once outside, Mr Smith exaggerated the difficulty of holding the Old Man.

'Hand me those photos, will you?' Mr Smith asked the first in line.

The man glanced at the snaps of the Old Man and he handed them to Mr Smith, murmuring, 'You're right. Nuttier than a fruit cake.'

Mr Smith acknowledged the observation, raising his eyes. What one has to put up with.

Once out in the open, Mr Smith backed himself into the corner of the concrete outer wall of the complex.

'Stand in front of me,' he ordered the Old Man.

'What?'

'As though I were undressing on a beach.'

The Old Man did as he was told.

In a flash, Mr Smith reappeared as an Arab, white robes and burnous.

'Who are you now?' asked the Old Man, bewildered.

'Ali Bushiri, and you are Amir El Hejjazi.'

'What do I have to do?'

'Nothing,' replied Mr Smith, spiriting a headdress from the air, and placing it over the Old Man's flowing locks.

'Luckily your robes could pass for a djellaba. All you need is this. And perhaps a pair of sunglasses.'

These were created with a wave of the hand, and in a trice the two of them looked passably authentic.

'Tell me my name again?'

'Amir El Hejjazi.'

'Where on earth did that name come from?'

'It was in the passport I stole. Quick. Which of these hideous photographs tickles your vanity?'

'I like them all,' admitted the Old Man, 'but then I have nothing to compare them with. You choose for me.'

'This one here, and one of mine. Can you help stick them over the real pictures?'

'Like this?'

'And now, come on. We'll catch the plane by the skin of our teeth, if we're lucky.'

'What about luggage?'

'Leave it to me—'

The two robed men entered the British Airways building and hurried up to the Concorde counter.

'We have our boarding passes already,' explained Mr Smith. 'We had to go out and phone long distance urgently.'

The girl belonged to the new shift.

She frowned. 'That's odd. Seats twenty-four and twenty-five are allocated already. Name of Friedenfeld. When did you register?'

'Not ten minutes ago,' said Mr Smith. 'Our luggage has already gone through.'

'Was it a blonde girl? Rather chubby?'

'Chubby? Stout, I would say.'

'Barbara, Barbara,' moaned the new girl. 'She never lets us down, does she?' she said to her neighbour, and then smiled sheepishly at Mr Smith. 'She got engaged only last week. Perhaps that's it.'

'Perhaps.'

'Would you mind forty-three and forty-four in the second cabin?'

'So long as the destination is London.'

'I hope it is, for all our sakes.'

Soon Mr Smith and the Old Man were seated in the Concorde and rising almost vertically into the air in virtually total silence.

'How long does it take to get to London?' asked the Old Man.

'Three and a half hours, I'm told.'

'That's awfully slow, isn't it?'

'By our standards, yes,' admitted Mr Smith.

The Old Man looked out of the window, which was slightly awkwardly placed for a man of his corpulence.

'I'm really in my element up here,' he said, and then added with a sigh, 'I'm almost tempted to get out here and abandon the whole disenchanting adventure.'

'You'll create havoc among the other passengers if you attempt it.'

'I wouldn't dream of doing any such thing, of course. To get out here would be tantamount to an admission of defeat.'

'And that you are not willing to do yet?'

The Old Man did not immediately answer. Mr Smith allowed the silence to continue for a long time, since it quickly acquired an eloquence of its own.

'Do you regret having come?' the Old Man broke the silence.

Mr Smith laughed. 'Can one regret such an experience? Hardly. I can only mourn the absolute decadence into which vice has fallen. Every vestige of hypocrisy has been erased from its presentation. It is as though foreplay had been discarded as a waste of time, instead of what it is, the measure of time, time's yardstick.'

'You speak of your discipline alone. Of vice.'

'No. No, it seems to me that, as usual, what applies to vice in fact applies to everything. Without healthy vice there can be no healthy virtue. They are as complementary as we are, and neither profits by the momentary deficit of the other. On the contrary, they both rise and fall together. They are indivisible. If I may say so, without being tasteless, they are the two sides of the same coin.'

The Old Man understood the allusion, but decided not to rise to it. He merely contented himself with an inner smile, and looked out at the clouds which seemed to be crawling by.

'So we got out of the United States without a single magic trick. Are you satisfied? Do I merit a quick vote of thanks?'

'No,' replied the Old Man. 'Admittedly there were no tricks, but there was subterfuge on a considerable scale. As a consequence, I am now Mr El Hejjazi. And what of the real Mr El Hejjazi, now finding himself in a land which can easily turn hostile towards those suddenly bereft of identity? And who has paid for our airline tickets?'

Mr Smith was beside himself. 'What utter humbug!' he screeched in a voice so un-Arabic that several real Arabs, discreetly dressed in expensive Western clothes, turned with evident displeasure to study such an odd representation of their culture and their heritage.

The Old Man even nudged Mr Smith, but there was no need. When he estimated that all the passengers within earshot were concentrating on other matters, Mr Smith spoke very quietly and to the point, expressing as little with his listless gaze as a ventriloquist.

'Once you have the power to do tricks, it is stupid not to utilize this power. It proves absolutely nothing to attempt to live and work by men's rules, which we have proved to be impossible without forgery, theft and total mendacity. What we have learned so far has been uniquely because here and there our true identities have been discovered. The ranger and his wife praised you only as what you are, and not for a moment because they were taken in by your ridiculous incognito. That poor pyschiatrist with his abandoned practice writes incomprehensible messages on his banner, because that is his way of acknowledging our presence in the world without attracting undue hostility. He is treated with the relative tolerance which greets a

140

harmless madman, and not with the hatred reserved for those who should know better. The others have all been models of pharisaical obtuseness. The higher up the social scale, the more crass has been its manifestation.'

The Old Man declined to answer, largely because he could furnish no argument to contradict what his friend had said, but also so as to pretend to sleep, a pastime which those able to afford the Concorde seemed readily able to indulge in.

Mr Smith grunted. He understood the motives and perplexities of the Old Man, and did not really wish to aggravate matters. Instead he looked at the British newspaper which had been lying on his knees since take-off, compliments of the airline.

'Your milkman could be God' screamed the headline.

Mr Smith read on with interest, picking his way among the pictures. The main illustration, which took up much of the front page, was that of a prelate, his mouth open, his hair in romantic disarray, pointing to a milkman, grinning loutishly, who had clearly been superimposed on the shot. When Mr Smith had finished his read, he nudged the Old Man in high good humour.

'Why wake me up?' asked the Old Man, not without self-pity.

'Because you weren't asleep.'

There was no arguing with this.

'Listen,' Mr Smith went on, 'this is a place we must visit while in London. It seems tops in entertainment value.'

'And where is that?'

'The Synod of the Church of England, at Church House, West-minster.'

'What are they up to?'

'One of their number, a bishop, Dr Buddle, has claimed that the public should always be on the alert, since even the familiar milkman might turn out to be God.'

The Old Man sat up, his interest rekindled. 'Full marks, I would say. But how did the others react?'

'Badly, but then Dr Buddle is apparently known as a maverick.'

'As a what?'

'It's an American word I think, meaning rebel, or lone wolf.'

'What was the outcome?'

'Uproar. The Primate of the Anglican Church, who is himself

known for his unconventional views, faced an amused but inquisitorial press.'

'Amused. Why amused?'

'The perplexity of the clerical fraternity, wallowing in the muddied quagmire of metaphysics and mysticism, will always amuse a largely agnostic press corps – who are, nevertheless, more than ready to adopt pious attitudes should the need arise.'

'I see. And what did the Primate say?'

'Dr Buddle has a right to his opinion as a son of God. As a high-ranking member of the Church, he should perhaps have been a little more circumspect in his choice of examples. He never intended it to be understood that the milkman *is* God. At all events, there is only one God and many milkmen. He only meant to say that there exists a possibility that the milkman in question might, under circumstances which are impossible to envisage, turn out to be God. He should certainly have made it clearer to the layman that the possibility of the milkman being God is highly unlikely, even if not entirely impossible.'

'Worthy of a Jesuit. No wonder the man's the Primate.'

'Shall we pay them a visit?' asked Mr Smith, brimful of mischief.

The Old Man thought for a moment. 'I think not,' he replied, a trifle sadly. 'It would only put an end to an argument which is delighting the nation by its agreeable absurdity. After all, what will our presence in Church House prove? The fact that he had all the right instincts will go to the good Dr Buddle's head, and he will be haunted by mirages of infallibility, the consequences of which could be quite disastrous, while the opposition will counterattack, on the slender premise that I am not a milkman, to prove that Dr Buddle is irresponsible and wrong-headed. By then, the intended sense of Dr Buddle's remark, which was simply to say that God is capable of appearing at any time in any guise, will have been deliberately forgotten by both sides.'

'Go as a milkman?' suggested Mr Smith.

'The last thing I should do. Why invest Dr Buddle's mind with the microbes of megalomania? And why humiliate the Primate and the Doubting Thomases? The world of ideas has no greater enemy than inescapable fact, just as the world of faith has nothing more ruinous than the physical appearance of God. The Jews have understood this. They await the Messiah with reverence, in the clairvoyant assurance that he will never turn up.'

'Then what the hell are we doing here?' cried Mr Smith.

'We are here for our sake, not for theirs,' snapped the Old Man, with surprising vigour.

Mr Smith half closed his eyes. 'Whatever happens, we must remain in physical contact. We must at all times be able to hold hands. Don't let them separate us.'

'Why do you say that?'

'The fact that we are here for our sake will not make it any easier. I have a feeling we will be less and less master of our own time, of our own wishes.'

'And who will influence us in any decisions? The FBO?'

Mr Smith had no wish or inclination to confirm or deny his suspicions.

12

The arrival at Heathrow Airport was efficient and uneventful. Several passengers who had been transported at twice the speed of sound for the first time could not get over their amazement, while those who were in the habit of taking the Concorde across the Atlantic remained distantly disdainful, much as members of an exclusive club might do at a sudden invasion of outsiders. Someone's guests, no doubt? The Old Man decided to record the same kind of disengagement expressed by the habitués. He felt that he could have walked the distance faster. Only Mr Smith was rather furtive.

'Don't forget you're an Arab,' he hissed in English.

'Why talk to me in English then?' asked the Old Man in Arabic. 'Aren't you an Arab, too?'

They left the plane, bending low to squeeze through the tiny door, and soon they were in line to show their passports to immigration. Naturally enough, they joined the wrong line first, until they decided that Saudi Arabia was probably not a member of the European Community.

'A stupid error on our part. Speed is all important.'

'All I do is follow you,' said the Old Man. 'Amir El Hejjazi is a very old and helpless Arab, relying heavily on his nephew for everything.'

Even Mr Smith had to smile.

The British official took his passport and seemed to photograph it by some mysterious process just out of sight of the passengers.

'You are Mr Ali Bushiri?'

'That is correct.'

'And for what reason are you intending to visit the United Kingdom?'

Mr Smith had not thought this question would be asked, and hesitated momentarily.

'I am Amir El Hejjazi,' declared the Old Man. 'I am going for a complete medical check-up.'

'Oh yes, sir. And where would that be?'

'Sir Maurice McKilliwray's private clinic in Dorking. He already has a huge collection of items I have contributed to his compendium of the human body, invaluable for students. Gallstones, kidney stones – he told me last time that I needed a geologist rather than a surgeon. He has that macabre English humour much appreciated in the remote parts of Saudi Arabia.'

'Is that so?' said the immigration official, his lips quivering and pouting with a sense of acute irony, without being able to apply it to anything which made the remotest sense.

'Ali Bushiri is my nephew, even if he seems at times even older than I. He is the son of my lamented sister, Aïsha, may her soul repose in a celestial oasis, who was nearly twice my age, although admittedly I was catching up with her towards the end. He accompanies me on all my check-ups. In case anything goes wrong, you understand.'

Since there were still a few passengers, who were beginning to grow impatient, the official waved them through, with a final observation, 'Your nephew looks far more in need of a check-up than you.'

'Tell him, tell him!' wailed the Old Man, with a sudden burning intensity which disturbed the official, who already had the next passport in his hand.

'Consider yourself told,' he said curtly to Mr Smith, who nodded fatalistically and shrugged.

'What's the matter with you?' he whispered fiercely to the Old Man as they hurried towards the luggage delivery hall. 'Such scruples about lying, and you suddenly go berserk. Your sister Aïsha, indeed, reposing in a celestial oasis.' He couldn't help laughing.

'You know I never wanted to wear a disguise. I knew that once I did, lying, or rather, invention, would take over against my better judgment.' The light of folly was burning merrily in the Old Man's eye. 'It takes me right back to the beginnings, this urge to create. Perhaps you remember vaguely some of my early excesses, before my sense of proportion had been honed down to the unique critical faculty it eventually became? The dodo, for instance, with its cumbersome eggs – it really couldn't survive. And the dinosaurs and brontosaurus, all these fruits of my early *folie de grandeur*, like movable temples to my ego. Movable, did I say? Well, only just. And you probably never saw some of my early sketches? Oysters that were intended to reproduce like humans. The design was faulty from the outset. And the prototype chicken could fly, did you know that? Cocks could swoop crowing out of an inky sky and wake up sleepers the world over. Insomnia was as serious a plague as ever visited mankind. Well, dressing up as Amir El Hejjazi brought it all back, this gift of invention. But I was not really reckless, was I? I only invented a dead sister, and you can't go far wrong with that.'

Mr Smith was not really listening, as they had things to do with despatch, and the Old Man's torrential memories were punctuated with sufficient puffs and gasps of effort as to make them a little incoherent.

They reached the hall where the luggage was delivered on clattering carousels, and Mr Smith grabbed a duffel bag coming from Lima and Mexico City.

'Had I better have one too?' asked the Old Man.

'I don't think you should steal one. One of your wives flew ahead with your luggage.'

'Oh.' Events were moving too fast for the Old Man.

'Mr Bushiri?' asked an officer in the Customs Shed, whose pallor and doubtful complexion declared his confinement to offices.

'Yes?'

'Mr Ali Bushiri is that?'

'Yes.'

'And Mr Amir – I'm afraid I don't know how to pronounce this –'

'El Hejja-azi,' said the Old Man.

'Em . . . well . . . would you follow me, please.'

'What for?' asked Mr Smith.

'Mr Goatley would like a word with you.'

He knocked at the door of a small office, and beckoned them in. Mr Goatley introduced himself as the Chief of Customs, and presented his deputy, Mr Rahman, who was black. He offered them seats.

'We are in somewhat of a hurry,' said Mr Smith.

'I'm sorry to hear that.' Mr Goatley studied the ceiling as though vaguely expecting something to materialize from up there. Then a sudden smile of startling insincerity appeared on his face, twisting his pencil-thin moustache into a shape similar to five to five on a clock face.

'Whether we can accede to your request to leave would depend largely on your ability to answer a few questions, wouldn't it?'

Mr Rahman seemed to be wracked with obsequious but silent chuckles.

'Now, first things first,' Mr Goatley went on. 'You insist that you are Mr Bushiri?'

'Why shouldn't I be Mr Bushiri?' asked Mr Smith hotly.

Mr Goatley consulted a piece of paper before him. 'May I see your passport, please?'

'We have already shown our passports.'

'I realize that. I have photocopies of them before me. I would now very much like to see the real things.' Registering Mr Smith's hesitation, he went on, 'You won't be allowed to enter the United Kingdom without showing them again in any case.'

Mr Smith and the Old Man surrendered their passports without much enthusiasm.

Mr Goatley examined them closely, helped by Mr Rahman, who pointed with his finger every now and then at items on various pages which caused amusement or disbelief.

At length, Mr Goatley spoke.

'Gentlemen, had you looked at the passports closely before you . . . you acquired them?'

'Acquired them? What are you insinuating?' rasped Mr Smith.

'We have a telefax from the authorities in Dulles airport stating that two passports in the names of Ali Bushiri and Amir El Hejjazi were stolen from the Saudia check-in counter about an estimated hour before the Concorde left.'

'That is preposterous! On what do they base their accusation?'

'The fact that Mr Bushiri and Mr El Hejjazi were unable to leave on the delayed flight to Riyadh, and are creating blue murder, since they claimed that they had surrendered their passports to the Saudia check-in counter. They were travelling as a group, you understand.'

Mr Smith became sly.

'I am the only Mr Bushiri of my acquaintance,' he said with a sincerity which was too evident to be true. 'What makes you think the other Mr Bushiri is not the impostor?'

'Well, sir, that is why I asked you if you had really studied the passports before utilizing them. It says here you are twenty-six years old.'

Mr Smith was finally taken aback. 'I have been extremely ill,' he muttered.

'And the suitcase?'

'It is mine,' claimed the Old Man generously. He felt that Mr Smith needed help.

Mr Rahman opened the zip.

'Anything of interest?' asked Mr Goatley.

'Six tennis racquets, sir.'

'Six?'

'All wrapped in cellophane. A collection of sports shirts and sweatbands.'

'And where did the bag come from?'

'Lima, Peru.'

'I see,' said Mr Goatley. 'Your passport says you are sixty-seven years old, Mr El Hejjazi, which is probably not too wide of the mark. I presume therefore that you are a player in the seniors' competition in Wimbledon, and that you have recently played in Lima. Do you appear on court in your robes? Aren't they a little restrictive, especially in singles?'

While speaking, he had been scratching at the photographs with a pair of scissors.

'As I thought,' he went on, 'there are the original photos underneath. A young bearded fellow – and someone dressed like you, but there the resemblance ends. Well. What shall we do with you? Care to make a clean breast of it?'

There was a long pause while the Old Man and Mr Smith shifted uneasily from foot to foot like children who had been caught red-handed in some dishonest pursuit.

At length the Old Man murmured, 'You are quite right, of course. It was a stupid subterfuge, for which we are neither physically nor morally suited.'

'Speak for yourself!' said Mr Smith, with a flicker of flame around the tongue which made the customs officers frown briefly, before they dispelled it as an ocular illusion. 'I still maintain that I am Ali Bushiri, and that the other Ali Bushiri is an impostor!'

Mr Goatley smiled, and his moustache swivelled. 'I am recording your allegation on tape for the eventual investigation. I hope you don't mind.'

'Now that we have made, as you say, a clean breast of it, may we go?' the Old Man asked, with a touching belief in man's innocence.

'I'm afraid it's not quite as simple as that. You see, I happen to know who you two gentlemen are.'

'Eh?'

'Yes,' Mr Goatley insisted tactfully. 'You, sir, are God the Father, whereas the other gent, alleging himself to be the real Ali Bushiri, is none other than our old friend, Satan.'

The Old Man was simply speechless with delight.

'At last! At last! The simple welcome I had longed for. No fuss, no fanfares. Just a smile of politeness by way of greeting! I thank you, sir. I shall always cherish your reaction to our presence. It just shows that the Old World is still capable of a certain objectivity, destroyed in the New World by the precipitate advance of technique, of – what do they call it? – "know-how". You, sir, have still preserved the precious "know-how-not", and we congratulate you. Now may we go? We have a lot to do.'

'I'm afraid not,' reasoned Mr Goatley. 'Now that we know who you are, we don't want to let you go so quickly.'

'I suppose that is flattering,' the Old Man observed, 'but rather inconvenient. Is it difficult for you to imagine that God has work to do?'

'Especially in the company of the Devil,' said Mr Goatley, not without sarcasm. 'May one ask what you could possibly have in common? I mean, what tasks bring you together? Correcting entrance exam papers to Heaven and to Hell?'

'What have we in common?' asked the Old Man, amazed. 'Only the Creation, existence, life, matter, manner . . .'

'I had nothing to do with the Creation. I refuse to take the blame for that,' Mr Smith intervened with some spirit, only to adopt a bitterer, more intimate tone. 'I'm so sick of your ingenuous nature. So happy to be recognized, you are, that your locks have curled, like cumulus clouds, and your beard is a-glint with silver, as though shrouded in Christmas decorations. You glow with appreciation for the fact that someone in this wide world other than a lunatic and a ranger has called you by your name. The other two fell to their knees. Why does not this gentleman?'

'He may be an atheist,' said the Old Man. 'He has a perfect right. I would find it difficult to believe in myself if I weren't sure I existed.'

'Do you not sense that all this has a reason other than simple reverence?' asked Mr Smith. 'That, in fact, we are being mocked?'

'Mocked? I hadn't noticed.'

'Very well then, humoured for the madmen we appear to be?'

Mr Goatley saw danger. 'Not madmen by any means,' he said, uncertainly, 'merely somewhat eccentric.'

'Eccentric?' The Old Man was bewildered.

'I can see the photographs upside-down on his desk when I stand up,' cried Mr Smith, 'photographs of you and I in that church in America, the first time you thought you were recognized for what you are!'

Mr Goatley pressed a button on his desk.

'You press a button. Now what? Hold my hand!' Mr Smith cried urgently, in a voice of ripping calico.

The door opened, and two men entered the tiny office.

'May I present Detective Inspector Pewter of the Special Branch, Scotland Yard and Lootenant Burruff of the CIA, from the US Embassy in London operating on behalf of the FBI,' said Mr Goatley, now businesslike.

'FBI?' asked the Old Man. 'Isn't that—?'

'It is,' replied Mr Smith curtly.

'We have here an international arrest warrant issued by Interpol,' said Pewter. 'You are to be handcuffed and sent back to face trial in Washington DC in the next available aeroplane.'

'Although I guess you know the charges, I will proceed to read them to you,' added the man from the Embassy. 'I guess you know you have rights, but I have to warn you that anything you say may be used in evidence.'

'Just a moment, before you subject us to the anguish of your official rigmaroles, tell us: are we being arrested by the British or the American authorities?' asked Mr Smith.

'Technically you are being arrested by the British authorities at the request of the American authorities,' replied the British detective. 'You will be sent back on an American airline. The moment you set foot aboard it, you become the responsibility of the US authority. Until such time, you are under our jurisdiction.'

'The charges are all American, and yet you apply them. Are you already so subservient?'

'That's the way Interpol works,' said Pewter. 'There is a warrant for your arrest in most developed countries. In the same way a British criminal can be apprehended within the United States.'

'And that does not preclude some British charges being added to the American ones already extant,' Mr Goatley stated. 'Falsification of documents, for instance, falsification of tickets, theft of luggage. And there will no doubt be others.'

'Let me get this straight, in language I can live with,' cried Mr Smith in gale-force voice. 'We are being sent back in custody to face the original charge of forgery?'

'Forgery for the other gentleman, just complicity for you,' said the CIA man.

'Aren't you going to put us on our honour not to vanish?' shouted Mr Smith, whipping himself into a frenzy.

'I'm coming to that,' the CIA man shouted back, leaning on the documents on the desk as the wind threatened to carry them away.

'Too late!' yelled Mr Smith, gripping the Old Man by the hand as the tempest swirled round the confined space, knocking the calendar on the wall and the coloured picture of the monarch sideways. All the documents that were unrestrained began taking flight like autumn leaves. It seemed to Mr Goatley that there were elemental forces pummelling his eyelids, and it was suddenly hard to breathe. At the height of this new situation, true to his training, the man from the CIA began shouting the charges incomprehensibly and at length.

The tape recorder burst into flames, as did all the electrical fittings in the room. Smoke began rising from the two passports, as well as from the desk. The case with the tennis racquets began crackling and popping.

The storm vanished abruptly, and with it Mr Smith and the Old Man.

'There goes the evidence,' said Mr Rahman, struggling with an extinguisher.

'Plus our clients,' added Mr Burruff, throwing down the indictment in disgust.

'It's really most irregular,' grumbled Mr Goatley, 'and just as we were getting to the culminating point—'

'I suppose I'd better warn the airline it's no go,' said Mr Rahman.

'I tell you one thing. I'd rather this sort of thing happened on the ground than in the air,' Mr Goatley added, his composure already halfway recovered.

13

It was a morning of exceptionally fine weather, a morning of beatitude, as close to perfect as possible. By mutual agreement, and by the means of communication at their disposal, they landed and materialized on undulent ground in the vicinity of Sunningdale.

'What a morning!' said the Old Man, exultant. 'This is the blueprint of my Creation, faithfully carried out. The world as I envisaged it before the elements began taking liberties with it, and claiming always greater autonomy.' He breathed deeply and seemed to shed the centuries as his eyes glittered with sheer pleasure.

'I admit it has its points, however unkindly I take to sunlight,' grumbled Mr Smith. 'Where are we going from here?'

'We're in no hurry, are we?' The Old Man hoped his good humour would be contagious.

'No, but I have better things to do than make my chronic cough worse by taking deep breaths. I like shade, and walls, and fire-places.'

'How can you say that when we find a little corner of paradise like this, all the more astonishing because it is situated in a largely built-up area? Houses everywhere, and yet here, what one would have considered the best land around, covered in luscious grass, cultivated, but totally unexploited.'

'It looks phoney to me.'

'Looks what?'

'Artificial. It doesn't look real. And that little pond over there – I bet it's man-made.'

'No, no. I, at least, should know nature when I find it.'

Just then, four people appeared in the middle distance in two small, silent vehicles. They were just visible as they began to busy themselves with some kind of obscure activity on the crest of a hill, among some trees.

'What are they up to?' asked Mr Smith nervously.

'Who?'

'Over there.'

The Old Man had not noticed the newcomers. 'Oh, I shouldn't worry,' he said, and went on, 'It would be completely unnatural not to see a few people out and about in weather like this. It must be so rare.'

'They are studying the ground. Could it be the beginning of a manhunt?'

'Please don't start developing complexes, whatever you do,' said the Old Man, almost sternly. 'You've done nothing to be ashamed of, and—'

'You know we're both hunted men. The planet's closing in on us. Everywhere I look I seem to see secret agents,' cried Mr Smith, half under his breath. 'Why are those people staring at the ground with such intensity?'

'They're probably planting something.'

'Or is it a clue they've found?'

'We haven't been up there, so that if it is a clue it's nothing to do with us. It's the wrong clue.'

'Even if it's a wrong clue, it's going to lead them to us. You mark my words.'

Just then one of the men shouted something in their direction and waved his arms.

'What did I tell you?' gasped Mr Smith, hoarsely.

'Don't lose your head,' said the Old Man. 'We are going to Moscow, in easy stages. I suggest we fly visibly, to conserve our energy—'

'Fly visibly?' questioned Mr Smith, as though the Old Man had taken leave of his senses.

'If we fly at a reasonable height, we can not only enjoy the splendid weather and the glorious landscapes, but also conserve vital strength.'

'We will occasion every air force in the world to take off!' cried Mr Smith.

'You know as well as I do, we can always become invisible if the occasion demands it.'

'So long as we do it in time,' murmured Mr Smith – then suddenly screamed, 'Look out!'

The Old Man spun round in time to see a small white ball spinning in his direction, seeming to hang back a little in the air as though too light to obey the exigencies of gravity. He caught it by stretching out his hand.

'What were they aiming at? Us?' he asked, mystified.

'There's a hole a little way behind you, with a flag in it.'

'Surely they didn't think we were trying to make off with their flag?'

'I don't know, but it just goes to show how easily one can be taken by surprise. Fall into a trap. I don't like it. It's an omen.'

'I wouldn't have felt anything even if it had hit me,' the Old Man replied stubbornly.

'A small ball, perhaps not, but a fighter aircraft?'

The Old Man cheerfully lobbed the ball back, but misjudged the distance, and it plummeted into the pond. The distant men let out a joint howl which could be heard clearly, and began running towards the immortals, waving what looked like spears.

'Let's take off,' cried the Old Man urgently.

'I know what it is. A game called golf.'

'I'll take your word for it. This is no time to learn the rules.'

'The pond is artificial,' Mr Smith spat out.

'D'you want a bet?'

They took off in perfect formation, and began rising slowly in the general direction of the Channel. The golfers stopped in their tracks, speechless at the sight of two elderly men, one of them apparently wearing a nightgown, rising gently over the trees, their arms out-stretched like wings. It so happened that the golfers were old group captains from the Royal Air Force, enjoying retirement in bungalows near Sunningdale, and their astonishment was somewhat mitigated by their appreciation of the finer points of the take-off.

'Must be shooting a film around here,' one of them remarked.

'That doesn't explain why the old boy in white lost my bloody ball for me,' said the other. Then he made a fresh start. 'Let's say we're the only ones to have seen them. Don't you think somebody on active service should know about them?'

'What's on your mind, Stanley?'

'We'll have to start the game afresh anyhow, won't we? I'm going back to the clubhouse to phone someone in charge.'

As they walked up the slope to rejoin the electric cars and the caddies, the one who had spoken first suddenly said, 'You don't think they could be witches on the way to Stonehenge, do you?'

'They need broomsticks, don't they? Those folks had no visible means of propulsion.'

Actually the two tiny but persistent dots had already been picked up on the radar screens of Heathrow Airport, before the group captains were able to raise the alarm. The reports said that two small private planes were flying dangerously close to one another at very low altitude, without permission. No radio requests for identification had been answered.

As the two of them approached the coast, the wonderful silence of the skies was invaded by a noise like that of a huge flight of migrating insects. Mr Smith, his face pushed into spongy shapes by the resisting wind, looked around him with difficulty, and saw nothing. The Old Man, much more relaxed, and enjoying his high place as usual, suddenly glanced up and saw a slow-moving aeroplane above them. A door opened and a man fell out, quickly succeeded by several others. They held hands, and formed a pattern like a stylized snowflake.

The Old Man veered off to the left to avoid the men who were falling like a tent in their direction. Mr Smith, alarmed, noticed the Old Man looking upwards as he performed his manoeuvre, glanced up himself, and immediately followed suit. The living snowflake passed within feet of them, and the Old Man waved at the newcomers in friendly fashion, but the sight of the two old gentlemen, not falling like any self-respecting mortals but proceeding in a southerly direction without any visible means of propulsion, quite spoiled the jump.

Down on the ground, their appearance during a routine practice of a new and extraordinary form of aeronautic art created its own consternation. At first the experts thought a couple of parachutists had become disgracefully detached from the main body, but when the snowflake formed perfectly it became clear that there were other temporary occupants of the air space. The cumbersome aircraft even tried to track the unwanted observers over the Channel, but it was recalled.

The British authorities co-ordinated their information with exemplary efficiency, and attempted to warn the French, but the latter were working to rule at that moment, as part of a synchronized strike action of their flight controllers against the government. The one man who was on duty thought that the information about two airborne men of advanced age seen heading for Calais at eight hundred feet, and both wanted for questioning by Interpol, so fanciful as to be either an elaborate joke or else symptoms of a nervous breakdown in the sender.

Nevertheless, addicts of Unidentified Flying Objects began to spot the old couple, and reports flooded in from all along their chosen path of what were assumed to be extra-terrestrials who had advanced to a point of no longer needing flying saucers for their journeys.

The couple overflew Paris, which sparkled majestically in the sunlight. So enticing did it appear, the fountains of the Place de la Concorde seeming to send showers of diamonds into the air, that Mr Smith slowed down with the intention of landing, but the Old Man prevented this with an imperiously negative gesture of his head, pointing upwards at the same time. Mr Smith looked up and saw airliners buzzing like hornets over their nest, all at different levels but looking distinctly menacing. They were all in a holding pattern, awaiting the whims of the control towers.

The Old Man veered off gracefully in an easterly direction, but Mr Smith was reluctant to follow. The temptation of the City of Lights, the reputation of which for the recumbency of its *grandes cocottes* was only a recent memory in terms of eternity, suddenly overwhelmed him. After all, he was in need of a stimulus for the dying embers of his enthusiasm. He prepared to land despite the peremptory gestures of the Old Man, who was in a holding pattern himself a kilometre away, waiting to be obeyed.

Suddenly Mr Smith felt a gale-force wind beneath him, accompanied by the sound of something beating his eardrums as though they were carpets. He glanced down and saw to his horror the rotors of a helicopter rising in his direction. He was just in time to avoid the blades. The helicopter contained two men and the letters on its side proclaimed it to be the property of the police. The pilot and observer made unmistakable gestures ordering Mr Smith to land. Mr Smith wanted nothing better, but not under these circumstances. The police even opened a glass panel to shout inaudible instructions. They rose higher and a rope-ladder came snaking out of their door.

Mr Smith rose himself, made an internationally recognized and rude gesture of rejection, and accelerated away to rejoin the Old Man, who shook his head wearily to greet the prodigal's return. Together they accelerated towards the Rhine, leaving the helicopter and its dangling ladder, as well as Paris, far behind.

At one point, the Old Man pointed south, where the Alps shone in the sunlight, like whipped cream on a distant array of pastries. Mr Smith mimed shivering with cold, and the Old Man smiled and nodded.

They crossed the border into Germany and flew over dense vineyards and romantic castles. The Old Man altered course slightly in a north-easterly direction. The land became flatter, but the greenery was interspersed with frequent forests and occasional broad roads like toothpaste squeezed out of a steadily held tube, a-glint with vehicles travelling at astonishing speed. Soon the roads became narrower and the cars slower. They reduced height to overfly Berlin. The *Fedächnisskirche* stared up at them like a rotten tooth, its gaping cavity filled with gunmetal. And over there, unexpected crowds, sitting on a wall, carousing and singing songs. The Old Man made urgent gestures for Mr Smith to join him. Together they cautiously approached the scene, even the Old Man having succumbed to his curiosity.

The wall was covered in coloured writing and pictures of the kind sometimes produced to demonstrate the unconscious genius of lunatics. It was art of a kind which seemed to suit the state of the picnickers who lay about on the wall and around it, paper cups and bottles everywhere, men stripped to the waist, but often wearing hats and braces, all of them singing with a dreary discordant insistence.

'How odd,' cried the Old Man into Mr Smith's ears as they hovered overhead. 'I had always heard that the Germans are such tidy people.'

Mr Smith dug his nose into the white curls of the Old Man's head in an effort to find the reciprocal ear. 'These are not tidy times,' he croaked.

Just then, somebody noticed the couple in the sky. A cry of astonishment went up, and before it had settled back into a buzz of excitement, several people had fallen, or been pushed, off the wall.

'Come on,' cried the Old Man. 'Gain height. This is the last attention we need!'

'It's your own damned fault,' yelled Mr Smith. 'If you have to come down, at least choose Paris.'

They flew at the usual height until the open countryside was reached once more. They were not on speaking terms, and each seemed unconscious of the other's presence, that is until the Old Man became aware of a disturbance on the horizon. He quite failed to recognize what the distant agitation implied, until a slight change in angle caused the sunlight to bounce off the sides of a squadron of fighter planes in a sudden blinding flash.

The Old Man held his hand out urgently, and agitated it. At the same time, he lost height dramatically.

Mr Smith cursed. 'Make up your mind,' he shouted, and lost height himself, converging on the Old Man.

As they joined hands, the aircraft broke the sound barrier in a series of ear-splitting explosions, and began to leave vapour trails.

'What did I tell you?' yelled Mr Smith.

'Invisible,' cried the Old Man, grasping Mr Smith's hand.

They both disappeared from sight, and from the radar screens.

A few moments later, they materialized in the ample gardens of the Kremlin, resplendent during one of the subtle seasons the country seems able to create, April showers in midsummer, floods of impatient snow long before the end of autumn. Now the sun was dazzling, bouncing off the golden domes against a hostile slate-grey sky, with a couple of ephemeral rainbows straddling each other in the humid haze over the Moscow river. Streams of tourists, many of them from within the Soviet Union, passed in glum profusion, the women dressed mainly in garish flower prints and the men in Sunday best with caps. Some of the elderly of both sexes wore medals or emblems of some kind, either merited or at least giving that impression. It seemed as though the trip was a reward for longevity at very least.

There were foreign groups too, of course. A woman without much voice stood shouting in peculiar Italian near the great cracked bell, while the tourists, having given up on understanding, looked around for themselves and reached their own conclusions.

Some Japanese bobbed and bowed with an astounding display of deference, muttering excuses and verbal filigree while squeezing the last ounce of sweetness out of their faces. When momentarily at a loss, they took photographs of each other. The Old Man had never seen anything like it before, and was hypnotized by this behaviour.

'Did I create all that as well?' he asked.

'You created what led to that,' said Mr Smith. 'There has been an evolution.'

'Where are they from?'

'Japan.'

'We must go there.'

'Very well, but not now.'

'They seem to have sublimated all their hostility, all their complexes, with the most exquisite, and, I must say, tiresome politeness. I could watch them for hours, and build up a most unusual kind of irritation.'

'No visit to this planet is complete without taking in Japan, or without visiting some of the richest of all mortals who live in imposed poverty, enjoying the denial of the immense power at their disposal.'

'That is sophistication indeed.'

'As for all aggression being sublimated into politeness, it was not always so. They used to forget to be polite at times, such as in their attack on Pearl Harbor.'

'On who?'

'No, it was not a defenceless maiden, but a naval base. Listen, we are here for quite another purpose, and that is to seek out the First Secretary of the Communist Party of the Soviet Union.'

'Oh.'

'If we continue to talk about Japan, it will only confuse you.'

'Yes, you may be right. One last look though. Please.'

'Oh, very well.'

While the Old Man took a last lingering look at the Japanese, Mr Smith tried to assess where to go in order to find the First Secretary.

'Amazing.' The Old Man had rejoined him. 'Tell me what to expect,' he said. 'Naturally I know about Russia, the revolution, the murder of the Tsar's family, famine, attempts on the life of Lenin, rise of Stalin, war, and from then on I'm rather lost. Peace, I suppose. Oh yes, and a man in a capsule circling the Earth. I remember that clearly. It was the first time it happened, and it gave me quite a shock. Now, of course, it has become a nuisance I have to put up with. These machines cross my line of vision with the regularity of saints on a cathedral clock. Some of them I have seen, weightless on the end of bits of string, doing callisthenics like great sad fish in an aquarium. But I distinctly remember the first one, because it was small, and the writing on it was in the Cyrillic alphabet.'

'The first one was actually American, but there was no one inside it.'

'Ah, I probably took that one to be a meteorite, or any of the zillions of particles which constitute a permanent rush hour up there in outer space.'

They were by now crossing some of the halls of the Kremlin itself, having found most of the doors unlocked and the halls themselves empty.

'I say, these murals are simply exquisite, but the arches are so low.'

'That was to encourage a servile attitude in those who entered the rooms, not least of them foreign ambassadors.'

'Extraordinary the weight accorded simple symbolism of that sort by some peoples throughout history. Even if they were incapable of inspiring awe by legitimate means, they went through the motions architecturally. I mean, dictators affect balconies, high places. Some rulers sit at huge desks, in comfortable chairs, forcing those that visit them to walk a great distance towards them, to sit eventually in a lower, less pleasant seat. Here they force even the unwilling to bow.'

'How strange you notice that, and not some of the salient facts of recent history.'

'I notice most of mankind's psychological quirks. They interest me. They are typical of what I created. Left on their own, men have exhausted every possibility of bamboozling each other with the means at their disposal – apart from war, of course. War is dull, to all those except the leaders. Those take the credit if successful. The men take the risks, and the blame if unsuccessful. War is not only tragic but simple-minded and, usually, sadly predictable. On the other hand, every way in which men attempt to get their way short of war is absolutely fascinating. As for recent history, it all moves too fast for me. Not so long ago, ambitious fools were still throwing themselves off church spires, convinced that they could fly. Today they do their languorous callisthenics in my eyelines. When, and where, will it end?'

'Before it ends, they will have conceived an existence without us. They already have in many parts of the world. Oh, they still pay you lip service, and pretend to fear me, but they accept society as being permissive out of office hours and rigidly obedient to the laws of science at other times. Neither of us plays any part in their existence any more. We had foreseen every possibility short of neglect. The ingratitude inherent in neglect is almost too much to bear.'

There was a break in the reverie while they bowed low to enter a room so dazzling in its lavish use of gold that they were forced to narrow their eyes to become accustomed to the light.

'It used not to be like that,' said the Old Man glumly. 'Look at all those images of me, such a profusion of haloes, such an overstatement of devotion. And where are you in all this?' he added, his sense of mischief returning.

'I have always inhabited the heart and groin – a dual appeal to the senses. I have no need for this kind of publicity,' said Mr Smith, disdainfully indicating the golden walls. 'The only times I have ever used a halo is as a subterfuge. Compared to you, my overheads are virtually non-existent.'

'Yes,' admitted the Old Man, 'your words have made me feel strangely old-fashioned and cumbersome. But it stands to reason, in a way. Immortality does not mean eternal youth. An immortal ages like everything else. The freshness of the beginnings cannot be maintained. I am old.'

There was no reply to this, which at first puzzled, and finally irritated the Old Man.

'You don't react?'

'I agree with you. I reacted.'

They made their way through other doors in silence. The rooms were modern, dating from the early nineteenth century. In one of them there was a man seated at a desk, but he was asleep. There were trays on his desk, overflowing with yellowing paper. They went through the room quietly, without waking him up.

The corridors were now suddenly full of people, but they appeared absolutely self-contained and uninquisitive. They seemed to walk along precise preordained trajectories, their eyes lowered, their expression non-committal.

'This must be the working part of the building,' said Mr Smith, and passers-by looked up in surprise that someone had spoken, then resumed their somnambulations. At the end of the next corridor there was a door. A red carpet led up to it. It was perhaps a little more ornate than some of the others. It had a stucco emblem above it, and a soldier before it, who was surreptitiously smoking a cigarette in the time-honoured way of the military, by holding it inwards into a cupped hand and going through mild contortions to take a drag. On the wall, fixed there by a drawing pin, was a peremptory notice not to smoke, and, as if that were not sufficient warning, a cigarette depicted in a black circle with a red bar across it.

Mr Smith pointed at the door. The soldier practically choked on the smoke in his lungs, and, beating his chest with his available fist, blurted out that it was in fact the door to the office of the 'Party Secretary'.

Mr Smith nodded, suggesting he wanted permission to proceed. The soldier coughed on, and brushed away the mute request. Mr Smith entered without knocking, followed by the Old Man.

The First Secretary, a pleasant-looking man of stocky build, dressed soberly in navy blue with a large badge representing an unfurled red flag in enamel on his lapel, sat at his desk signing a mountain of documents.

'I'll be with you in a minute,' he said in colloquial Russian, without looking up.

Mr Smith and the Old Man stood deferentially before the desk. The First Secretary added his signature to the last document with a flourish, and looked up, smiling genially. His smile lost some of its intensity when he took in the appearance of his visitors.

'Who are you?' he asked.

The Old Man could hardly believe his ears. 'You want to know who we are?' he enquired.

'Have I not that right, in my own office?'

'Of course, of course. It's just that we were in Washington – at the White . . . White House . . . with the President. He wasn't in the least interested in who we were, but only how we got in.'

'Ah, they are very security-minded over there. Here, we are pursuing a policy of openness, and the Kremlin is today full of people who could well have no right to be here at all, but after many centuries of hermetic secrecy, it is a pleasant and necessary change, like airing bed linen. Still, we must not forget that this is Russia, a country of obstinate traditions. In the light of this, it may well be much more difficult to get out than to get in, and I will therefore prepare you documents to guarantee you safe conduct.'

'Yourself? You will prepare these documents yourself?' asked Mr Smith, incredulous.

'Why not? I am sick of those who consider certain tasks beneath their dignity. In a land of fraternal ambitions, everyone must be prepared to do anything, so long as it is useful. Now, to prepare such *laissez-passers*, I will need to know who you are.'

'This is where the difficulties begin,' said the Old Man.

'Why?'

'Because what I have to tell strains the credulity. At least, that is what our experiences have led me to believe.'

The First Secretary smiled. 'Who could you possibly be to provoke such reactions? You are not Anastasia by any chance? The Tsar's daughter? And the beard is merely a clumsy disguise?'

The Old Man gazed at the First Secretary with all the repose, all the serenity he could muster.

'I am God,' he said.

The First Secretary's eyes narrowed for a moment, then he broke out in soft, infectious laughter.

'What a joke if it were true,' he said, and added quietly, 'We have been waiting long enough it seems to me. We were very rude to God after centuries of devotion which was probably too fervent, too irrational. A godless society was the consequence. Oh, it was never really aimed at God, but against the hierarchy of the priesthood. And it led nowhere, it was purely negative. Now we are once again bringing the ikons out of their hiding places. My parents were devout. I, frankly, am not. But I see the utility of belief, if only of belief in oneself. And who knows, perhaps in the final analysis belief in God and belief in oneself are one and the same, without one even noticing it. Unfortunately, I have no time now to investigate the truth of your claim, but one fact is evident to the naked eye. You are both old.' He made an expansive gesture. 'Sit. Rest!'

Both Mr Smith and the Old Man sat down obediently, slightly mystified by the First Secretary's manner, which seemed both frank and direct, while never seeming quite free from a glozing of astuteness.

'First of all,' declared the First Secretary, 'I will write you out your documents. Don't lose them! Everybody in the Soviet Union has to have documents. This was true throughout history, even under Ivan the Terrible, when hardly anyone could read. Pretending to read documents was one of the great activities of the period. Especially before other people who couldn't read. It gave a man status, and was one of the first of the Russian self-deceptions which have poisoned our heritage.' He began writing the document. 'What can I call you? I can't call you God. It would seem pretentious in any case. Boguslavsky.' (The Russian word for God being *bog*.) 'Sviatoslav Ivanovitch. And you, sir? I have no need to ask who you are. Your very appearance proclaims your identity.'

'Really?' asked Mr Smith, surprised. 'People in general, while not believing that either of us is genuine, based their disbelief on the presumption that God would never allow himself to be seen in the company of Satan.'

The First Secretary laughed agreeably. 'May I draw your attention to the old Russian proverb, "Praise God, but do not neglect the Devil?" I think we have always seen in them some sort of friendly competition for our souls. We find it difficult to separate them. And, in fact, when God fell into disfavour, nobody even mentioned the Devil, in order not to give him an unfair advantage. At all events, we had Stalin. What did we need with the Devil? Saving your presence, of course.'

'Stalin had nothing to do with me,' said Mr Smith hotly. 'He was a kind of pragmatic maniac who regarded those around him as though they were flies on a tablecloth, ready to be swotted at any time. In order to lead people into temptation, I must have a higher regard for them than that!'

The First Secretary grinned. 'You know, I am beginning to believe you. Curious how it seems easier to believe in the Devil than in God.'

'Oh, that has always been the case.' The Old Man waved it aside. 'The Devil has for ever appeared to cater for immediate human needs much more than God, who is by the nature of things more abstract, more indefinable. It's my own silly fault if that is so. That is the way I arranged it, and I can see this fact faithfully reflected in the difference between our characters.'

'Now, Comrade Boguslavsky, I need your help. What shall we call your colleague?'

'Chortidze . . . Chortinian . . . Chortmatov . . .' suggested the Old Man (*chort* being the Russian word for Devil).

'I would prefer to avoid all racial allusions at this time. No, keep it Russian-sounding, then all the others can sound off at it. And where shall we say you come from? The Chirvino-Paparak Autonomous Region, perhaps. Good idea.' And the First Secretary wrote, mouthing the words silently, so as to make no mistake.

'Does such an autonomous region exist?' asked the Old Man.

'Of course not,' replied the First Secretary, 'but our country is so vast that it may as well exist, in Central Asia, of course. Where they wear the kind of clothes you have on. Made by themselves from ancient looms. All apart from your T-shirt, Comrade Chortkov, which was given you by the United States Cultural Attaché, eager to make contacts in your region, for reasons it is no longer fashionable to invoke.'

'And what will we do with these documents?' asked Mr Smith, as he took delivery of his, and passed the other to the Old Man.

'Present them whenever challenged. The fact that I have signed them brings with it not only advantages. I am both very popular and very unpopular by turns, depending on the region and the kind of events which take place at any given time. You see, throughout history we have been a closed society, which in itself is a permanent vote of no confidence in the capacity of people to think for themselves. Illiteracy was both complained about in public and secretly encouraged. Apart from some intellectuals and a few enlightened landlords, no one saw any virtue in the peasant except for muscle. Then came the revolution. Dawn broke for the masses. They believed for one giddy moment that their time had come – and in a way, it had. The most important of its victories was that over illiteracy. Even if all could not yet understand, at least almost all could read. But apart from these brief few years of enlightenment, Stalin supplanted the Tsars with an autocracy both more ruthless and even far less flattering to the public intelligence. Now, after centuries of hibernation, we have dared to awaken the people. Wake up! we have exhorted them. Have opinions, dare to think, to act! Our troubles arise from the fact that many of them are not yet able to do so. You know how difficult it sometimes is to wake up after a single night in midwinter. Think of it, they have slept for ten centuries, more. They are grumpy, still clinging to the idea of sleep although now irrevocably awake, turning over in bed for one brief rediscovery of oblivion. We are passing through these waking moments at this time.'

'What single fact has driven you to try such a dangerous experiment?' asked the Old Man, fascinated.

'The theorists of revolution always referred to a class war, the toiling masses, a conflict of huge anonymities. But if you reflect, the individual is at all times more important than the mass, for what is the mass but millions of individuals who have, for the purpose of political theory, lost their personality? Yet, every idea, good or bad, every invention, constructive or destructive, has emanated from a single mind as surely as an embryo can only be brought to birth in a single womb. Ideas and inventions can be adapted, ruined, even improved by committees, but they can only be the brainchildren of the individual. And it is the individual, manifesting himself or herself by some unique or distinguishing marks, which sets the standards for those other individuals who seem to constitute the masses. Why are we undertaking these fundamental changes in our society? Because we have rediscovered the individual.'

'That is nothing new to us, of course,' said Mr Smith. 'We have only dealt in individuals from the beginning. It is very difficult to lead the masses into temptation. For that I need the help of some particularly quiescent dictator who does my wishes obediently and without question while seeming to dominate his followers. But my most exquisite successes have all been with individuals.'

'Mine also!' warned the Old Man. 'And with me there are absolutely no cases on record of collective virtue. Not one. Virtue is far too personal a commodity to be shared among groups or sects, let alone masses. But let me say that if you have, as you say, rediscovered the individual, that is the automatic reason why you no longer find it necessary to persecute the Church.'

'Correct,' smiled the First Secretary. 'I will go further and say that I speak to you as though you were God. I have no idea whether you are or not, and frankly, I don't consider my opinions on the matter important. As someone brought up in this society, I am automatically sceptical about such a possibility. But, once I treat you with the respect that I owe to another individual, it seems to make normal conversation a possibility.'

The Old Man was amused by the proletarian openness of the First Secretary's approach. 'You are in luck,' he said, 'since I am in a mood to underplay celestial privilege, and address men on terms of equality. But to revert to your discovery, or was it rediscovery of the individual? How did you ever lose this understanding, if you did lose it?'

'Do you know what winter is?' asked the First Secretary slowly. 'I don't mean sleighbells, hot grog, Father Christmas – I mean the deep winter of the soul. Dark skies, dark thoughts, the overdose of vodka, anything to keep the spirit alive. In January, in February, there is no difference between our Russia or that of Stalin or that of Boris Godunov. It is in the spring you see the difference. We had given in to the winter all year round. Now we encourage ourselves to be infected by the spring. But how can you ask such questions? Have there not been long periods in which those responsible for orthodoxy have not frowned on individual reactions to even simple things, seeing in them the machinations of the Devil?'

Mr Smith nodded with a deep satisfaction. 'There were times in which I needed to make no effort. They saw me all over the place, especially there where I wasn't. But don't let me interrupt you. You are giving me too much pleasure,' he said.

'The Inquisition, the excesses of the missionaries, even today, fundamentalism and the kind of thoughtless obtuseness it engenders, the burning of books and people, the witch hunt of the individual as traitor to as rigid and awful a truth as ever enslaved mankind. And you can express surprise that we succumbed once, but for a long time, where you succumbed so frequently and so variously?'

'There is, of course, truth in what you say,' admitted the Old Man gravely. 'Liberty is an essential part of belief. Belief is worth nothing if it is compulsory. It is only of value if it is the result of choice, the outcome of predilection.'

'That is true of the kind of belief which I inspire also,' said Mr Smith, with the dignity of a negotiator.

The First Secretary nodded with a sort of pragmatic satisfaction. 'May I say that God and the Devil approve of the principles of coexistence?'

'My dear boy,' replied the Old Man, 'Satan and I invented coexistence long before you ever coined the phrase. We had to. The alternative would have been disaster.'

'It is very flattering for us if we feel we have been inspired by as high authorities as you. And now, my friends, I have to go to address our new parliament on the question of economic reform. As the delegates of the autonomous region of Chirvino-Paparak, population two, you are very welcome. Come in with me, and sit where you can find a place. I hope your eyes will be opened to the great changes we are undergoing.'

'I must warn you, however, that we know very little about economics,' said the Old Man, rising.

'In that case, you will be in very good company,' laughed the First Secretary.

'Speak for yourself,' snapped Mr Smith. 'I spend a lot of my time dabbling in the market. It is the area in modern society most prone to my influence.'

'I can believe that,' remarked the First Secretary as they walked down the corridor. 'The Americans spread the rumour that we are bankrupt, and that Marxism is incompatible with a free market. There is a grain of truth in this. But any system can be made to work if it allows personal initiative. We wish to see whether it is possible to create a society in which pride is satisfied without greed being encouraged, or indeed rewarded. Is it possible to instil a certain morality into a society without insisting on it? What we have done up to now is to enforce rules which made our state inefficient, and the more inefficient it became, the more we trumpeted our success. What success? Merely success in enforcing such idiotic rules. Now all this must change. Every citizen should work for himself, on condition it is for the general good.'

'You are asking for the impossible,' Mr Smith remarked.

'But I will be delighted with the possible,' said the First Secretary.

'Ah, there you are!' cried a young man, coming in the other direction. 'They are growing impatient. There is a slow handclap in progress. They're like schoolchildren banging their spoons against their plates.'

'Good description,' grunted the First Secretary, walking faster. 'But, frankly, that is what we are trying to encourage, precisely what normal politicians try to avoid: dissatisfaction, impatience, protest. Anyone who causes a disruption is to be congratulated – for the time being. Later? Who knows for how long our patience will last?'

They came round the corner to find two men fighting. One was streaming with blood. They fell to the floor. Both were quite formally dressed.

The young man who had come to fetch the First Secretary spoke to them. 'Make way for the First Secretary, please, comrades. Differences should be settled in a democratic manner, by conversation.'

'We ran out of conversation,' said one of them, panting.

'When you still had a conversation, what was it about?' asked the First Secretary.

After a pause, the bloodier of the two replied, 'I can no longer remember.'

The First Secretary smiled, and looked at them both penetratingly. 'Are you both from the same part of the world?'

'He's from Azerbaijan,' said the bloody one.

'And he's from Armenia,' said the other.

'Ah well, then it's a miracle you had a conversation at all. I'm very relieved you took your differences out on each other. You could so easily have laid an ambush in these narrow corridors and leaped on me.'

He waited to let this piece of schoolmasterly tolerance sink in, then added, 'Do you both work here?'

'We are delegates, comrade.'

'Oh, then you have plenty of time to fight during office hours. It's a pity to waste all your energies where no audience could possibly be accommodated. Come with me. Have you a handkerchief, comrade? No? Take mine please. If you go into the Congress covered in blood, some Western media man is bound to start spreading rumours, and I detest rumours, more especially when they are true.'

As they walked towards the auditorium, the First Secretary spoke softly to the Old Man.

'I am really not qualified, as an atheist, to separate ethnic agitators. Sometimes ethnic is a convenient misnomer. You see, one is Christian, the other a Muslim. Their Communism was never more than skin deep. It takes you to keep them apart.'

'Or bring them together?' said the Old Man.

'You're an optimist then, like me?'

'In that I know from experience what a sad, wasteful, stupid and contradictory place the world can be, yes, I'm an optimist.'

'What does a pessimist know?'

'Nothing. He finds out the deceptions anew every morning.'

Mr Smith felt it was time to intervene. 'At the risk of displeasing both of you, I am an optimist too. I live in the hope that this will get even worse, and I let all that you dislike be my inspiration.'

The Old Man sighed deeply. 'I hope optimism is not all we have in common,' he said.

14

The First Secretary began his declaration, and was frequently interrupted. The Old Man and Mr Smith sat right at the back of the huge
auditorium, and huddled together behind the sea of humanity which
stretched before them, down to the long, curved desks facing them, at
which the high officials sat.

'We're in a trap,' whispered Mr Smith.

'Why?' whispered the Old Man, surprised.

'You'll see. We'll be called on to speak. Can't you see us now? The
two of us coming back to Earth on tiptoe, as it were, both incognito
and hoping for a kind of intimate recognition by selected people, now
called upon to address the Soviet parliament on the subject of the
economic difficulties of the Chirvino-Paparak Autonomous Region,
which doesn't even exist? It's just like the First Secretary, as I already
feel I know him, to take such an initiative in order to alleviate the heat
of real problems.'

'If that should happen, you'll speak first, of course.'

'Why should I?'

'Oh,' replied the Old Man, his mouth twitching with mischief, 'you
know far more about the region than I do. You have every fact and
figure at your fingertips. It's the sort of situation you cherish.'

Mr Smith grinned with satisfaction at the accuracy of the Old Man's
assessment, and they settled momentarily to follow the debate.

An elderly General was extolling the virtues of a one-party system.
'Where would the Army be if every man-jack followed his own
inclinations instead of obeying orders?' he asked.

'To the devil with the Army. The boys would be home with their
parents or sweethearts, where they belong!' cried a woman deputy,
covered in medals.

'Why do you invoke the Army? We are not the Army! We are freely elected delegates!' cried a thin man with a beard and pince-nez, who looked, perhaps deliberately, not unlike Trotsky.

'The heroic dead of the revolution would rise up in horror if they knew that the one-party system of workers and peasants has been betrayed,' cried another elderly military man, so liberally sprinkled with orders that there was a fierce tinkling every time he breathed or gestured.

After that, arguments for both sides began to be heard simultaneously; heard, but of course, not understood.

The First Secretary hit the top of his desk repeatedly with a gavel, and the noise diminished slowly, then ground to a ragged halt.

He spoke with both a quiet energy and a discernible effort to keep the door open to as wide a range of opinions as possible. The delegates had inherited the discipline of the previous regime, and were not yet prey to the hardened arteries and conditioned reflexes of party politics, since opinion was nearly invariably personal, and not yet subject to loyalties other than that of coherency. Unlike scenes in other parliaments, there were no organized claques. It was too soon. There were even odd moments of silent reflection, during which nobody wished to talk.

But whereas in the past they had sat stony-faced, thinking other thoughts while the geriatric brigade of old Bolsheviks droned on, reading their own uninspired words with such hesitancy that they imbued even unadulterated boredom with a sense of insecurity, they now shifted in their seats or else expressed a frustrated eagerness to intervene.

One man of professorial appearance underscored the resemblance of this assembly to a school perilously close to a breakdown of authority when he released a model aeroplane made of folded paper from one of the back benches. It flew serenely over the gathering, even seeming to gain height mysteriously, until it veered sideways, corrected itself, and made a perfect landing in the lateral aisle, at the foot of the First Secretary's podium. At the beginning of its flight, it naturally attracted every attention, and successfully silenced the First Secretary. The delegates followed its graceful flight in silence. Then, as it landed, there was applause mixed with laughter.

The First Secretary smiled. After all, had not good nature won him every conflict up to now? 'Will the prankster please identify himself?' he said.

The professorial gentleman rose. 'I am no prankster, and I was never, even at school, reduced to such methods to attract attention to myself. My name is Professor Ivan Feofilactovitch Gruschkov.'

There was immediate and prolonged applause, in which the First Secretary dutifully joined.

'By profession I am a designer of aircraft, including the Grusch 21 and 24 fighter bombers, the Grusch 64 transport plane and the Grusch 77 supersonic prototype passenger plane.'

'You have no need to tell us,' cried the First Secretary. 'We know.'

'Well, now, you will perhaps agree, esteemed First Secretary, that it is not easy to attract your attention—'

'Especially when I am speaking myself!'

'An activity which you enjoy, and I don't blame you. It takes all sorts to make the world, and therefore, by definition, the Soviet Union. Well, I like speaking rather less, unless it is highly technical, with either students, or my peers. Which is part of the point I wish to make. There is a peculiarity in the Constitution of our mother country which, like so much that we have endured, looks logical enough on paper, although in practice it leaves much to be desired. Government, especially by a single party, honoured the best brains of the Soviet Union by elevating them to the status of politicians. In other countries, the best brains are left to their own devices, and politics are generally in the hands of people with few qualifications other than for the thrust and parry of political life, and by now, judging by the statistics of the proportion of votes to non-votes, these people are largely discredited. I am not sure that the situation in these countries would be any better if their best brains were dragooned into service in such congresses, and forced to waste their time at the expense of the taxpayer – because, dear comrade, the time of the best brains in any country is important. Here, not only are they forced to listen to a great deal of verbal histrionics, most of which is profoundly uninteresting, the result of rampant ambition and thought improperly analyzed, but at the same time they are denied the time which would be usefully spent at their test benches, their drawing-boards, or their offices, depending on their discipline. I came here today determined not to lose time by listening to arguments I neither understand nor respect, about subjects which are outside my competence. Consequently I constructed, out of order papers, a model of the Grusch 77A supersonic airliner with a revolutionary wing configuration, which will eventually employ amalgams new to aircraft construction. I am gratified to note that even a rough model made out of porous paper, unpleasant to the touch, reveals great qualities of stability and malleability, and that the landing, even on a carpet, was well-nigh perfect.'

His statement was met with a torrent of applause, delegates rising as though a milestone of some sort had been reached. Gradually they all, including the First Secretary, rose to their feet. Professor Gruschkov waited for a restoration of order. Then he waved at the assembly.

'It is not out of lack of respect that I am now going back to my factory. On the contrary, to be given a voice in the destiny of the mother country is most flattering. That is the trouble with it. Beware of honours which are heaped on the deserving. To be an expert in one field doesn't mean that one is therefore an expert in them all. I understand nothing about the subject of today's debate. Of what value is my voice? Of what value is my ear? I could also cover my heart in medals, comrades. I have many, but they are at home, in a drawer. I find they tear the linings of my suits. And I want to be known for what I can still offer today, not by a mosaic of what I managed to achieve in the past. And on that note I take my leave of you. Will you excuse me?'

Another outburst of applause greeted his departure, followed by six or seven delegates who decided to follow his example. The old military man struggled to his feet despite the weight of his garland of medals.

'If you have earned your medals, it is your solemn duty to wear them!' he screamed, until his protest was lost under the weight of unruly derision which began to swell, only to engender a reaction from all right-minded conservatives and medal wearers, who began clapping rhythmically.

The First Secretary banged his gavel, and, when a degree of order had been re-established, he spoke.

'There are many aspects of an administration which bear re-examination and re-appraisal. It is too soon for me to say whether I agree with Comrade Academician I. F. Gruschkov or not, but his manner of drawing our attention to his words was both highly original, as one would expect, and effective, which shows that, despite his protestations, he possesses considerable political skills.'

There was appreciative laughter, and a handclap or two. Many orators claimed the floor.

'Comrade Mehmedinov, I would willingly surrender the floor to you, but must warn you that if you insist on speaking in Uzbek, as you did the last time, you are defeating your own ends, since we all admit your right to your own language, but cannot admit a situation in this forum where the words of speeches in languages other than Russian cannot be generally understood,' the First Secretary declared.

Comrade Mehmedinov sat down again with a shrug, a tacit admission that he had been prepared to filibuster in Uzbek once again. There were calls and catcalls in practically every minority language of the Soviet Union.

'Of course, as the largest constituent unit of the Soviet Union, the Russian republic is open to all sorts of innuendo and banter from the smaller units. We bear these continual taunts with laudable humour, and even understanding—'

Cries of 'Speak for yourself' from the expected quarters.

'It is time we spoke of Russia again!' yelled the officer with the medals. 'The Soviet Union is Russia and nothing else!'

'Order! Order!' insisted the First Secretary. 'We are gathered here to discuss the economy, and the possible cures for the chaos in our bureaucracy, which has assumed the proportions of a national emergency. Despite – despite the urgency of the situation, we always become bogged down in this fruitless antagonism – antagonism between integral parts of our great federation, which for years have lived in a harmony which may well have been enforced – may well have been enforced, and was therefore never allowed to add to difficulties existing at the time.'

The First Secretary had trouble in restoring respect for the chair. His speech was often punctuated by outbursts and single words, shouted incoherently.

The Old Man nudged Mr Smith. 'If I'm not much mistaken . . .'

'Oh, nonsense.'

The First Secretary's eye swept the upper reaches of the auditorium as a searchlight spotting those on the run.

'Very well,' he said, 'if you insist on making my job impossible, which does not speak highly of your sense of the common interest, I will give the floor to none of those who have made it a habit to occupy it, as though it were a right accorded your quality of mind, but I will instead give the floor to one of those delegates from the remoter parts of our nation, the Chirvino-Paparak Autonomous Region.'

The First Secretary had a moment of misgiving when it was Mr Smith who rose instead of the Old Man, but he showed nothing on his face except subdued energy. The delegates turned to look at Mr Smith, and there was something about his appearance which commanded the attention.

'Comrades,' said Mr Smith, 'without further ado, I bring you the greetings of those of the Chirvino-Paparak Autonomous Region less privileged than we.'

There was the statutory applause here, and the Old Man looked appreciatively at Mr Smith.

'We have naturally followed the events of the democratization of the Soviet Union with great interest and a growing sense of responsibility. It would, of course, have been possible for us to address this honourable assembly in the language of the Chirvino or Paparak peoples. (I am a Chirvino, incidentally, who tend towards sallowness. My colleague here is a Paparak, who are plump and fair.) We have been most antagonistic towards each other historically, standing morally and politically for values which are diametrically opposed – which is why Stalin, in his infinite cynicism, lumped us together in our miserable homeland. Now, as I say, we could bore you further with our quarrels and do so in one or other or both of our native languages. We will not do so. We will speak in Russian.' (Applause.) 'It could be construed by virtue of our appearance here together that here is proof that people with very different traditions can live peaceably together' (Silence from most delegates from national minorities. Excessive applause from Russians, led ostentatiously by the First Secretary.) 'This is not the case.' (Thunderstruck silence from the Russians, who registered feelings of betrayal. Shouts of exaggerated stridency from the minorities.) 'The antagonism between the Chirvino and the Paparaks is as alive as ever, but we, believing in the necessity of coexistence not only between nations, but between peoples, have reached a sometimes awkward, but reasonable, accommodation. We not only tolerate each other, but even, at times, search each other out for company, for what you would call, in your vernacular, interdependence.' (The First Secretary, sensing a piece of unusual oratorical ability, applauded Mr Smith's train of thought. The Old Man, however, who knew Mr Smith better, noticed a subtle and disturbing shift in both matter and manner of delivery. The voice was becoming imperceptibly harsher, the coal-black eyes more febrile.)

'Now, what have we noticed about you from greener pastures? We, from the slate-grey steppe? You have begun your precipitous race from the mental prison in which you have been incarcerated for centuries towards the anarchy of your dreams.' (A worried stir among the listeners.) 'Yes, like it or not, the freedom set out in dreams is nothing but anarchy, the sudden lack of responsibility towards anything but the mood of the moment. The last stop on the road to anarchy is the platform of democracy. Will the train of thought have the brakes to stop there instead of plunging on into the abyss where logic counts for nothing, loyalty for nothing, devotion for nothing?

'What we see in this chamber is the struggle between anarchy and order, between brilliant improvisation and bovine subservience, between recklessness and discipline. I do not think you will have the strength of character as a body to know when to stop.' (Mingled protests and approval.) 'But why make it all so difficult for yourselves?'

The Old Man was alert as Mr Smith's voice changed to a trenchant and unmusical sound, his eyes darting hither and thither as though he were shedding his skin, like a snake, to reveal an identity which might be taken to be his true one.

'I can't help it,' he croaked in an aside. 'My true self is screaming for self-expression. Damn it, I'm not here to serve you or sweet reason! I am . . . myself!'

Those sensitive to ugly sounds winced, and with the final claim to being himself, one or two elderly delegates, their brows knitted, nervously crossed themselves in an imprecise and fugitive manner.

'You are so bleak!' cried Mr Smith, with a mocking cadence. 'So puritanical! So stiff! Didn't that mad monk have fun, filthy as a pigsty, his hair reeking of fat, as he had his will of his pick of naked women, doused in lavender, every pore white as milk, avid for the corruption which follows when nature is recklessly left to its own devices!'

Many of the delegates could hardly listen to this sudden catalogue of vice, gift-wrapped in nostalgia, so unpleasant were the vibrations of Mr Smith's voice. The First Secretary rapped his gavel, but to no avail.

'No, you shan't interrupt me! Not when I remind you of your secret traditions – not those you speak about with vibrant voices and the tinkling of medals – but the real traditions of this land of horizons – *droit du seigneur* – the knout – alcohol – deceit – venality – indolence – procrastination – mendacity – make of these things your allies. They were always a force, not only a weakness! Even if it gave you a bad reputation, its badness was incidental, dependent on the vices of others, *their* lying, *their* hypocrisy, *their* venality! A nation's personality is but a reflection of the world's personality with a little local colour thrown in, an eternal battleground for evil and good. You thought I'd say good and evil? Well, no! I know what's important!'

There were signs of riot, delegates struggling out of their rows in order to have a free hand, others grasping their ears in pain, and, insistent as a metronome, the gavel.

As men clambered close to Mr Smith, ready to seize him, to struggle with him, the Old Man rose to his feet, and appeared twice as tall as he really was. He drowned out the crazed croaking of Mr Smith, who appeared to shrink into a bronchial outburst on the edge of vomiting. The Russians have always been at the mercy of rich bass voices, and now the Old Man's rang out with the diapason of a mass of cellos, caressing and crushing by turns. Peace returned briefly to the discordant assembly.

'I will not tell you who we are. That was not the intention of our visit. The fact that I was compelled to intervene against my better judgment when vice was extolled as a necessary adjunct to virtue may give even the sceptical a clue as to who I am. I believe passionately in the final triumph of good, even if I admit to an absurd penchant for risk. I am, perhaps, at heart, a gambler, but only because I believe the path to final triumph must, of necessity, be a thorny one. There is no virtue in facility. The threat of failure is the condiment which makes the fruits of victory desirable. Forgive us for our show of what may seem superiority to you. For those who believe only in themselves – you, Mr First Secretary – I advise you to turn the other way as we disappear from your midst – not necessarily to the Chirvino-Paparak Autonomous Region. Remember only that doubts are necessary to progress, and that a twinge of conscience is a glimpse of God.'

'A glimpse of me is on offer at all times!' called Mr Smith.

'Shut up,' said the Old Man, devoutly, seizing Mr Smith's hand,

and very slowly they faded from view, the Old Man bathed in a kind of leaden radiance, Mr Smith red and flickering.

Chaos erupted. Some delegates, especially from distant parts, fell to their knees, crossing themselves and kissing the ground, as though they had observed a miracle in the twelfth century. Fighting broke out among others, some dogged upholders of atheism, others more sensitive to psychic phenomena. After ten minutes a semblance of order was restored. The First Secretary was allowed to speak. His manner was, as always, rational and terse. To listen to his resumé, one would imagine that nothing at all had happened.

'I feel, comrades, that I owe you a report on the events of this morning, although I am quite unable to offer you an explanation. The entry of these two individuals into my office was almost as mysterious as their disappearance from our midst a few moments ago. They expressed a desire to speak with me, and the old man in white told me that he was God, a statement which I had some difficulty in accepting since, like the majority of you here, I was brought up an atheist. However, if, for the sake of argument, one was willing momentarily to accept the veracity of the statement, then it didn't stretch the imagination unduly to imagine who the other fellow was. They both seemed, apart from this controversial issue, to be well educated and relatively well informed. As such, they expressed a wish to experience the workings of our Congress. It was for this reason that I extended an invitation to them, in conformity with our ancient tradition of hospitality, and gave them documents as delegates from the Chirvino-Paparak Autonomous Region, which, may God, if he exists, and my dear comrades forgive me, is a figment of my imagination. Such a region simply does not exist.'

The laughter grew with the realization of the hoax played on them, worthy, as one delegate called out, of Gogol in his *Dead Souls*.

'Finally, make of this morning's episode what you will, comrades. Those sensitive to divine or diabolical intervention are free to react in their own way, as the hysterical and the impressionable have learnt throughout our long and troubled history. To those more rational, I would only say that there was no conclusive victory, no knock-out surrender in today's battle of giants. We find ourselves now with the same problems, the same prospects as we did before our senses were jarred by the one or our musicality cajoled by the other. Nothing, comrades, has changed. And that is why we will now break for an early lunch, in which we have time to reflect on this morning's events, and we will meet again at two o'clock sharp, when the subject of debate will be the economic situation facing us, with special reference to the production of radishes and the bankruptcy of several enterprises, especially the one which failed to meet its targets of doorhandles in Semipalatinsk. No deviation from this agenda will be tolerated.'

He was about to bring the gavel down when the Foreign Minister slipped a piece of paper before him. He read it briefly.

'I have just been informed that the American Ambassador has sent a memo to the Foreign Ministry to the effect that the men describing themselves as God and Satan have warrants out for their arrest in the United States on a charge of forgery and resisting arrest by disappearance.'

'Forgery? Bring them back! They could help us with our hard currency problem!' called one delegate, to a roar of laughter.

'Don't blaspheme!' yelled another, on his knees in the aisle, crossing himself with insistence.

The gavel fell, and it was lunch for everyone.

During the lunch break, bells began chiming all over the Soviet Union. Since nobody was in the habit of accepting the responsibility for anything, there were none willing to admit having given such an order. It was therefore assumed throughout the Union that the bells had begun peeling of their own accord; yet another unexplained phenomenon in the long tapestry of Russian history, already rich in the unexplained, and unexplainable.

15

Although they had left Moscow at lunchtime, they did not land until after nightfall. It was a dark night, but they sensed that they were in an olive grove. The air was warm, and even the soil had not cooled off entirely after the heat of the day. Had they been able to smell, they would have enjoyed the mixture of rosemary and thyme which filled the air at the spot where they landed.

'Why did it take us so long?' asked the Old Man, disturbed.

'Are we suddenly as slow as the Concorde?' remarked Mr Smith, uncannily.

'First of all, where are we?'

'Close to the Equator, that's for sure.'

'Wait, wait. I seem to recognize the night sky. The constellations. All my little signposts in their fixed positions. Oh, look! There is a shooting star! Always on the verge of rebellion. But judging from the angle at which I am contemplating the debris of the Creation, I would put us not far from Babylon. The outskirts of Ur of the Chaldees, perhaps. Even Damascus.'

'Are we on the road to Damascus by any chance? Oh, I hope not. You will be intolerable there. Dictating your memories into my ear for hours on end.'

'Have I ever . . .?'

'No, but you will, you will. I know you. A tireless propagandist for mumbo-jumbo which places you in an attractive light. Look what happened in Moscow. Drowning my voice with sheer volume. Was that fair? And all that subliminal advertising about a twinge of conscience! I ask you!'

'I must point out that I didn't have to raise my voice to its full volume, since you were already choking on your own vivid description of carousing with mad monks and the like. My function was not advertising, but restoring order. They were like drunkards who had to be restored to sobriety before taking to the road. I did what had to be done. But what worries me far more is, are we losing our capacity for disappearing? And as for travel, are we losing our speed?'

Mr Smith shrugged ungraciously. 'Don't ask me,' he said. 'You made the rules by which both of us exist. Your instinct must tell you what is possible and what is not. After all, there is a rumour that you are omnipotent. If it is true, there must be a way round practically everything in this existence. Whatever rules you made, you can always bend.'

The Old Man replied in a heartbroken voice. 'I can't remember. Isn't that awful? I've never put any of it to the test before now. I was quite content to lie across the world like a blanket, basking in my own cozy reflections on this and that, smiling and frowning according to the mood of the moment, engendering hurricanes and heatwaves, snowstorms and doldrums.' Suddenly he smiled. 'Oh, I know where we are, with pin-point accuracy. That star, over there, the one which seems to be winking slyly. It is in its prescribed place. We are in the land of Israel. Somewhere a few kilometres north-east of Bethlehem. Between there and Jericho I would say.'

Mr Smith grunted. 'That means trouble.'

'Trouble? Why? The Romans have left.'

'Listen!'

From far away came the sounds of baleful revelry, music in a fatalistically minor key, thumped out in a sour parody of joy. There was a distant clapping of hands, a kind of sombre rowdiness.

'Yes, I must say, it does sound somewhat grim, like an invitation to dance by those who are not choreographically inclined by nature,' said the Old Man. 'What are they up to?'

'Judging by the morose music, they are celebrating some happy event. Their milk curdles as it is poured out, the tears turn to salt. All is predestined. What is birth but a start on the road to death?' reflected Mr Smith.

'Let us meditate a while before we go and investigate,' suggested the Old Man.

'It sounds like the kind of party which will go on all night. I have an absolute conviction that we are not missing anything,' said Mr Smith.

'I agree with you. What have we left to see, apart from practically everything?'

181

They thought for a moment.

'You know,' said the Old Man at length, 'I shall regret not seeing Africa.'

'Why regret? Why not go?'

'I must be honest. I feel my strength is waning. I am most surprised, and most disheartened. Like you, I had heard everywhere that I was omnipotent, Lord God Almighty, I seem to remember from the Anglican hymn, sung with the same inspired lack of musicality acquired by the cherubim over the ages. Well, I wonder. It's a question of stamina. When I tried to engineer a quick exit for us from the Kremlin, it suddenly took hours to disappear. Hours, I exaggerate. At least two and a half seconds. That is unheard of. I very much fear that Africa is a luxury we can ill afford.'

'You can go in spirit, can you not?' asked Mr Smith.

'Of course, but it's not the same as putting your feet on the naked soil and contemplating the activity. Mind you, Africa is probably the continent which would least surprise us. It is, I imagine, more closely as we created it than any other.'

'How kind of you to include me in the Creation. But I want no part in it. It has never been a blueprint of which I was asked for, or for which I would accord, my approval.'

'How pompous you are, after all this time! Well, out with it, what would you have done?'

'It was never my job to do anything,' replied Mr Smith, with cool logic. 'My brief, if I understood it correctly, was to react against what you did with all the means at my disposal, which I have done, most conscientiously, until quite recently.'

'Until quite recently?' asked the Old Man, with some anxiety.

'Evil becomes quite as monstrous as good after all the initial excitements. Man came of age some time ago, and, as far as my department is concerned, he can be left quite safely to his own devices. He has even found it in himself to invent certain things I would never have thought of, for the simple reason that it is the kind of evil which gives no satisfaction whatever. The nuclear weapon, which is about as evil as one can get, is far from being erotic, and evil without the necessary stimulus to the senses is quite simply inadmissible. There are those of mediocre intelligence, prime ministers and the like, who speak about a nuclear deterrent, which is as perspicacious as talking about

182

loud noises as a sleep deterrent, or public executions as a crime deterrent. First of all there are those who are merely stimulated by the idea of a deterrent aimed at their heads, and secondly there is no deterrent for lunacy, and if there were one, the last thing it would be is common sense.'

'To what do we owe this sudden outburst of spite against nuclear weapons?' asked the Old Man tactfully.

'They are beneath my dignity as a tempter. They are even beneath my dignity as a commercial traveller. They are, quite frankly, frightfully dull – when they are not being used, of course. Half a century ago the victor condemned a whole dockful of ageing men to death for war crimes, do you remember?'

'Not with any clarity,' admitted the Old Man.

'They had to invent the rules of the game before deciding that the war criminals had lost it, and these were hanged in an atmosphere of outraged piety. Whoever is the first to use a nuclear weapon will make those ageing men in the dock look like juvenile delinquents, and yet the possibility of nuclear defence is bandied about in rational terms, with no hint of a moral posture. Of course, there is no difference between nuclear defence and nuclear attack. One is as blasphemous as the other, but I want no part of these monuments to human stupidity in my arsenal. Do you want them?'

'Certainly not. They can never be invested with even a shadow of a moral purpose. I disown them as maledictions.'

'You see!' cried Mr Smith. 'The human race is beginning to escape from the intimate battlefield of ours, where souls are claimed or rejected individually by the two of us. They have invented vices unknown, unrecognized, unthought of by us two. Vices which not only surpass their imagination, but what is far more terrible, even succeed in surpassing ours!'

'So?' asked the Old Man, slowly, wishing to face whatever truth it turned out to be.

'So? We are luxuries which a world in hasty evolution can no longer afford. You could not be expected to foresee *everything*. We have been outgrown.'

'But the ranger?'

'An isolated case. He can afford the purity of his belief, the sanctity of his family, because he lives far from society. He has chosen, and found, a monastic isolation. He need not recognize the passage of time, up there on his mountain. He possesses the greatest gift left to men, distance.'

'And Dr Kleingeld, the psychiatrist?'

'He has lived so close to madness all his life, and made so much money from it, he's merely paying back a debt he recognizes that he owes his fellow men by plaguing the White House police with his charming banner expressing confidence in us.'

'Maybe. And the English cleric who is ready to prostrate himself before the milkman?'

'Oh, English clerics have become wildly eccentric ever since they shook themselves free from Rome. They have never really recovered from the delirium of freedom from that constraint. It would be dangerous to take their utterances too seriously. Besides, they don't expect it.'

'But I have seen churches, mosques, synagogues and temples wherever we have travelled. Well, seen them – sensed their existence –'

'Lip service is still one of man's great industries. An American president is bound, by the nature of his employment, to invoke prayers at regular intervals. He shuts his eyes in meditation, but he may well be doing nothing more than calculating the moment when it is judicious to open them again. Since it is a free country, we will never know. All over the world, your name is invoked to witness this or that, people swear by you, kill each other because one or some of them have apparently offended you. You are still a yardstick by which all moral values are publicly judged, but privately, where it really matters? Less and less. Less and less.'

'You paint a depressing picture,' said the Old Man, and sighed so deeply that the silver leaves on the olive trees caught what light there was, shivered on their branches, and the sigh was transferred to other trees out of sight in the darkness.

'I still feel curiously guilty about Africa,' he remarked suddenly, eager to change the subject.

'Africa?'

'Yes. I wonder if I gave them a chance, if I finished my work as I should have done, and didn't just leave the continent to its own devices a bit too much.'

'I don't think so,' ruminated Mr Smith. 'They have splendid landscapes, superb animals.'

184

'It is not enough. There was not the wherewithal with which to advance unaided, and that gave rise to all the curious attitudes of man to man, judgment not by quality, or virtue, but by colour, and beliefs that those of darker hue are nature's children, who can never grow up.'

'Most of that's in the past, and there's absolutely nothing that can be done about it retrospectively. You will serve no purpose whatever by going there now. If your strength is really failing, as you say, then perhaps you should rather, like a politician, visit those constituencies where you can be sure of a majority.'

'I feel some frightful heresy coming,' muttered the Old Man, and went on, 'Such as?'

'Such as Rome,' said Mr Smith, his lips twisted into a baroque expression of derision.

'Trust you to express such disturbing thoughts. Why Rome? Why not Mecca? Or the banks of the Ganges? Or Lhasa?'

'In Mecca you run a real physical risk as a result of your blasphemy in daring to pretend that you are who you are.'

'But, dear boy, I am who I am, and one of my terrible regrets is being immune from all harm.'

'You may be immune, but they'll find a way to hurt you all the same. While being addicted to tolerance, and a very beautiful form of belief, some of them are among the most professional of religious fanatics in the planet, who brook neither change nor the most infinitesimal variant of their version of the truth. I know. They are practically untemptable, and trying to tempt them is more trouble than it's worth. All blazing eyes and no sense of fun. You stand less chance there than as Messiah with the Jews.'

'We will soon know,' murmured the Old Man grimly. 'In any case, I cannot go to Rome. I'm not nearly well enough dressed for the Vatican.'

'Rubbish. You are dressed almost exactly like His Holiness, except that you affect tennis shoes instead of soft slippers.'

'In that case, my appearance would no doubt seem to be *lèse-majesté*.'

'Perhaps. In any case, you would come under no physical threat in those quarters. They would merely consider your claim to be God, argue about it for about four hundred years, and then, with luck, accept you as beatified as a first step to sainthood, after which it shouldn't be too long before the end of time itself before you make the grade you possess anyway by the nature you created. All of which proves that the seats of organized religion are not places for us. They are like ministries, in the secular sense, far too busy with the daily ramifications of belief to bother with the root of belief itself. You and I do not belong in the cloisters and the court-yards and the shrines. Meditation is an abstract activity. Staring at the likes of us is a disappointment which no fellow with mystical aspirations is likely to accept. He felt closer to the truth before.'

The Old Man suddenly began rocking with uncontrollable laughter. It was a great release of anguish and anxiety, of a brow suddenly unfurrowed like a flag caught in the wind; of a spirit abruptly illuminated from within, as by a sunburst; of a huge trumpeting of merriment, a herd of jolly elephants at the discovery of a waterhole; all Heaven breaking loose. Even the bleak clapping of the distant revelry hesitated for a moment as the night announced some mighty therapeutic force, pumping away somewhere out of sight. Mr Smith joined in as the contagion caught him in its wake, bouncing him like a child on a well-upholstered knee, but his laughter resembled the simpering of a shy schoolgirl in the grip of puberty. On those rare occasions when his mood was clement, he produced only little noises, a far cry from the rattle and the blaze of cacophany he could diffuse when provoked by opposition.

The Old Man must have done the impossible: not merely rested, but slept. His last memory before sweet oblivion was a strange sensation, unknown before, of the pricking of tears in the eyes. Not enough to worry an immortal, perhaps, but worthy of passing note. Mr Smith had been unable to stay awake, and joined the Old Man in the snug refuge of dreamless slumber. At least he had a precedent, the escape road he had taken in the presence of the prostitute in New York. No need to feel for his wallet now, even in sleep. He had the consolation of knowing they had nothing in their pockets.

They awoke at the same moment at dawn. Cocks were crowing over the undulant countryside, a ferocious sun was clambering its way to the rim of the horizon, and the olive trees had shed a few stiff little leaves on them. But the cause of their awakening seemed to be the noise of conflict. Raucous voices, the screams of women, a little wailing, violence.

The Old Man and Mr Smith exchanged a brief look and, without further ado, arose and began to hurry over the hillside. They soon saw a patchwork of squat houses, as blindingly white as teeth on an advertisement, separated by courtyards and patios. There were banners and streamers with Hebrew writing on them, a few wires with coloured electric light bulbs criss-crossing a sandy area, trestle-tables, chairs, an improvised dance floor, the untidiness after a celebration.

Moving round the agglomeration, which made it look like a fortress rather than a residential area, were men in shirt-sleeves, all of them wearing yarmulkas. Some of them carried rifles. Far away in the valley there was another group of houses, a village, but here the buildings were yellowed with time, half sunk into the surrounding earth. Between the two settlements, there was a road of no great importance, snaking its way into the distance among the hills. On this road, there was a procession of veiled and masked men, women and children carrying banners, inscribed in Arabic. Some of the men and all the children were breaking ranks and running up the slope, armed with stones, which they lobbed into the midst of the defenders of the new buildings, who were Jewish settlers.

'I have no idea who the participants are, but it is outrageous to use little children in such fights,' said the Old Man.

'And what if the little children have opinions which they deem it honourable to defend?' asked Mr Smith.

'Oh, nonsense. At that age? They can't know what it's all about.'

'In that sense, they resemble you. The men below, up on that hillock, are Jewish settlers. Those stoning them are Arab villagers.'

'But who does the land belong to?'

'A moot point. The Arabs say it belongs to them, because they have lived on it for so long. The Jews believe it belongs to them because it says so in the Bible.'

'Oh, not again!' exclaimed the Old Man, pained. 'What that poor book has had to put up with. If you search long enough, and with a modicum of ill will, you can find a justification for almost any action conceivable to man, especially in the Old Testament.'

'It is not my bedside book,' said Mr Smith. 'Here come others to complicate the issue. Look.'

And a series of military vehicles arrived in clouds of dust, caused by those sections of the road where the tarmac had surrendered to the pressure of nature and subsided into sand.

'Who are they?' asked the Old Man, earnestly trying to follow the plot.

'Israeli soldiers.'

'Come to drive the Arabs back!'

'Not necessarily. These Jews have broken the law by building this settlement.'

'Gracious. If they were really breaking the law, there would have been plenty of time to stop them before they had laid the foundations, let alone finished the buildings.'

'Agreed. It is an equivocal kind of law – the kind of law they are encouraged to break.'

'By whom?'

'By the very people who made the laws.'

The Old Man sighed. 'It hasn't changed, has it.'

'No. The Romans were glad to go.'

The Israeli troops fanned out over the side of the hill, some of them firing rubber bullets at the Palestinian villagers, but sparingly, while a voice speaking Arabic through a microphone urged them to retire to their village. Meanwhile, other soldiers, armed with night sticks, belaboured the settlers, who screamed with an intensity which transported their show of passion over the tenuous border into the ridiculous. Nobody seemed keen for anybody to be hurt. Then a shot rang out, two. Nobody knew from where the shots had come, but they had a different ring to them than rubber bullets. At almost the same time an Arab woman held a wounded child aloft and began a horrifying hymn of hate, and an Israeli soldier was lifted from the ground, evidently hit. The battle began in earnest, with grimmer aspects than could be discerned in the original demonstration.

The Old Man thundered down the hill without a word of warning. Mr Smith, at first caught unawares, was bound to follow, with a rasping curse at such an impetuous act. The Old Man rushed between the combatants, his arms outstretched in imperious supplication. He then seized the wounded child, held aloft by its shrieking mother as evidence, and in a trice restored it to its original condition. It would be indelicate to describe the mother's reaction as merely astonished, although under such circumstances, and with human values at a low ebb, this was a more normal state of mind than gratitude, which had been so neglected as to become inoperative. The Old Man received a hail of jagged stones from the settlers, and a few punitive rubber bullets from the soldiers, the price of interference. Turning, the Old Man caught the last of the stones and playfully threw them back as though at baseball practice. As for the few rubber bullets, he volleyed them back with the palm of his hand, creating a couple of minor wounds among the soldiery. The wounded soldier suddenly rose from the ground. There was no trace of his injury.

Thinking he was creating a diversion, Mr Smith set fire to a military vehicle. The available soldiers began dousing it with extinguishers.

By now the mother was kneeling beside the recovered child, crooning words of maternal love and singing the praises of Allah. '*Allah es akhbar,*' chanted the villagers, with the renewed conviction that God was with them. Some of the settlers looked towards Heaven, their arms outstretched, as though appealing to an unseen umpire of a corrupt encounter.

'What have we done to you that you should succour one of their offspring?' one old fellow, with an acute sense of celestial accountancy, was heard to say.

Meanwhile, things fell back into place. The Arabs went back to their village, chanting. The settlers barricaded themselves in their settlement, and the Old Man and Mr Smith, outnumbered, were dragged into the presence of Major-General Avshalom Bar Uriel, the commander of the military district.

The General, a fine-looking man in his late thirties, greeted them in a meagre whitewashed office, which was his command post. There was an indefinable melancholy about him, expressed not only by the deep furrows on either side of his mouth, but also by the leaping arch of his black eyebrows, which met above his nose where the portal of a frown rose towards his hairline, romantically unkempt.

'They tell me you cured a child which had been wounded by a bullet. One of our men also. May I ask how you did it?' he enquired of the Old Man.

'Oh . . . nothing. Nothing much. A trick I picked up somewhere.'

'A trick?' The General smiled, ironically, but without humour.

'With tricks like that at your disposal, you deserve to be in charge of our medical service. You speak Hebrew.'

'Yes, I do. Even if I'm a little lacking in practice.'

'You speak a very good Hebrew, if I may say so. A very pure Hebrew. Not the Hebrew which is spoken today. A Hebrew from biblical times.'

'You are very kind.'

'No. It's a fact. No Israeli general is merely a general. When I'm not on active duty in this hateful job, I'm a professor of philology. You speak the Hebrew of King Solomon, and I'm intrigued by it.'

'I'm intrigued by the fact you called your job hateful, or was that a slip of the tongue?' continued the Old Man.

'Not at all. It is hateful. Everybody here is willing to fight, even to die, for the country. But what we are forced to do here is destroying the souls of my soldiers. We are forced to behave as colonial powers used to behave towards us. What a lesson! What bitter medicine we are forced to swallow, and with every local victory our moral defeat becomes more evident. Take today. It is a success so far. Not a single demonstrator has yet been killed, either in Gaza or here. Two were wounded, but have since been restored to health, thanks to you. By one solitary gesture, or whatever it was, you have deflected the disgust of the world for one more day. You deserve a decoration.'

'Oh no, thank you,' laughed the Old Man. 'I have seen enough of those in Russia. When you have as many as they have, you might as well invest in a suit of armour.'

'Another reference to history,' the General said quickly, and then added, 'Incidentally, our crew carried out a cursory examination of the burned-out personnel carrier, and could find no reason why it should have burst into flame. Was that your initiative also?'

'No, it was mine,' said Mr Smith, with cool vanity.

'Yours? Why? For what reason did you destroy a military vehicle?' The General spoke with an unexpected hardness.

'I, too, have a range of useful party tricks – I beg pardon – party miracles. And once you have them at your disposal, it's a pity not to use them, don't you agree?'

'You speak Hebrew too. The same kind of Hebrew.'

'We were great friends when we were boys.'

'And now?' The General looked perspicaciously from one to the other as they looked at each other, no longer noticing the General.

'Were you in Russia together?'

'Yes,' said Mr Smith, staring at the Old Man.

'Where else?'

'England,' said Mr Smith.

'The United States,' added the Old Man, with a wonderful tenderness, as he contemplated Mr Smith.

They were all of a sudden like lovers remembering the places where they had been happiest.

'I think I read about you in the *Jerusalem Post*,' the General said quietly.

The Old Man chuckled. 'I wouldn't be a bit surprised.'

'A gift for disappearance . . . and for forgery perhaps?'

'That's it, and for flying through space a little quicker than that old slowcoach, Concorde.'

'And now, saving a child's life . . . and setting fire to the property of the Israeli Government.'

Mr Smith laughed. 'We can only reimburse it in forged currency, I'm afraid.'

The General smiled, as sadly as ever. 'If you wish to escape now in your usual manner, be my guest. It's now or never.'

'Why do you say that?'

'This is a land of miracles, you know. Which is another way of saying it is a land of the deepest scepticism. Nothing is ever taken at its face value. Like a piece of gristle in the mouth, it is chewed over and gnawed to tastelessness before it is admitted that it was inedible in the first place. Being such a country, but also virtually under martial law, I am forced to take various steps as a general which are profoundly distasteful to me. First of all, I am compelled to destroy a couple of Arab houses, arbitrarily selected, as a warning to them not to demonstrate in the future. This is not an accurate reflection of justice as I understand it, and not only I know it. We can beat the *gush emonim*, the settlers, gently on the head, but we can't touch the houses, although their increasing number is the most arrant provocation.'

'And what is your second duty?' asked the Old Man, slowly.

'In view of your miracle, and other details of the sort, which will be enumerated in my report, you will automatically have to appear before a religious court. Once you dabble in the supernatural, you understand, you are beyond my competence. My mandate is to deal with military intervention, retaliations, and the kind of retaliations which pre-date the initial attack, and which, in the verbiage of contemporary hypocrisy, are called pre-emptive strikes. I am also empowered to act in cases of assault, reprisal, and death, but salvation, transfiguration, ascension, I must leave to others.'

'We have no intention of escaping, General,' the Old Man said.

'The Sanhedrin! What fun! After all this time!' cackled Mr Smith.

'As you wish,' said the General, 'but since you have no fear or complex about the religious court, I strongly advise you not to go without prayer shawls, or yarmulkas. I can supply you out of military stock.'

'No, thanks all the same,' said the Old Man reasonably. 'After all this time, I have an aversion to pretending to be what I am not.'

'What do you mean by what you are not?' asked the General slowly. 'What are you not?'

'Jewish,' said the Old Man.

The General lost his composure for once. 'You're not going to tell them that I hope? You'll be there till the end of the century arguing about fine points of interpretation. They're all very old. You don't know them. They'll make a point of not dying until they've got you where they want you.'

'And where is that?' the Old Man enquired.

'Probably on a plane out of Israel.'

'That is a punishment?'

'The way you said it . . . and what you said . . . I find it impossible to believe that you're not Jewish. And in such choice Hebrew, yet.'

16

They spent the night in a kind of prison, in which hundreds of suspects were temporarily incarcerated, although every effort was made to give them a little extra comfort in view of their age, miracles, and disturbing air of distinction. In the morning, they were transported to Jerusalem in a spartan vehicle used by the military to move prisoners, and ended up in front of a squat doorway, which they entered, only having a glimpse of the Old City, straddling its hilltop like a grounded battleship.

They waited for a while in an anteroom, until a door opened to release a black gentleman into the room, dancing with anger and frustration. His eyes flashed and rolled as he spoke at the top of his voice in an accent of the southern states of America, which was all but incomprehensible as his fury lengthened even further the already over-extended vowels. He wore a couple of yarmulkas on his head, one over the other, and a variety of prayer shawls; black ringlets hung like exhausted springs on both sides of his otherwise Afro haircut. All this over blue jeans shorts and a T-shirt spelling out a saucy message in Hebrew. He was evidently at great pains to prove his Jewishness, and it was also clear he had been turned down. He was quickly shepherded out by a guard who had somehow mislaid him after his examination was over.

'I still feel guilty about Africa,' said the Old Man. 'He awakened all my culpability. What did he say?'

'He has nothing to do with Africa,' explained Mr Smith. 'He is from the southern part of America.'

'America?' The Old Man registered surprise. 'Then why didn't he speak American like the others?'

'Many Americans speak like that. We just didn't meet any.'

'What? Hopping about and clicking their fingers, as though about to go into a ritual dance? Is that part of the language?'

'Very much so. And then he was particularly annoyed because they'd just turned him down as an applicant to be a Jew.'

'I wonder why,' reflected the Old Man. 'You don't think it could be anything to do with his colour? That would be too reprehensible. What is the criterion for being a Jew?'

'We'll soon know,' replied Mr Smith, indicating an usher, who was already beckoning them into an august presence.

The examination room was quite small, containing an elevated podium and a long desk, behind which five learned men sat, pondered, and doodled. Below them, and before them, at a lower level, there were two chairs. There were also provisions for a recorder. Through the large modern windows lay the Old City once again, bathed in sunlight.

The learned men had one feature in common, their extreme pallor. They looked as though no ray of sunlight had ever been allowed to contaminate their skin, which bore all the signs of infinite labours in underlit rooms, the trials and tribulations of great learning, acquired under the most austere and unhealthy of conditions.

The central figure of the five had the sharpest nose ever seen on man, shaped like a paperknife, and aimed unnervingly at whoever he was talking to. Three of the others had all the outer signs of intractability, the last remaining one, probably the Sephardic influence, was rather more lustrous and awake to the ways of the world.

They shuffled their papers for a while, and then the forbidding father figure spoke in a high wheezing voice which was a flagrant contradiction of his imperious manner. He spoke in English, not daring to assume that the Old Man and Mr Smith spoke Yiddish, the language of orthodoxy, before their Jewishness was beyond doubt.

'Who you are, I won't even ask. I have no wish to begin this investigation with a blasphemy.'

'So you know?' asked the Old Man with a twinkle.

'I have heard. We have all heard. And we have all deplored.'

'It is depressing when someone you have been waiting for for so long actually turns up. It throws your arrangements into disarray.'

'I did not hear the last remark. The other rabbis not either. I will explain to you your situation. We are under pressure from the United States for many things: we should not molest Arabs in our own

194

territory; we should buy from the United States what we can make ourselves better; and only this morning comes the request, we should arrest you and send you back to America to face trial like forgers. Such requests and others we resist if it can be proved that you are Jewish.' A trace of subdued hysteria was stoked among the embers of his means of expression. 'To us,' he said angrily, 'it is more important that you are Jewish than that you are a forger.' The others nodded sagely.

'In other words, a Jewish forger will benefit from greater understanding before this court than a man who, while not being a forger, is also not a Jew?' asked the Old Man.

'A lay court, it should decide if it is a forger, a man. A religious court is only concerned, yes or no, he is a Jew.'

Mr Smith interrupted. 'Ask me who I am. There's no risk of blasphemy in my reply.'

The President, whose name was the Rabbi Tischbein, hit the desk with a gavel. 'Do not attempt you should dictate to us. One at a time, I'm asking. Each case must be judged on its own merits. Now, please, your mother was Jewish?'

'Mine?' the Old Man asked.

'Who else?'

'It is difficult for me to reply.' The Old Man hesitated.

'You never knew your mother?'

'I certainly never knew my mother . . .'

'In childbirth, she passed away?'

'No. It may seem dramatic to you, Rabbi, but it was quite natural to me – in that anything can be said to be quite natural for someone who is justified in claiming nature as his responsibility.'

'You speak in riddles.'

'The fact is, I had no mother. Put it that way.'

The President took a sharp intake of air, and tore his lapel. The others rocked their heads from side to side, and wailed a little under their breath. Mr Smith cackled. 'Oh, ecstasy! Remember them in older times? It all comes back to me now. They were in honour bound to tear their clothes every time they heard a blasphemy! By the evening, in the Sanhedrin, they had heard so many that their clothes were in tatters.'

The four other rabbis looked quickly at each other, and tore minute rents in their clothing.

'You speak you could have been here to that time?' asked Dr Tischbein, his eyes narrowed.

'Oh, I was, I was. You can say that I witnessed the birth of the great Jewish tradition of tailoring, with its later development of invisible mending.'

'That it should be good for commerce should make it bad for religion?' asked the Rabbi, not without a glimmer of caustic humour.

'On the contrary. Most religious shrines do a roaring trade in souvenirs.'

'Even here,' sighed Dr Tischbein. 'But those are not Jewish shrines.'

'May I ask a question?' the Old Man interposed.

'Here, the questions, it is we who ask,' snapped Dr Tischbein.

'It is I who wait for the answers,' the Old Man replied. Since there was no question immediately forthcoming, the Old Man took this as a sign of subtle acquiescence, and asked the question he had in mind.

'Why is it so important to be a Jew?'

The Rabbi was shocked, and the others murmured.

'You can be, what you are not?' he wheezed. 'Or be not, what you are?'

'That was not my question. Why is it so important to be what you are?'

'We were chosen by God!'

'That is, of course, entirely possible. I can't really remember. I took so many initiatives in my youth.'

Dr Tischbein tore a bit more of his lapel. The others followed suit.

'I am not saying for a moment that I made the wrong decision!' said the Old Man hastily. 'I am sure that by your single-mindedness, your intelligence—'

'Your suffering,' Mr Smith interrupted surprisingly, and sincerely.

'—you thoroughly deserve to have been chosen.'

'It was God's will, not yours.'

'How can you prove that I am not – no, no, leave your lapels alone, I implore you! – who I say I am?'

'We would all know God if he came back. Not our minds alone, our hearts would tell us.'

'A profusion of miracles? The blind able to see? The lame throwing away crutches? A confusion of bakery and fishmongery?'

'In the circus we are not,' Dr Tischbein hissed.

Mr Smith spoke with evident loss of patience. 'I told you it was a waste of time,' he said. 'Religious authorities are the last ones we are able to convince. The whole of theology stands between us. They expect nothing because nothing can live up to their expectations. It's as simple as that. As abstractions, you command devotion, I, at least respect. As physical appearances we are a dead loss, jostled by customs' officers, wanted by the FBI, bullied by hobos. It needed someone as sceptical by nature as a psychiatrist to accord us the credence we deserve. Here we stand not a ghost of a chance. Let's give it up and move on. At this rate, the poor rabbis will have no clothes left. Everything will be torn to shreds yet again.'

'Your sympathy, please keep.'

'I admit that all of what you say is true, but I am still fascinated by the point. What makes you think you are so different to other people?' asked the Old Man.

The rabbis murmured, as the Bible might say, one with another.

'We are different. It's a fact.'

'All people are different.'

'Not so different like we.'

'In choosing you, can you not imagine that God also chose the human race?'

'The human race he created. Us, he chose.'

'Does not creation imply choice?'

'No. Creation, it is before choice. You make your choice once there is something to choose, not before.'

'I don't follow.'

'Which comes first, the cloth or the suit?'

'They both come before the blasphemy,' said Mr Smith, tearing his T-shirt mischievously. 'Come on, hold hands, and disappear.'

'No,' said the Old Man, 'I must get to the root of this conviction, which destroys equality. And once there is not the concession of a sense of equality, it makes dialogue with others quite impossible.'

To his surprise, the rabbis nodded.

'It gives arrogance,' said one.

'Also persecution,' warned another.

'Hatred,' remarked the third flatly.

'Jealousy?' enquired the fourth.

'All this is true,' reflected Dr Tischbein, 'but that is God's will, not ours.'

And all the rabbis nodded once again.

'Oh, that is too easy. You blame—' And the Old Man stopped in his tracks, since he noticed the hands rise to the lapels in anticipation. Instead, he asked, 'How do you know?'

'It is written,' replied Dr Tischbein. The others approved.

'Who wrote it?'

'Prophets.'

'Which prophets?'

'Many prophets. It is written.'

'And that is enough? The word of a prophet is always in doubt until his prophecy is confirmed by an event. This is not always the case. The words of many prophets would be that much more doubtful.'

Dr Tischbein held up a hand, white as marble, with long, tapering fingers. 'It is written!' he said, with the inflection of finality.

The Old Man and Mr Smith looked at each other, the Old Man exasperated, Mr Smith with exaggerated patience.

'Listen.' It was Dr Tischbein who spoke again. 'No people it is who has clung to their ancient traditions with such obstinacy. Our manner of prayer is different to others, the things we are eating, the laws governing Sabbath and Feast Days. Even our God is our own, and no one else's. Others send out missionaries to convince, to convert. We keep it ourselves, and let no one should come in without proof they belong, even lost sheep like you, it is possible. Our tradition is so strong, it is existing to the time of Babylon just like it should exist today. When we had not had this discipline, this law, we would no longer be here. We were dispersed, thrown like chaff to the wind, hunted to the ends of the Earth, we are still here. Please, now tell us we are not different?'

'Everyone is different.'

'Everyone is different it could be. Only we are, from them, more different.'

The Old Man tried once again, making it sound as though it was the last time he would. 'Tell me, do you still remember the first slight to your people, the first wound it ever suffered in history?'

Rabbi Tischbein answered slowly, after lengthy consideration. The irony inherent in his personality was discreetly in evidence.

'No, we do not remember,' he said quietly. 'At the same time, we can never forget.'

The other rabbis captured the spice of his reply on their palates, and nodded fatalistically and with the appreciation of gourmets.

The Old Man was touched at this implied admission of vulnerability. He was eager to make a reciprocal gesture. 'Then let me try to meet you halfway,' he cried. 'I *am* Jewish!'

A great cry of delight went up from the court, not sounding much like delight as usually expressed, but more like a moan.

'. . . among many other things,' the Old Man went on.

The moan shattered into atonality and chaos before it was left hanging in the air, unresolved and miserable.

'Either Jewish, or not Jewish!' cried Dr Tischbein at the top of his wizened lungs. 'Between is not anything!'

'What did I tell you?' cried Mr Smith, exasperated. 'Let's go. This reminds me of so much I'd rather forget.' He looked skyward. 'The *endless* arguments. Or better, the arguments to which there was no logical end!'

'Please?' Dr Tischbein blinked in disbelief, his pink eyelids falling over his eyes like those of an ostrich, to shut out the pain and disappointment of the world of surprises.

Mr Smith turned on Dr Tischbein with his usual vindictive wildness. 'Dispersed, thrown like chaff to the wind indeed—' he shouted. 'Hunted to the ends of the Earth! Which made of your diaspora a tragedy in your minds, instead of the blessing it was!'

One of the rabbis rose in protest.

'Yes, blessing! Would you have spawned Maimonides or Spinoza, Einstein or Freud if you had stayed here, wallowing in struggles with your neighbours? Of course not! The fact that you are now all crowding back to your ancestral home is a gesture more sentimental than practical, and merely proves my point. To acquire your fame, your notoriety, you had to seek out broader horizons, and once they had been acquired elsewhere, you now think you can afford to return, and set up risible courts like these. Good grief! Haven't you suffered sufficiently at the hands of those seeking to prove that the purity of a race can be defiled by alien elements not to indulge in a parody of the same heresy? And to what purpose, this exclusivity? If I wished to stay here, I could prove I am a Jew to everybody's satisfaction within a minute. If it took me a minute, it would take my old friend thirty seconds or less. But the fact is, we are honest, each in his own way. We do not need to prove anything to anybody. We are above nationality, above creed or religion.'

One or two rabbis tore their tunics.

'Not above religion, beyond it—' corrected the Old Man, ever conciliatory. One rabbi tore his tunic again, to be on the safe side.

'We have done without tradition, without roots, from the beginning of time,' Mr Smith rasped. 'Why should we be sympathetic towards such silliness now?'

Dr Tischbein kept his head. 'You think you could prove you should be Jewish to our satisfaction? I doubt it. Even when I am conceding it would be more easier for you to prove you was African.'

'Really?' asked Mr Smith, turning himself into an African, with a couple of yarmulkas on his head, and a saucy Hebrew message on his T-shirt.

'Oh, don't waste your precious energy on miracles,' cried the Old Man. 'We'll need every volt, every ohm we possess!'

'A minute, I'm asking,' Dr Tischbein interrupted. 'Ago a moment, when I spoke with you, you was not black.'

'Earlier on I was, remember?' said Mr Smith, clicking his fingers in obedience to some rhythm only he could hear. 'I came in here like in search of roots, see. Well, I guess it just didn't work out the way ah'd hoped. No hard feelings, man.'

The rabbis huddled like pigeons in the park, pecking at imaginary crumbs as they muttered their reactions to these disturbing events into each other's ears. It was the Sephardic rabbi who was the first to break away from the conclave. His general appearance avoided the texture of parchment which seemed the hallmark of the others. Velvet, rather, one would have said. And an almost excessive richness of voice, like a singer speaking.

'And where are you going from here?' he enquired.

'You know we are not staying?' asked Mr Smith.

'If you had wished to stay, you would have stayed. You said so yourself.'

'But how could I know you believe us?'

The Sephardic rabbi smiled. 'There is no need to continue your African charade any longer.'

'I'm sorry, one so easily forgets,' said Mr Smith as he reverted to his usual hideous self. 'We are going to Japan.'

'Japan?' The Old Man was annoyed.

'It's a beautiful country,' said the Sephardic rabbi.

'You have been there?'

'No.' The Sephardic rabbi smiled. 'Belief counts for something in this sad world. You have to believe people are not lying when they tell you that Japan is a beautiful country. One has to believe that people are not lying when they tell you almost anything.'

Mr Smith made to respond, but the Old Man silenced him with a gesture.

'Does that mean . . .?' he began with a quiet intensity. 'Does that mean that you believe us?'

The Sephardic rabbi smiled more caressingly than usual. 'In court we may ask questions, and expect direct answers – but our training in law prevents us from answering directly ourselves.'

'What will you say of us after we have gone?' Mr Smith ventured.

After a moment, the Sephardic rabbi replied, his smile as magnanimous as ever, 'A good riddance.'

'But why?' stammered the Old Man, perplexed.

'You are outside our experience. It makes no difference if we believe you or not. You are, frankly, not what we expected, and therefore not what we have been waiting for. You lower our threshold for exultation, you reduce praise to conversation, psalmody to prattle. We are bitterly disappointed.'

'And I thought the way into men's hearts was the ordinary, the workaday,' said the Old Man in the merest whisper, and added with a hint of malice, 'I assure you, the disappointment is not all on one side.'

Mr Smith held out his hand to the Old Man.

'What does that mean?' asked the Old Man, irritated.

'Japan?'

'What will you tell the Americans, the FBI?'

'We will tell the truth as always,' replied the Sephardic rabbi. 'We will say you disappeared. That can cause them no surprise.'

They all looked at each other for a considerable time, expressing variously pain, grief, regret and, in the case of the Sephardic rabbi, a distant, hardly perceptible amusement. Then the Old Man let his hand slide into the open palm of Mr Smith, and their fingers interlocked.

Then they slowly disappeared from view.

At once, Dr Tischbein began nodding his head while intoning a prayer. The others followed suit. Hebrew scholars would recognize the words instantly as a litany of thanksgiving.

17

They landed clumsily and painfully in a vast open space which was cruelly paved, amid a crowd of people who shied away with the first rush of their coming.

The Old Man lay flat for a moment, seeming concussed. Mr Smith, while dishevelled and distraught, appeared less immediately affected by the rigours of the trip.

'Why on earth you choose such obesity as a mortal shell whereas you could have chosen an infinity of more athletic disguises is beyond me,' he scolded.

The Old Man lay inanimate, while an oriental crowd regarded him with an awe which prevented any move in his direction.

'Snap out of it,' barked Mr Smith. 'I know you can't possibly be dead, or even wounded, so don't try to scare me, especially in front of people we have never seen before.'

'Is this Japan?' asked the Old Man at length, in the smallest of voices.

Mr Smith tried his best Japanese on some of the bystanders, without result. He then ventured Vietnamese, Thai, Burmese, Laotian, Kampuchean and Indonesian. People tended to recoil cautiously as he practised his knowledge of South-East Asian linguistics on them. It only occurred to him as a last resort to try Mandarin Chinese.

A pretty girl with a boyish figure and a white headband, which looked ominously like a bandage, stepped towards them.

'You are in the so-called People's Republic of China,' she said. 'In Beijing to be precise, in Tienanmen Square.'

'Tienanmen Square,' echoed Mr Smith in horror.

'Why does that word seem to inspire such dismay in you?' asked the Old Man, now fully aware.

'Get up, get up, stop imitating a traffic accident,' grumbled Mr

Smith, as he helped the wincing Old Man to his feet.

'Tienanmen has had a recent past of great sorrow, when the Army massacred a large number of students demonstrating peacefully. This action alarmed and depressed many foreign countries which had thought that China was on the way to becoming a more liberal society. Am I correct?'

'I cannot answer for the reaction of the foreign countries,' said the girl, as though addressing a meeting, 'but your description of what occurred in the square is, in the main, correct.'

'I must apologize for the questions of my friend,' Mr Smith explained. 'He shows only scant interest in events in the last ten thousand years.'

'In that case he would be well equipped to serve in our government,' said the girl.

'You called it the so-called People's Republic of China. What is it in reality?'

'The Dictatorship of the Geriatric Ward.'

Mr Smith laughed a little guiltily. The Old Man did not laugh at all.

A couple of policemen instructed everyone to keep moving.

'It is a technique they learned from the Americans,' said the girl.

A young man joined the girl, indicating by a transparent possessiveness that they were emotionally linked, and that he had a jealous and unstable nature. There were Chinese symbols on his headband, suggesting that he preferred the facility of slogans to the greater challenge of words.

'My friend tells me they are taking photographs again, as evidence in future events,' the girl said furtively, her restless gaze seeking to penetrate the shifting crowd. Her friend pulled a sock over his face as a precaution, like a terrorist, only his eyes remaining visible.

'Taking photographs as evidence of what?' asked the Old Man.

'Us. That's what happened the last time. We gave the soldiers flowers, and gained their sympathy. The Old Guys played for time. When they saw that we were winning, they sent in soldiers from the provinces, who only had orders to go by, and no emotional contact with us. They murdered a great number of us, and hunted the rest, on the basis of photographs and videos *agents provocateurs* had taken of us during the preceding days. They are still after us, to bring us to cursory trial, and to execute us.'

'Execute you?'

'Yes, as rebels against the authority of the Party, of the Old Men. They never thought their actions would be so widely known, as accurately interpreted. They thought it was still possible in this day and age to sweep us all under the carpet, and pretend we had never existed, as would have been the case in all preceding centuries. They were amazed, and horrified, when certain countries temporarily abrogated treaties, or even imposed limited sanctions in their anger at what had occurred. The only calculation in which they were right was one of utter cynicism. They guessed how the temptations of the huge potential Chinese market was too great to allow the fury to last longer than a symbolic period, and that before long all would fall into place again, with the flower of our youth under the ground. Apart from that, and the fact that the old were older, everything is exactly as it was. But – we served a purpose towards the family of man. Without our sacrifice, and the pig-headedness of our leaders, the peaceful revolutions of Poland, Hungary and, even more so, of East Germany and Czechoslovakia could not have taken the form they did. For a period after Tienanmen, no police force could lift a weapon against students. So we are testing the water today, to see if, even here, another Tienanmen is possible or not.'

'If it is?' asked the Old Man, cautiously.

'We will catch up with the other nations.'

'If not?' Mr Smith enquired brashly.

'Those who escaped last time will die.'

Before any more could be said, the young man in the stocking headgear spun round and swung an accurate fist at a passer-by, who let a camera slip down his tunic and onto the paving stones. For a moment both struggled for the camera. Curiously enough the other man, although not as young as the student, also wore a headband with an inflamatory slogan written on it.

'*Agent provocateur*,' explained the girl.

The student managed to expropriate the camera, and threw it to the girl before grappling with the photographer again. The girl removed the film expertly, then placed the camera on the ground.

'Come on,' ordered the girl.

'Where to?' asked the Old Man, perplexed by the speed of developments.

'We have been ordered to keep moving. My friend will probably be arrested. We have the film. It must not be found. You must be on it too. That is bad for foreigners.'

Not even the Old Man could guess just how bad it was, nor that there was another eye prying into his affairs, and from the least expected quarter, outer space, normally his own bailiwick.

* * *

As the enlargements of the spy satellite's photographs dried, the man in charge of that technical department somewhere near Washington expressed his surprise conventionally, with a low whistle. He then proceeded as per instructions, by putting through a few heavily coded and mysterious telephone calls which resulted in a rapid convocation of interested parties in a heavily screened briefing room somewhere safely out of range of everything but coffee in paper cups.

Less than an hour after the initial discovery, Lougene W. Twistle stood before the huge enlargement of the aerial photograph, a pointer in his hand, holding forth to a handful of experts who craned forward like sprinters on their blocks.

'This is photograph AP dash MS dash 11.932.417, taken at fourteen twenty-one hours local time, over Tienanmen Square, Peking, otherwise Beijing, on the 4th, 11th. As you can see, the square shows unusual activity, the space having been largely empty or sparsely occupied since the events some months ago. I refer, of course, to the student rioting and the intervention of the Army.'

'Let's get down to the nitty-gritty,' commanded Milton Runway, one of the heads of the FBI. 'None of us have much time.'

'I am acting on instructions, sir. Not all my clients are as well informed as you gen'lemen are. Senators, congressmen, the like,' Twistle explained.

'We appreciate that,' snapped Runway.

'Before we start, does anyone want their coffee replenishing?'

There was no consensus, so Twistle went on at his own measured pace.

'Reasons for the enlargement. Well, there were many small touches of white, usually student headbands, or, in some cases, banners, which are, in the main, rectangular, even seen from a distance of a few thousand miles. There was one white patch which was rounded, however, and which even under a magnifying glass looked incompatible with a headband – it was too large – and not of a nature to be extended between two poles. I decided for maximum enlargement. Here, gen'lemen, is the result of the fine work of our laboratories. Here—' And he waved his pointer over the mass of humanity '—are the students, a few militiamen and others, whose purpose in the square could not be established with any accuracy – but here—' And he pointed to the specific white rotundity '—here we find a man of moderate to considerable corpulence, who seems to have fallen to the ground, being the reason for his occupying an abnormally large area. By him, if you gen'lemen look carefully – he's a little tough to make out on account of he's dark, and against a dark background – is a small guy with long hair and what looks like a kind of unkempt beard. He's stretching out a hand, maybe to help the portly party rise to his feet. At first you'd be entitled to think this guy Chinese like the rest, but when you take a good look at the aforementioned portly party, you notice a white beard and bald or sparsely covered cranium, also the considerable amount of space accorded his centre section, or belly area, being all the more noticeable by virtue of his recumbency, whereas every other party in the portion of the square under review is, or are, on his or her feet.'

'I seen enough to convince me,' said Runway. 'That's them.'

'I was just going to refresh you gen'lemen's memories of how the two wanted men looked at the time they were still in the United States,' remarked Twistle, as an illuminated slide machine began to run through shapes of the Old Man and Mr Smith on television with Joey Henchman and their passport stills from the confiscated Saudi Arabian passports, among other shreds of evidence.

'I don't have to see them again. Christ, could you guys forget a couple o'jerks who handed out the biggest humiliation in the FBI's history? That's them OK. Now—' And with a surge of bile at the continuing parade of memorabilia, 'Will you please turn that goddam machine off, mister!'

Twistle, a little sullen like all technicians who have had their day in court interrupted by those who imagine themselves too highly placed for thoroughness, switched the machine off, while leaving the enlargement brightly lit.

'If you gen'lemen should require my presence, I'll be on extension 72043,' he said, and left discreetly. His job as an eloquent and lucid cog in a vast machine was done.

Runway stood up and began pacing. This was evidently his routine for deeper contemplation. 'Now listen fellows,' he said, his voice presaging a great satisfaction, 'we're back on track. According to Israeli Intelligence, these fellows told their Israeli interrogators that their next stop was Japan. They end up in China. Now, question is, was that a change of plan, or, is their range limited, as that of an aircraft?'

'I don't see what difference—' began Lloyd Shrubs, another member of the group.

'Every difference in the goddam world,' shrieked Runway, in his endless impatience, his eyes shut, grimacing. He relaxed in order to explain his vision of things.

'A change of plan anyone can have. Right?'

'Right,' echoed Shrubs.

'But let's say, their plans had not changed. They wanted to get to Japan. But they plain ran out of whatever gas they operate on. Get it? And they force-landed in Beijing!'

'What does that tell us?' Shrubs pursued doggedly.

'It tells us the range of which they're capable!' enunciated Runway, as if to an idiot. 'Extend a compass between Tel Aviv and Beijing on the map. Now turn that compass over the map, its point remains in Beijing. You now have the precise distance they can travel from Beijing without landing!'

'In other words,' said Shrubs, 'we know that they can't get further than the Yukon, or Djakarta, or Bangalore, or back again to Tel Aviv without taking a short rest. Some information.'

'OK.' Runway calmed down dramatically, and tried another tack. 'We know they crossed the North Atlantic on a Concorde. Why? It was an absurd risk to take, in view of their status as felons. Were they forced into this decision by a knowledge of their own limitations? Was there a real risk of being forced down at sea?'

'I can't answer that,' said Shrubs.

'I know you can't. And I can't either. But isn't it our solemn duty to study the nature of the beast? Should a good intelligence operator not attempt to know all there is to know about his adversary? Can you tell in advance what shred of information is going to come in handy at what precise moment?'

'Of course not,' agreed Shrubs, 'but there's got to be degrees of likelihood, and you've got to take even hunches into account, gut feelings.'

'I'm not discounting them,' replied Runway serenely.

'OK, so what's your gut feeling about where they're heading?' asked Shrubs, slipping a piece of chewing gum into his mouth as an aid to reflection.

'My gut feeling?' Runway enquired as though appealing to his own highest authority. 'Japan. That's where they said they were going. That's where they would have gone if they hadn'a run out of combustible material.'

'Japan? I got another scenario for you.' Shrubs was relentless.

'Oh?'

'They lied to the Mossad. The whole Japan pitch is just a king-size red herring. Catch of the day. They're in Egypt, or Jordan, or Eye-rack, one of them countries.'

'You forgot one angle,' muttered Runway, playing one of his seemingly endless supply of trump cards. 'The fat guy says he's God. Now God don't lie. And a guy says he's God don't lie either. Why? Because he wants his God story to stick. On top of which, people don't lie to the Mossad. They assume you're lying in any case, and you'll do anything not to confirm their lousy opinion of you.'

'So?'

'So, we're opting for Japan. And alerting all our agents within the radius of the presumed flight capacity of our couple.'

'There's gonna be a lot of sleepless nights.'

'Better than let them get through our fingers again. It's no longer just a question of law enforcement, Lloyd. It's a question of goddam honour.'

'One angle we can discount,' said Stanley Rohdblokker, who knew better than to interrupt until then. 'The allegations that the felons was working for the Russkis, and, in fact, getting their classified means of propulsion from them.'

'I don't want to discount anything, however preposterous it may seem,' Runway insisted. 'On the face of it, the theory appears implausible. Why, the Reds don't even have solid fuels for their missile programme. How could they be so advanced in some respects, and so retrogressive in others? Apart from which, they are known to be more adept at the larger, less subtle fields of science and engineering than at the miniaturized ones. That being said, the old guy and his companion did visit Moscow, if only briefly. Now, was this in order to consult with the KGB, and receive new instructions? It's too soon to know, although it does appear from our information that their stay in the Soviet capital was no longer than three hours or so, which included most of a morning session at the Congress, in which they both made speeches. There seems hardly time for a briefing as well. However . . .'

'Where did we get this information?' It was indefatigable Shrubs, at it again.

'Russian sources, and some of our own.'

'We now have to rely on *Russian* sources for information *about* Russia?' Shrubs made it sound incredible.

'Those are the terms of our treaty of mutual assistance, the facts of life, Lloyd. Naturally, we double check whenever possible.'

'*Whenever possible?*' enquired Shrubs, making it sound even more of a betrayal.

'Yes. Goddam it, what are you insinuating, Lloyd? That we sold ourselves down the river by signing any kind of a document with them?' shouted Runway.

'You got it.'

'Think of a better way.'

Into this charged atmosphere came Declan O'Meeaghan, pronounced O'Mean, and as devious a performer as his name suggested.

'To change the subject for a moment, while still remaining within the framework of our terms of reference, is there any proof for or against a prevalent supposition about our two renegade forgers, i.e., that they are gay?'

'Oh, for Christ's sake Declan, what would it help us to know that?'

'Such people are often open to temptation, which could be strewn subtly in their way as they proceed across the world. We could, I'm ensured, entrap them if we played our cards correctly.'

Runway cleared his throat. 'First of all, we have the confidential medical reports from the hospital to which they were taken when originally arrested. I don't want to go into those in any detail. Suffice it to say, they seem not to possess the wherewithal for any deviation from a vegetative form of existence. I don't know if I make myself clear?'

'No,' said Shrubs.

'They had no veins, no arteries.'

'Are you serious?'

'Absolutely. How they tick remains a mystery. Once this is so, it is tougher to conceive of them having any kind of physical life, with the temptations that go with it. That being said, Declan, although we have many brilliant minds in our outfit, with many wonderful qualifications, I can't offhand think of anyone capable of laying a trap for faggots in the People's Republic of China.'

'Tomorrow it may be Japan, Nepal, Kamchatka . . .'

'Is that any easier?'

'There has to be a way . . .' muttered Declan, biting the top of a pencil like a schoolboy, a mesh of coal-black hair falling over an ice-blue eye, the image of a corrupt cardinal on the verge of being unmasked.

* * *

Back in the square, the girl kept moving the Old Man and Mr Smith as though she knew what she was doing, and in full control of some infallible procedure. The atmosphere became vaguely oppressive.

'Why do we keep moving in this tiresome way?' asked the Old Man.

'It would be folly to stay still,' the girl replied.

'If we must move, can't we move out of the square?'

'That would be suicide. They will arrest anyone who leaves.'

'How do you know they won't arrest anyone who stays?'

'I don't.'

'How do you feel?' asked Mr Smith anxiously.

'As well as is to be expected. Why did we land here of all places?' the Old Man enquired, panting.

'We ran out of steam, juice, whatever you like to call it. We didn't just land. We fell. Two mortals would have hurt themselves badly.'

'It may be only my imagination, but I fancy I did hurt myself.'

'If you must talk, do it in Chinese,' said the girl, grimly.

'Chinese? But we don't look Chinese,' remarked the Old Man.

'There is a great deal of anti-foreign feeling now that foreign powers are tending to behave as though Tienanmen never happened.'

'Have you the strength to reach Japan if we should have to vanish in a hurry?' Mr Smith demanded.

'I don't know,' replied the Old Man in Cantonese, his eyes shut in sheer misery.

'Not Cantonese!' snapped the girl. 'They are as unpopular as the foreigners for the time being.'

'We may have to leave at a moment's notice,' Mr Smith warned, in Outer Mongolian.

'If things get desperate enough, one always finds the strength,' wheezed the Old Man.

'Why do you speak Uzbek when I address you in the slang of Ulan Bator?'

'I know Mongolian, of course,' sighed the Old Man. 'That is one of the principal perks of omniscience. But I've never heard it spoken. I have no idea how to pronounce it.'

'I did a lot of basic temptations out there in better times. Poor darlings, they were sitting ducks. They had so little. And they responded to every emotion – gaiety, slapstick, charm, tragedy, desire – with wild shrieks. It was often difficult to decipher their true feelings.'

Mr Smith was interrupted in his reverie by a net which seemed to unravel between two lampposts, falling over them all like a huge bell. It quickly tightened with the effect of a noose, driving the twenty or so people within its radius into violent contact with each other. They were prisoners of the militia who gathered round, grinning with satisfaction and taking evident pleasure in brandishing their weapons.

The girl cursed. 'The oldest trick in the repertoire, and I didn't see it coming.' Then she became her usual glacial self. 'That film must never fall into their hands. They will strip me. They enjoy that.'

'Give it to me,' said the Old Man softly.

'They may desist from searching you because you are a foreigner, although I doubt it in their present mood.'

'Let's have it. I can look after myself, have no fear.'

They were pressed so close to each other the girl had some difficulty in reaching into her pocket and passing the film to the Old Man.

'I feel like setting a few fires,' screeched Mr Smith, isolated from the

Old Man by several students, who were struggling hysterically against the raw strands of rope pressing in from all sides.

'Don't do anything rash!' appealed the Old Man. 'Let's get out of the square first. One false move on our part, and the whole place could go up like a bonfire.'

The students outside appealed to the police, passing flowers around, but ears were deaf. A truck backed into the area emptied of demonstators. Its back flap fell to the ground, and the pressure of the net eased. The hem was raised, and the prisoners were allowed out one by one, cudgelled by the militia as they bent low, and pushed rudely toward the truck, into which they were forced to mount, encouraged by rifle butts and truncheons belonging to other militiamen. The girl was tripped as she emerged, and savagely beaten as she lay on the ground. Then she was isolated from the other prisoners. The Old Man received his ration of poking with a rifle barrel by a militiaman who was inspired to playfulness by the sheer size of his target. The Old Man gently seized the rifle, twisted the barrel into a knot, and handed it back to its user with a smile.

'Now explain that to your sergeant,' he said in Mandarin.

The militiaman looked at his weapon in amazement, his eyes wide, his mouth twisted into a joyless grin of disbelief.

'I have the necessary energy!' the Old Man called out to Mr Smith as he clambered into the truck. 'It all depends if the mind is engaged.'

Mr Smith received a savage cuff as he slid under the net, and a gob of spittle full in the face, presumably as a hated foreigner. Mr Smith paid his tormentor back in kind, landing an arrow of saliva into his eyes. The militiaman screamed, clutching his hands to his face in agony.

'You saw too much in any case,' declared Mr Smith, also in Mandarin, and added, 'Now go and make a Chinese proverb out of that.'

As he was climbing into the truck, he let out a terrifying scream, the sound of a nail file in action, amplified beyond the point of human endurance. The militiaman, who had been rubbing his eyes, suddenly doubled up in sheer anguish, placing his hands over his ears to protect them, only too late.

As the truck moved away with a jerk, the Old Man asked Mr Smith, 'What have you done?'

'He can still talk,' Mr Smith stated with a total lack of expression. 'He'll be able to tell his kids about it.'

The Old Man looked at his colleague, at times so invaluable, so understanding, so surprising, and saw only the green and blue veined pallor of a ripe gorgonzola, lips wet as a winter pathway, nostrils like caverns in eroded limestone cliffs, eyes as flecked as reflections of the moon in stagnant pools on nights of scudding cloud. All he could find it in himself to say, with the monotony of responses, was, 'Smith, Smith, Smith . . .'

The truck creaked and groaned as it moved slowly through the surly crowd. The Old Man and Mr Smith had nothing to say to one another until a sudden proximity of houses on both sides indicated that they were on a normal road at last.

'We have left the square,' murmured the Old Man. 'Any time you wish . . .'

'You feel up to it?' asked Mr Smith, concerned.

'On those rare occasions when I am angry, I feel up to anything. But why Tokyo?'

'There's one man we both ought to meet before our adventure comes to an end. Matsuyama-San.'

'Who?'

'Quiet,' yelled the guard from the back of the truck. 'You'll have time enough to talk when the Colonel asks you questions in his own inimitable way.'

Mr Smith sidled up to the guard through a few students who seemed either broken in spirit or keeping their energies intact. He spoke Mandarin in a very low undertone.

The guard strained to hear. 'What?'

Mr Smith repeated his question, which was almost certainly about his need to visit a toilet.

The guard bent even lower to catch the question.

In a flash, Mr Smith had seized his ear between his jagged teeth, and hung on like a dog.

The guard screamed, and could not even struggle to free himself, so fragile did his ear seem to him under such circumstances. Suddenly a new pain of similar intensity made him divide his attention. Both his boots were on fire. Mr Smith tore half the man's ear off with a vicious shake of the head, and tossed the unresisting guard over the tailgate and into the roadway. Soon the man with the burning boots was lost to view as he writhed and howled in the deserted street.

Mr Smith lowered the tailgate and made a magnanimous gesture to the students. One after the other, they leaped free of the truck in gathering excitement. Soon the Old Man and Mr Smith were alone.

'Now?'

Mr Smith merely shook his head negatively.

'What is that repellent object in your mouth which is preventing you from talking?'

'Oh.' Mr Smith had quite forgotten that there was something in his mouth on which he had been nervously nibbling. He took out the part of the guard's ear, and tossed it away like an empty packet of cigarettes.

'Just give them a few moments to make their getaway.'

After a long pause, Mr Smith said, 'Give me your hand.'

'What's in your mind?'

There were cries of alarm from the front of the truck.

'What have you done?' the Old Man asked, as the vehicle screeched to a halt.

'The engine and all four of the tyres are on fire.'

The driver and a couple of guards who were in the front cabin gabbled furiously as they appeared in the roadway and registered their consternation at seeing the body of the truck empty and the tailgate hanging limply down.

'You know,' the Old Man said, 'when I first conceived the human ear, I thought of it as an object of unutterable beauty ... and balance ...'

'Not now. Later,' said Mr Smith tactfully, and they both quietly disappeared, while the guards emptied a couple of submachine-guns into the space where they had been.

18

It was raining miserably in Tokyo as they made a perfect soft landing in a depressing alleyway somewhere in the poorest, most claustrophobic area of the city.

'You did that perfectly,' said Mr Smith, in a surprisingly tender recognition of the Old Man's capability. 'Are you still angry?'

'Angry, no. But my sensibilities were sharpened by our Chinese adventure. We had no intention of going there. What drove us there? Yes, yes, I know you are going to say we ran out of energy, but why Tienanmen Square? Why not anywhere else in that large country, some isolated paddy field, some temple destroyed during the Cultural Revolution?'

'You know about that?' asked Mr Smith, amazed.

'I'm always fascinated by old men who lose their heads, who declare war on impotence, or enforced immobility, on clouded minds. Mao Zedong attracted my immediate attention. He elected to swim when walking became a problem. Like another old codger in Africa.'

'Bourguiba, in Tunis.'

'That's it, swam everywhere to show he could still move, the most eloquent of returns to the womb, swimming in placenta. Only Mao did one better: swam with one hand while holding his little book of platitudes in the other, a pretty sordid sales pitch for a volume which was no good anyway. Then, when his desire for immortality became unbearable, he instructed his young people to go out and destroy everything old except himself. The final revenge, the final proof of senility, of a mind rusted away by usage.'

'You seem to have made quite a study of your subject.'

'Do you wonder, at my age?' murmured the Old Man, ruefully, and then added, with knitted brows ... 'Why Tienanmen Square? Presumably we still had something specific to learn. But what took us there? Destiny? But we are destiny . . .'

They stood in silence for a moment under the driving rain. Water was splashing from drains into barrels, and then onto the cobbled roadway, while the occasional old woman passed by on her resonant clogs, echoing down the narrow street.

'Where are we going?' asked the Old Man.

'It is difficult to know in Japan, since the houses are numbered according to the year of their construction, but I believe it to be that black aperture over there.'

'There is no door in that aperture.'

'That should not surprise one in the poorer parts of the city. But do you see that small shining object under the roof? We are already under electronic surveillance.'

'They can see us from inside?'

'Our every move is recorded.'

'And what do we expect to find there?'

'Matsuyama-San.'

They began to cross the street, stepping cautiously over the gushing water, yellowed by dislodged soil, which cascaded down the hill, finding its way arbitrarily between the cobbles. As they picked their way towards the house of Matsuyama-San, squeezed tortuously between other houses on different levels, the Old Man suddenly said, 'Oh yes, the human ear. I remember. It was a difficult decision, how to make it both functional and beautiful. Quite a problem. After many trials and errors, I was rather pleased with the result. Vaguely inspired by sea shells, I admit, but no poorer for that. On the whole it was more successful than the foot, a part of the body which gave me trouble from the outset. I tried to make it as harmonious as the hand, but the average body just couldn't balance on such a fragile base, and I was reduced to coarsening it until it became the functionally efficient and yet somehow stunted object it is. But the ear . . . ah, the ear . . .'

'I apologize for my behaviour. It must have shocked you,' said Mr Smith, as he extended his hand to help the Old Man negotiate the slippery descent.

'I had become used to something else,' the Old Man admitted. 'At times I had even quite overlooked who you are. But contact with a civilization which may be, for all I know, just a trice too old, brought out a kind of primeval callousness in you, a recklessness, a savagery you had made me forget.'

'Why does a man need sight and sound when he has profited so little from these privileges when he possessed them?'

'In that case, it was a cruelty not a kindness to leave him with his power of speech.'

'Of course. Let him bore others with the accounts of his calamity until his dying day.'

'And what about the ear, now we're on the subject. Was that necessary?'

'He only needs to grow his hair long. It's quite the fashion these days. I found the whole incident rather disappointing. There's not much meat on an ear. I suppose it could become an acquired taste, like squid.'

Despite his squeamishness, the Old Man chuckled softly. 'You really are a wild, unprincipled little fellow.'

'You have to be in this job,' said Mr Smith, preening himself in the warmth of the compliment. 'The order of the day is an unsentimental view of life and an inherent toughness to back up your integrity with action.'

The radar had moved like the eye of a cyclop, and as a result of its investigation, four ferocious Akita dogs now rushed into the street from the sombre aperture, stern, silent, unforgiving. Mr Smith shrieked, and sought shelter behind the Old Man.

'It's no use changing yourself into some impressive beast. These dogs are afraid of nothing.'

'What are they?' whispered Mr Smith, whose teeth were chattering with fear.

'Akitas. With four of them, there is no need for a door.'

The Old Man held up his hand, and said, 'Sit,' in Japanese, of course.

The four Akitas obediently sat, awaiting further instructions, their light eyes alert.

'It's remarkable. But they could easily get up from a sitting position,' suggested Mr Smith.

The Old Man lowered his hand, and turned the palm down. 'Lie,' he said, in Japanese.

The four Akitas lay down, their eyes as vigilant as ever.

'Perhaps they could have a short nap,' suggested Mr Smith, 'or even a long one. An eternal one, perhaps.'

'Are you sure you don't want a bit out of one of their ears first?' asked the Old Man.

'I'm sorry.'

The Old Man moved his fingers slowly, as though languorously playing a scale in the air.

'This is going to be more difficult,' he said, and then his voice acquired a dreamy quality. 'You are very sleepy,' he informed the Akitas. 'You wish to dream of bones . . . bones . . . bones . . .'

The dogs did not seem to grow drowsy, but fixed the Old Man with their habitual alertness.

'I told you this would be more difficult,' the Old Man commented.

'May I make a suggestion?'

'What is it?' The Old Man was a little irritated that someone in Mr Smith's perilous condition should actually give advice.

'Would it not be more effective to continue speaking Japanese, instead of breaking into Polish as you have done?'

'Is that what I have done? That just shows that I'll be swimming myself soon, holding aloft my tablets with one hand.'

The Old Man changed to a kind of dog-Japanese. 'You are very sleepy . . . You wish to dream of bones . . .'

One by one the light eyes shut.

'You dream of intruders.'

In their sleep, sixteen canine legs began twitching.

'You have bitten their ankles.'

Four fangs were bared, and snapped together, some foam flecking their muzzles for a moment.

'Now you think only of sle-e-ep . . . sle-e-ep . . .'

The four Akitas flopped over as though drugged.

'What if they wake up before it is time to leave?'

'They won't. Come, let us enter.'

When the two men appeared in the threshold, there was panic from several tiny women, and a young man or two who rushed hither and thither, bowing, muttering and expressing medieval deference.

'Matsuyama-San,' said Mr Smith, with the arrogance of a *samurai* seeking a single combat which is his due.

The domestics parted like waters to let them through. The rooms were absolutely bare except for an occasional folded mat or low table, but there were more of them than one could have guessed from outside.

In the final room, perched on cushions and held in place by a wickerwork chairback, was a man of extreme old age. So old was he, in fact, that the features of the skull were more salient than what was left of the features of the face. It was as though skin had been stretched over the bones as tightly as the surface of a drum. This made Matsuyama-San practically incapable of any movement. His mouth was almost permanently open, since there wasn't the skin available to allow him to shut it. A thin trickle of wetness was visible on one side of his mouth as his jaws sought to formulate words with a flickering uncertainty. His eyes, on those rare occasions when they were visible, were clay-coloured. They moved about within apertures which looked as if they had been slashed into the face with a dagger. A few isolated hairs were left on his ravaged pate, like reeds at the edge of a pond.

'Matsuyama-San?' enquired Mr Smith.

The smallest of nods acknowledged the question.

Mr Smith squatted on his haunches, and he invited the Old Man to do likewise. The Old Man felt safer sitting on the floor.

'We are friends from foreign parts,' Mr Smith said in a loud voice, on the fairly safe assumption that Matsuyama-San must be deaf.

Matsuyama-San lifted an agued forefinger. That was always the signal that, whether one could hear him or not, he was speaking. He spoke English to foreigners, Japanese to dogs and other servants.

'I saw your treatment of my Akitas.'

'How?' called out Mr Smith.

The same febrile forefinger searched for a knob among a whole keyboard of them. He pressed it, and the entire bamboo wall disappeared upwards, to reveal a battalion of no fewer than forty television sets, all of them showing different activities in various workplaces. Only the first one showed the courtyard with the four Akitas, asleep where the Old Man had left them.

'Powerful medicine,' Matsuyama-San muttered.

'It's no medicine,' replied Mr Smith, 'but some of God's best magic.'

Matsuyama-San found this irresistibly droll, and shuddered with silent mirth.

'What makes you laugh, if I may ask?'

'God.'

The Old Man tried to look dignified, and distant.

Suddenly Matsuyama-San appeared to snarl. His mood change was sudden and perplexing.

He pushed a button which lit up.

A young man in traditional costume entered, bowing low. Matsuyama-San held up three fingers, then two.

The young man looked at the screens, muttering, 'Number thirty-two,' then produced one of those traditionally Japanese sounds, expressive of exaggerated disapproval, a sustained note on the lower register of a trombone.

'What's wrong?' asked Mr Smith.

The young man looked at Matsuyama-San for permission to reply. It was accorded by a gesture so small as to be invisible to those who were not of the household.

'In factory number thirty-two, in Yamatori Prefecture, where we make submarine turbines and electronic organs, the morning break has been over for two minutes, and still some employees are laughing in the canteen.' He picked up a phone and dialled only two numbers. It was evidently a direct line. He spoke shortly and forcefully, then transferred his gaze to screen number thirty-two. The female employees were just dispersing to go back to work. Matsuyama-San twisted a knob, and their conversation became audible. A man entered the area of the small screen, barking officiously and ticking off names on a list. The two scolded employees bowed and seemed on the verge of tears, as though suffering punishment in some hellish kindergarten.

'What is going on?' Mr Smith enquired.

'Employees in keyboard section of electronic organ department get punishment for laughter after end recreation,' explained the young man.

'What punishment?'

'Only half-salary pay this week. If happen twice, dismiss, and once dismiss, no can find employment in any other major Japanese corporation for five year. Is agreement between majors, initiative Matsuyama-San, biggest of majors.'

'All that for giggling after the end of the recreation period?'

'Equal punishment for giggle before recreation period.'

'And during recreation period?'

'Recreation period called name so can get rid of all giggle during.'

'It seems very tough on the inveterate giggler.'

Matsuyama-San didn't understand this, but thought he would like to make his own contribution to the briefing, without relying too heavily on a proxy.

'Matsuyama-San employ over two million person,' he said of himself, while holding up two fingers.

'Two million!' exclaimed the Old Man, hardly able to believe his ears.

'You God?'

'That is correct.'

Matsuyama-San cackled playfully, and held up one finger.

'My name, Mr Smith,' shouted Mr Smith.

'Amelican.'

'Not necessarily.'

'God also Amelican.'

The Old Man and Mr Smith looked at one another.

It was hard to decide whether Matsuyama-San was very silly or profoundly ironic.

'What else God can be but Amelican?' he asked with the limited joviality at his disposal. 'Am not Amelica God own country?'

The Old Man decided that there was a distinct malevolence behind the cutting edge of these allusions.

'How strange to find a man of enormous wealth and power living in such a relatively popular quarter of the city,' the Old Man remarked.

'God not understand?' Matsuyama-San asked, and then his mood darkened, so that he began to resemble death itself. 'Japanese got no one god,' he purred. 'Japanese prefer to keep worship in family, worship ancestors. I not worship ancestors; ancestors not good; compel me do everything myself. I born here, in this house. My ancestors born here. Cooks, carpenters, plumbers, thieves, all share. Many people. Old, young, new born, uncles, aunts, cousins, all live here. Much noise, much commotion, no silence. Now, I, alone. Much silence, much contemplation, much reflection. My brothers, all dead. My sisters, all dead. My children, some dead, some live big houses, swimming pool, barbecue, wooden bridges over artificial waterway, all luxury. Two my sons, kamikaze, sink ships. One, kill self at war end. Full of disgrace. Luck of game. I survive war. Continue Japanese tradition. Employ two million people. Soon perhaps more. No more sink enemy ships. Old times. Now sink enemy automobiles, television, camera, watch, hi-tech, new times. Good and evil criteria of past. Old times. Polarity of future, efficiency and inefficiency, have and have not. Today, *samurai* live again, but in industry, not in single combat but in boardroom.'

'Just a minute,' bellowed the Old Man, 'are you suggesting that good and evil have been supplanted by efficiency and inefficiency? Did I understand you accurately?'

'Most correctly. This is new dimension in human behaviour. Rivals speak much of efficiency, but never carry idea to logical conclusion. Appoint quality control, other gimmick, but allow giggle during working hours. Two incompatible. Can be no exception in quest for total efficiency. Equation as follows. Total efficiency equal total virtue.'

'Curious,' reflected the Old Man. 'We do our best to speak like mortals, in order not to give any impression of superiority, out of politeness you understand, as a social grace. You, on the other hand, Matsuyama-San, speak like an immortal, for a motive which I do not dare to understand.'

A ghost of a smile fell over the toothless mouth like lace. 'Most acute observation,' Matsuyama-San whispered, his index finger feeling its way to another switch. The bamboo screen behind his throne disappeared downwards, unveiling a strange machine.

'This state-of-the-art life-support machine. The last step on the road to immortality. Within five years, my factories have the order to master technique of everlasting life. Confidential report yesterday give me great happiness. Tell me work going well. Take perhaps less than five year.'

'But what happens if you should die before your experts have finished their work?'

'I go at once on life-support machine. Holes already bored in my flesh to receive sensors. Also have slot in back skull. Receive disk. Record all thoughts during coma. Can give coded instruction while unconscious. One last step all needed to open prospect of immortality to all deserving.'

'And this prospect gives you pleasure, you poor fool?'

Matsuyama-San took a moment to absorb the insult like medicine.

'For years I dispense with pleasure. Pleasure replaced by achievement.'

'Have you never loved?' enquired the Old Man.

'Hated?' Mr Smith threw in, in order not to be left out.

'Ah so. For last half century at least reserve one hour a day for wife, one hour for geisha, one hour for prostitute. I have no idea whether these females are the same as they were when I made the rule. I believe improbable. But they are under instructions to be good friends, whoever they are.' A frown grew on Matsuyama-San's emaciated face as he hesitated. 'You see,' he admitted slowly, his index finger in the air, 'for some years, I have difficulty in recognizing people. I recognize only achievement, and misdemeanour.'

'How many children did you have?' The Old Man was as tactful as a doctor.

'Don't ask me the impossible,' scolded Matsuyama-San. 'I have no idea. In a sense all my employees, two million, two hundred and forty-one thousand, eight hundred and sixty-three of them, are my children, to be praised and punished. The young men in the house here may well be children of mine. I treat them badly enough. On the other hand, I can still, with failing eyesight, distinguish between my four Akitas. I know them by name. Divine Thunder, Celestial Volcano, Vengeful Lightning and Imperial Warrior. And I remember their parents with respect. Dragon Breath and Fragile Bloom.'

'You say your eyesight is failing. How will you replace your eyes, even in immortality?' asked Mr Smith.

Matsuyama-San reverted to his sketch of a grin. 'Special lenses already tested, with plastic replacement for optical nerve, housing special sensors. Hearing too, techniques evolve from hi-fi, with microphones the size of half a garden pea implanted in drum. Hear and see better than child.'

'And have you no fear of the effect of arrogance on your character?' the Old Man elocuted slowly.

'What kind of question is that,' Matsuyama-San croaked derisively. 'Arrogance? I know nothing else. I command. I order. Arrogance is my existence.'

'You enjoy it?'

'Enjoyment is a weakness, a vice, self-indulgence. Bad word. I enjoy nothing. I am. That is all.'

'Then I will teach you humility,' cried the Old Man in his most

224

fulgurant cadence. 'I will place you on the defensive once again, where you belong. Look at me!'

'I look, God.' And there was a trace of mockery in his voice.

'You are sure? I can't see your eyes from here. Don't make me do this more than once. I too am old, and it takes some effort. Are you ready?'

'What you going to do? Prove to me that God still have remnant of power?'

'Precisely. When I count to three, you may notice a transformation in me. Keep watching me. Nothing else.'

'I thought you hated relying on miracles for your effects,' hissed Mr Smith.

'There is no other way in the face of such obtuseness,' thundered the Old Man. 'One. Two. Three!'

And he vanished into thin air.

His absence hardly seemed to register with Matsuyama-San, although it made Mr Smith distinctly nervous. The prospect of being alone in this quiet madhouse hardly reassured him, and he spent his time during the Old Man's absence eyeing screen number one, on which the Akitas were still mercifully asleep. After ten seconds which seemed like ten minutes, the Old Man reappeared, in serene mood.

'Well?' he asked.

No reply was forthcoming. Nothing about Matsuyama-San had visibly changed. He still sat there, stiff as a ramrod, a non-committal expression on his face, but there was no movement whatsoever.

'He's asleep,' said the Old Man flatly.

'Or dead?' suggested Mr Smith. 'It may have been the shock of seeing you disappear. Should I call that young man to put him on the life-support machine, or shall I have a go? There is a tangle of wires down there.'

'He's asleep,' the Old Man repeated, and cleared his throat with the sound of a not-too-distant earthquake.

Something in Matsuyama-San's face twitched. 'I apologize,' he muttered, 'out of politeness, not because I have to. I fell asleep. At my age it is for practical purposes all that is left which is unpredictable this side of death.'

'Did you see nothing at all?' cried the Old Man.

'I had the impression, perhaps quite erroneous, that you left the room for some purpose, and that, after a while, you returned to your original position on the tatami matting.'

'Once again through the door?'

'How else?'

'That's the point,' shouted the Old Man. 'Now you've had your rest. This time there's no excuse. Keep looking at me. I'm not going to do this a third time. I'll just leave you to stew here in your own unwholesome juices, is that clear? Now. Watch me!'

He waved his hands in Matsuyama-San's eyeline.

Matsuyama-San acknowledged the gesture with a feeble nod. 'I am awake,' he confirmed.

'Right. Now concentrate. One, two, three!'

And he vanished.

This time Mr Smith fancied he saw Matsuyama-San looking cautiously round the room, and especially up to the ceiling. After the statutory ten seconds, the Old Man reappeared, giving Matsuyama-San a visible tremor.

'Well?'

'How much?' came the terse reply.

'I beg your pardon?'

'How much, for the rights?'

'I don't believe it,' murmured the Old Man, deflated.

'I pay well, but not excessively,' said Matsuyama-San. 'It's a good trick, but not essential to perform. Say one hundred thousand US dollars. If you refuse, know that we will master the technique ourselves at a later date, so it is in your interest to conclude deal now.'

'Accept it!' pleaded Mr Smith. 'At least we'd have some legitimate money at last. A hundred thousand US!'

'I can't,' cried the Old Man. 'I know how to do the trick, but I've got nothing to sell. I can't give anyone instructions. It is inherent.'

'Does that matter? Can't you pretend? I'll do it then. I'm as good at disappearing as you are. I'll sell anything.'

'You will be cheating him.'

'He deserves to be cheated!'

'That is another question, and outside the ethical spectrum.'

'To hell with the ethical spectrum.'

Matsuyama-San held his finger aloft. 'I see you arguing, but cannot hear a thing. I will make you my final offer. One hundred and twenty thousand US dollars or yen equivalent for worldwide rights in disappearing trick.'

'He has debased it to a trick! That is the final straw!' roared the Old Man, only to be interupted by a hysterical squawk from Mr Smith.

'Look, look, screen number one. The police!'

In effect, screen number one showed several policemen in riot gear cautiously approaching the house. One of them kicked an Akita, which woke up and grabbed his ankle.

'The dogs are awake!'

'Oh, I can't think of everything,' said the Old Man, disgusted.

'I call police when I first see way you dominate Akita,' Matsuyama-San revealed, his finger indicating a red knob. He turned another knob, and the conversation outside the house amplified. The ferocious growling of the awakened Akita, the cries of the victim, and the efforts of the other policemen to free their companion all came through the loudspeaker in confusion. A large fair-haired man suddenly loomed into sight together with a small Japanese policeman with some characters on his helmet, presumably indicating his superior rank. The fair-haired man's face was distorted by the slight fisheye configuration of the lens.

'OK, so we're agreed. You people go in first. I follow. We don't want to give them the opportunity to vanish before we have a chance of reading their rights to them. Whatever you do, don't scare them. Give them the impression that yours is merely a routine check in response to a false alarm. In other words, lull them into a sense of security. Then I come in, in my own time. I'll try to make a deal with them.'

The Japanese officer nodded.

'The FBI!' exclaimed Mr Smith. 'Them and the dogs! It's too much.'

'How did they find us?' said the Old Man tensely. 'There must be electronic devices already in existence which can trace us. Perhaps this fellow's right.'

'The one thing nobody but us can do is disappear.'

'It's not the most constructive of ploys,' said the Old Man, giving his hand to Mr Smith.

Just then the first Japanese police broke into the room with a great deal of lithe machismo, and the attendant grunts of effort.

'Oh, I do miss my television,' crooned Mr Smith.

'Where's it to be?'

The Japanese officer strode in, holding up a hand. The others lowered the submachine-guns.

'India.'

'India?'

'Our last stop before we shake off this mortal coil.'

'That's pretty. Who wrote that?'

The tall fair-haired man wandered into the room with studied negligence.

'OK, fellows. This is the end of the road for you guys. I guess you know that.'

Their eyes shut, and with beatific smiles on their faces, the Old Man and Mr Smith levitated slowly through the roof, a variant on their usual practice.

'Shit!' cried the fair-haired man. 'One of you guys must have scared them!'

Matsuyama-San's youthful assistant had entered in time to witness the last exchanges, and the ascension. He studied his master with some foreboding. Then he raised the alarm while the police were still awaiting instructions, and the Akitas were yawning drowsily on screen number one.

'Quick. Matsuyama-San is dead. I got to put him on life-support system within two minutes. One of you hold instructions while I plug him in!'

As the assistant manhandled Matsuyama-San, while trying to find the holes in the ancient's back, the latter awoke with a start.

'Idiot! I only dropped off to sleep for a moment. What happened?'

19

Their penultimate journey, while not being the furthest, was nevertheless by far the most taxing, probably because of their battle-scarred condition. They had no idea where they landed, since they fell into a deep slumber almost before they had both hit the ground. How long their sleep lasted they did not know, but by the time the Old Man opened an eye, only to close it again at once, the midday sun was beating down on them relentlessly. The Old Man felt his stomach, which was exposed owing to the upward displacement of his robes during landing, but he quickly withdrew his hand again.

'Good gracious,' he mumbled, 'my belly seems to be white hot. I've never possessed such sensitivity in my hand before.'

Mr Smith stirred. 'What's that? Belly white hot? I thought that was my prerogative during medical examinations!' And he laughed. 'I needed that sleep.'

'Have you ever needed sleep before?'

'We both have. It has become, gradually, a prerequisite for successfully shamming the mortal condition. With me it started with that dreadful hooker in New York City. I can see the elastic marks on her body to this day, like tyre tracks in the snow. There, sleep was inspired by the sheer boredom of being compelled to share her experience of sex. Mark you, I never went through with it, but I could see it coming in the mind's eye, and that was enough to seek the escape road. All that theatrical panting, the mist-filled eyeballs, the rhythmic bouncing, the commercial litany, "it feels so good," the simulated orgasm as the statutory fifteen minutes approaches its end.'

'These are hardly experiences I can share with you with any degree of comfort, or of comprehension . . .' reflected the Old Man.

'I only mention it because it was a kind of milestone for me, the first time I ever slept in my existence, my first taste of that sweet oblivion which has been denied us—'

'We have other advantages.'

'Very few. The ability to disappear, that's all.'

'To travel without tickets, without standing in queues, without relying on public transport—'

'Is that a worthy counterweight to a life without dreams, without rest, without end? I doubt it . . .'

'It worries me, however . . .'

'What?'

'That in simulating mortal existence, we are slowly becoming mortal – at least, certainly more successfully and even more gracefully than Matsuyama-San was becoming immortal.'

'Which means, I suppose, that it is time for us to go,' said Mr Smith slowly.

'It has been time to go for quite a while now. Put your hand on my belly.'

Mr Smith did as he was asked.

'Does that not seem to you almost unbearably hot?' he asked.

'No. No, that is quite a reasonable temperature for a belly, in this climate.'

'I chose the wrong example. But the climate, you do feel the climate.'

'Temperate for me, which means it is painfully hot for most normal people.'

'I never knew what it was to feel heat or cold. Now I have at least an inkling. If this goes on, I begin to worry about our powers to return where we belong.'

'Once we have those powers, they never go, of that I'm sure. All we could lose is our energy. The bedridden remember how to walk, but they can no longer do it.'

'A joyous example, as usual,' remarked the Old Man, as he readjusted his robes, and rose on one elbow. His eyes grew accustomed to the intense, the ever vibrant sunlight, which made the background of shrubbery shimmer. In the shadow of an immense tree, he noticed the silhouettes of what he took at first to be animals, absolutely motionless, yet disturbingly vigilant.

'What are they?' he asked confidentially.

Mr Smith sat up. 'People,' he replied.

'Are you sure?'

'Absolutely. They are practically naked. All men. Thinner than I am. Bald. Wearing metal-rimmed glasses.'

'All of them? How many are there?'

'Five, unless there are others hidden in the tall grass. Five visible.'

'My word, your eyes have lasted well.'

Mr Smith smiled, diabolically. 'They have often been trained on such delights. I think that has kept my eyesight sharp and eager.'

'Keep the reason to yourself. My next question. Who are they?'

'Holy Men.' The answer came from one of the group, in a high, querulous, but gentle voice, in the singing cadence of Mother India.

'Can they hear us from there?' asked the Old Man, perplexed.

'I wouldn't have thought so,' whispered Mr Smith.

'We can hear every word,' came the voice, 'and it confirms us in our opinion that you are also Holy Men of great power and influence, and we are gathered to hear your vurds of vizdom.'

'How did you know we were here?'

'We received a mystic message, all of us, telling us where to come. There are, no doubt, others on their way who have further to travel. Then when we saw you tumble from the sky into the middle of a field, and lie there under the cruel rays of the midday sun, in a part of the country infested with serpents, and to which the tiger is no stranger, we said to ourselves, these are indeed Holy Men of the very first rank, at the very top of the echelon, as it were, and we gathered under this tree to protect our more fallible pates while awaiting your avakening.'

'How did you know we were still alive?' called Mr Smith.

'We could hear you breathing, of course.'

'Which means, no doubt, our snoring,' added the Old Man.

'I will admit, the odd snore punctuated the breathing.'

It was not clear if it was always the same Holy Man talking, or if they had taken it in turns.

'Well, this is certainly quite new,' whispered the Old Man to Mr Smith. 'Having been chased all over the globe by the FB whatever it is, arrested in England, attacked by aircraft over Germany, apprehended in China, entrapped in Japan, stood trial in Israel, been forced by circumstances to assume the disguises of hornets, a grizzly bear, Arab travellers, and delegates from an imaginary part of Soviet Siberia, here

231

we are at last welcomed for more or less what we are. Why so late in our adventure?'

'Because we are not like other people,' came the reply from under the tree.

'You could hear my whisper?'

'On a good day we can even hear each other think,' the voice answered, with a friendly chuckle, and went on, 'You must know that India has for long been a place where the material possibilities are so remote, at least for those of lower caste, that we have tended to direct our energies towards the spiritual goals which are within the grasp of everyone, but towards which government officials, politicians, industrialists, and other corrupt or corruptible stratas of society, or those few, like maharajas or hereditary rulers, above corruption, have no need to apply their minds.'

'That was a very long sentence,' remarked the Old Man.

'We do tend to be long-vinded, for the simple reason that we have extremely long vinds. That is one of the attributes of dominating nature from the lowest level. We breathe very much less than normal people without spiritual goals, and this, coupled with the fact that we are extremely well educated, with very little opportunity to display that education, leads us to be extremely boring when the need arises.'

'I see,' reflected the Old Man. 'You make the best out of the little you have.'

'Brilliantly put, if I may so. Humanity, as we see it, has many common denominators, however diversely it may express them. If mankind sees a ladder before it, or, in the case of India, a rope, there is an irresistible desire to climb it, wherever it may lead – in India's case, nowhere. The entire symbolic weight of the rope trick is inherent in this observation. But the common instinct of society is an upward one. In our case, we recognize with a shudder not only how much is gained by climbing, but how even more is lost.'

'We have just come from Japan, where this was brought home to us,' said Mr Smith. 'There was an old man there, he must have been close to a hundred years old, and he employed well over two million people.'

'That, in itself, is immoral, on condition they are paid. If two million people are paid by the same man, they are never paid enough. That is almost a rule. In order to keep such employees in line, the employer must behave both as a skinflint and as a cruel father, activities which are by no means incompatible. He will lose his soul in increasing his profits.'

'But what did you mean by saying it is immoral to employ two million on condition they are paid? Surely it could be argued that not to pay two million and still derive the benefit of their work is even more immoral, since it's nothing other than slavery?' asked the Old Man.

'Slavery in that sense is a thing of the past. It still exists in many other forms. But I was, of course, referring to our Lord Buddha, who employs considerably more than two million souls, who are unpaid, and therefore fully free of corruption.'

'I see what you mean,' mumbled the Old Man. 'What you are really doing is to reiterate the old saw that money corrupts.'

'How brilliantly, how succintly, you put it.'

'Thousands have put it as brilliantly, as succinctly before me.'

'That in no way dulls the radiance of your remark. I had never heard it before. Money corrupts.'

'The Japanese centenarian told us his factories were on the point of developing a machine which could prolong life indefinitely – in other words, an immortality machine,' Mr Smith explained.

'It will fail.'

'How can you be so sure? It worried us not a little.'

'No, no. A little thing will go wrong. A defective plug or a switch with a short in it. Something insignificant. And what kind of life can a man enjoy when he is dependent on an electrical contact? It is bad enough to be dependent on a liver, or a kidney, or a heart, but those you can forget in the course of the day, however great a hypochondriac you are. A defective contact you can never quite get out of your mind. A toothache causes pain, but never the same kind of anxiety as the instability of a false tooth. What is part of you never causes the loss of sleep occasioned by an artificial adjunct to your person. Since that Japanese geriatric only made that machine for his own use initially, in view of an eventual commercialization at a later date when he can continue to give orders from his pillow, the whole mad initiative will fail miserably, in the pop of a fuse, in the flash of a blackened bulb. It is too insolent to succeed.'

'That is very reassuring. But tell us, how do you manage to acquire such a vision of the world, you who have nothing?' It was the Old Man who spoke.

'We have nothing, and everything. But even if you have everything, you can never have enough of everything. That is why we are here to follow you, and to know even more.'

'And if we do not wish to be followed?'

'We will respect your wishes, of course. But you will never be quite rid of us again.'

'That is comforting,' said the Old Man, with irony. 'But while you are about it, you might as well tell us how you have managed to make so much out of nothing.'

'By resisting that temptation to climb out of reach of our perceptions in that mad rush called progress. But examining that which is closest to us, and bothering to understand it, is the first step to the understanding of all things.'

'You refer to—?'

'The human body. Master it and you are far closer to an understanding of the world than you are milling around in the stratosphere on the end of a wire.'

'And you have mastered it?'

'We have nibbled at the outer shell of comprehension, but even there, we have had a modicum of success. First of all, all of us are certainly a little older in years than your Japanese friend. Most of us are well over one hundred years old, and although our bodies may be vizened, they are not corroded by anxieties. They are spare, and functional. Even in desert areas, we have no fear of dehydration, since we can absorb the dew through the pores of our skin. We can make a meal of a blade of grass, and enjoy the myriad subtleties of its flavour. Two blades of grass is a banquet, a sign of greed, the road to ruin. We can, if need be, empty a small pool of water by absorbing it through the rectum, and vomiting it out a few kilometres away. This we only practise privately, since it tends to revolt the sensitivities of people deprived of this capacity, although I must say we have been at times used by the fire departments of remote rural areas. Every aperture or sphincter of the human body can be used as a valve to intake or to expel. Thanks to yoga and its variants, the senses are sharpened to the point of being able to hear well out of earshot and to see round the curve of the horizon, especially if there are low clouds around to

234

deflect the vision. There is no need to develop our voices to a disagreeable magnitude, since we have mastered the use of wavelengths. None of our perceptions are extra-sensory. They are not arbitrary for a moment, but guided by the full application of developed natural science to the anatomy.'

'Well,' pondered the Old Man, choosing his words with care, 'I cannot reveal to you exactly who I am for fear of offending you – which is a ridiculous complex on my part in view of your reverent attitude towards me – but there it is. I can only say that I am delighted to see the extent to which you have improved on the original blueprint in which I had a hand. I never for a moment guessed the extent to which the design could be improved, even streamlined. It was never designed to run on a single blade of grass at a filling, but if you have managed it, and to slake your thirst by exposing your skin to the early-morning dew, more power to you. What you have done is infinitely flattering.'

'No, we don't know who you are, as you are evidently in heavy disguise, as is your henchman. And we are not sure we really want to know. The only part of your anatomy which is more than familiar are your smiling eyes and the friendly fullness of your stomach. We saw it rising from the shrubbery like a golden cupola after your landing, reflecting the sunlight in a manner which was painful for the eyes. We noticed its majestic contours, and the fact that its smoothness was nowhere indented by signs of a normal birth. It was at that moment that we decided to listen to you as a first step to adoring you.'

There was a long silence, after which the high-pitched voice went on, 'We sincerely hope those are tears of joy.'

The Old Man covered his face with his arm.

The saccharine atmosphere of unadulterated piety was too much for Mr Smith, who was literally bursting at the seams with iconoclasm.

'I am not a henchman,' he shrieked at length, in a voice so disagreeable that the Holy Men flinched.

'We chose the wrong word, and we are full of contrition. Would fellow-traveller do the proverbial trick, in a manner of speaking?'

'I am of equal status, of equal influence.'

'That is evidently a matter of celestial semantics, a field in which our minds are unqualified to graze.'

'You must forgive us,' said the Old Man, suddenly sitting up, 'but we really must be off. We are both weary. Our time here is up. We are called elsewhere . . .'

'We don't both come from the same place,' cried Mr Smith. The timbre of his voice attracted the attention of a tigress, who suddenly appeared in the middle distance, in the belief that the occasional outbursts of ear-grating stridency heralded some rare and succulent form of game which bore investigation.

'If you don't shut up, I'll disappear, and leave you alone with the tiger over there,' muttered the Old Man.

'Tiger? Where?' whispered Mr Smith.

'Sitting still over there with its nostrils in the wind.'

'Don't do that, or I'll disappear myself!'

'And we'll never find one another again.'

This effectively silenced Mr Smith, who began shivering.

'It is a tigress, which is far more dangerous. Judging by her inflamed nipples, she is feeding a litter of cubs,' said the voice of a Holy Man. 'A tiger merely hunts for himself, like a British sportsman, self-indulgence, for the hell of it, as it were, don't you understand. A tigress hunts for her offspring, in a spirit of fearless altruism. She is coming slowly this way.'

'Aren't you afraid?' asked the Old Man.

'We have, over the years, developed an odour emanating from the human body which, while indistinguishable to the average nostril, is deeply repellent to that of a tigress or tiger.'

'My dear, you have been active with your researches.'

'Unfortunately, many Holy Men were devoured by tigers before we had got the formula right, while we were still in a stage of development. They were martyrs to the cause.'

The tigress began to move cautiously forward, head low, conserving her energy for the final pounce.

The Old Man stood up.

Mr Smith shrieked, clinging to the Old Man's cloak. 'Don't leave me here!'

The tigress stopped and blinked, as the shriek stimulated her salivatory glands.

'Not another word, or shriek,' commanded the Old Man, as he stretched out a peremptory hand with caressing motions. The tigress turned on her back, her paws limp, as though expecting to have her chest rubbed.

The Old Man and Mr Smith strode off along a little path, while the Holy Men waved, and a voice rose from their midst, accompanying the travellers with an unchanging intensity even though they were further away with each step.

'We have indeed witnessed a great power for good, which confirms us in our belief that all of nature is one, and that every part of it is as sacred as the whole. Wherever you wander, travellers, we will not be far away. Never again.'

* * *

It was the Old Man who broke the silence over half an hour later. Mr Smith still held a fistful of his robe.

'All of nature may well be one, and every part of it may well be as sacred as the whole. My only regret in the whole beautiful balancing act is that those wretched tiger cubs will have to wait for their supper.'

'As a potential part of that supper,' said Mr Smith, 'I am quite satisfied with the present arrangement.'

'I hope we are, by now, out of earshot.'

'Unless, of course, they can read lips over the curve of the horizon.'

'We have our backs to them.'

They gradually entered what they took to be a village, but which turned out to be the outskirts of a small town. The holy cows wandered about, obstructing traffic and eating lazily off vegetable counters of wayside shops, their expressions being precisely those of somnolent dowagers to whom nothing can be refused. All that was missing were the tiaras. Mr Smith was uncomfortable in the presence of the pariah dogs who looked up with furtive and guilty eyes, and which appeared to be miniature airports for fleas and sinister termites.

'Go away. Dirty,' he kept muttering as he clutched more and more of the Old Man's robe, and tried to avoid contact with the poor scabbed creatures who were permanently in search of something friendly to rub up against. The crowds became more and more intense as the heat of the day blended into the more equable light of the afternoon. They crossed and recrossed the yellow dirt road, steering their way between the tricycles, with their fevered bells, and piles of holy cow excrement. Without warning, Mr Smith let go of the Old Man's cloak, and said, 'Wait for me a moment if you will.' He then walked briskly to a small shop selling everything from electric fans to cones of sherbet, and disappeared inside.

This sudden determination worried the Old Man not a little. For Mr Smith to conquer his cowardice, there had to be a major temptation. The Old Man was forced to move by a holy cow which chose to walk through the spot on which he was standing. The 'let them eat cake' look on her blasé face brooked no compromise. The Old Man looked as though it had been his intention to move in any case, which was far from the truth.

He then saw a man lying in the gutter, a man in such a state of disarray that he made even Mr Smith appear groomed. The Old Man addressed the fellow in Urdu. The man, who was not only caked with filth, but had left his hair to its own devices for many years, replied in a voice dulled by alcohol or drugs, in the pomaded tones of the English landed gentry.

'Don't speak a word of that bloody lingo. The Queen's English, if you please. Or for ever hold your peace.'

'I beg your pardon. I thought you'd left.'

'Left? Left what?'

'India.'

'My old man left. I'm back. Worst luck. Would you believe it. I was a film star. Benedict Romaine. Phoney name. Ever heard of me? Of course not. I was doing too well among the very young for anyone else to have heard of me. Then I did the fashionable thing. Found myself a guru and came to India, paying my keep. Damned expensive considering I ate nothing and only drank a great deal on the quiet. Now I haven't a bean left to my name to go home. Somewhat of a flaming tragedy, wouldn't you say? While we're about it, you wouldn't have the odd rupee to spare, would you?'

'I'm afraid not. Money's the only commodity I have absolutely none of,' said the Old Man compassionately.

'That's what they all say. I'm quite used to it. A beggar here has to be Indian and a Buddhist. I tell you one thing, they've found a caste even below the proverbial untouchables for a beggar whose colour is due to dirt rather than pigmentation, and who is unrepentantly Church of England, by confirmation rather than conviction. Is there anything else I can do for you while I'm alive?'

'This sounds absurd, I know, but I'm looking for Mount Everest.'

'You wish to scale it, do you, in a nightdress? Some people will stop at nothing to enter the *Guinness Book of Records*. I tell you, it's a crazy enough idea to be damn good in this nuttiest of all ages. If I felt halfways myself, I'd join you, but I'm afraid I wouldn't get much further than Camp One. Tell you what you do, go on in the direction you're going until you run out of town. Then you turn right, and keep on straight ahead. You won't have to ask again, you'll see it, but don't get it confused with some of the other mountains, which often look higher from some angles.'

'Thank you very much indeed.'

'Think nothing of it. Give my respects to the old folks if you should pass that way. General Sir Matthew and Lady Tumbling-Taylor, Rabblestock Place, Stockton-on-Tees. Tell them I'm probably dead by the time they get the message. Benedict Romaine. Well, I couldn't call myself Robin Tumbling-Taylor on the screen, could I? And I can't call myself either in the gutter.'

The Old Man was terribly confused by this tale of woe. He could hardly pass such decrepit dignity by without it rankling in his conscience, another of his temporary acquisitions while on Earth. Looking around furtively to be sure nobody was staring at him, he dug deep into his pocket, and discreetly let a shower of rupees rain on the vagrant, who seized them or gathered them up where they fell with febrile fingers.

'And you said you hadn't any!' giggled the vagrant hysterically.

'I haven't really,' said the Old Man. 'Be careful how and where you spend it. It's all counterfeit. I know, I made it myself. Invest in a bar of soap first, and some scissors. They will improve your credit considerably.'

'I saw that,' announced Mr Smith, with venom, arriving on the scene. He was clutching a cardboard box under his arm. 'Oh no, no pocket money for poor Mr Smith, is there? Just for total strangers.'

'What's in that box?' asked the Old Man with misgiving.

'A television set. Japanese.'

'Have you borrowed it? To what purpose?'

'Because you would never dream of making *me* some money, I had to steal it, as usual. And we'd better mingle with the crowd before the man in the shop finds out it's missing.'

'I do beg your pardon for all this,' said the Old Man to the vagrant.

'Oh, it's lovely to hear a flaming row between a couple of queens. Takes me back home.'

'Come along.'

As the Old Man gathered up Mr Smith, and they both began walking quickly away from the scene of the multiple crimes, the Old Man scolded, 'I wish you wouldn't behave in quite such an effeminate way. It gives us both a most unfortunate reputation.'

'It gives *you* that reputation. I already have it. In any case it's your own fault for bringing out the worst in me.'

'And what do you need with a television? You'll never get it to work without an aerial, and since you live in an unventilated place, you won't be able to have one.'

'I'll make it work. I must! Now that we are going back to the monotony of our operations rooms, I have begun to think what I will really miss. Television. I have become hooked on television. It is one long commercial for my point of view, my lifestyle. Arbitrary destruction, deceit in high places, unadulterated vulgarity and mindlessness. My regret is that it's all what they call hokum. All the dead have their make-up removed at the end of every programme, and go home to their wives, mistresses or whoever, to rest up for the next day's fantasy projection. My consolation is, however, that morons watch television in their stultified droves, and a few of them derive their inspiration from it to turn these fetid nightmares into reality. They go out and kill. The idiots think life is like that, and they want to be part of it. Even those deprived of a personal imagination can fall back on a public imagination – called television. If there were any fairness in the world, *your* world, they ought to pay me a royalty!'

'It's most disturbing and, yes, disillusioning,' said the Old Man, a little out of breath with walking, 'that the fact you are going back to your lonely realm is enough for you to revert to your true colours, and become hostile and frankly disagreeable. Gracious me, do you realize that there were moments during our adventure when I actually completely forgot who you were – or rather are?'

'That's better,' said Mr Smith, in a slightly better mood, clutching his television as a disturbed mother might hold a baby prone to screaming.

Suddenly the Old Man stopped dead. 'What's that?' he asked.

'I heard nothing,' replied Mr Smith, on the qui vive.

240

'It's not a noise. It's a smell. I can actually smell something.'

Mr Smith sniffed. 'Nothing,' he said. 'I can smell nothing.'

'Cooking,' the Old Man announced. 'Oh, by all that's holy. I'm hun-gry!' And he began to shake like a small boy with an urgent need.

'I'm not hungry, but you remember when we hurried through the high grass while avoiding the tigress?'

'Yes.'

'There were some savage thorns near the soil. Look at this—'

Mr Smith pulled up his tattered trouser legs to reveal criss-cross lacerations above his ankles.

'What's that?' asked the Old Man, bending down.

'Blood.'

'Blood?'

There was an electric pause while their eyes met.

'One more night on Earth, and we have to part,' declared the Old Man in a choked voice.

20

They spent their last night on the steps of a ruined temple rising out of the tangled undergrowth of a jungle. The hardness of the steps was softened by tufts of grass which had forced their way through the stones. It was a decor which flattered Mr Smith's sensibilities on his last night on Earth, since the murals were largely of advanced eroticism, even if you had to be something of an expert in the matter to disentangle the multitude of bodies, which seemed at first glance to be made up entirely of buttocks and kneecaps with toes like beads on an abacus.

Night was falling rapidly as they settled for their ultimate meditation and sleep. The chatter of jungle livestock filled the evening air, weird cackles and hoots sounding like a lively parody of human communications, while hordes of monkeys flung themselves in a wild delirium over the ruins of the temple, silhouetted against a fading sky.

'I hope you are satisfied with the locale I picked out for our final hours on Earth,' said the Old Man.

'It shows unusual understanding,' replied Mr Smith, as he struggled with the cardboard box of his television set.

'Why are you taking it out of its box?'

'It will be lighter to carry. And then, if it's out of its box, I can always say I bought it. In its box, it looks awfully stolen to me.'

'Still bothering about appearances where there are no people?'

'I will have to go to the lowest place I can find tomorrow. I'm bound to find people on my way. It's easier for you. You only have to go up to the highest place. It is almost bound to be empty. Remember Olympus?'

'What have we learned on this journey, misguided or inspired as it may seem at difficult moments?'

'Oh. Are we going to be serious?'

'Otherwise, what was the point in coming?'

'Ah. She's a little beauty!' cried Mr Smith, as he lifted the television set from its cradle, and examined it more closely.

'It's called a Petal. Made by the Matsuyama Group of Companies. Featuring Matsuyamatic Peta-lite Controls. It's enough to make you vomit!'

'There could not be a better theme for our reflections, could there? In one sentence you have gone from unrestrained delight to the deepest revulsion. Nothing is as it seems.'

Mr Smith thought for a moment.

'No, nothing is as it seems. Remember America? Everyone hankers to go there, to make a fortune, to find freedom—'

'Is that true?' asked the Old Man cautiously.

'Why did you choose to go there first?'

The Old Man nodded, and remained silent.

'The mirage is one of untold wealth, of hard work rewarded. There is no mirage which includes even a suggestion of the people lying in the street, either drugged, or drunk, or dead. Nothing is as it seems. Ask why this state of affairs exists, and you will be told it is the price of freedom. Freedom extends its tentacles even into the gutter. The poor wish to be poor, the homeless wish to be without shelter, the destitute have selected their lifestyle. Freedom, you see, is compulsory. But if freedom is compulsory, the individual is no longer free. That is a point beyond their comprehension.'

'You really are brutal.'

Mr Smith smiled engagingly. 'Don't misunderstand me. Of all the countries we have visited, it is the one in which I would most like to live. The one in which I could prosper. They like nothing better than to wash their dirty linen in public, on television. And when there isn't sufficient dirty linen to satisfy the national need, they invent it, in deliciously nauseous serials about the corruption of the rich, an example to them all. Freedom abounds all right, but sometimes in strictly controlled, regimented segments.'

And here Mr Smith gave rein to his gift for waspish imitation. '"In the thirty seconds left, Mrs Tumblemore, would you tell the listeners exactly how the doctor broke the news to you that you were terminally ill." Or, "There are only twenty seconds left, Mr Secretary of State. Within that time slot, what should our message to fundamentalist terrorists be?"'

The Old Man began to laugh merrily, quite his old self again.

'The Japanese centenarian was right, you see. Efficiency is all important in a society of self-appointed winners, but when there are only twenty seconds left in which the Secretary of State must formulate a message which will be taken up by every wire service in the world, their efficiency goes out of the window. Efficiency is the creed, but the practice is full of endearing blunders, negligences and sacrifices to sheer haste, as though a traffic cop was continually speeding up traffic by blowing his aggravating whistle and waving his arm. Freedom is also giggling after the recreation break, freedom is the right to be inefficient.'

'But to suffer the consequences?'

'Of course, freedom in its fullest sense leads straight to the park bench. Or to the ownership of untold wealth. There's the catch, and the temptation. A criminal is free to cheat, to embezzle, to cook the books until he is caught—'

'Not very tactful, that last observation—'

'Listen, if you were to recreate the world because it displeased you, the FBI would no doubt charge you with forgery of the old one.'

'But why do you suppose there is so much destitution in a land so fundamentally rich, and in which the inherent wealth is often brilliantly exploited?'

'There is an advanced sense of personal salvation, thanks to the need for some kind of spiritual criteria in a civilization normally utterly bereft of it, and in which culture is a dirty word reserved for gays and pacifists. There is no shortage of volunteers to do the work which any self-respecting government should claim as its aim. But then, government is another dirty word, and as for the majority who think like that, there is no obligation to recognize the jungle around you. There is always the freedom not to see that which offends.'

'And you tell me you could live in that jungle, among the moaning sirens and machine-gun fire?'

'I'd wallow in it. And I'd make my fortune – easily – as a syndicated gossip columnist, writing with the self-assurance of an oracle about things I do not necessarily need to understand, or I could make it as a money launderer, or any one of the new professions corruption has thrown up, or better still, I could exploit the greatest corruption of all, and become an evangelist on television, with an audience of millions, the Reverend Smith, with his chorus of angels with beehive hair-dos and gowns from a provincial ballroom dancing derby, welcome guests in any Christian home. Poor John the Baptist, with his intimate circle of sceptics in the wilderness. What could he know of the big time?'

'That you should be fascinated by corruption and the opportunities it offers, I can understand,' interrupted the Old Man. 'It is a vocational matter as far as you are concerned, and I do not question it. But tell me, is corruption an inevitable consequence of unbridled freedom?'

'Corruption, as you know, exists everywhere. It is one of the spurs to progress. Obviously it comes into its own there where there is freedom as a surfboard to ride the waves on. Corruption in Japan was the private privilege of Matsuyama-San, and he had forty television sets to nip it in the bud wherever else it should appear. In America, it is a temptation for all, and let me say that corruption in a world of plenty leads to greater prosperity for all. It is only where there is little to share that corruption serves one at the expense of the other.'

'Disguise your ideas a bit, render them a little less comprehensible, and you could make it as a top economist as well,' growled the Old Man appreciatively.

'You let me do all the talking,' said Mr Smith.

'I like to listen to you, even if I do not always agree. But I have little to add until I have indulged in some deeper meditation, and for that I must be alone. Suddenly, when I have no more corporeal form, everything becomes clear and limpid. While I am confined to this tub-like shape, I am all at once afraid to express myself. I seem to make errors of judgment unworthy of a deity.'

'You are not a deity,' corrected Mr Smith. 'You know perfectly well who you are, and you owe it to yourself not to lose your confidence. If you do that, I'm in honour bound to lose confidence too, and I will feel lost. Remember that I depend on you.'

The Old Man passed his hand over his face, white as that of a clown. 'Perhaps I am just exhausted. All these rapid displacements. From one civilization to another. From one hemisphere to another. I'm beginning to feel that . . . it's a long time since the Creation and all those indomitable dreams. Tell me – honestly – in your opinion – have men found a way or lost it irrevocably?'

'Why such pessimistic thoughts?'

'I gave them aggression as an afterthought, as a cook will add salt and pepper to a meal. I never expected them to make a meal out of the condiments. Remember the military in the Soviet Union, the marks of their lethal achievements twinkling away like oriental temple bells on their chests, and the General in Israel, neglecting his studies of philosophy to blow up a few cottages in a meaningless reprisal? What a waste!'

'Don't let anything depress you, sir.'

The Old Man looked up. 'You call me sir?' he asked, incredulous.

'I do,' said Mr Smith, playing a part, but playing it very well. 'What lives longer in the mind – the gratuitous cruelties of Tienanmen Square, or the serenity of a T'ang horse? The debates in the Soviet parliament, or the diapason of an Orthodox Church choir? And is not God the Milkman but a nod in the direction of Lewis Carroll's surreal genius, fit to sit at the same table as the Mad Hatter and Alice, sipping tea, with, thank God, milk?'

'You really are a fool,' chuckled the Old Man, 'but you certainly restore a sense of values. Culture outlasts everything, of course. Even the building on which we are resting our temporary mortality. The fun and games were over long ago, but the images remain for the benefit of the baboons.'

'Every potentate of the past boasted a fool. It's a privilege for one to play the part of yours, sir.'

'Don't overdo it, or I shall think there is an element of sarcasm in your civility.'

'You know me well enough to know that, with me, such an impression at least, is inevitable.'

They looked at one another with affection and amusement, as equals. It was, curiously enough, Mr Smith who became grave first.

'There is just one element I would like to clarify,' he said.

'Yes?'

'There is so much condemnation in the various holy writs about praying to false gods, to idols with feet of clay, all that internal propaganda, publicity put out in favour of one belief at the expense of all the others. This seems to be entirely erroneous, in that it is belief itself which is important, not the objects of belief. Belief entails a lesson in humility. It is good for a man's soul to believe in something greater than himself, not because he magnifies his god, but because he shrinks himself to size. Now, if this is so, a primitive man who worships a tree, or the sun, or a volcano derives the same benefit from his act of moral prostration as a cultivated man would do before the god of his tradition, and the effects on the worshipper are identical. It is the act of worship which is important, at no time the object of that worship. Heresy?'

'All I can say is that which is self-evident to everyone except a theologian. Since I am everything, it follows that I am the clay of the false gods' feet, to say nothing of the volcano, the tree, the sun. There are no false gods. There is only God.'

'Many heretics have been burned and hideously tortured because they worshipped false gods. They should have been congratulated for worshipping at all.'

'Don't. Please don't ask me the impossible, a comment on the imperfections of the past. I am not in the mood to rake up the embers of conflicts in which convictions won battles over doubts. Remember only that mankind is united by its doubts, divided by its convictions. It stands to reason that doubts are far more important to the survival of the human race than mere convictions. There. I have said too much already.'

'You do not think ill of me for bringing up the subject?'

'I would have thought ill of you if you had not.'

The Old Man stretched out his hand, and touched Mr Smith's shoulder. 'Why are you good to me? So tolerant of my lapses? So eager for my welfare?'

Mr Smith answered with a simplicity which was disarming. 'You forget that I was trained as an angel.' And as a barely audible afterthought, he added, 'Sir.'

The Old Man closed his eyes in evident contentment. 'Let us sleep,' he said. 'I wanted food for thought. You have given me a banquet. We need all our strength for tomorrow.'

Mr Smith shut his eyes, made himself comfortable with the visible quest for ultimate comfort of a gun dog after a good day's hunting.

'Good night,' he said, but the Old Man had already slipped off into sleep.

After an untroubled moment, a flickering picture appeared in the subconscious of both sleepers. The Holy Men were still sitting like pixies under their ample tree, but their number had by now grown to well over twenty. The newcomers were seated in the dark, just as were the original five, but they seemed to be as glistening-bald and stripped as their fellows. Their metal-rimmed glasses shimmered in the inky darkness under the tree.

'We are, as you will notice, still, as it were, in touch with you,' said the reedy voice.

Both the Old Man and Mr Smith stirred in their sleep.

'We feel we ought to inform you that we have had a visit from the Indian police, that section which is charged with the welfare and protection of Holy Men. They had had reports of a considerable concentration under this tree, and came to investigate. It appears the American authorities at New Delhi have sent out a general alarm for a couple of gentlemen answering your description who are wanted for some unspecified crime in Voshington. Now I must say that we were all a little alarmed by the fact that your assistant stole a flagrant symbol of today's tawdry values in the shape of a television set, but we are somewhat reassured by his subsequent exposé of the full horror of a consumer-oriented society. Some of us were tempted to help the police in their search for you, others placed more reliance on our usually infallible instincts about other Holy Men, and we sent them packing in the opposite direction.'

'But how do you know all this?' cried the Old Man in his sleep. 'How can you hear our confidential conversations?'

'We are on the wavelength of your subconscious,' declared the voice. 'We only need a quorum of Holy Men who have mastered the technique for us to pull off this quiet hallucination.'

'You mean our most intimate thoughts are within the range of your scrutiny?' cried the Old Man, outraged.

'So long as you remain within reasonable distance.'

'That's terrible.'

'We know who you are. Or at least, who you think you are. You may be right. You may not be.'

'But how did the police know that we were here?' cried Mr Smith. 'And the Americans?'

'From what we could gather from a confidential telephone call outside normal hearing range, from their jeep, your last word on leaving Japan, relayed by the Japanese police to their Indian counter-

248

parts, and by the American intelligence to their correspondents in the United States Military Mission, was the single word "India", to which your accomplice allegedly replied, "India".'

'And as a result of that simple indiscretion, this entire operation was set in motion, and with such despatch?' asked Mr Smith, aghast. 'It seems hardly credible.'

'Communications have become almost uncannily rapid,' said the caressing voice. 'Information can now be transferred from one end of the Earth to the other at a speed far in excess of that of sound. It stands to reason that misinformation can travel as fast. The lie has an equal opportunity to the truth. By electronic means man has accelerated the transference of thought. All he has singularly failed to do is to improve the quality of that thought. Fancy using such wonders for the simple purpose of informing other policemen that both you and your accomplice had uttered the word "India"! It is like idle banter between gaolers! What a waste! One could almost say, what a sacrilege!'

'I am not the old gentleman's accomplice,' rasped Mr Smith.

'We realized that,' purred the voice, 'and it was that which persuaded us to send the police away on a false scent. Listening to the conversation between you, we arrived at the conclusion that you are some kind of complementary power, that together you cover the spectrum of human choice, of human aspiration.'

'Correct!' cried the Old Man.

'And since we have managed to extract possibilities from the mortal mechanism which are, over the short range, more effective than electronics, we were able to direct attention from your activities.'

'I am sure we are extremely grateful,' said the Old Man nervously. 'You see—'

'Stop!' snarled Mr Smith, his anxiety bringing out once more all the discordant notes in his voice in one sour chord. 'You are about to tell them things you have even denied me, things you may not discuss until after you are disembodied once more!'

The Old Man awoke with a start. His forehead was beaded with perspiration.

'Oh heavens, I had the most frightful dream,' he muttered.

Mr Smith was already awake, the tone of his voice having startled even him. 'Are you sure it was a dream?'

'Don't be absurd,' said the Old Man nervously. 'Of course it was a dream. It was so dreadful, it couldn't have been anything else.'

'I believe I shared that dream with you,' Mr Smith suggested, soberly.

'Nonsense. Dreams are not for sharing.'

'Close your eyes and tell me. Are they still there?'

'Who?'

'Under their tree?'

The Old Man shut his eyes, and reopened them at once. 'They are still there. All of them,' he whispered in a horrified voice.

'We dare not sleep again,' Mr Smith announced, categorically.

'You mean, they have invaded even our solitude to that extent?' the Old Man asked slowly.

'Look!'

'What?'

'The screen of my television set,' murmured Mr Smith, only looking at it out of the corner of his eye.

A pale image of the great tree had appeared, with a vague impression of the Holy Men, but the picture kept disappearing upwards, as though being endlessly shuffled, like cards.

'Turn it off,' begged the Old Man.

'It's not turned on,' replied Mr Smith.

'But how—?'

'In some way, they generate their own electricity. We can even see them in the dark.'

'Try another channel. Remember how it works?'

Mr Smith did as he was told. The Holy Men occupied all the available channels.

'It will be a fitting punishment for my theft if, when I get home, all I can see on my set are the Holy Men sitting under their tree.'

'Oh, thank you for your sense of humour. It takes the curse off most situations.'

'What do we do?'

'We part now.'

'Now? In the dark?'

The hint of a deep-red sun peeped through the clouds like the waking eye of some huge monster.

'It will be light enough soon.'

'And until then?'

'We meditate, but for goodness' sake, not transcendentally. Just unambitiously, even superficially. Don't give them anything to cotton on to. Was I about to say something terribly foolish when you woke me up?'

'It sounded more like something terribly profound, which had been denied even me, but which flowed out of the mouth of a somewhat foolish . . . elderly person.'

'Thanks for stopping me, in my confusion. It was yet another proof of your intrinsic loyalty.'

'I only did my duty,' said Mr Smith, with a somewhat excessive piety.

And both of them meditated superficially for a while.

When the red sun turned orange, and the monkeys were celebrating the fact by performing incredible acrobatics against the re-established background of the sky, the Old Man stood up abruptly.

'Perhaps it is just as well that we leave each other under these circumstances. The fact that we are observed prevents our parting from being too emotional.'

'Thanks for having thought of me.'

'No regrets?'

'How can one have regrets?'

They looked deep into one another's eyes.

'It's probably against all the rules and usages, but . . .' said the Old Man, and clasped Mr Smith to him in an emotional embrace.

Both shut their eyes to enshrine the moment in their memories. Inevitably, with their eyes shut, the Holy Men reappeared.

'Are they still there?' asked the Old Man, under his breath.

'They are still there, but there seem to be fewer of them.'

'Can they read our intentions as well?'

Mr Smith smiled satanically. 'What a revenge!' he cackled.

'Revenge?'

'We are being driven from this world much as I was driven out of the garden while eavesdropping on the first copulation in history.'

The Old Man struggled his way out of the embrace. 'I don't want to hear about it,' he said, annoyed and disappointed.

'And it wasn't even sinful yet, just a little experiment in the best of taste. It only became a sin after the invention of the fig leaf.'

'There's always a sting in the tail, isn't there?'

'You only say that because, when I was a serpent, you couldn't tell one end from the other.'

Despite his annoyance, the Old Man laughed. 'Incorrigible,' he said in a robust voice, and strode away.

Mr Smith watched him go with tears welling up in his eyes, then turned to the television set, picked it up, and said in a voice deprived of emotion, 'You are my companion from now on.'

He then walked away from the erotic temple without so much as a glimpse at the carvings, in the opposite direction from the Old Man.

* * *

Although he was trying to save energy, the Old Man did indulge in one or two considerable leaps forward in disembodied form, since he reckoned that if he did not take a few short cuts, he would never reach the peak of Mount Everest before evening. Once or twice he shut his eyes experimentally, and saw nothing but blackness. He was thankful to be out of the range of the holy vigilantes. The air became rapidly more rarefied, and since the Old Man had gradually become susceptible to temperature, he began to shiver as his wet feet, in their fragile tennis shoes, began to sink into snow. More energy was consumed in stoking up the internal boiler so that he might be impervious to cold, a contingency he had never foreseen.

He reached the peak of Mount Everest fairly late in the afternoon. His white hair and beard, as well as his eyelashes, sparkled as crystals formed in abundance over their surface, giving him the tinselled look of a Father Christmas in a department store. He felt weak, and unprepared for the ascension into his realm. He spoke aloud for a while to try to banish the loneliness he was already beginning to feel.

'Pull yourself together. There's nothing to it. All you have to do is to visualize your destination in your mind's eye, and then, let go! You don't even have to give the matter much thought – that merely leads to complexes, to inhibitions. It's your birthright, as walking is to mortals. Have a go! You'll be grateful when it's over.'

He had entertained the sentimental notion of one last look at the Earth in all its glory, but there was nothing but impenetrable fog, swirling mists, and buffeting winds. A hostile send-off.

And so it was with a feeling of resentment and annoyance that he suddenly blasted off, taking even himself by surprise. At first, all went well. He climbed slowly at the start, then with augmented speed, like a rocket. It was only after he had been under way for a minute or so that a great fatigue overwhelmed him, as well as a desire not to expend all his available energies in an aborted leap, so he relaxed, and with an immense sigh, began spiralling to Earth again. His landing was only soft in that he sank into a huge pile of snow and had to struggle not to sink in even further. On his way down, he fancied he saw a quantity of black dots on the slopes of the mountain, like currants on a bun. But he admitted that it may have been his imagination.

He was free of the snowbank, and tried to analyze his situation rationally, and without panic. His shortage of celestial fuel was a new situation he had not been confronted with before. Were there, in fact, limits to his powers, or was it merely a fear imposed on him by his adoption of human form? He tried hard to think these ideas through, but was interrupted by what he imagined were the shouted voices of women, carried in the wind. He broke off his concentration and looked over the edge, only to see a long line of women, linked by ropes and armed with picks, who were making their way painfully to the summit.

'No privacy,' he muttered. 'More and more like Olympus all over again.'

Now there was an added incentive to escape. He looked into the sky, made himself mentally weightless, and shot off into the air like an arrow. But instead of gaining momentum, he once again began to level out, and then, after an agonizing wait, he turned downwards again, searching desperately for air pockets like a bird, but, finding none, he was thrown against a jagged rock at the same level as the painfully climbing women. They saw him, and began shouting to each other, speculating that he was an eagle, or a meteorite. The language they were communicating in was Swiss-German, and large letters on one of the knapsacks proclaimed that they were schoolteachers from Appenzell, climbing Everest as a holiday task with some of their advanced pupils.

The Old Man had no time to devote to them. He had broken out into a cold sweat as the pain in his body was numbed by the terrible feeling that he would never be able to leave Earth again; that he was predestined to hover around the peak of Everest making endless attempts at departure, each one ending more embarrassingly than the other. He was overwhelmed with a quite uncharacteristic wave of self-pity, and he wept, his tears turning to icicles on his cheeks.

Suddenly his blue eyes regained their composure and a twinkle of recognition invaded them. He let out a huge bellow of triumph, which made the Swiss ladies, many of them suspended upside-down, like bats, look over in alarm, and share their feelings in the patois of Canton Appenzell.

There was no resolution to their perplexity. That is, they never saw what happened next. It was just that the Old Man, prone to the forgetfulness of age, had clean overlooked the need to be invisible. Whereas visible flight was economical once the requisite altitude had been reached, it added prohibitive weight to a take-off. The Old Man became invisible at once, and since nobody ever saw him again, it is to be assumed that his third and final attempt was in every way successful. Suffice it to say that when the Swiss ladies reached the summit just over an hour later, planting the flags of the Helvetic Confederation and that of Canton Appenzell on the crest, and laying a small armoured box between the flags, containing a wristwatch, a piece of cheese, and a bar of chocolate, they did not fail to notice the huge crater caused by the Old Man's landing. They took photographs of it from all angles, with a flash. Was this proof, at last, of the yeti's existence?

At roughly this time, in the Ganges, the empty case of Mr Smith's body flowed with the tide like the rejected skin of a reptile. His features were plainly recognizable despite their transparency, and in his arms, the consistency of oilskin, lay cradled the empty shell of a television set: no screen, no dials, just the outer casing.

The skin was followed by a sea of flowers and floating candles, placed lovingly or thrown carefully by at least a hundred Holy Men who had known where to come, and now followed the relics in long narrow boats.

'We are united in our sorrow at the passing of great spiritual forces,' said the querulous voice, carried far and wide over the twilight regatta, 'which have given us much to ponder, much to decipher, much to unravel. We know that this is not death in its habitual form, there is no cause for a funeral pyre here, or chanting, or vailing. It is merely the passing from one season to another, as symbolized by the shedding of a skin. But, coupled with our deep reflection, let us be thankful that no greater truth was revealed. We are as ignorant of the deeper purpose of life as we ever were. Even though, by our perseverance, we may have fashioned the key, the lock is, as ever, elusive. We have our ignorance to thank for the fact that we can continue to be Holy Men as before, to quote the Old Man, giving our doubts the freedom they need, and keeping our convictions on a short rein.'

Slowly they began to intone a chant, starting with the lowest of registers, gradually blossoming into a dense but cautious harmony, like an organ wiling away the time, measured, full of acidulated tonal resonances, utterly unrelenting. The perfume of joss-sticks rose into the air, while on the riverbank, from a slowly moving jeep, a hulk of a man with an iron-grey crew cut was taking shot after shot of Mr Smith's mortal remains, in the available light, through a zoom lens.

EPILOGUE

The immediate consequences of the return of Mr Smith and the Old Man to their habitats were many and puzzling, although very few people, apart from Dr Kleingeld and a handful of Indian Holy Men, ascribed the events to the ascension and to the descent. Ecologists the world over tended to blame the criminal negligence of the human race in failing to respect certain natural laws.

Perhaps the most immediately dramatic occurrences were the violent snowstorms which assailed the Sahara Desert, and the terrible floods which followed. Pictures appeared in newspapers of a miserable camel standing knee-deep in mud, pain and perplexity apparent on its woebegone face. Pop groups everywhere rallied to the call for help as they always do in an emergency, and an organization called SESAFF (Sahara Emergency Snow and Flood Fund) began soliciting financial contributions from the public, as did an even more raucous group known as RARFADS (Rock and Rollers for a Dry Sahara).

The Canadian Government began operating a shuttle to hospitals and rest camps along the southern borders, transporting Eskimos and Inuits overcome by sunstroke well north of the Arctic Circle. These unfortunates, who were found prostrate on disintegrating sections of pack-ice as they watched their igloos inexorably melting, were brought south by seaplanes. Vast seas hammered the western coasts of Europe, sending deckchairs as far inland as Wolverhampton and Limoges, while an entire catamaran crashed into a field near Cognac. The outbreak of malaria near Gothenburg puzzled the Swedish authorities, as well as the identification of tsetse flies in Switzerland, with outbreaks of sleeping sickness. Bilharzia turned up without warning in the crystalline waters of the Barrier Reef, there was a major earthquake near Düsseldorf, high on the Richter scale. Authorities did their best to reassure the public that there were valid reasons for all these unexpected upheavals, one man of science even going as far as to claim that it was a veritable miracle that the region of Düsseldorf had not been struck by tremors before. Some superstitious people consulted Nostradamus, and claimed they found all that was happening insinuated between the lines; others blamed nuclear energy, underground testing, the hole in the ozone layer, the greenhouse effect, and acid rain. Finally nobody knew precisely what they were talking about, but as usual, that did not prevent them from talking. On the contrary, the wilder speculations gathered the most aggressive following, and there were angry demonstrations in most large cities. In Bulgaria, a crowd blamed the government for the bad weather, and this was greeted in Washington as a confirmation of the popular enthusiasm for the democratic process.

In Washington itself, things were unusually calm. Dr Kleingeld still arrived every morning at eight sharp, with his thermos and sandwiches covered in tinfoil, outside the White House. He was accompanied as always these days by the enormous oaf who had killed two men while believing he was God, by name Luther Basing, who now followed Kleingeld slavishly in the absence of the Old Man, before whom he had kneeled and felt the tug of adoration. They unravelled their large banner stretched between two poles, and displayed it to all comers:

God and the Devil
Are on the Level.

One day a car drew up in front of them. At the wheel was the formidable Miss Hazel McGiddy, the erstwhile receptionist of Dr Kleingeld's hospital. She was now dressed in the smart uniform of a female major in the US Army.

'Coo-ee. Remember me?' she called in her baritone voice, looking rather like a Mayan god with peroxide hair.

'Good God. Miss McGiddy, isn't it?'

'It sure is. Only it's Major now. I've been seconded to the staff of Colonel Harrington B. Claybaker, PA to the CS of the USAF.'

'I have no idea what that all means,' said Dr Kleingeld.

'You think I have, honey?' she laughed. 'It doesn't matter. I tell you, it's so overstaffed, if ten of us died tomorrow, they wouldn't realize it till the end of the year.'

'You left the hospital?'

'Oh sure. I didn't like that job. Fifty per cent of the people admitted weren't going to come out again alive. Maybe I'm exaggerating, then maybe I'm not. I did a stint in the armed forces when I first gave up the roller-derby, so now I thought I'd go back in. I work part-time in the Pentagon, part-time at a secret venue in West Virginia. It's all maximum security, but since there are no secrets in Washington, it's good for a gossip.'

'No secrets in Washington?'

'Naah. It's a city of show-offs. Guys who know better. Who make up what they don't know. And secretaries with confidences for sale, and bodies, and there's a price for the two; who photocopy all that goes in the shredder, in case it has a price.'

She made up her mouth in her car vanity mirror, and changed her tone.

'I often think of you, honey, and I always think what a damn shame it is that that brilliant Doctor Morton Kleingeld, who could have won the Nobel Prize for Medicine, should be standing out there in front of the White House in the company of God Three, just because a couple of crazy cats crossed his path and turned him away from his real work.'

'You don't understand, Major . . .'

'Sure I do. You were a *great* doctor. You were making *so much money*. What else is there, after all? Personal satisfaction? Don't make me laugh. What did I think of in the roller-derby after I'd knocked a coupla girls unconscious and landed flat on my ass as some vicious bitch ducked under my sideswipe and landed a piledriver to my jaw? Personal satisfaction? No, sir. The one thing kept me going as I spat out my teeth was the thought of my pay check. Hey, God Three's put on weight. I didn't think that was possible. And how d'you get him out of the nuthouse?'

'They castrated him, which was part of the sentence. Since then he's much calmer, and inevitably he's putting on weight, like most eunuchs. Mrs Kleingeld left me when I decided to alter my way of life.'

'Oh, I'm sorry to hear that.'

'She's much happier now, and so am I. It's not much fun being married to a psychiatrist. She's gone up in the world, which she always wanted. She's shacked up with a croupier in Las Vegas. They never see each other, and they're perfectly happy. I adopted God Three since she left. He sleeps in a hammock in the garage. I don't have a car anymore.'

'Gee.' Major McGiddy did not really know how to react to so much misfortune, especially since it was presented as though it were all fortunate. 'That's tough,' she said, but quickly changed her tone in her usual mercurial style.

'Hey, do I have some dirt for you about . . . about the two crazies you been rooting for.'

'God and the Devil?'

'Whatever. The FBI's still after them, you know.'

'I'm sure they are.'

'Oh sure. Almost caught up with them in England, then in Israel, then some other places, what I hear, and finally India. They've gotten photos of Smith, dead, floating in that river they have out there, and one of a dent in the snow, a picture I mean, which corresponds in size to the shape of the old guy, Godfrey.'

'I find it awfully difficult to follow what you are saying, Major. Where was the dent in the snow?' asked Dr Kleingeld.

'Atop Mount Himalaya.'

'There is no such mountain.'

'Well, give me some names.'

'K2, Annapurna, Everest.'

'That's the one. Atop Mount Everest.'

Dr Kleingeld laughed aloud. 'Who on earth could have taken a photo of a dent in the snow atop Mount Everest?'

'A team of Swiss female schoolteachers. It was more than a dent. It was a regular hole, the size of the old guy. They sent the picture to *National Geographic* thinking it might be proof of the abominable snowman's existence. The FBI got copies for their files from the magazine.'

'So where does this lead them?' asked Dr Kleingeld, still amused.

Major McGiddy moved closer on the front seat of her car. 'I don't know whether you know that the FBI has been working together with the Massachusetts Institute of Technology on a project which has cost the *earth* so far. See, they were just about fed up that everytime they caught up with these two felons, the felons would disappear. This made them fighting mad, and now – only what I'm telling you's about as secret as you can get, y'understand – they've managed to make a mouse disappear, and make it visible once more. The technique could be applied to a man, or a woman, but what's holding them back now is the sheer cost. If they were to go ahead, it would mean cutting millions of dollars out of defence, out of welfare, and out of education. Is it worth it? Some, like the big guns at the FBI, like Milt Runway and Lloyd Shrubs, regard it as a question of honour, and believe the experiments should be pursued at any price. Others, like Senators Polaxer and Del Consiglio, and Congressman Tvanich, of Nome, Alaska, can't see why the nation should run to such astronomic expense in order to apprehend first-time felons who have only forged a relatively small quantity of banknotes.'

'"Make an exception, and it is the vital first step to abolishing law and order in the nation," was what Runway declared.

'"So we can seem to get rid of a mouse, and then bring it back again. Any competent conjuror can manage this trick. Only it's most times done with pigeons. Big deal." That was Polaxer's reaction.

'Del Consiglio saw it differently. "There's photographic evidence they're gone. Left. Quit. From up the Himalayas and the Ganges."

'This is exactly what that miserable shit heel like Shrubs was waiting for.

'"Gone? Quit, have they? Well, maybe they have and then, once again, maybe they haven't," he said, and looked each one of them in the eye like he was giving them a last opportunity to amend their statements. "OK," he went on, sounding reasonable as all hell, "let me see if you can live with this scenario. They come back, see, as they always have done whenever they seem to have left. They come back, manufacturing billions and billions of false dollars in Cuba, Nicaragua – even in friendly Panama. Or else in the Soviet Union, Japan, China, Korea, places we don't have the possibility to send in a coupla airborne divisions to apprehend them. They've improved their counterfeit techniques since the first time – and they turn out enough of the stuff to undermine our financial dominance in a single afternoon, to sink our economy, to shatter confidence in the greenback. Can we allow this to happen? Can we take the risk? Don't we have certain responsibilities towards the human race?"

'That did it, I'm telling you. That mention of the human race.

You know how they all feel about the human race.'

'What did they do to give expression to their feelings about the human race?' asked Dr Kleingeld discreetly.

'They adjourned the meeting,' said Major McGiddy with gloomy finality.

'And the President?' Dr Kleingeld was no longer amused.

'He's undecided, as usual,' replied Major McGiddy.

Just then a policeman on a motorcycle rode up to the car. 'You can't stay here, Major. I'm sorry.'

Major McGiddy just took time to light a cigarette, indulge in a brief but violent coughing fit, and blow Dr Kleingeld a kiss before accelerating slowly away.

Dr Kleingeld sighed. Then he smiled agreeably at God Three.

'Isn't that just like the human animal?' he asked. 'For ever trying to come closer to God, even with the help of the FBI.'

God Three failed to understand, but nodded all the same.